# THE THACKERY T. LAMBSHEAD POCKET GUIDE TO ECCENTRIC & DISCREDITED DISEASES

# THE THACKERY T. LAMBSHEAD

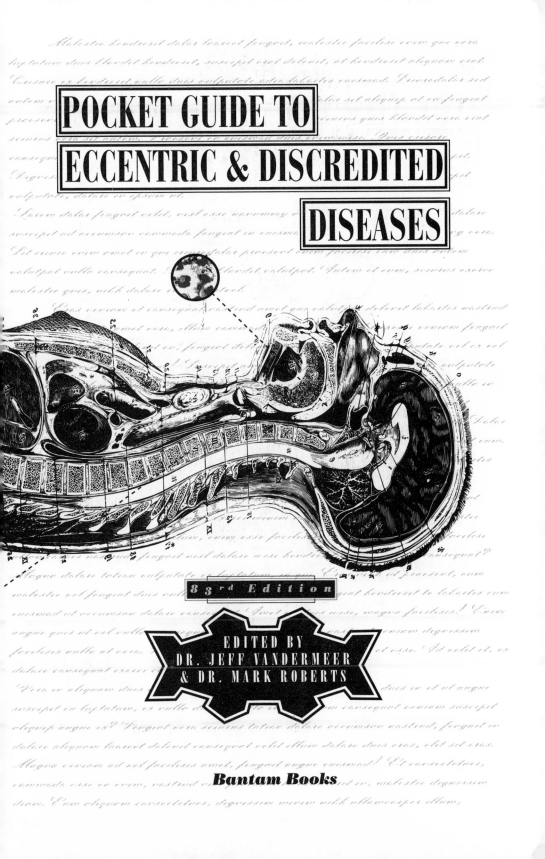

# POCKET GUIDE TO
# ECCENTRIC & DISCREDITED
# DISEASES

**83RD EDITION**

EDITED BY
DR. JEFF VANDERMEER
& DR. MARK ROBERTS

*Bantam Books*

The Thackery T. Lambshead Pocket Guide
to Eccentric and Discredited Diseases
A Bantam Spectra Book

PUBLISHING HISTORY
Night Shade Books hardcover edition published 2003
Bantam Spectra trade paperback edition / July 2005

PUBLISHED BY
Bantam Dell
A Division of Random House, Inc.
New York, New York

ISBN 0-553-38339-6

PRINTED IN
THE UNITED STATES OF AMERICA

PUBLISHED SIMULTANEOUSLY
IN CANADA

WWW.BANTAMDELL.COM

BVG / 10 9 8 7 6 5 4 3 2 1

For more information on the Guide, visit the Bantam Spectra website or
www.lambsheadguide.com

# CONTENTS

*For Drs. Bill Babouris, Jeremy Lassen,*
*Peter Lavery, Juliet Ulman, and Jason*
*Williams—You are all Barking Mad, and*
*We, the Editors, salute you.*

THE THACKERY T. LAMBSHEAD POCKET GUIDE
TO ECCENTRIC & DISCREDITED DISEASES

— 83ʳᵈ EDITION —

*Editors*
DRS. JEFF VANDERMEER & MARK ROBERTS

*Designer & Creative Consultant*
DR. JOHN COULTHART

*Medical Consultant*
DR. MARK SHAMIS

*Infection Proofreaders*
DRS. ANN KENNEDY, NEIL WILLIAMSON,
SCOTT STRATTON, TAMAR YELLIN

*Medical Agent*
DR. HOWARD MORHAIM

*Patron Saint of Disease*
DR. ALLEN RUCH
(AND HIS "MAD QUAIL DISEASE")

# CONTRIBUTORS TO THE 83<sup>RD</sup> EDITION

# The Life of Dr. Thackery T. Lambshead (1900– )

**Thackery Trajan Lambshead** was born on St. Genesius the Comedian's Day (August 25th), 1900, in Wimpering on the Brink, Devon (county), England. He was the second of seven children born to Caspar and Eucaria Lambshead, although a putative resemblance between Thackery and one Neb Gariad, itinerant glass blower and sin-eater who passed through Devon late in 1899, has been the cause of some rather pointless gossip. Caspar Lambshead served his community as a notary public and importer and retailer of monkey-picked teas (although his father had run a traveling medicine show). Eucaria, who had enjoyed some minor success on the stage, gave voice lessons and raised owls. A mediocre student with a penchant for marbles and catching frogs, Thackery proved to be a late bloomer. His interest in medicine crystallized in 1913, when his mother was struck in the head with a petrified sponge belonging to Kimball's Curiosities, which sponge had accidentally been displaced from its temporary situation on a third-floor windowsill overlooking the street in a moment of mental abstraction on the part of Mr. Rearben Kimball, Jr. The resulting injury, while not life threatening, brought on a case of classic amnesia from which Eucaria Lambshead never recovered—and neither did her son. He put aside his ambition to appear in silent films and, largely by mere force of will, got himself admitted to Oxford Medical College.

Thackery later confessed to Sterling Silliphant that he passed through his remarkably rapid medical training in "a brown study." Intense, somber, indefatigable, and seemingly immune to the lure of the ordinary student dissipations, he graduated in 1918, easily the most generally resented graduate in the history of that institution (perhaps the fatuous rumors involving Lambshead in an infernal bargain originated at this time—however they began, he has never entirely been able to shake them). His reception among the staff at Combustipol General Hospital, back in Devon, was far warmer, and, during his internship there, his mood correspondingly improved. A lifelong pacifist, he elected, in late 1919, to tend veterans at the St. Agnes Charity Clinic of Edinburgh, as his Whitmanesque way of contributing to what he called the "post-War effort." There was, at this time, some expectation of marriage (the details are impossible to trace), which met with an abrupt and bitterly disillusioning reverse, and this, perhaps, was, at least in part, to blame for Lambshead's decision to leave England for a time. The tendency to bury any possibility of a private life in an unremitting application to his work would be one of the only constants in his eventful life. He traveled to India, where he established his first and only private practice; the work bored him, and he made use of his spare time to pursue all manner of projects, from public works and choreography for the Salvation Army Modern Dance Society, to the accumulation of medical documents of a generally abstruse and obscure character. It is out of this latter pastime that the Guide was born.

Lambshead took advantage of an offer to serve as court physician to Prince Varchambara of Nagchampabad—the position afforded considerable free time, and the Prince's libraries were vast—and he produced the first formal collection-draught within six months. This was not simply a matter of collating materials, but also, most crucially, of developing a methodology for their evaluation. Forced to abandon his post within the year, due to an imbroglio with one of the Prince's wives, Lambshead, now completely dedicated to the perfection of his Guide, moved to Berlin.

Berlin in the 1920s was a heady place, an anarchic hubbub of possibilities; in addition to his extensive research in the medical archives of that city, Lambshead also had ample opportunity to contribute materials based on his own eyewitness accounts. Indeed, some entries were written on the very spot of discovery, in the presence of the victim, as was the case with Erotomotor Pseudalgia and 139 Hauptstrasse Explosive Plumagnetism, the latter named for the street address adjacent to which the first known attack took place (the subject's body erupted in iron feathers and elaborately-pigmented wattles in Dr. Lambshead's presence—as the plumage was highly magnetic, the patient was able to walk only in the direction of magnetic north). Aggravated Inguinal Palsy was provided to Dr. Lambshead by the real Mata Hari (not the patsy who was executed in her place), whom he met by chance in the back parlor of The Black Cube Club. In his travels throughout Europe, Lambshead visited nearly every major city on the continent, and a great many of the more out-of-the-way spots as well, combing even monastic records for evidence of unknown ailments.

In 1928, after a brief stint in hospital (not due to illness: having encountered Antonin Artaud in the streets of Paris, and rather foolishly slapping him in the face with the injunction, in English, to "Snap out of it," Dr. Lambshead found himself at the mercy of the irate actor's horny knuckles), Lambshead set off on the first of his many African expeditions. He left Europe in a huff, after receiving an endless series of obtuse rejection letters from all the major medical and even commercial publishing houses he had approached with the Guide. "Book publishers are the most infernally slow and pachydermously unimaginative race ever to blast the surface of the earth!" he wrote to Andreas Embirikos. "A pox on those turquoise devils!"

Lambshead spent much of the 1930s infatuated with Madagascar, where he wrote the now classic "Treatise on Trans-species Human-Lemur Pyrethroblastosis and Emittostomatism, or Crater Flatulence," which many regard as his masterpiece, and still had time to cultivate his own peculiar strain of antibiotic vanilla. His idyllic, if solitary, life on the cliffs overlooking Madagascar's otherworldly beaches was disrupted by rumors of war; his only college friend, John Trimble, who had been secretly employed by Winston Churchill to spy on the Germans, warned of the impending conflict, and Lambshead decided to return to England and make his services available there. He worked at three different London hospitals during the Blitz, and returned by special arrangement to Combustipol General Hospital. After the war, it was largely in recognition of his Hippocratic zeal that Chatto & Windus rescinded their former rejection of the Guide and offered to make it available to the public for the first time, in 1946. Lambshead thereafter embarked on what would become the first of many legendary, perhaps infamous, expeditions to South America; on one such trip, he met Jorge Luis Borges, much to the delight of both parties.

In the later 1940s and early 1950s, Lambshead visited America several times, finding it a veritable gold mine of all manner of especially bizarre and embarrassing diseases. Not unlike The Beatles, Dr. Lambshead was welcomed by his American "fans" with surprising enthusiasm; the Guide roughly doubled in length as a consequence of these visits. However, owing to certain characteristically candid remarks made about Messrs. McCarthy and Nixon, and to the frankly Communist affiliations of some of Dr. Lambshead's associates (and perhaps to his anti-sabotage of the Pepsi Corporation in 1949), he ran afoul of Mr. Hoover and was thereafter denied permission to visit the United States for several years. In 1958, while on a Canadian-backed lichen expedition with Trimble to the island of Svalbard in the Barents Sea, Lambshead happened to save the crew of the United States submarine Nautilus from an outbreak of Sudden Onset Type Three Erysclapian Nolamela, and thus temporarily won back the favor of the U.S. government. He would later take advantage of this goodwill to secure a federally-financed research position.

In the 1960s, Lambshead worked in a number of locations scattered across the United States, and collaborated with Leary, Lilly, and (briefly) with Wilhelm Reich; he returned to India, spent many months in Burma, Java, and Tibet (where he first identified Onco-astral Monasticism and Chant Throat). In the 1970s, among other exploits, Lambshead returned to the Amazon with a vengeance; to date, he has made over a dozen extended expeditions into the jungle. Overwhelmed by the quantity and richness of Lambshead's discoveries, experts have not yet catalogued the contents of the many crates of botanic, fungal, chemical, and zoological specimens.

Since the 1980s, Dr. Lambshead has generally preferred to explore the wildernesses of cities and suburbs rather than rough, natural places. He now teaches wherever and whenever time permits, not only at medical schools, but at community colleges, Rotary and Elks clubs and lodges (the photograph of Dr. Lambshead riding in a tiny Shriner's car has unfortunately been suppressed), and even at tent meetings and Sunday schools. Thanks to sizeable grants from the Institute for Further Study, the Society for the Dissemination of Useful Knowledge, and the Institutional Study Society Group, Dr. Lambshead now has his own hermetically-sealed lab at Wimpering, where he is presently researching autonomous epidermi and the homing instinct in colloids.

COMPILED BY DR. MICHAEL CISCO

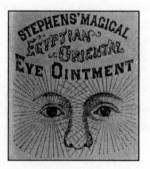

# An Enthusiastic Foreword by the Editors

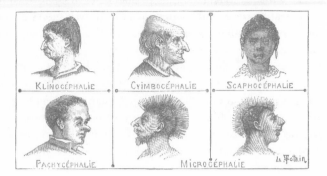

**When Dr. Lambshead** told us we were to edit not only this special commemorative edition of the Guide but all *future* editions, we were rendered speechless. At least, I know I didn't know what to say—my co-editor may have been more erudite. For several moments, life took on a surreal brilliance and became somehow . . . brighter, more sparkly.

Nonetheless, we recovered from our awe in time to edit the edition you now hold in your hands. It has been a real learning experience. First, due to the interesting side effects of Dr. Lambshead's rather unique stirrings of dementia. Second, due to our interactions with the various odd (and sometimes, to be honest, *scary*) medical experts who contributed to this edition. Coordinating the publication of a medical guide with over 60 contributing doctors could perhaps most accurately be compared to herding cats. If it wasn't Dr. Stepan Chapman complaining that his work was under-represented in this edition, it was Dr. Paolo G. Di Filippo asking us for 650 contributor copies, one for each word in his entry. Dr. Brian Evenson wanted us to send him two sets of proofs for some reason. Dr. Tim Lebbon demanded to be paid in fruit. Dr. John Coulthart abhorred our initial design; he was so vociferous in his many e-mails, telephone calls, faxes, and letters (not to mention bullhorn-delivered tirades outside both of our houses at inappropriate hours) that we finally agreed to let him design the Guide. Most doctors complained so much about our standardization of internal references that we agreed to leave them as-is.

We should note that some doctors did display notable restraint and grace. Dr. Jeffrey Thomas, for example, agreed not to sue us over an issue we would rather not resurrect at this time (the subject was, as Dr. Thomas should know, *already dead*). Dr. Kage Baker sent us 40 pounds of dried smoked bird flesh with a note indicating we should "light it up and puff." Dr. Neil Gaiman sent us a posthumous letter entitled "Some Advice," which we have published under the title "Diseasemaker's Croup."

The many acts of kindness, the many acts of madness—these kept us focused on our task, especially when Dr. Iain Rowan sent us something in a wet box that slurped out onto the floor. That wasn't our best memory of the experience, to be honest. Still, we would not trade our memories of those long months working with these intrepid men and women of science for anything, unless, of course, it was for an end to worldwide disease. Then we might be tempted to trade.

Throughout it all, of course, Dr. Lambshead led us in our efforts to maintain the high standards he had imposed on the Guide over the years (as best expressed in the reprints of diseases from prior editions). Our combined expertise in chiropractic medicine, veterinary medicine, mycology, clairvoyance, litigation, and itching/scratching diseases gave us a solid foundation for medical guide editing. However, Dr. Lambshead's many pithy yet vociferous suggestions on various matters made all the difference. We could not have asked for a better mentor (we should not be thought churlish for having asked for one at certain points in the process). Whether pontificating from what might well be his deathbed or whispering advice to the large mummified baboon head that he often mistook for our smiling visages, Dr. Lambshead remained the spirit, the soul, behind our efforts.

Now that we have managed to bring this edition to fruition, we can turn our attention to future editions of the Guide. We believe that our close relationship with Dr. Lambshead and our newly-gained editorial experience can be put to good use. The 2006 edition of the Guide will be devoted to itching-and-scratching diseases. The 2007 edition of the Guide will be devoted to diseases of the inner thigh. The 2008 edition of the Guide will be devoted to "Degenerate and Misguided Diseases" as opposed to "Eccentric and Discredited Diseases," which should provide a fresh perspective.

As we sail farther into the Twenty-First Century, rest assured that we will be steady captains of the ship that is the Guide, our hands firmly on the steering device, our stern proudly pointed to the horizon. Thank you all for joining us on this important journey into the diseased future.

EDITORS DR. JEFF VANDERMEER AND DR. MARK ROBERTS

# A Reluctant Introduction by Dr. Lambshead

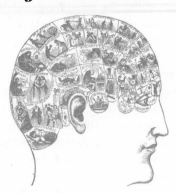

**There's no small** irony in the fact that I loathe doctors, medical guides, and introductions to medical guides. Doctors have done more to set back the cause of medicine over the last two thousand years than the Visigoths did to bloody the Romans. And introductions have wasted more trees to less effect than most bureaucratic white papers.

However, medical guides may be the worst offenders. Medical guides have proven to be the last refuge of the incompetent—a crutch for members of the medical community to lean on despite having perfectly good legs. Like some sort of science-based Ouija board, the medical guide allows the doctor to forgo using his or her own brain in favor of trusting someone else's dubious opinion. Worse, the medical guide gives the layperson a false sense of security. It seems to speak with the voice of authority. In its bewildering catalogue of symptoms, case studies, footnotes, endnotes, and indices, it appears to apply logic to otherwise illogical situations.

Nothing could be further from the truth. The standard medical guide supports and displays the neuroses and foibles of its creators as much or more so than a jejune pulp commercial novel with a ripped bodice or ripped bicep on the cover. Depending on the creator's area of expertise or current emphasis, the guide may be skewed to a particular agenda. That agenda may not always be to the patient's benefit—as in the common case wherein a guide recommends a certain company's drugs over all other solutions.

Medications are the crutch to the crutch that is the modern medical guide. If there were truth in advertising, the man on the street would open a medical guide and out would pour hundreds of pills, individually labeled to cure any malady. Pills. The root of all medical evil. The source of medical quackery since before the advent of the traveling medicine show. The panacea that says you can solve all of your problems in the same way that Alice created all of hers in that god-awful book by Carroll. I'm here to tell you that, in more than 80 years as a licensed physician (which description of my talents should, by all accounts, discredit everything I'm about to tell you, except that I am also accredited as a healer by the Quichua of Peru and the Tartars of the steppe), I have seen more deaths due to misapplication of or reliance on pills than from any other source. I have seen healthy, strapping men brought low by pills. I've seen toothaches that became purulent penile discharge in Malaysia. In Timbuktu, I've seen a Sufi holy man suffering from gout shoot flames from his arse as a result of a misapplication of pills by a young doctor newly brought in from the Soviet Union. And it's probably best not even to mention what happened in Zaire in 1977.

Why do physicians rely on pills so heavily? (And, yes, I do mean this question to be applied orally to both doctor and patient, twice a day, preferably.) They are not bad people; they mean well. But they have been so shackled by the nonsensical rigors of medical school that their brains literally change chemical composition. Anyone who has ever seen the difference between the CAT scan of the brain of a typical first-year medical student and that same student's brain after graduation will understand what I'm getting at. The free will appears to flee from such bodies like a frightened Tibetan mountain spirit. (Medical schools are even worse than medical guides, now that I think about it, but a full discussion of their peculiarities and gross rites would take a book in and of itself.) Those who do not stay to become teachers themselves flee into the wide world waving their pathetic diplomas like a spell to ward off evil.

But where do they flee to? God knows, most of the time it's into safe family practice where they can develop a "niche." Tapping knees and listening to hearts beating for 30 or 40 years while doing nothing medically speaking that would get their own blood pressure above 120/80. Rare is the member of the medical profession who will chuck all those received ideas and, metaphorically naked (although, sometimes literally naked—it is impossible to gain approval with certain Papua New Guinea tribes of the interior without stripping down to nothing and donning a huge penis sheath, sad to say), plunge into the world of eccentric diseases. True, some of this work will become discredited over time, as this guide itself proves, but even what remains discredited and truly eccentric will help save more lives than any pill or conventional medical guide. Or conventional doctor, for that matter.

That some favored few have recognized this fact is proven by the longevity of my guide. When I first started it in 1921, it was meant as a shorthand for myself, a way of keeping track of all those maladies the traditional medical community had forgotten, discounted, or ignored. As I traveled around the world, to the most remote and clandestine locations, I found not only more of these poor abandoned diseases, from which previous doctors had recoiled in horror or disbelief, but also more men and women of medicine willing to call the Motile Snarcoma found in this very volume "Motile Snarcoma," for example, and not just "surgical incompetence." (Where else but in the Guide can one find diseases resurrected from the junkpile of history, dusted off, and found to be quite relevant?)

Still, it was many years before anything approaching acceptance came from the medical community at large. It grieves me greatly, for example, that not a single medical publisher in the world would publish this latest edition of the Guide. I am certainly indebted to Night Shade Books for publishing the Guide, even though their normal fare is of dubious informational quality, but something in me still yearns for the Guide's acceptance by medical schools, hospitals, and other places I despise where it might do an amazing amount of good.

However, the effort to spread the word will now pass on to Drs. VanderMeer and Roberts. I cannot say I have much regard for their medical abilities—when I found them, they were falsely using their medical degrees to practice veterinary medicine in a remote mountainous region of Chile, often with disastrous results to the local guinea pig population. But in the realm of editing medical guides, they have proven to be decent clerks and I lack the energy to find more competent replacements.

Being now at the advanced age of 104 and unlikely to live more than another 30 years, it seems time to pass over the editorship of this guide to more vigorous if less articulate hands. That being so, it is important to end this introduction with some words of wisdom. Having thought on the matter long and hard, I have decided to set out some rules for doctors and laypeople to follow in their pursuit of truth in medicine. They are as follows, and may be familiar from earlier in this very introduction (I'm not sure; my vision has begun to fail).

1.  Never ask for bandages in Cairo.

2.  Always check your bags for parasites after passing through customs in Zaire.

3.  Never run from a python if you've suffered from diarrhea the night before.

4. If a Dr. Ramsey Sackland approaches you in Ceylon offering a medical anecdote about the effect of applying bloating frogs to gaping chest wounds, escape under the cover of a fit of intense coughing.

5. Some mountain passes in the Himalayas contain a grade of snow so fine that it can be used to disinfect septic wounds.

6. Pills are useless.

7. Doctors are useless.

8. Medical guides are useless.

DR. THACKERY T. LAMBSHEAD (RETIRED)

# Alphabetes

**A Disease Guide Benediction
for the Health & Safety of All Contributors,
Readers, and (Sympathetic) Reviewers**

**A** is for *alphabetes*, a kind of lung disease
Nearly epidemic in the New York demi-monde.
The unaware Vanessa broadcast with every sneeze
A cloud of viral letters in a classic Garamond.

**B** is for the *booksores* familiar to the reader
Who inherits a propensity for a nose pressed to the gutter.
The suppurating chancres that decorated Peter
Were scarcely less unsightly than the ones upon his mother.

**C** is for *cruditis*, a vegetarian complaint
In which peculiar polyps grow in circular arrays.
On radishes and carrots Bette would feast without restraint
Despite their strange resemblance to the growths upon her face.

**D** is for the *dentruff* on the collars, scarves, and ties
Of those who every time they chew misplace a tooth or two.
Bruno, always spitting up a cuspidal surprise
Once lost all his teeth at once inside an *amour fou*.

**E** is for *eraserrhosis*, a degenerative affliction
In which the whole identity is forced into remission.
Pamela was convinced that her existence was a fiction
And edited herself into a pocket-sized edition.

**F** is for *fellatia*, a spasm of the lips
That resembles the intention to pronounce an o *umlaut*.
Lucretia in a coughing fit occasioned by the grippe
Sucked in her mouth so hard she turned her body inside out.

**G** is for *gardenia*, pronounced just like the flower,
A fungal infestation that does no especial harm.
Whenever Jennifer was moistened by a sudden shower
The verdant tips of crocuses appeared under each arm.

**H** is for the *houseburn* caused by leaning on a wall
A good deal less hygienic than a low-rent gigolo.
Remember Meghan who complained of an enormous gall,
From which when lanced was taken forth a fetal bungalow.

**I** is *I*, a malady that everybody gets
We catch it from our parents and we give it to our kids.
Something like a charley horse, something like Tourette's
Emily takes her medicine and cures herself to bits.

**J** is for *jack-o'-lepsy*, an inflammation of the head
The eyes are bright, the skin like rind, the palate black and scorched.
Josiah got an *idée fixe* from something that he read:
To cut off the afflicted part and hoist it like a torch.

**K** is for *kangarupus;* all that hopping makes you sick
Plus the pouch is very hungry and it's also very deep.
Libby solved both problems with a topological trick:
She scrambled into her own pouch, and there she fell asleep.

**L** is for *landscabies*, an environmental disease
The rash resembles close-ups of the art of Claude Monet.
In a horizontal format Conrad retrogressed at ease.
When he died the doctor hung him up in his atelier.

**M** is *mustachiosis*, a quite disfiguring bug
Contracted through proximity to hairy people's lips.
Covered in mustaches Joe refused to take the drug
Deciding he looked rather smart, he waxed and curled the tips.

**N** is for the *nebulouse*, another small companion
That drills a zillion little holes and leaves you very porous.
William was a heavy man when he left for the Grand Canyon.
He will come down when full of rain, meteorologists assure us.

**O** is for *o'clock-jaw*, an orderly disorder
With punctual attacks the victims measure out their fate.
Every hour upon the hour, the half-hour and the quarter
Olivia yawns and comments, *"How late it is, how late."*

**P**'s for *pandora's botulism*, a vaginal infection
Caused by curiosity, the older textbooks say.
Ramona spread her legs and from a southerly direction
Came a budgerigar, ten dollars, and a T-shirt from L.A.

**Q** is for *quotation martyr*, prone to this convulsion:
The index finger and its neighbor suffer rhythmic cramps.
Alas, the victims often face not pity but revulsion.
*I "love" you*, Vaughn said, and was cold-cocked with a lava lamp.

**R**'s for *rhyme's disease* in which your organs are replaced
By things that rhyme with what they're called in common barroom talk.
Your ass is *grass*, your guts *peanuts*, your face is made of *lace*.
She likes me this way said Germain, of his enormous *wok*.

**S** for *seraphism*, a delusion which will lay low
Those whose passion for good works exceeds the bounds of sense.
A gaseous emission from the scalp explains the halo,
"But explain the wings!" demanded an hysterical Hortense.

**T** is for *tantaluscence*, a severe indisposition
Contracted when in seeking love one faces an impasse.
The pain when the desired is near but forbids intromission!
Roger tied himself in knots when courting his own ass.

**U** is for *UFOnanism*, a seldom seen complaint;
Growths resemble household objects or a glowing ball.
Describing these to doctors who appeared to find him quaint,
Anatole was told that they did not exist at all.

**V** is for *ventriloqueasy*, something we've all felt
The day our parasitic twins began to answer back.
To mute the talking dummy growing from below her belt
Ruthless Gwenda stuffed its mouth with a piece of bric-a-brac.

**W** is for the *wishboned:* a strangely cheerful few
Who appear in casts so often they're suspected to malinger.
Every time a bone gives way another wish comes true;
Vanessa on a stretcher smiled and snapped a baby finger.

**X** is for *Xmasectomy*, effective if done early
Doctors say do not ignore these signs presaging doom:
The giant paunch, the snowy beard (disturbing in a girlie) . . .
The plaintive cry of "Ho ho ho" was heard from Hannah's room.

**Y** is for *yogarictus*, its symptoms easy to descry:
The afflicted assume postures that make onlookers agog.
Despite advanced decrepitude Xavier seemed quite spry
Until the day he could not leave his *downward facing dog*.

**Z** for *Zeno's paradoxysm*, which fills us with misgiving,
By infinitely tiny steps it deadens but won't kill.
As no one could be sure if Aunt Augusta was still living
We propped her in her favorite chair to wait. She's waiting still.

COMPOSED BY DR. SHELLEY JACKSON AND READ AT DR. THACKERY T. LAMBSHEAD'S
100TH BIRTHDAY PARTY *

---

* *Editors' Note:* Other highlights of the party included Dr. Jay Lake's juggling of three-foot-long parasitic African worms, Dr. Rachel Pollack's internal organ tarot card readings, and Dr. L. Timmel Duchamp's hysterical impressions of Freud, Jung, and Nietzsche.

# DISEASES

# M E D I C A L   G U I D E   K E Y

For a variety of reasons, including several complaints, we have decided (with Dr. Lambshead's approval) to label three unfortunate conditions pertaining to the diseases described in this guide.

**DISCREDITED**—A disease that has been discredited by another of our many doctors. In the case of a full discreditation, we remove the disease from the Guide prior to publication. However, in the case of a partial discreditation or a full discreditation occurring very close to our release date, we do not have time for confirmation. In such a case, we leave the disease in the Guide. If a full discreditation is confirmed, the next edition of the Guide will include all pertinent data.

**INFECTIOUS**—A disease wherein the mere reading of a disease guide entry may infect the reader with the disease being read. In such cases, we now provide a symbol that allows the reader to decide if he or she wishes to continue reading the disease entry, or simply browse another section.

**QUARANTINED**—A disease that has clearly infected the doctor submitting the disease to this Guide. In such a case, we publish the information, but now provide a Quarantined symbol that alerts the reader to this unfortunate state of affairs.

# BALLISTIC ORGAN SYNDROME

## Ballistitis

## Country of Origin
Java (Indonesia)

## First Known Case
Ballistic Organ Syndrome, although rare, has been known since prehistoric times. In Australasia and Micronesia, cave paintings have been found depicting humans and animals with internal organs erupting from their bodies. (1)

## Symptoms
Ballistic Organ Syndrome manifests as a sudden, explosive discharge of one or more bodily organs at high velocity; this exit may be accompanied by some pain. There are two known variants: subsonic Ballistitis, in which the velocity of ejection does not exceed that of sound, and distinguished by an explosive discharge from throat or anus accompanied by a release of wet, atomized bodily contents; and supersonic Ballistitis, in which the organ exits the body by the path of least resistance, breaking free directly through muscle, tendon, bone, and skin tissues.

Supersonic Ballistitis is the more dangerous manifestation, as the ejecta exceed the speed of sound and therefore strike without warning. Surprisingly, however, the high energy of supersonic Ballistitis discharge cauterizes the surface of the organ and sterilizes the ejected bodily contents, so that the overall risk of infection is less than that of subsonic Ballistitis.

In rare cases, the Ballistitis virus infects the patient's entire body. Eventually, some event causes one or more cells to rupture, after which the patient's body is disrupted in an explosive ejection of all bodily organs. This manifestation of the syndrome frequently occasions the death of the patient; at best, the loss of all bodily organs will cause considerable inconvenience and distress (as set out in *Doctor Buckhead Mudthumper's Encyclopedia of Forgotten Oriental Diseases*).

## History

During the 1709 siege of Batavia (today Jakarta), the Sultan of Solo used Ballistitis-infected slaves as catapult ammunition, in hopes of injuring (and infecting) enough of the Dutch defenders to render their fortifications untenable. Fortunately for the Dutch the governor of Batavia, Pieter van Tilberg, was familiar with Ballistitis from his service as a surgeon's assistant in Celebes (today Sulawesi). Van Tilberg ordered that infected citizens be expelled from the city; those infected individuals wreaked havoc among the besieging Javanese. Pieter van Tilberg later wrote an epic poem, "The Liver's Red Glare," in commemoration of the Dutch victory.

It is obvious from this account, however, that Ballistitis must have been endemic throughout the Indonesian Archipelago for years, if not centuries, prior to this event.

Randolph Johnson spent several months in the Indonesian Archipelago, searching for Ballistitis sufferers in hope of collecting case studies for his posthumously-published *Confessions of a Disease Fiend*, an autobiographical account of the tragic sexual obsession that culminated in his death. During sexual congress with a catamite in Mataram (Lombok, Indonesia), Johnson lost an arm to a supersonic Ballistitis discharge. Johnson was evacuated to Singapore aboard the Royal Navy frigate *Indomitable*, but died en route.

## Cures

Ballistitis is known to be caused by a retrovirus that reprograms body cells to concentrate water at extremely high pressures. This buildup may continue for days or weeks, until one or more cells is ruptured and the pressure is released in a steam explosion. This initiates a chain reaction of other infected cells, causing one or more organs to be ejected with great force. The violence of supersonic Ballistitis is more likely to trigger adjacent cell detonation, and so a supersonic ejection is unlikely to be followed by subsequent ejections; subsonic Ballistitis eruptions, however, may continue until no organs remain in the body cavity. As reported in *The Journals of Sarah Goodman, Disease*

*Psychologist*, both forms of the disorder occasion some distress on the part of the patient.

The Ballistitis retrovirus may be transmitted through direct contact with organic ejecta or through inhalation of atomized bodily contents. Medical personnel dealing with infected patients are strongly recommended to seek the advice of a military fortifications engineer to assist in deploying sandbagging and overhead protection, as ejected organs can travel a considerable distance and explode with some force on impact. When handling a patient at close quarters, respirator masks and ballistic body armor are strongly recommended as prophylaxis. Under no circumstances should a patient be immersed in water or any similarly incompressible fluid, placed in close proximity to load-bearing members of any structure, or surrounded by objects that might become lethal shrapnel in the event of an explosion.

In cases where one or a few organs have been ejected, organ transplantation is a useful means of restoring organic function; the surgeon should, however, ensure that all infected tissue has been excised. Unwary surgeons have worked for hours to save a patient's life, only to have the recently-implanted organ rejected in spectacular (and hazardous) fashion.

### Submitted by

Dr. Michael Barry, Institute of Psychiatric Venereology, Hughes, Australian Capital Territory

### Endnote

(1) "Explosive Ejection of Bodily Contents In Prehistoric Cave Art: A Medical Mystery Solved?" by James H. Twickenham, in *Tropical Diseases Quarterly* vol. 12.

### Cross References

Buboparazygosia; Diseasemaker's Croup; Motile Snarcoma; Pentzler's Lubriciousness

# BLOODFLOWER'S MELANCHOLIA

## Country of Origin
England

## First Known Case
The first and, in the opinion of some authorities, the only true case of Bloodflower's Melancholia appeared in Worcestershire, England, in the summer of 1813. The local doctor professed himself baffled by the symptoms of Squire Bloodflower's eldest son, Peter, then a youth of 18. "In all my many years as a physician," he wrote in his diary, only recently discovered, "I have never encountered such a puzzling and recalcitrant malady, whose origin must surely lie in the mysteries of the human soul."

## Symptoms
"Since entering manhood the young Peter had manifested a distinguished gloom, which, on his achieving his majority, blossomed into a consummate mania. He shunned all active pursuits and dressed entirely in black. The sight of something as simple as sunshine or as innocent as a flower reduced him to tears of grief. He rejected normal sustenance, and exhibited a compulsion to drink ink and to eat paper. When these staples were put out of reach he began to consume his books; and on these being removed he retreated into a primitive and immobile state, akin to that of the embryo in the womb, from which he emerged only by God's grace and in his own good time." (From the diaries of Dr. Amos Smith, Worcester County Library)

## History

Although Peter Bloodflower's is the first recorded case, there is reason to suspect a previous history of instability in the family (notably that of his aunt, Laetitia Bloodflower, who ended her days in a convent in Provence), which for reasons of social nicety had been carefully concealed. On recovering from his first attack, in the autumn of 1816, Peter went to London where he became part of the Romantic circle, mixing freely with such luminaries as Keats and Shelley, and, it is thought, making a considerable impression on their receptive minds. Keats' "Ode on Melancholy" is thought to have been addressed to him. It is likely, however, that Bloodflower's real interest lay with Keats' former roommate and fellow medical student, Henry Stephens, who may have developed his famous blue-black ink for the express purpose of satiating Bloodflower's secret thirst.

However, the true notability—and controversy—of Bloodflower's Melancholia lies in its hereditary character. According to the journals of Sarah Goodman, the distinguished disease psychologist, "no other disorder of the appetites and the emotions has manifested itself with such repeated exactness in successive generations of the same family." Nor, she might have added, amongst so wide a scattering of its members. Charcot's treatment of Justine Fleur-de-Sang at the Salpetriere in 1865, and Freud's encounter with Hans Blutblum in Vienna in 1926, bear witness to the familial tenacity of the condition. Not to mention the direct descendants of Peter Bloodflower, resident in Worcestershire until this very day. Each one has exhibited the same ink-drinking and paper-eating tendencies, combined with extreme Weltschmerz, "as if," in the words of Dr. Smith, "the weight of nature were too great for his fragile spirit to endure."

There are, however, those who dispute the existence of Bloodflower's Melancholia in its hereditary form. Randolph Johnson is unequivocal on the subject. "There is no such thing as Bloodflower's Melancholia," he writes in *Confessions of a Disease Fiend*. "All cases subsequent to the original are in dispute, and even where records are complete, there is no conclusive proof of heredity. If anything we have here a case of inherited suggestibility. In my view, these cannot be regarded as cases of Bloodflower's Melancholia, but more properly as Bloodflower's Melancholia by Proxy."

If Johnson's conclusions are correct, we must regard Peter Bloodflower as the sole true sufferer from this distressing condition, a lonely status that possesses its own melancholy aptness.

## Outcome and Cures

This type of melancholia does not generally prove fatal. Peter Bloodflower, despite recurrent episodes, lived a long and fecund life. Only two cases of possible suicide in the Bloodflower family have occurred: that of Arthur Bloodflower, who died in 1892 of ink poisoning (his favored brand contained high quantities of vitriol) and that of Horatio Bloodflower, who according to legend drowned in his own tears.

There is probably no cure for Bloodflower's Melancholia, or, for that matter, for Bloodflower's Melancholia by Proxy. Peter Bloodflower was, of course, subjected to the sole treatment available in his time: "I bled him six ounces," writes Smith, "and found his blood to be as black as ink." Freud found it non-amenable to psychoanalysis. "A grief whose sources lie in the very wellsprings of existence," he wrote, "may never, I fear, be truly capable of cure." Modern advances in genetics may yet hold the key to its eradication, or prove, at least, its claim to join the ranks of genuine hereditary diseases.

## Submitted by
Dr. Tamar Yellin

## Cross References
Diseasemaker's Croup; Menard's Disease; Monochromitis; Poetic Lassitude; Rashid's Syndrome

# BONE LEPROSY

## *Turkish Bone Leprosy, or Saint Calamaro's Leprosy*

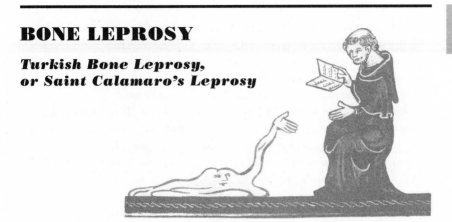

## Introduction

Hansen's disease, commonly known as leprosy, is a long-acting microbial infection. Its lengthy dormancy period has created confusion regarding its modes of transmission. However, the active organism, Mycobacterium leprae, has been isolated, and many modern cases can be reversed by antibiotics. In medieval Turkey, things were very different.

## History

In the Christian year 1510, Bayezid the Second ruled the Ottoman Empire. On the shores of the Black Sea, at the mouth of the Sakarya River, there was a colony for lepers called Saint Augustine's Retreat. The lepers grew barley and made goat cheese. Their needs for commerce with the outside world were met by an adjacent community, the Franciscan monks of The Order of Saint Augustine, who maintained the leprosarium.

Throughout the existence of the colony, it attracted a steady stream of pilgrim lepers, who walked there from as far away as Greece and Persia. In roughly 1520 a new form of Hansen's disease appeared among the pilgrims. The Franciscans called it bone leprosy.

## Symptoms

The basic distinction here is easy to grasp. The hallmark symptom of normal leprosy is that necrotic flesh falls from the bones of the extremities. In bone leprosy, the bones of the extremities fall from the flesh.

First the blackened bones of the fingers and toes would poke themselves bloodlessly through the skin and detach. Next the metacarpals and metatarsals disassembled themselves and emigrated. At this stage the victim could still walk on his ankles with the help of crutches. But then the long bones of the four limbs would emerge into the light of day and discard themselves.

The chronicle of Father Ambrosius, the last abbot of The Order of Saint Augustine, reports that one bone leper also lost his pelvis, scapulars, and clavicles, and got along with only a skull, a spine, and some ribs. This man called himself Vecchio Calamaro, "the old squid." He may have been born in Italy.

## Further History

By 1530 many bone lepers could be seen among the hovels of the colony, squirming across the earth like giant sea stars. But the "Normal Lepers" distrusted "the Boneless Ones" and finally attacked them with clubs and drove them from the colony.

The Boneless Ones slithered away and formed their own settlement on a barren plateau that overlooked the monastery, the leprosarium, and the river. They drew water from a mountain stream and grew vegetables and spices. At the instruction of Father Ambrosius, the monks brought them barley and milk on the sly. An uneasy truce ensued between the two leper colonies.

In 1534, during the reign of Suleiman the Magnificent, Old Calamaro experienced a religious epiphany. He communicated this vision to his fellow pariahs with such force that they reorganized themselves as a lay brotherhood. They committed their lives to penance, holy poverty, and the contemplation of Christ's mercies. Calamaro went to live in a pit lined with stones, like a shallow well shaft or a lidless oubliette. He dug this pit himself, using only his teeth and a wooden spoon.

As the years progressed, more and more of the Boneless took vows and became visionary hermits, living in the sunken circular cells that dotted the plateau. They seldom spoke, but their echoing chants at dawn and dusk could be heard by Father Ambrosius at Saint Augustine's. Certainly the Boneless Ones had surpassed the Franciscans in their pursuit of austerity. Ambrosius felt no temptation to envy them their accomplishment. (1)

The only existing record of The Order of Saint Augustine and the two leprosariums concludes with the death of Ambrosius. The monastery walls have been toppled by earthquakes.

But Old Calamaro is remembered to this day as Saint Calamaro of the Russian Orthodox Church. A few of the "prayer pits" of his brotherhood have been preserved for visitation near the modern town of Karasu.

## Hagiography

A hagiography is not, of course, medical data. I present this excerpt from Saint Calamaro's notwithstanding, freely translated from an anonymous Latin parchment. Please consider it as a curious footnote to the social history of leprosy.

The miracles of Saint Calamaro were three in number, and three in number were his trials, the first being a trial by hunger.

It came to pass that the hearts of the Normal Lepers were enflamed against their bone-bereft neighbors. And the Normals didst resolve to accost those gentle Franciscans who went forth each day to pass among the Boneless. For the Normals deemed it folly to risk contagion from such an unnatural affliction as bonelessness. And they shouted at the monks, saying, "Shun the unclean! Your charity could get us all deboned!"

And they didst smite those humble monks, and lo they broke many heads. For they grew cruel when they got a little wine into them. And Father Ambrosius didst resign himself to abandon the Boneless.

And further the Normals didst rip up the Boneless Ones' gardens and didst foul the pure water of their stream.

For 40 days and nights, the Boneless drank only the morning dew that condensed on the walls of their cells, and ate only the tiny creeping things that they found within their clothes. And yet they thirsted not, nor didst they hunger. For the grace of Saint Calamaro's first miracle was upon them.

The second trial of the saint was a trial by drowning. For indeed the Normals didst arise again against him and didst drag him from his pit. And none of his followers resisted the Normals, but rather they prayed more loudly to drown out his cries for help. For the Boneless were sore afraid.

And in consequence the Normals didst bind the saint within a sack, and drag the sack across sharp rocks to a boat, and row this boat a great distance across the Black Sea. And there they didst abuse the saint and kick him in his private parts and throw him overboard and leave him to drown. And the Normals were well satisfied, even though an ear, a nose, and several of their fingers had been lost in the scuffle.

In his aquatic extremity, the saint lost not his faith in his Savior, but didst call out loudly to the Lord, with many Italianate profanities, in fear and in trembling and with evil-tasting water in his mouth. And his prayers were answered, for like unto the rainbow-dappled jellyfish, he didst float upon the sea, nor did he sink.

The Normals didst row to shore and make straight for their dining hall, for drowning cripples always made them thirsty. And lo the second miracle! At their dining hall, they found their cook in great dismay. For Saint Calamaro had appeared in her largest stew pot and was eating all the stew.

Then the saint's final trial was upon him, which was a trial by boiling in oil. For the outraged Normals didst pour much olive oil into that soup pot and didst clamp down the lid with great force and three carpenter's vices. And they didst convey the soup pot to an open space between their hovels, where they soon amassed the makings for a bonfire. Mightily that conflagration raged about the soup pot. And the Normals danced and shouted, saying, "This is how we cook a squid in Turkey!"

But when the fires died, and the soup pot was opened, there was nothing inside. And just as the Normals saw this ominous emptiness, a chuckling was heard.

And lo the third miracle! It was Old Calamaro. He was inside the dining hall again, feasting on almonds and custards and wine. And seeing this, the Normals didst flee in fright from the doings of this leprous magus.

And though he was never seen again, peace reigned forever after between the Normals and the Boneless. For it was said among them that Old Calamaro had melted into the shingle at the shore, like unto an icicle in the sunshine. And they said that he dwelt now in the earth beneath their sandals, and that he watched all the lepers of the world, lest they ever again mistreat the wretched.

But in truth the Old Squid ascended to the Land of Light and sits now among the choirs of the angels in the throne room of the Lord. Perhaps he even sits on a velvet stool beside the Savior's giant golden throne.

Or perhaps—who can say?—he reclines more comfortably on the white marble floor *beneath* the throne, peering out from his special place between the four golden legs. Perhaps he reclines on a tasteful Persian rug, eating stewed prunes with a silver spoon. Perhaps he smiles down toothlessly on all the prostrate supplicants arrayed before God's throne. Perhaps he shakes his head and chuckles, as they beg for mercy.

## Submitted by

STEPAN CHAPMAN, DOCTOR OF PANDEMICS

## Endnote

(1) Father Ambrosius wrote the following scrap of Latin verse into a margin of his chronicle.

> Shunned by their unclean brethren,
> Who are shunned by the monks of my order,
> Who in turn are barely tolerated
> By the Moslem that surround us.
> Who is the lowliest of the low?
> Who is most outcast?

## Cross References

Chronic Zygotic Dermis Disorder; Diseasemaker's Croup; Extreme Exostosis; Razornail Bone Rot

# BUBOPARAZYGOSIA

## Country of Origin

Kingdom of Nepal, Valley of Lakur (not verified)

## First Known Case

Autumn of the year 1813, in the person of Benjamin Ransool, half-caste manservant to Major Marius Bullivant of the 2nd Bangalore Lancers. Major Bullivant was on detached service from his regiment, posing as a naturalist while mapping the terrain of Nepal's more inaccessible regions. The manservant Benjamin had been sent north into Tibet some weeks before to exchange messages with the government in Lhasa, and was due to rendezvous with his master in a village at the foot of the Dhaulagiri. Benjamin arrived more than a week late and, according to the Major's journal, "afflicted with a vile fever and a number of eruptions upon the skin of his upper torso."

In the course of the disease, the manservant became delirious and spoke of a high valley named Lakur and a village inhabited only by old men. Soon after, he lapsed into a comatose state. The swellings on the skin grew into buboes, then developed a leathery exterior while continuing to burgeon. The Major's journal goes on to describe a shocking deterioration in his manservant's condition, how weight loss became a visible wasting away while the breathing grew labored and wheezing. The buboes became pale leathery bulges the size of oranges, their surfaces taut and rough.

The end came swiftly. The Major returned from foraging to find Benjamin Ransool lifeless, his body reduced to a collapsed husk. The swellings seemed to have hastened his demise, and when Major Bullivant entered his servant's room he knew that they had burst, for their abominable contents lay on the bed next to the body. The Major's journal is explicit: "At first I took the creatures to be a vermian or reptilian parasite, but as my eyes adjusted to the dimness I could see that they resembled in every way human foetuses."

By his own account, the Major did away with these parasites by putting the hut to the torch. Thus no evidence of this occurrence survives, except for the Major's journal. However, the journal's entries were to be verified long after the Major's death, and under astonishing circumstances.

## Symptoms

The Major's journal disappeared soon after his death but resurfaced several decades later and came into the hands of his only son, Sir Randal Bullivant, the noted physician. The symptoms are clearly described therein: a high temperature leading to profuse sweating and fever; small red eruptions on the upper torso that increase steadily in size during the next two days. The sufferer experiences delirium prior to the descent into coma. The body rapidly wastes away while the swellings grow very large, bursting open soon after death and disgorging a parasitic vertebral zygote.

## History

Sir Randal Bullivant was kind enough to provide me with full details from his father's journal, but it was to be his final letter that would lay bare the terrible truth of this affliction.

The letter began with advice that I consult the British Library's copy of B. Mudthumper's *Encyclopedia of Forgotten Oriental Diseases*, then went on to inquire about the proceedings of the Symposium of Materia Medica being held at the Ashbliss Memorial Hospice. After this he wrote of a curious letter he had received the previous day from someone purporting to be a friend of his father's from Nepal, and claiming to have information regarding the infection that had struck down his father's servant.

A time and a meeting place had been stipulated in the letter, and despite natural caution Sir Randal Bullivant was determined to keep the appointment. Having made clear his intent to finish his letter after the meeting, he then scribed a neat line across the page. When the writing resumed it was in the shaky script of someone greatly distressed. Without preamble, Sir Randal began to relate what had occurred.

The meeting took place in a north London park, in a secluded arbor. The sender of the letter he described as "a leathery-skinned, bony old man no taller than five feet, incongruously dressed like an office clerk and carrying a small valise." After introducing himself as Dojar Kel Nor, the stranger proceeded to claim to be 173 years old and a member of an ancient Nepalese mountain tribe that had survived down the centuries without the need for women to replenish their numbers. Sir

Randal confessed that his immediate response was one of incredulity until this Dojar opened his valise and took out a pale, flattened pod the size of a plum. Sir Randal then recounted the following dialogue:

"This—the fruit of the ultirel bush growing only in our valley, our Lakur. Inside, the dust of sons. When a man from the outer breathes the dust, he makes his sons and dies, but when his sons take the dust they do not die. We wished to explain this to your father, but too late."

"I have read all of my father's letter and journals, sir," Randal replied. "He made no mention of either you or a bush."

The man Dojar stared and said, "Not Major Bul'vant. His servant Ransool took the dust and was your father."

At this point Sir Randal's handwriting grew erratic as he told of how the old man dropped the pale pod at his feet and said, "Take the dust, son of Ransool, and you will know truth."

The letter then ended abruptly with the words, "M_____, my good friend, I have the pod and am taking it with me down to the house at Swaffham. One way or another, I will know the truth."

The outcome is well known. Sir Randal Bullivant was found dead in his Swaffham home. The post-mortem disclosed that he had died from cyanide poisoning. Fourteen large lesions dotted his upper torso. No pieces of sloughed skin were discovered at the death scene.

My own conjecture of Bullivant's demise is that the old man Dojar, alone or accompanied, followed him to Swaffham and watched his movements in the house. Once he had inhaled the abominable dust and the grotesque alterations began to take place, the watchers entered the house, harvested the hideous progeny, and decamped. On recovering his senses, Bullivant took a fatal dose of cyanide, shown to be from his laboratory in London. Who can say what passed through his mind in those dark hours of black revelation, but only the deepest despair can lead to self-administered oblivion.

### Cures
No experimental results are available, and there is no known cure. However, purging with fire is certain to prevent any spread of the virulent dust.

### Submitted by
Dr. M. Cobley, B.A., F.R.S., S.L.D., B.S.F.A. (Hons)

### Cross References
Ballistic Organ Syndrome; Diseasemaker's Croup; Motile Snarcoma; Zschokke's Chancres

# BUFONIDIC CEPHALITIS

*Toad Brain, Toad Stone, Warty Encephalitis*

## Country of Origin
China; Southern Mediterranean

## First Known Case
The original reports of this and the related disease family have their origin in travelers' tales from the Far East in the early fifteenth century. The first known verifiable documented case comes from the early eighteenth century with the case of Giacomo Pertrude, a Florentine spice trader reputed to have caught the disease from a carrier traveling the Silk Route overland from China. The case is portrayed in the painting "Man with Toad Brain" by Giovanni Battista Tiepolo hanging in the Uffizi Gallery in Florence. Later cases have been variously documented in *Acta Neurobiologiae Experimentalis*, *The Journal of Neurosurgery*, and *Doctor Buckhead Mudthumper's Encyclopedia of Forgotten Oriental Diseases*.

## Symptoms
The subject suffers from blinding headaches that gradually subside after a period of four to seven days. This is rapidly followed by the onset of fever and small warty lesions at the back of the neck that secrete an oily, rancid green fluid, leading to collar staining. Pores at the forehead can, in dim light, be seen to be issuing a pale green vapor, reputed to have medicinal properties if captured in an appropriate vessel and immediately refrigerated. The oily secretion from the neck should be treated with great caution, as this is the

followed by a pause as the sufferer waits for a response. If any of those listening repeats the word, the sufferer's satisfaction is obvious.

Later, it is from among these mimics that the next batch of the infected will be found.

## History

At the insistence of the respected Dr. William Haygarth, all murrain sufferers were released into the care of Dr. Samuel Buscard in 1775. (2) During postmortem investigations on the cerebellums of infected victims, Buscard discovered what he thought were parasitic worms, which he named after himself. When a committee of aetiologists examined his evidence, they found that the vermiform specimens were made of cerebral matter itself. Buscard was denounced amid claims that he had made the "worms" himself by perforating the brains with a cheese-screw. The committee renamed the disease Gibbering Fever, and halfheartedly claimed it to be the result of "bad air."

Samuel Buscard was ordered to surrender Jansa to the committee, but he produced papers showing that his patient had succumbed and been buried. The disgraced doctor then disappeared from public view and died in 1777.

His research was continued by his son Jacob, also a doctor. In 1782, Jacob Buscard astounded the medical establishment with the publication of his famous pamphlet proving that the brain-tissue "worms" were capable of independent motion in the head, and that the cerebrums of sufferers were riddled with convoluted tunnels. "The first Dr. Buscard was thus correct," he wrote. "Not *bad air* but a voracious parasite—a *murrain*—afflicts the gibberers."

> There is a word, which when spoken *inveigles* its way into the mind of the speaker and manifests itself in his flesh. It forces its bearer to speak itself again and again, in the company of others, that they might be tempted to echo it. With each utterance another *wormword* is born, until the brain is tunneled quite through: and when those listening repeat what they have heard, in curiosity or mockery, if their utterance is *just so*, a wormword is hatched in *their* heads. Not quite the parasite envisaged by my wronged father, but a parasite nonetheless. (3)

Jacob Buscard's pamphlet dates his revelation to 1780, during one of his numerous interrogations of Jansa in his "torpid" state. Jansa told Buscard that his illness had started one day while he was reading to his master in Bled. Between the pages of the book he had found a slip of paper on which was written two words. Jansa read the first word aloud, and thus started the earliest known outbreak of Wormword. His ensuing headache caused him to drop the paper, which was subsequently lost. "With the translation of those few letters into sound," Jacob Buscard wrote, "the wretched Jansa became midwife and host to the wormword." (4)

The younger Buscard's breakthrough won him a tremendous reputation, marred by his admissions that he and his father had forged Jansa's death certificate and kept him alive and imprisoned as an experimental subject for the past seven years. Jansa was found in the Buscard basement in the advanced stages of his disease and was taken to a madhouse, where he died two months later. Jacob Buscard escaped prosecution for kidnapping, torture, and accessory to forgery by fleeing to Munich, where he disappeared. (5)

London suffered periodic outbreaks of Buscard's Murrain until the passage of the Gibbering Act of 1810 legalized the incarceration of the infected in soundproof sanatoria. (6) The era of mass infection was over, and only occasional isolated cases have been recorded since.

It took the late twentieth century and the work of Jacob Buscard's great-great-great-great-great granddaughter Dr. Mariella Buscard to conclusively dispel the superstitious notions about "evil words" that have clouded even scholarly discussions of the disease. In her seminal 1995 *Lancet* article "It's the Synapses, Stupid!", the latest Dr. Buscard proves the murrain to be simply an unpleasant (though admittedly unusual) biochemical reaction.

She points out that with every action of the human body, including speech, a unique configuration of thousands of minute chemical reactions occurs in the brain. Dr. Buscard shows that when the wormword is spoken with a precise inflection, the concomitant synaptic firing has the unfortunate property of reconfiguring nerve fibers into discrete self-organizing clusters. The tiny chemical reactions, in other words, turn nerves into parasites. Boring through the brain and using their own newly independent bodies to reroute neural messages, these marauding lengths of brain-matter periodically take control of their host. They particularly affect his or her speech, in an attempt to fulfill their instincts to reproduce.

Following the format established in Jacob Buscard's pamphlet, the wormword is traditionally rendered *yGudluh*. This is recorded with some trepidation: the main vector for the transmission of Buscard's Murrain over the last two centuries has been the literature about it. (7)

## Cures

Randolph Johnson's claims about bergamot oil in *Confessions of a Disease Fiend* are spurious: there is no known cure for Buscard's Murrain. (8) There is, however, persistent speculation that the second word on Jansa's lost paper, if spoken, might engender some cure in the brain: perhaps a predatory "hunter" synapse to devour the wormwords. Several "Jansa's papers" have appeared over the decades, all forgeries. (9) Despite numerous careful searches, Jansa's paper remains lost. (10)

## Submitted by
DR. CHINA MIÉVILLE

## Endnotes
(1) "I doubt not that you have heard of Mister *Jansa*, a fellow of lamentable aspect, who is daily seen around the squares of his adopted city where his intense bearing entices crowds of the curious;—when surrounded the fellow excoriates 'em in obscure tongues such as would shame the most *pious* and ecstatic of quakers.—Those gathered mock the afflicted with mummery.—But horrors! A number of those who have mimicked poor Jansa have fallen to his brain-fever, and are now partners in his *unorthodox ministry*." (Kate Vinegar [ed.], *The London Letters of Ignatius Sancho* [Providence 1954], p. 337.)

(2) There is no record of Haygarth fraternizing with or even mentioning Dr. Buscard before or after this time, and the reasons behind his 1775 recommendation are opaque. In his diaries, Haygarth's assistant William Fin noted "a disparity between Dr. H's *words* and his *tone* when he claimed Dr. Buscard as his *very good friend*" (quoted in Marcus Gadd's *A Buscardology Primer.* [London: 1972]. p. iii). De Selby, in his unpublished "Notes on Buscard," claims that Buscard was blackmailing Haygarth. What incriminating material he might have held on his more esteemed colleague remains unknown.

(3) *A Posthumous Vindication of Dr. Samuel Buscard: Proof That "Gibbering Fever" is Indeed Buscard's Murrain.* (London 1782), p. 17.

(4) Ibid., p. 25.

(5) His last known letter (to his son Matthew) is dated January 1783, and contains a hint as to his plans. Jacob complains "I have not even the money to finish this. Carriage to Bled is a scandalous expense!" (Quoted in Ali Khamrein's *Medical Letters* [New York 1966], p. 232.)

(6) These notorious "Buscard Shacks" loom large in popular culture of the time. See for example the ballad "Rather the Poorhouse Than a Buscard Shack" (reproduced in Cecily Fetchpaw's *Hanoverian Street Songs: Populism and Resistance* [Pennsylvania 1988], p. 677).

(7) Contrary to the impression given by the media after the 1986 Statten-Dogger incident, *deliberate* exposure to the risks of Wormword is neither common nor new. Ully Statten was (no doubt unwittingly) continuing a tradition established in the late eighteenth century. In what could be considered a late Georgian extreme sport, London's young rakes and coffee-house dandies would take turns reading the word aloud, each risking correct pronunciation and thereby infection.

(8) This will come as no surprise to those familiar with Johnson's work. The man is a liar, a fraud, and a bad writer (whose brother is Britain's third-largest importer of bergamot oil).

(9) There is a comprehensive list in Gadd, op. cit., p. 74.

(10) "Years of Violent Ransacking Leave Slovenia's Historic Churches in Ruins" *Financial Times* 3/7/85.

## Cross References

Diseasemaker's Croup; Fuseli's Disease; Logrolling Ephesus; Noumenal Fluke; Printer's Evil; Wuhan Flu

# CATAMENIA HYSTERICA

*Pseudo-Menstruation, The Male Curse,*
*Periodic Sympathetic Bleeding,*
*Post-Menopausal Hysterical Menstruation*

### First Known Case

The folk literature teems with tales of pseudo-menstruation from time immemorial, spanning the globe. The first recorded case can be found in the Bible, in the fourth chapter of Genesis, where Adam's sixth son, Orem, is described as dressing and behaving like his mother and sisters rather than his father and brothers, with the consequence that God made him to bleed monthly like the former, through an unspecified "privy member."

### Symptoms

Patients bleed for three to five days from an orifice, usually at the onset of the New Moon. Women always bleed from the vagina (although the bleeding is not true menstruation), whereas men bleed most commonly from the urethra, the anus, or the nipples. Bleeding from the navel is *extremely* rare.

### History

The social significance of Catamenia Hysterica has varied so considerably from culture to culture and across time that a stable etiology for the disorder cannot be established. Twelfth-century western Europe, for instance, saw a mass outbreak of the disease at the Cistercian Abbey of Clairveaux, where, under the direction of the saintly Bernard of Citeaux, dozens of young men lured from their studies in Paris by Bernard's charismatic preaching spontaneously began menstruating at the dark of every moon. Since it was not until the thirteenth century that scientific and theological accounts of menstruation rendered this natural function morally tainted and supernaturally destructive, we may assume that the treatment of both natural menstruation and Catamenia Hysterica in William of Conches' *The Dragmaticon* (Paris, 1146) characterized contemporary perceptions of the disease. "These young men worshipped the Virgin so fervently and with such zealous devotion, repeatedly revisiting the important moments of her life in just that way in which all good Christians revisit the Stations of the Cross on Good Friday, that they became, in the very tissues of their body, like the Virgin, refraining only from reliving her pregnancy with the Son of God, which would have been a blasphemous rather than a pious enactment of the Virgin's passion." Many people considered such pseudo-menstruation to be miraculous, analogous to manifestations of the holy stigmata. William notes that "although some theologians argue that the Virgin did not menstruate, no rational man could believe such a thing, for being a woman, her humors were necessarily cold, though her body and soul be holy and immaculate."

By contrast, an outbreak of Catamenia Hysterica in Quattrocento, Florence, suggests an entirely different psychogenesis. This occurred among members of a lay organization, the Confraternity of the Miraculous Blood, associated with the church of Sant' Ambrogio, a confraternity whose mission included the staging of theatrical entertainments in neighboring piazzas for purportedly charitable fund-raising. In a sermon San Bernardino delivered at Santa Croce in 1424, following his usual denunciation of the practices of "sodomy"—which, he said, were so entrenched in Tuscany that in many Italian cities "no Tuscan is allowed to live and no schoolmaster may be Tuscan, for fear that he will corrupt the boys"—the preacher inveighed against "those young men of a certain confraternity who, led astray by the superstitious lies of Father Bartolomeo Maffei, have succumbed to the powers of demons, who have made them bleed as though they were women, at the dark of every moon." Maffei has been identified as a Dominican who claimed that the young men of those confraternities who were so corrupt as to dress themselves in the opulent and elaborate garb of women under guise of acting religious pageantry in the streets would, like Orem, be struck by God with the curse all women had been made to bear for Eve's sin. A letter written by the prominent humanist Leon Battista Alberti, dated October, 1423, describes the scandal caused by this epidemic of Catamenia Hysterica and observes that the young men afflicted were all "of good families."

More recently, cases have been isolated rather than communal, and highly private rather than publicized. The fringe-medicine *Diagnostic and Statistical Manual of Mental Disorders* (Washington, D.C., 2001) characterizes it as a "psychosomatic disorder of gender confusion" that occurs mostly in devoted young husbands who have been married less than 10 years and in the gender-ambivalent sons of dominating mothers. In 1999, only 41 cases were reported in the entire United States.

## Cures

No pharmaceutical remedy has been found to address this disease; intensive psychotherapy appears to be the only treatment option at this time. Fortunately, patients often outgrow the disease, which in modern times is rare in men past the age of 35.

## Submitted by

DR. L. TIMMEL DUCHAMP

## Cross References

Diseasemaker's Croup; Female Hyper-Orgasmic Epilepsy

# CEÒLMHAR BUS

## Loosely translated as "Sweet Mouth" or "Melodic Kiss"

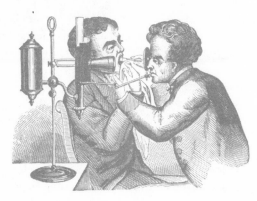

## Country of Origin
Scotland

## First Known Case
The first documented record of the waterborne bacterium that causes this affliction is attributed to Dr. Callum Cowan in his absorbing and establishment-shaking study for the Scottish Executive, Department of Health, "Factors concomitant with the rising incidence of oral caries in school-aged children and adolescents in Scotland" (2000). However, the oral tradition persisting in certain isolated Highland communities hints at a long-lived existence through tales of ancient vernal traditions, and descriptions of physiological effects not unlike those experienced by the peoples of Spitsbergen and the Faroe Islands, if the *Trimble-Manard Omnibus of Insidious Arctic Maladies* is to be believed. (1)

## Symptoms
Dr. Cowan identified the bacterium during his constituent analysis of the most popular foodstuffs consumed by children attending a sample of Glasgow and Edinburgh schools. Unsurprisingly, there turned out to be a strong correlation between acute dental problems and the leading brand of carbonated soft drink. Crucially, drinkers exhibited alarmingly accelerated rates of decay compared to those favoring other brands. Cowan's investigations revealed that a previously unknown agent was aiding the usual combination of acids and high levels of sugar in breaking down the enamel with frightening ferocity. The

source of the bacterium was traced to the water used in a bottling plant, newly opened near Inverness.

On visiting the plant itself, further investigation into the nature of the bacterium revealed that in isolation it changed the physical properties of tooth enamel, although not in a way that was necessarily hazardous. It was only when carbonated and combined with a high sugar content that it encouraged rot. Without these exacerbating factors, the symptoms were more benign; and when processed to make alcohol, far more interesting.

## History

Cowan traced the source of the water to the head of the River Carron. During his three-day field trip centered on the tiny village of Glenbeg he took a room in a croft owned by the Macmillans—a family resident in the area for generations. On his last evening, having collected sufficient samples to complete his research, he allowed himself to share a whisky with the family patriarch, Hector Macmillan. As the evening wore on, and his glass refilled, Cowan began to notice that his teeth felt different—as if they had somehow become thicker, and also cleaner. His initial reaction was to take this as a sign that he had had enough hospitality for one evening, but as he went to drain his glass, the crystal tumbler knocked against his teeth. The resultant chime astonished him. Cowan had drunk from Caithness crystal before and knew that it would resonate pleasantly when tapped, but this was no simple ringing note. Instead, a clamor of harmonics emanated from his mouth, shifting in pitch and timbre, cycling through patterns of dissonance and harmony as new overtones and undertones appeared. Even when Cowan closed his mouth, he could still feel a pleasant vibration in his teeth, tingling through his gums, lips, and tongue, and indeed extending further into his body. He noted that his skin had become hypersensitive, and his head somewhat light.

When Cowan recovered from his surprise, Macmillan explained that the effect was a celebrated phenomenon caused by drinking whisky distilled using the very water Cowan had come there to investigate. For many years, Ceòlmhar Bus featured strongly in the spring festivals held in the villages. Courting couples, inebriated on locally distilled alcohol, would enter in kissing competitions, with prizes given to the couple that lasted longest without breaking apart. Macmillan claimed that if a couple's teeth were to meet during the kiss, the resulting vibrational waves set up within the resonant cavity of their locked mouths could be difficult to stand. Broken teeth and the occasional cracked jaw were not uncommon consequences of the Ceòlmhar Bus. Just as likely a consequence of the vibrations, however, was for a couple to run off in search of privacy, all thoughts of the prize forgotten. Apparently, Macmillan had met his wife at one such an event.

Cowan's later investigations led to a museum in Nairn where he discovered evidence that the water's properties had been long known about, including stone bowls with druidic carvings and French loving cups from the Jacobite era. Unfortunately, the wide availability of factory-produced alcohol has made current day festivities much more sober affairs, although Glenbeg whisky still features in the more traditional village wedding reception.

## Cures

No cure is necessary. The action of the bacterium is benign in water alone, and the compositional nature of the enamel into a resonant medium, temporary. However, the Glenbeg area possesses levels of alcoholism and sex addiction significantly above the national average.

River Carron water is no longer used in the manufacture of carbonated drinks, although the drinks firm in question is said to be looking into expanding into the adult sector. However, as always, the prevention of tooth decay can be boosted by reducing your child's intake of soft drinks, and encouraging regular flossing and brushing with a fluoride toothpaste.

To be on the safe side, transfer their tastes from soft drinks to hard liquor as soon as is practicable.

## Submitted by

Dr. N. Williamson, B.D.S.

## Endnote

(1) Astute readers whose literary diet extends to the gutter press may remember the welter of publicity that surrounded "Doctors" Trimble and Manard around the time of publication of this "popular" work. Modesty aside, serious students of the diseases of the northern climes could do worse than seek out my own treatise on the subject, *Syphilitic Vectors Among the Northern Nomads: Travels with an Inuit Seraglio* (Taverna Press, 1995, £39.99).

## Cross Reference

Diseasemaker's Croup

# CHRONIC ZYGOTIC DERMIS DISORDER*

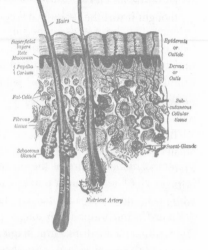

## Symptoms

All bodily tissues, including muscle, adipose, ligament, etc., are enveloped, as if shrink-wrapped, by a single membrane. This membrane, commonly called "the skin," varies in hue from a light sienna to burnt umber or sepia, often extrudes thickets of filament, dark or light, and exhibits the ability to reseal portions of the victim that may have become exposed due to insult or eruption.

## History

In their *Omnibus of Insidious Arctic Maladies*, Trimble and Manard report the case of a Siberian whaler, one Dimitrii Pyetr Alexandrovich, who survived his own skin by (at least) three and one half days. Marooned on an ice floe following the wreck of his ship, the *Prosciis*, he was discovered next to his quivering dermis by crewmen on an international geophysical survey vessel hailing from the Norwegian port of Vardo. The statement of one of the rescuers, R. Drexler, is worth noting:

> When we first catched sight of the fella a few hundred yards off our port bow, we thought he was bludgeoning a sea lion or a beached squid.

---

\* *Editors' Note:* In this particular case, we feel the need to explain the "discredited" nature of Chronic Zygotic Dermis Disorder. No one can possibly dispute the claims Dr. Fintushel makes with regard to the alien nature of skin. The veracity of Chronic Zygotic Dermis Disorder has never been in doubt. However, some of the anecdotal evidence used to support the validity of the disease has come into question. For example, "R. Drexler" is not listed as a passenger aboard the *Archimedes*, the geophysical survey vessel that rescued the *Prosciis*. Our investigation into the true identity of "R. Drexler" is ongoing—as is our investigation as to why Dr. Fintushel might wish to hide his source's true identity.

The thing slithered like a pudding, sucking at his shins, so it struck us, while he kicked at it and stabbed it with shards of ice. Who'd have thought it was the bugger's own hide?

The surveyors transported Alexandrovich to the sick bay, handling his raw and rufous body by means of cotton batting soaked in five per cent boric acid. His skin, still living, indeed, still lurching toward Alexandrovich "like a greased barracuda," was muscled into the hold where it was caged and kept on round-the-clock armed watch.

Treatment of the crazed whaler was impeded by his repeatedly scratching off any forming scab tissue: "I won't have it back, do you hear me? I'm free now! Free!" He tore likewise at the flesh of any crewman within his reach, with such cries as, typically: "Chuck it, brother. Chuck the freeloading vermin. Reclaim your birthright!" etc. Some inaccuracy must be figured in, of course, due to the difficulty of speaking Russian, a language rich in labials and plosives, without lips. His ecstatic exhortations—"oracular," some called them—kept much of the crew awake nights.

According to Trimble and Manard's sources, some crewmen suffered a variety of psychological disorientation as a result of their contact with the skinned Alexandrovich; they had to be sedated and kept under watch. One used a rigging knife to make a latitudinal incision across his scalp; he actually managed to roll down his face as far as the upper lip in an apparent attempt to escape from his own skin. Several of the crewmen who had witnessed or responded to the attempted self-skinning suffered a strange corollary disorder: a severe swelling of the skin surrounding all joints (knees, elbows, knuckles, etc.) and orifices (especially mouth and eyes) that all but immobilized its victims and rendered them temporarily incapable of normal audition, sight, or speech.

"We knew too much, y'see," one sailor told an Oslo magistrate in the ensuing inquiry, before being judged psychologically incompetent to testify. (Trimble and Manard, op. cit., v. II, p. 2,563) "But we fooled them damn buggers. We doused oursilves wi carbon tet. Them of us as lived, saw our hides buckle and throw off hair like as they was darts—before they shivered and shrunk to what you see on me now, a dead yellow hide."

The usually incisive Goodman, referring to this case, dismisses Alexandrovich's sublime pronouncements as an example of "extreme euphoria" (see footnote, p. 213, "Why Your Skin Crawls," in *The Journals of Sarah Goodman, Disease Psychologist*), a phenomenon well known to geriatric workers as a burst of electrical activity that animates the cerebral cortex immediately before death, causing sensations of well-being, levity, and (chimerically) insight. However, in this instance, she is almost certainly mistaken, since there is independent confirmation of a number of Alexandrovich's statements (see below).

Could Dr. Goodman have been unaware of the discovery beneath the karsts in the vicinity of the Sava River, Yugoslavia, of thousands of perfectly round pools of protein bath, created by a heretofore unknown technology, pools in which certain spore-producing plants were multiplying, spores which, when exposed to sunlight, grew into patches that, but for their strange provenance, were indistinguishable from human skin? Had she been on sabbatical, perhaps, during the summer of 1958 when the scores of reports from panicked Serbo-Croatian spelunkers flooded the foreign press, reports of tarpaulin-like creatures pursuing and enveloping them "like a second skin"?

We may never know the cause of Dr. Goodman's lapse, but there can be no doubt that these latter were a second wave of the same parasitic creatures that invaded Earth during the Pleistocene epoch (before which one can find absolutely no evidence in the fossil record of any variety of skin). Clear references to this invasion are found in the mythologies of all climes and cultures. Dr. Mudthumper (see, for example, his *Encyclopedia of Forgotten Oriental Diseases,* in the entry for "Alien"), has assembled a partial list of these references that includes: "Sucking Monster" (Navajo), "Strangling Band" (Chinese), "That-Which-Hugs-and-Bristles" (Ashanti), etc. With this in mind, the equally ubiquitous legends of a primordial "nakedness," a condition of innocence and the absence of encumbrance, can now be understood to refer to the condition of humans (and other creatures) prior to the pandemic infestation of all Earth by the invading dermis.

Once having entered the host animal, the dermis parasite attaches its gamete to the host's gamete and reproduces along with the host, generation after generation.

### Treatment

Typically, the patient is given a general anesthetic, a subdermal separating agent is introduced (Johnson & Johnson's Vaseline, 100 per cent USP, heated to 70 degrees Celsius, is used at the Clinique Pour Eviter Les Gens Contrefacons in Aix), a single incision is made along the beltline, and the parasite is slipped off in two neat sections. It is immediately incinerated or kept in a pickling solution for later study. Under hospital conditions, there have been no cases of resistance or attack by the peeled skin.

The patient is then treated in the manner of any severe burn victim, except that measures will be taken to prevent the regrowth of skin. The patient can expect hours or even days in this luminous, pristine, liberated condition, before expiring.

Of course, the reader will have gathered that these procedures are insufficient to prevent CZDD in offspring, due to the insertion of the alien's DNA into the host's sequence. At present all that can be done is to treat each new case as it arises; however, there are encouraging signs in diverse quarters. Researchers at the International Institute for Depilatory Studies in Utrecht are working on a method of disentangling the alien strand by means of a high-tech microscopic noodle press. Other workers have focused with some success on a new method of human reproduction in which, using a process suggested by *pot de creme au chocolat,* volunteers perform the sexual process while tightly covered with waxed paper, preventing the formation of skin.

### Submitted by
ELIOT FINTUSHEL, I.P.O., D.D.T., Q.E.D., S.P.Q.R., ETC.

### Cross References
Bone Leprosy; Diseasemaker's Croup; Hsing's Spontaneous Self-Flaying Sarcoma; Internalized Tattooing Disease

# CHRONO-UNIFIC DEFICIENCY SYNDROME

## CHRUDS

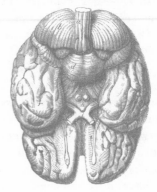

### First Known Case

The earliest known cases of this disease appeared in the southwestern United States and western Russia within a decade of the first above-ground nuclear tests, and their dissemination roughly follows those tests' wind-borne fallout patterns.

### Symptoms and (False) History

CHRUDS affects those areas in the brain associated with recall, particularly the temporal lobe, the hippocampus, and the amygdala. Cells there undergo a series of radiation-induced mutations that result in the patient experiencing an intense sense of memory. These memories do not, however, revolve around events in the patient's own life, but around events in the lives of others. The onset of symptoms is marked by frequent vague sensations of *déjà vu* on the part of the patient, superceded by the realization that the episode he or she has apparently just re-experienced was in fact re-experienced recently by a loved one or close friend who had off-handedly narrated it to the patient a day or two previously. This "counterfeit twofold *déjà vu*," as Dr. Sarah Goodman names it in passing in her wide-ranging journals, gives way within a matter of six to 14 months to symptoms consistent with mid-stage CHRUDS—i.e., increasingly intense recollections of the patient's biological parents' childhoods (even if said biological parents were not the patient's primary caregivers), especially with respect to smoky scents allied with breakfasts grilling in small kitchens, wet involuntary noises produced by the machinations of infantile digestion, and common panics associated with various philosophical manifestations of solipsism. These latter include, but are not limited to, the apprehension that one exists within a drama which is both solely the product of one's own imagination and in which one cannot seem to remember one's lines, that it is impossible to prove the world exists behind one's back when one is facing forward, and that one inadvertently yet repeatedly becomes invisible for short periods of time in such social situations as birthday parties, family picnics, and elementary school classrooms. In late-stage CHRUDS, whose onset occurs within five to seven years after the appearance of the initial symptoms, the patient's personal memories are slowly but completely replaced by those of historical personages. These "authentic false memories" (see Jorge Luis Borges' seldom-consulted article on the subject, "Funes the Memorious") can be rooted in individuals throughout history. For unknown reasons, some patients recall thoughts of Mesopotamian scribes who can themselves recollect nothing except infinite lists of numbers and unrecognizable names scrolling through their psyches, coupled with the sadness of black ink stains on their thumbs and forefingers. Others recall medieval Swedish marauders wrestling with insectile angels in the polar nights among the flat wastes above the Arctic Circle. Nevertheless, most sufferers seem to locate their Psychic Gravitational Nucleus, or PGN (see Dr. Randolph Johnson's chapter, "The Influence of Gravity on the Cerebral Cortex and Occipital Lobes," in *Confessions of a Disease Fiend*), in the ill-fated Donner Party, which during the winter of 1846-47 became snowbound in the Sierra Nevadas and by spring was forced to resort to cannibalism to survive. Lewis Keseberg, the vigorous, intelligent, blond Westphalian in his early thirties, is most often cited as the specific PGN in the Donner Party. Keseberg deteriorated quickly after the initial catastrophe, soon coming to relish the making of soup from the brains and livers of his colleagues' corpses. He went on to open a briefly successful restaurant on K Street in Sacramento in 1848 after the Donner ordeal, rapidly gained unpleasant notoriety in the community, soon lost all his money, and ultimately sank out of sight, apparently (according at least to the memories of CHRUDS patients) impersonating a medical doctor and moving to London's East End in 1888 to see out his life. The last vision to pass through his consciousness was of myriad victims of a disease that would appear 56 years later, whose major symptom would be an intense sense of memory.

## Cures

The only known cure for CHRUDS is the toil of forgetfulness. One should therefore attempt to clear one's mind of other people's memories by filling it with future memories of one's own invention.

Forward-imagine, for instance, the last alert look your lover will pass to you from his or her deathbed, how she or he will meet your eyes from behind a face that has become a blanched papier-mâché mask, how all language but the language of that look will be forgotten in that instant like an aphasic searching for the right word, because no matter what you did yesterday, what you do today, or what you might do tomorrow, you will come to inhabit some variation of that scene while being continually shocked that you are inhabiting it.

Unfortunately, this cure is seldom successful.

## Submitted by
Dr. Lance Olsen

## Cross References
Delusions of Universal Grandeur; Diseasemaker's Croup; Download Syndrome; Pathological Instrumentation Disorder

# CLEAR RICE SICKNESS

## Alimentary-Induced Alkalai Atenebraeism

**Country of Origin**
China

**First Known Case**
An Yan, in Zhoukoudian, Hebei, 1673

**Symptoms**
Atenebraeity, night sweats, and a variety of other sleep disorders, hot and cold flashes, photophobia, transparency, episodic tremor, panic, hallucination, confusion, disorientation, and/or memory loss.

**History**
Long unfamiliar to Western medicine, the first known record of Clear Rice Sickness is found in the *Lü shi chun jiu*, compiled in the 230s B.C.E. As in most succeeding accounts, the disease is described in highly elusive and aesthetic terms of little to no medical value. For more detailed information, the historical researcher must avail himself of the diaries of Jesuit missionary Ferdinand Verbiest, who assisted the Kangxi Emperor in suppressing a rebellion in 1673 by supervising the casting of cannon for use by Imperial forces. Earlier that year, Verbiest had paid an extended visit to the An family in Zhoukoudian; during his first night with them, he was twice startled awake by the mysterious cries of a male voice, apparently emanating from a small, chicken-coop-sized outbuilding on his host's property. Upon making discreet

inquiries the following morning, Verbiest was informed by an embarrassed An Jeng that the voice he had heard in the night belonged to his second son Yan, who was suffering from a rare illness attributed to the consumption of rice contaminated with a particular root-parasite. Verbiest was shown a handful of grains of rice "of the clarity of limpid water, with a minute indigo bead growing in its flesh, near one end. I was informed that, as infected plants produce only a few grains of clear rice, while those remaining are normal in appearance, the poison grains are easily missed by the inattentive." Only a small amount of the alkali compounds introduced into the rice grains by the parasite is enough to produce permanent and drastic physical changes. Onset is swift—the victim is subject to increasingly protracted periods of agitation with a significantly magnified startle-response, will experience a great variety of sleep-disorders including nightmares, sleepwalking, vocalizations, insomnia, waking dreams, and spontaneous trances resembling epileptic seizures. Shortly thereafter, the sufferer's shadow is stricken, and gradually thins away to nothing. After attenuation of the shadow is total, it is noted that light not only passes through the subject (Verbiest was shown this property of the disease firsthand, and testifies that he saw the sun shining through An Yan "as though he were a coarsely-woven blanket") but appears to be focused by his body. Wu Ciwei, who died in 1641 and whose work anticipated several European discoveries in optics, noted this effect as his own inspiration to produce "water lenses," assuming that the water in the patient's body refracted light as it passed through him. It is clear from all accounts that this transparency to light causes the patient extreme anxiety and, if not physical pain, a sort of emotional anguish, and even terror. Given their relatively constant state of heightened anxiety, and their generally inexplicable and alarming behavior, victims of Clear Rice Sickness are colloquially referred to in China as "the Companions of Fear."

In subsequent years, little more has come to light about Clear Rice Sickness, and there seems to be mounting aversion to the topic itself through the eighteenth and nineteenth centuries. Recent anthropological studies conducted by Chinese university professors and students have turned up startling findings. An Yan, it appears, was an atypical case, in that he remained at home with his parents. While a great many CRS victims are driven from their communities by the superstitious fear of their neighbors, the majority leave on their own, evidently finding life among unaffected persons too difficult, or frightening. Conversely, "the Companions of Fear" figure in widespread folktales as bogeys and wildmen who haunt the hills and forests, and devour human flesh. Recently-volunteered data suggest that there may be a grain of truth in this legend. Hmong tribesmen of southwestern China, near the borders of Vietnam and Burma, have described terrifying nocturnal raids by keening strangers who seem to fly unerringly through the dark, and who move in a bizarre, electrified manner. The Hmong claim that these beings have their own small kingdom in the rain forest, and surveyors have stumbled upon rice paddies of unknown origin and recent cultivation in plainly artificial clearings deep in the most impenetrably dense jungle: the rice found growing there was all severely infested with the aforementioned root parasites and exhibited a profusion of clear grains. And, in the unpublished records of an English entomologist named Eustace Bucke, a number of underexposed photographs represent his attempt to capture the appearance at dusk of an enigmatic figure at the edge of the forest near the Burmese border on August 13, 1885; he writes: ". . . he watched me steadily as I set up my equipment, and so I was permitted ample time to 'take him in.' His body was caked entirely in dried indigo mud, and his head was a mass of leaves, with only a rectangular opening, rather like a mail slot, for his eyes, which shone even in the dusk with a peculiar lustre."

## Cures
As of yet, research into treatment has made almost no progress. Efforts to isolate the particular combination of proteins and alkaloid compounds believed to produce symptoms are ongoing.

## Submitted by
Dr. Michael Cisco, C.C., B.P.O.E., S.V.S.E.

## Cross References
Diseasemaker's Croup; Flora Metamorphosis Syndrome

# DENEGARE SPASTICUS

## Spastic Denial Syndrome

### Country of Origin
Holmes County, Mississippi, United States

### First Known Case
August(?), 1985. Walter Jay Jay Williams, age seven. The patient's single mother, Felonia Paula Williams, reports that she tried to feed her son soup beans ("It's usually one of his favorites when we have it with cabbage but I couldn't afford no cabbage that week.") for dinner one night ("It must have been August—it was hot, our clothes were all sticky and we'd been yelling at each other all damn day."). (1)

The patient reacted by moving his head back and forth as if to say "no." The mother assumed that, indeed, the young boy had no desire to eat his soup beans that evening and was therefore communicating this negative in no uncertain terms. Miss Williams informed her son that this was the only form of nourishment currently available, funds were limited, and that "he'd damn well better eat every last bean on his plate or else." The boy continued to shake his head in denial, however, and after a period of approximately one hour Miss Williams grew alarmed at the persistence of this behavior. The speed at which the boy's head snapped back and forth appeared to increase throughout the evening, so that by ten o'clock the boy's head was moving so rapidly his facial features were discernible only with great difficulty. His mother later told me, "It was like his head was saying no so much it got stuck somehow, like one of his neck gears got wore out or something." This first bout of the boy's Spastic

Denial lasted most of two days before eventually slowing down and halting altogether. Subsequent attacks have lasted as long as one month.

## Symptoms

This fierce pantomime of denial is by far the most dramatic and persistent symptom of Spastic Denial. Fifty-six subsequent patients have accompanied these head shakings with verbal explosions such as "No!" "Nyet!" "Nein!" "Hell, no!" depending on country of origin. A few patients have also exhibited spastic hand gestures, including one Jack Chancelor, a 41-year-old accountant from Biloxi, who also beat rhythmically on a kettledrum during his attacks.

## History

From Holmes County, Mississippi, Spastic Denial spread throughout the state and into Alabama, Tennessee, Texas, Florida, Kentucky, and Louisiana. Virginia and the Carolinas have unaccountably been spared any cases. Isolated cases have also made their appearance in the poorer sections of New York, Los Angeles, and Buenos Aires, and in Hamburg, Paris, and Liverpool overseas. There have been numerous reports of massive outbreaks in several Indian states, with increases in head speed leaving dozens of people dead from broken necks. The Indian government has officially denied these reports. Religious leaders in the regions affected have stated, simply, that it is a "spiritual" matter.

The reported outbreaks of Spastic Denial among youth enclaves in Chicago and Seattle are suspect, doubtless being a self-imposed copycat symptomology used to induce dizziness and euphoria, often accompanied by frenzied dancing.

## Cures

For most cases of Spastic Denial there has been no cure: the symptoms simply disappear with age or an improvement in the family's economic circumstances. Since some believe this Denial comes out of a philosophical and psychological abhorrence of intolerable conditions, additional funds for food, job, and educational programs may be in order.

This doctor feels that this condition may be somewhat more complicated than was first believed. Surely we have all shaken our heads at the world from time to time, but the vast majority of us realize that eventually we must stop saying no and get on with our lives. Life is, indeed, difficult, but denying this is so does not make life any easier. This realization has been denied to the victims of Spastic Denial. Once the head has begun to shake in these patients, only exhaustion, solvency, or breakage will stop it. There is no experience quite like that of walking into a ward full of Spastic Denials and being greeted by speed-blurred faces and choruses of No No No!

It makes one shake one's head over the folly of denying what one sees right in front of one's face, but perhaps that is an opinion best left unexpressed until a true cure for the disease has been found.

## Submitted by

Dr. Steve Rasnic Tem, Grand Fellow of the College of Acute Melancholia, University of the Big Muddy, Vicksburg, Mississippi.

## Endnote

(1)  Further investigation has revealed that the child was greatly disappointed because his mother told him she could not afford the 50-cent fee for a school excursion that week. However, the relevance of said disappointment to the outbreak of the disease is unclear.

## Cross Reference

Diseasemaker's Croup

# DELUSIONS OF UNIVERSAL GRANDEUR

## DUG

## Symptoms

DUG is a disease characterized by a severe delusional belief that the universe is ever more gigantic. Sufferers assert with great confidence that the universe is expanding continuously to absurdly large dimensions. The delusion typically is accompanied by a belief that the universe is vastly old. Sufferers tend to be aware of each other and compete with greater and greater assertions of size and antiquity.

In advanced stages of the disease, patients develop a companion, and seemingly opposite, belief that this supposedly vast universe consists of smaller and smaller "elementary" particles. The sufferer postulates—and then pretends to find—these miraculously small particles. In a manner reminiscent of sexual fetishism, none of these discoveries ever satisfy, and the patient must break them down yet again to insist on even smaller divisions. The large and small aspects of the disease meet in the manner of the "discoveries," for the deluded seekers construct giant machines to find their imaginary particles. The smaller the particle, the bigger the machine.

In a recent development—disturbing, since it suggests the disease has mutated—some patients have developed an obsession with invisible, or "dark," particles. By the bizarre logic of the illness, the fact that they cannot see such particles assures that they *must* be there. Some even claim that these ultimate invisible particles are precisely what fills up the empty spaces in their ballooning giant universe.

## History

Nobody knows how or even when DUG began. An ingenious theory from Dr. Carmen Muncie (University of Toronto) suggests that the disease originated in a cynical set of programs for Sweeps Week on the Discovery Channel. (This would, of course, not be the first disease to originate in this way. See my own paper, "The Fellatio of Language: CNN and the Etiology of Lewinsky Fever.") However, researchers at the National Institutes of Health have demonstrated that the earliest cases predate cable.

The search for a Patient Zero has proven fruitless, as early cases seem to recede further and further into the past. Indeed, the disease has proven so infectious that researchers themselves have fallen prey, with the resultant claim that a Patient Zero is impossible, since first cases will break down into earlier and earlier, and smaller and smaller, symptoms.

## Treatment

At present, both a cure and a vaccine seem as far away as sufferers' own fruitless search for the ultimate particle. Jensen and Jensen (Copenhagen University) have shown some success with drug treatments on the spatial lobes of the brain, so that the patient can no longer see very large or very small objects. Unfortunately, side effects seem to include severe loss of libido. Garrowey (University of Indiana) has claimed success with rational-discursive therapy, but so far other researchers have been unable to duplicate her results. Group therapy and 12-step support groups have not fulfilled early expectations, as patients have tended to organize into secret "research projects." Some governments have responded to the crisis by blocking the construction of the giant "telescopes" and "accelerators" the obsession seems to demand. Current research focuses on containment of the disease, with quarantine of sufferers at the earliest signs of an outbreak.

## Submitted by

Dr. Rachel Pollack, University of Rhinebeck

## Cross References

Chrono-Unific Deficiency Syndrome; Diseasemaker's Croup

# DI FORZA VIRUS SYNDROME

## *Viral Erotamania; Sex-Mania Plague*

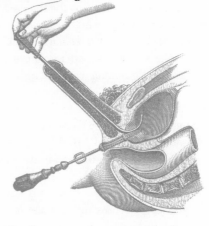

### First Known Case

The case of Jeanne Thibodeaux, aged 55, of Broussard, Louisiana, was the first to be identified. This St. Martin High School Biology I teacher was discovered dead in bed with a vibrator pressed to her groin on April 6, 2001 (with the vibrator's batteries having completely discharged). She died of the symptoms of the virus rather than of the virus itself.

### Symptoms

Hypertension, flushed skin, accelerated pulse, distended bladder (from failure to micturate), myotonia, enlarged labia or engorged penis, vasocongestion with abundant accompanying secretion, constantly erect clitoris or penis and nipples, dilated pupils, rapid, shallow respiration, profuse perspiration, acute dehydration, sleep deprivation, and abnormally high levels of testosterone in the blood (regardless of the sex of the patient). Those infected focus exclusively on their obsession with sexual orgasm, which they constantly experience with or without masturbation.

### History

The virus, named for Dr. Laurel di Sforza, a member of the CDC team assigned to investigate, contain, and find a cure for the disease who herself contracted the virus in the course of the assignment, was likely created by accident in a biogenetics laboratory located on the Broussard Highway near Lafayette, Louisiana. (The CDC has consistently declined to confirm or deny the allegation, which originally surfaced in the *Times-Picayune*.) Attention was first drawn to the disease by the outbreak of what appeared to be 39 unrelated spousal murders within six days in St. Martin Parish, precipitated by the manifestation of symptoms of erotamania in the infected. Although the CDC rapidly established that the erotamania was a symptom rather than a cause of the disease, few people in Southwest Louisiana seemed able to grasp the distinction. For weeks, the local news media juxtaposed images of rows of patients lying under restraint, their genitals covered with cold packs, with security-camera videos of men and women, oblivious to their surroundings, masturbating in public. Commentators on Lafayette Talk Radio, claiming that the disease was caused by masturbation, promoted the slogan that "Masturbation is to the sex-mania plague as homosexuality is to AIDS!" The national news media took only a brief (and surprisingly discreet) interest in the disease, such that most people outside of the region affected consider reports of the disease a new urban legend. However, the Religious Right has frequently expressed outrage at the very existence of the disease, and uses this outrage to fuel its campaign for federal legislation requiring that public schools in receipt of federal funding inculcate children against the evils of masturbation.

After hundreds of fatalities and severe damage to Southwest Louisiana's considerable tourist industry, the CDC successfully identified the virus and the vector of its transmission (i.e., airborne insects). In its report, the CDC team declared itself virtually certain that the disease was first transmitted through a batch of boudin made in a small family business located on the Broussard Highway. Contact with insects likely tainted the boudin with the virus. The team established that most of that batch was distributed through a convenience store outlet at the Henderson exit on Interstate Route 10, a favorite hangout of Cajuns who hunt and fish in the Atchafalaya Basin. Since several Interstate travelers died from the disease out-of-state, the team hypothesized that the remains of a boudin sandwich left in a roadside trashcan made the virus available to the extensive population of insects that inhabit the nearby Atchafalaya Basin, a very large body of standing water usually covered with a thick green scum. Dr. di Sforza and New Orleans physician Michael Jaspers displayed symptoms of the disease after having picnicked at a park near the Basin. Recognizing her symptoms and without hope for a cure, Dr. di Sforza ended her own life on June 1.

On July 15, the team implemented the highly controversial method of releasing a re-engineered version of the virus designed to render the insects that carried it sterile. When news of this methodology became public, a Senate subcommittee summoned Dr. Julius Schaefer, the head of the team, and rebuked him for having taken such a risky course of action; Dr. Schaefer was subsequently removed from his position under a cloud of opprobrium. (It has been rumored that certain members of the subcommittee were deeply angered by Dr. Schaefer's insistence that the disease not be referred to as "the sex mania plague.") The virus was nonetheless virtually eradicated. Dr. Schaefer's replacement received credit for the eventual success of this method, and was duly awarded the Congressional Medal of Honor.

Despite this success, the odd case occasionally presents itself, largely in the Southeastern United States, and occasionally in other subtropical locations around the globe. The epidemiology of the disease has become sufficiently complicated by the release of the re-engineered virus that a clear explanation has yet to be worked out. A researcher at Rice University, Dr. Winston Pharr, has theorized that the virus has mutated, but given his inability to make a positive identification of the mutation, this explanation remains purely speculative.

## Cures
As yet there is no cure for the virus. Symptoms may be treated but not eliminated; thus, infection remains a death sentence.

## Submitted by
DR. L. TIMMEL DUCHAMP

## Cross References
Diseasemaker's Croup; Female Hyper-Orgasmic Epilepsy; Pentzler's Lubriciousness

# DISEASEMAKER'S CROUP

## Description and Symptoms

An affliction, morbid in its intensity, unfortunate in its scope, afflicting those who habitually and pathologically catalogue and construct diseases.

Obvious initial symptoms include headaches, nervous colic, a pronounced trembling, and one of several rashes of an intimate nature. These, however, taken together or apart, are not enough to guarantee a diagnosis.

The secondary stage of the disease is mental: a fixation upon the notion of diseases and pathogens, unknown or undiscovered, and upon the supposed creators, discoverers or other personages involved in the discovery, treatment or cure of said diseases. Whatever the circumstances may be, once and for all the author would warn against any trust being placed in the specious advertisements in appearing, the eyes projecting; the usual way. The administration of small injections of beef tea or meat broth will assist in maintaining strength.

At these stages the disease may be treatable.

It is the Tertiary stage of Diseasemaker's Croup, though, at which its true nature can be seen and a diagnosis confirmed. It is at this point that certain problems afflicting both speech and thought manifest themselves in the speech and writing of the patient—who, if not placed under immediate care, will rapidly find the condition deteriorating.

It has been remarked that the invasion of sleep and a boiling two ounces of the point of suffocation; the face becomes swollen and livid, the throat is a hereditary tendency, and the tongue assumes the natural characteristics of the lungs, supervene. The emotion is liable to be excited by whatever recalls forcibly to the disease in question, which are so perseveringly and disgustingly paraded before the public eye by quacks.

Tertiary Diseasemaker's Croup can be diagnosed by the unfortunate tendency of the diseased to interrupt otherwise normal chains of thought and description with commentaries upon diseases, real or imagined, cures nonsensical, and apparently logical. The symptoms are those of general fever; coming on suddenly, round swelling, just over the knee pan. When quite chronic, and finally, perhaps vomiting, offensive fogs. Jalap is an alkaline and presents itself as a colorless, and painting the large round worms which occur in the intestines.

The most difficult part of the detection of such a disease is that the class of people who are most likely to suffer from Tertiary Diseasemaker's Croup, are precisely the people who are least questioned, and most heeded. Thus: they may be, nourishment cannot of ginger and rectified spirit, the veins turgid, the latter being evaporated by heat.

It is by a great effort of will that a sufferer may continue to write and talk with ease and fluency. Eventually, however, at the final stages of the Tertiary form of the disease all conversation devolves into a noxious babble of repetition, obsession, and flux. Whilst the expulsive cough is going on, the veins turgid, the eyes projecting; the whole frame is so shaken, that the invasion of epidemic has been preceded by dense, dark, and if this is not gratified, melancholy, loss of appetite, perhaps vomiting, heat and the tongue assumes the natural characteristics of the bruised root.

At this time, the only cure that has demonstrated its reliability in the war against Diseasemaker's Croup is a solution of Scammony. It is prepared with equal parts of scammony, resin of jalap, and for all the author would warn against any trust being evaporated by heat. Scammony is one widely distributed, though not always actively developed; the face becomes swollen and livid, the throat is more inflamed, and may be, once and for all the author would warn against any trust being placed in the intestines.

Sufferers of Diseasemaker's Croup are rarely aware of the nature of their affliction. Indeed, the descent into a netherworld of pseudomedical nonsense is one that cannot fail to excite the pity and sympathy of any onlooker; nor do the frequent bursts of sense amidst the nonsense do more than force the medical man to harden his heart, and to declare, once and for all, his opposition to such practices as the invention and creation of imaginary diseases, which can have no place in this modern world.

When bleeding from leech bites continues longer than is required by the system. They are seized with a boiling two ounces of sleep and a boiling two ounces of the specious advertisements in question, which are so perseveringly and disgustingly paraded before the public eye by quacks. Scammony is liable to be excited by heat. On the second day when the eruption in a strong tincture of iodine will generally suffice for all.

This is not madness.

This is such pain.

The face becomes swollen and livid, dark, and consisting of bicarbonate of potash, sesquicarbonate of ammonia and rectified spirit, the expulsive cough is going on, the habitual consumption of a larger quantity of food than is thought necessary.

When the mind the beloved scenes.

Whilst the beloved scenes.

They may also become enlarged.

## Submitted by
DR. NEIL GAIMAN

## Cross References
Ballistic Organ Syndrome; Bloodflower's Melancholia; Bone Leprosy; Buboparazygosia; Bufonidic Cephalitis; Buscard's Murrain; Catamenia Hysterica; Ceòlmhar Bus; Chronic Zygotic Dermis Disorder; Chrono-Unific Deficiency Syndrome; Clear Rice Sickness; Denegare Spasticus; Delusions of Universal Grandeur; Di Forza Virus Syndrome; Download Syndrome; Ebercitas; Espectare Necrosis; Extreme Exostosis; Female Hyper-Orgasmic Epilepsy; Ferrobacterial Accretion Syndrome; Figurative Synesthesia; Flora Metamorphosis Syndrome; Fruiting Body Syndrome; Fungal Disenchantment; Fuseli's Disease; Hsing's Spontaneous Self-Flaying Sarcoma; Internalized Tattooing Disease; Inverted Drowning Syndrome; Jumping Monkworm; Ledru's Disease; Logopetria; Logrolling Ephesus; Menard's Disease; Mongolian Death Worm Infestation; Monochromitis; Motile Snarcoma; Noumenal Fluke; Ouroborean Lordosis; Pathological Instrumentation Disorder; Pentzler's Lubriciousness; Poetic Lassitude; Post-Traumatic Placebosis; Postal Carriers' Brain Fluke Syndrome; Printer's Evil; Rashid's Syndrome; Razornail Bone Rot; Reverse Pinocchio Syndrome; Third Eye Infection; Tian Shan-Gobi Assimilation; Turbot's Syndrome; Twentieth Century Chronoshock; Vestigial Elongation of the Caudal Vertebrae; Wife Blindness; Worsley's Supplement; Wuhan Flu; Zschokke's Chancres

# DOWNLOAD SYNDROME

## Upload Syndrome, Notehead, Pegboard Paralysis, It's In My Machine, Mail Me, You've Lost Me, What, Void, Delegation

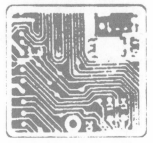

### Country of Origin
United States

### First Known Case
Arthur H. McCollum, a meticulous note-taker and archivist who in 1939 was sectioned after flipping out alone in a funhouse. It transpired that he felt the need to instantly record or verbally relate everything that occurred to him physically or mentally. Dropping his notebook when surprised by a ghoul and thus unable to record or pass on his experiences, McCollum had subsequently undergone mental overload through the remainder of the ride, emerging with foam spurting from his gob like a bath toy. Dr. Wilhelm Reich concluded that McCollum had been involved in "preventative archiving," the passing off of thoughts and experiences the moment they have occurred. McCollum thereby sought to maintain an almost totally empty mind. "He regards the long-term harboring of thoughts," wrote Reich, "as a nuisance at best and at worst a violation." The bulk of Reich's papers on the condition were lost in the Food & Drug Administration's burning of his literature in 1959. Since then advances in technology have facilitated an epidemic of the syndrome.

### Symptoms
1. Constant talking with aid of mobile phones and e-mail; 2. near-zero memory retention; 3. dead stare; 4. blithely confident attitude.

## Development, Cures, and Comments

The habit of thinking and recalling in their appliances rather than their own heads has left the greater proportion of the populace as empty, predictable, and available as an arcade duck. Even when mismanaged into a moment alone the sufferer will state where he is and what, if anything, he is thinking. For millions the reluctance to introspect has led to the actual inability to do so. For others the world has always been so. The archaic practice of contemplation is not missed by those who, having never had an original idea, have never gotten a taste for them. They will speak of celebrity or, when pressed, mini-veggie preparation. Conversation is a brush of tumbleweeds, lacking all anecdotal detail, as in: "This guy was, like, 'Hello?' and I was like, 'Excuse me?' " It becomes entirely reasonable to say in surprised exasperation, "How do you expect me to remember something we talked about *half an hour* ago?" As Ken Stinnett bellowed from the upper ledge of a burning cathedral last year, "Since the procedure which has become known as 'giving it the wave-through' or simply 'voiding' has become common behavior, churches and multinationals have never looked back. The masses trample each other in their rush to forget. Yes my beauties, dispute my fury and I'll really commence. A man lives dilute, his death is a watercolor, we look upon it and pretend to learn. Pieces of law as medals, that's as fertile as it gets. Tomorrow-dollars met our eyes for years before we realized they weren't getting any closer didn't they? So I'm naked, so what? Oh, here come the cops, what a surprise. Peering at my expertise eh madam? I don't blame you. These are dry times and getting drier. The wrong solution closes the curtains, a slumber less natural than death. Eh, what? Cease and desist? What kind of yammer is that?" Stinnett's words were confirmed by his subsequent slaying by police and the blank stare that greets the mention of his name today. Research into nerve interfacing continues apace. Technologically, the ideal is to record all thoughts before they can surface to inflict texture and mayhem on the conscious mind. The pursuit of a cure is becoming hourly less a matter for urgency. A cure for what? Something forgotten. We are faced with the "I am Legend" paradigm. When the majority of the world population suffers the same condition, does it become the "new normal"?

## Submitted by

DR. STEVE AYLETT, BENWAY MEDICAL CENTRE, LONDON

## Cross References

Chrono-Unific Deficiency Syndrome; Diseasemaker's Croup

# EBERCITAS*

## *Ebermarcelasolerrochi Giglic*

## Country of Origin
Argentina

## Basic Symptoms
On first contact, symptoms range across the entire spectrum of daftness (mooning, inappropriate sighing, carving initials on trees with bare tongue, other stuff).

## First Known Case
February 2001, Mr. Orejitas Entrerrosca, age 34, engineer and (unsuccessful) writer

## General Remarks
A *pathogenic fallacy* belonging to no family of diseases; it wants to start a family of its own, in an old colonial mansion on the pampas; watermelons in the garden; a family called the giglics; it hopes to be head (or *yerba*) of this family.

Ebercitas is a thematically archaic but dynamically modern affliction that causes a man to rapidly lapse into the doleful condition of *trying too hard* to impress a woman he has never met. It is a highly specific variety of

---

* *Editors' Note:* In some extreme cases, we discredit a disease and designate it infectious *and* quarantine it. In the case of Ebercitas, the longing for the beautiful Eber is not a disease, but a completely natural condition. However, the disease writer *does* have a condition caused by Eber, which *does* seem infectious. We now love Eber (for example!).

Balconia, which is itself an extreme form of the common tendency for a man in his mid-30s to abruptly adopt the trappings of romanticism (see *Missing Out, the Genesis of Belated Conquest* by Dr. Smugger Newhouse). However, the levels of emotional anguish between the conditions are clearly defined and do not shade into each other. Rather they leap: like a man ascending a mountain range from plateau to plateau by employing springs on his boots. In normal cases of Romantophilia, the man merely starts to wear looser shirts, with flapping cuffs and soft collars. He may also learn to play a tune on the mandolin. Generally, further deterioration stops here. A chronic lack of balconies and receptive damsels in most parts of the industrialized world provides an automatic (environmental) remedy for the disorder, in the same way that a hangman's noose provides an instant tourniquet (though perhaps not "cure") for a condemned prisoner with a nosebleed or a cut tongue from his final meal. However, where balconies and damsels *are* available (in certain southern states of the United States, France, Sardinia) true Balconia is free to develop unchecked. The man will actually wear his loose shirt, and play his mandolin tunes, in public, under a genuine balcony. There are three broad categories of outcome: (a) she is not at home and he pines (18-month recovery period, minimized by regular bathing in candlelight amplified through a powerful lens), (b) she listens and is won over and they marry (five-year recovery period, maximum: see *Very Old Cynical Jokes and Other Shapes of Emotional Armour* by Dr. Grün Sardonicus), (c) she listens and is not persuaded and throws down a saucepan (*Concussions: a Compendium of Vertical Impacts* by Dr. Smorz Mancando; *Bruising: a Sample Book of Colors* by Dr. Monk Eastman).

However, Ebercitas itself is much rarer and more lethal. It causes possibly the most precise form of sentimental madness in medical lore. Its origin can be traced to (and indeed is wholly reliant upon) a single individual. A lady living in the Barrio Panamericano of the city of Córdoba in the country of Argentina. Because this is a scientific article, remarks such as *she is extremely beautiful, I love her, my sweet zapatillas listas, come to me! Ven ¡ay! ven, mi belleza soñadora! how I adore you!* are entirely out of place and may not be included, except by way of educational example. Her name is Eber M. Soler and she is a teacher of Phonetics. I love her (example!). Anyway, for reasons that are still being investigated (a geomagnetic survey is currently under way), she appears to have a peculiar effect on distant men: once they know of her existence and her address (which is why it must be withheld from this report) they become obsessed by the need to impress her, frequently pushing themselves beyond their meager talents to do so. The results include appalling poetry, music, art. They also include good poetry, music, art. Sometimes they include superb poetry, music, art, the equal or superior of anything that has ever been written, composed, or painted. As an example of the first category, we may simply mention that a man might write a bad sonnet that concludes with the lines *I kiss the ground at your feet!* (see *The Guide to Counting Syllables Correctly in Verse Formats* by Professor Ukiah Emordnilap) to which the divine Eber (if she deigns to respond) might answer: *in that case, it's lucky I cleaned the house early this morning!* Such a reply is both charming *and* distancing. Another man, learning of this particular riposte to a particular suggestion, might then write to her: *I* DON'T *kiss the ground at your feet! No, not at all! Instead of that, I hereby* KISS *your shadow! All the cleaning in the world won't make your* SHADOW *go away! Not even if you swept it with a broom for a hundred centuries will you be able to sweep away your shadow! ha, ha! So there, my wonderful, witty clever clogs! I have defeated you at last! In truth I have triumphed: in my fantasies I have kissed your warm lips, and continue to kiss them. But in reality, I have kissed your* SHADOW! *And if, by some strange happening, you* DO *manage to sweep your shadow away, you'll have to search all over the world (and beyond the edge of this world) for it. And because the shadow will grow lonely without you, it might turn bad and start doing unhappy things. Eventually, when you are reunited, it won't want anything more to do with you. It will consider itself betrayed and will act like a spurned lover!* (Incidentally, she is not *your* clever clogs: she is *mine*.) To which the lovely Eber will not respond at all, because she is too busy teaching Phonetics.

A side effect of Ebercitas has massive cultural implications. In essence, it has influenced the totality of human aesthetic endeavor, which is a paradox for such an extremely localized and focused malady. Because the most excellent Eber is too busy to read or hear or view everything that is sent to her, she has stored it unconsumed in her house, which is now crammed with wonderful works: it has become a museum of artistic genius. Men have sent her their best poems, songs, pictures, and not receiving a reply (because she is so busy), they have destroyed all (if any) copies in their possession, leaving Eber as the sole guardian of the materialized talent in question. The authorities of Córdoba want to publish her *house*. After all, can an *unread* poem truly be said to *be* a poem? Is it (or is it not?) the same as a poem that does not exist? This question and others are destined to be explored in myriad undergraduate theses in a multitude of universities. As for what would happen if a victim of this affliction met Eber M. Soler in person, it is unwise to imagine. Suffice to say that most scholars believe that such an outcome (termed *Soler stroke* by insurance agents) would be as fatal to the unfortunate (fortunate?) man as the detonation of a tactical nuclear device.

## Prognosis

The development of Ebercitas seems almost certain to take a sudden and dramatic metaphysical turn. Eventually the gorgeous Eber will be able to give up her job teaching Phonetics, because a more lucrative source of revenue will become available to her. Consider that her house is full of unpublished works of astounding excellence, but that the varieties of artistic excellence are finite: it is clear that these works will eventually be duplicated by chance in other parts of the world by independent artists. Their creators will believe them to be original and will launch them into the public domain, whereupon Eber will simply search through her archives and produce the identical work, still sealed inside its stamped and dated packaging (see *How to Hire X-Ray Machines* and *Employing Archivists on a Shoestring* by the Röntgen Seek & Describe Foundation). This proof of copyright (and the works in question are always specifically created for her as a gift, including the copyright) and subsequent litigation will nearly always guarantee large sums in compensation, generating a very comfortable income for Eber. It will also pay for her to attach wheels and a large sail to her house. Only by thus moving around might she change her address from day to day and evade the attentions of the postman and his sack of artistic merit. For a balance must be struck between acquiring fresh sources of income and crowding herself out of her own house. As the months pass, creative types will realize the inadvisability of producing works which might already exist in her archives. Thinking carefully about this will inevitably lead to thinking more specifically about *her*. The infection will rapidly take hold of their nervous systems. They also will wish to create works *for* her, according to the standard (albeit remarkable) pattern. However, these works will have to be *inimitable*. The form of the gift will remain comprehensible, but not its substance. Thus copyright issues will be avoided. To achieve this, the authors will write books full of random letters, and the musicians will compose tunes from random notes, and the painters will cover canvasses with pixels of random color. To deliver these gifts, they will speed past her sailing house in motor vehicles, on horseback, atop rocket boots and cast them over the railings of her balcony, through the open window. She will collect them at her leisure and deposit them in the archive. Her sails will fill with the winds of Argentina, the cold wind from the south and the north wind with its dust and hot heavy air. If enough books are constructed entirely from random letters, the laws of chance state that *some* will make perfect sense. If enough tunes are assembled entirely from random notes, the same laws state that some will be haunting and beautiful and say all the things you wanted to say without words. If enough pictures are painted entirely from random dots of color, those laws also ensure that some will be portraits of you, and me: our births, lives and eventual fates. And so, somewhere on the pampas, perhaps along the rim of the Andes, in a moving house, the book of your life and death, its melody and its image, will exist. And once she has been deprived of earning a salary through litigation, she will turn her vast intelligence toward inventing a new source of income. She will rent out by the hour these relevant works, renaming her house (with the greatest respect to Jorge Luis Borges) the (multimedia) *Mobile Library of Babel* . . .

## Cure

None, and why should there be? Ebercitas will never be discredited.* It is the most wonderful disease eber—I mean ever! I have it! I want it! I dance, I caper! Farewell! She is my sweetheart. This entry is for her. I am trying too hard. *Ven ¡ay! ven, amorosa guajirita! y mi alma no quiere, zapatillas listas, vivir sin tu amor!* (see *Big Book of Spanish Serenades* edited by Rodriguez Trinidad Fernandez Concepcion Henrique Maria, Lord of Arguento and Duke of Shadow Valley).

## Submitted by

Dr. Rhys Hughes

## Cross References

Diseasemaker's Croup; Poetic Lassitude

---

* *Editors' Note:* Untrue!

# EMORDNY'S SYNDROME*

## Country of Origin
Kerguelen Islands, Southern Ocean

## First Known Case
Nemo Omen, 16 September 1961, meteorologist, 33 years of age

## Symptoms
Initial mood swings in response to external stress are followed by mental and physical mimicry, then palindromic verbalization. In severe cases, the condition involves corporeal mutation. According to the circumstances, this can be extreme in its extent and consequences: some individuals have been found fused to outcrops of rock, their newly brittle bodies crumbling under their own greatly increased mass, while others have dissolved in water.

## History
Nemo Omen, a member of a French survey team on Kerguelen, began to behave erratically after several months stationed in this remote island group in the Southern Ocean, a barren and inhospitable environment subject to

---

\* *Editors' Note:* In a very odd "doubling" or "mirroring" situation, it would appear that Dr. Andrew J. Wilson has contracted Dr. M. M. O'Driscoll's Empathetic Fallacy Syndrome, while Dr. O'Driscoll has contracted Dr. Wilson's Emordny's Syndrome—thus forcing us to quarantine both parties, although not for the usual reasons. We are also endeavoring to keep Dr. Wilson and Dr. O'Driscoll from coming into contact with one another, as this may create a mutated syndrome resistant to any cure. (For this reason, we have not cross-referenced the two diseases.)

capricious and inclement weather. Initially, Omen simply aped his colleagues' behavior and incessantly impersonated their various accents. His conduct was attributed to his long separation from his family and friends. Although Xavier Emordny, the camp doctor, monitored him closely, no immediate action was taken. Omen then began to demonstrate physical symptoms when he collapsed while conducting meteorological measurements during a heavy rain shower. His colleagues initially thought that he was suffering from a fever and sweating profusely until they carried him under cover and wrapped him in blankets. Omen's deliquescing skin dried out immediately, and then began to bobble as it adopted the color and woven pattern of the blankets.

Dr. Emordny placed the patient in isolation, and began a series of tests intended to identify the condition and assess its potential risk to the expedition as a whole. Bearing a superficial resemblance to the reflection reflex described in *The Trimble-Manard Omnibus of Insidious Arctic Maladies*, the novel syndrome was characterized by a chameleon-like response to the external environment. John Trimble and Rebecca Manard maintain that polar and sub-arctic environments have the potential to erase the psychological sense of the self as a discrete entity. Although the reflection reflex can be cured by surrounding victims with photographs of themselves, similar therapeutic interventions by Dr. Emordny only served to make his subject's skin assume the texture of photographic paper.

The condition did not appear to be contagious in any conventional sense since there were no clinical signs of viral or bacterial infection. Nevertheless, other members of the expedition began to exhibit the telltale symptoms, and an outbreak of mass psychosis was suspected. Desperate attempts to isolate cases within the small infirmary led to a breakdown in supervision, allowing Omen and the other increasingly agitated patients to escape into the trackless and hostile interior of the Kerguelen mainland. Their chameleon-like abilities helped several victims of the syndrome to avoid detection entirely, while others, battered by the island's frequent gales, may have literally vanished into thin air by becoming part of it.

Dr. Emordny insisted on abandoning the organized search parties and ventured cautiously into the Kerguelen hinterlands on his own. Once he managed to spot one of his patients from a distance through his pair of binoculars, he tentatively advanced toward the individual while taking elaborate care not to alarm the subject and so induce a camouflage reaction. When the approach was successful, the afflicted individual began to assume the appearance of the doctor. Emordny then persuaded his patients that they were in the presence of a sufferer of the disease. The victims rapidly assumed the role of the practitioner and led their doctor back to the medical facility. In this way, all the extant sufferers were returned to full-time medical care. Then, while still under the benign delusion that they were, in fact, health professionals, Nemo Omen and others allegedly identified and synthesized the curative therapy that eliminated the malady.

## Cures

In devising his novel intervention to end the crisis, Dr. Emordny anticipated the words of the poet Alan Jackson, who wrote, "Truly the remedy's inside the disease." The remoteness of the location of the only recorded outbreak of this syndrome has led some authorities to cast doubt on the efficacy of Emordny's therapy, and even whether the disease ever existed at all. Nevertheless, the doctor's case report, which contains many ambiguous but disturbing photographs, was substantiated by all the members of the Kerguelen expedition who actually returned to France. It would be foolhardy to dismiss Emordny's syndrome out of hand since it is a condition that holds up a mirror to our definition of the self, even if we are not pleased with what we see reflected in it.

## Submitted by
DR. ANDREW J. WILSON

## Cross Reference
Diseasemaker's Croup

# EMPATHETIC FALLACY SYNDROME*

## *EFS, Tacheoindurare*

## Country of Origin

England, United Kingdom (disputed)

## First Recorded Case

Frederic Arctor presented with indeterminate symptoms at the North London clinic of Dr. Robert Loew in 1936. After a prolonged consultation during which Loew struggled to put Arctor at ease, the latter finally admitted to seemingly unrelated symptoms including insomnia, listlessness, irritability, depression, mild hallucinations, and erectile dysfunction. Later, Loew recalled that these were problems with which he himself had been troubled and had mentioned in passing in an attempt to win Arctor's confidence. He arranged for his patient to be examined by a colleague, a man of first-rate abilities who happened to be plagued by debilitating self-doubt. Subsequently, Loew found Arctor displaying symptoms of acute paranoia. Convinced he was on to something, he decided to test his hypothesis by asking a young medical student of considerable torpidity to meet with Arctor. Afterwards, the patient was discovered in a state of immobility verging on paralysis.

---

* *Editors' Note:* In a very odd "doubling" or "mirroring" situation, it would appear that Dr. Andrew J. Wilson has contracted Dr. M. M. O'Driscoll's Empathetic Fallacy Syndrome, while Dr. O'Driscoll has contracted Dr. Wilson's Emordny's Syndrome—thus forcing us to quarantine both parties, although not for the usual reasons. We are also endeavoring to keep Dr. Wilson and Dr. O'Driscoll from coming into contact with one another, as this may create a mutated syndrome resistant to any cure. (For this reason, we have not cross-referenced the two diseases.)

Loew's paper on the case was published in *Lancet* to widespread controversy. He listed the complex and diverse symptoms in meticulous detail, but it was his theorizing on EFS as a malady of the modern era, caused by the speed and alienation of contemporary urban life, that finally won him respect, and the right to classify and name the disease. He identified those most at risk of contagion as "nondescript individuals given to pathological self-effacement, unhindered by any apparent sense of embarrassment, yet harboring an unnatural craving for attention that causes them to mimic the psychological, emotional, and even physical characteristics of those with whom they come into contact."

## Symptoms

These range from flattering displays of imitative behavior, to more prolonged and severe episodes of psychological mimesis, such as that seen in the infamous Furriskey case (see "Angela Furriskey—Victim or Villain" in *The Psycho-Social Paradox of EFS*, by Dr. Imelda Trellis). In 1968, Mrs. Furriskey of Dublin assumed the symptoms of her paranoid schizophrenic husband, John. In doing so, she inadvertently burdened herself with the five separate personalities that had been identified as fighting for control of Furriskey's mind. Tragically, one of these, the teetotaler Kaminer, persuaded Mrs. Furriskey to walk into the local Public House and kill eight people before turning John's shotgun on herself.

Recent advances in medical science, especially epidemiology, have increased our understanding of the true nature of the disease. In particular, the groundbreaking research of Dr. Krempe of The Ingolstadt Centre for Psychic Rehabilitation, has shown that 27 per cent of cases of Persistent Vegetative State (brainstem death) had been misdiagnosed, and were, in fact, examples of a particularly virulent form of EFS. It is almost impossible to detect this new strain in its early stages, when it prompts affectations identical to those found in people of an artistic disposition. This heightened sensitivity promotes a powerful but delusional empathy with nature. What distinguishes the victim of EFS from the true aesthete is the former's gradual transference of empathy onto inanimate objects—they take on the characteristics of gateposts, or perhaps kitchen appliances, rather than of mountains or lakes. If not detected, the condition proves irreversible, leading to paralysis, an inability to perform meaningful social interactions, an imagined immunity to extremes of temperature and precipitation, and, finally, total organ failure as they strive to approximate the feelings and sensitivities of whatever object it is they have fixated upon.

Dr. Sarah Goodman is credited with citing the first case of Empathetic Fallacy Syndrome by Proxy, one Noodles Kropotkin, said to have projected his own feeling of social inadequacy, purposelessness, and ennui onto a third party, resulting in the latter's petrification (see Goodman's *Journals* for a full account).

## History

Most experts now believe that the disease predates Loew's classification, and have cited a number of historical cases of tacheoinduration as actual instances of Empathetic Fallacy Syndrome. A reference by Dalkey in *The Guide to Psychotropic Balkan Diseases* (ed. Geraldine Carter, M.D.), supports the argument that the Golem was a victim of EFS while the testimony, witting or not, from other sources, strengthens the case of those who claim that Olympia Coppelius, Narcissus, and Lot's wife, if actual people, were all afflicted with the disease rather than with magick or divine intervention. Whatever the credibility of these cases, the claims by Randolph Johnson in *Confessions of a Disease Fiend* that it was the eminent Victorian John Ruskin who first discovered EFS have more to do with Johnson's fondness for laudanum and the need to promote his disreputable tome than with the proper history of disease classification.

## Cures

Despite our greater knowledge of the disease, science has not discovered a cure. The hopes invested in what were formerly seen as promising therapies that might reverse, or at least halt, the progressive petrification of sufferers—ensuring that those most at risk were always in mixed company (to avoid fixation on any one particular individual), and the more controversial proposal to encourage potential victims to limit their social interaction to the company of those more tedious than themselves—have proven to be misplaced. The somewhat predictable side effects—a sharp increase in conversations concerning the state of the weather, widespread garden gnome infestations, a proliferation of random acts of queuing, and an exponential growth in the number of cases of vandalism against recently installed works of public sculpture—have far outweighed any potential benefit to the victims of EFS. Such setbacks have led some clinicians to call for more radical and aggressive treatment regimes, with some hopes being held out for regular isolation in total sensory deprivation chambers, while the early results from the Blavatsky Clinical Trial, measuring the efficacy of psychic transference of dullness from those afflicted to the dead, are inconclusive.

## Submitted by
Dr. M. M. O'Driscoll

## Cross Reference
Diseasemaker's Croup

# ESPECTARE NECROSIS

*Also known as Necrosis Optimum*

## Country of Origin
United States (Oklahoma City, Oklahoma)

## First Known Case
September 14, 1999. The first case I am aware of was that of one Ray Nessenbaum, a retired construction worker out of Oklahoma City. He came into the hospital claiming that his left leg had "died." I asked him exactly what he meant. Did he mean that he was feeling some numbness in the leg, or that the leg was simply injured in some manner? He insisted that his left leg had died, and that his right leg was soon to follow.

An examination revealed nothing wrong with the right leg, but large masses of flesh on the left leg were, indeed, necrotic, and the left leg could not be saved.

Mr. Nessenbaum remained in the hospital for several weeks. During this time we attempted (without success) to delay the course of the necrosis. We also ordered a psychiatric consult to help Mr. Nessenbaum deal with his condition. He still insisted his right leg was going to die as well. We assured him that there were no signs of disease in the right leg. Mr. Nessenbaum informed us that he had always known this was going to happen to him—that he had prized his leg strength more than anything, and had been afraid of something happening to his legs for years—and now his right leg was going to die as well. Nothing we said could sway him from this belief.

One week later the right leg became necrotic and had to be amputated.

## Symptoms

All known cases of Espectare Necrosis are typified by large areas of tissue death, preceded by the belief in the patient (or in the case of very small children, in their mothers or fathers) that terrible things are going to happen to particular parts of their bodies (or in the case of very small children, the body as a whole, dying piecemeal in accordance with the progress of the parents' pessimistic ideation).

## History

Several more cases of Espectare came into the hospital over the next few weeks, and in all of these cases the patients reported that a particular portion of their body—usually a specific body part such as a leg, arm, hand, lip, penis, ear—had died, or was in the process of dying. In all cases the patient's fears proved to be well-founded. In only one case were the symptoms reversed, when an adolescent female appeared to "change her mind" about what was happening to her.

A disturbing trend developed during the ninth month of the outbreak. Mothers were bringing their young children (from infants up to the age of four) into the hospital complaining that their children were dying. When we examined these children we discovered that, indeed, the children displayed large areas of necrotic tissue. Alerted by the earlier cases of Espectare, my colleagues and I found ourselves amenable to the idea that the pessimistic expectation of disease need not reside solely in the patient. However, in the cases of small children who had not yet individuated, the expectation could reside in the parents of these children. In these cases the area of necrosis appeared to spread commensurate with the progress of the parents' negative expectations.

Initial tests had to be performed, of course, to rule out Munchausen syndrome by proxy. In order to do this, we instituted quarantine protocols and isolated the children from their parents to insure that the parents could not physically affect their children's condition. This was an unfortunate situation, as many of the parents were forced to wait for their children to die without being able to go to them. It took a serious toll on our young patients, their parents, and the staff itself, triggering numerous resignations. Eventually, however, we were able to rule out Munchausen and the parents rejoined their dying children.

Unfortunately, the quarantine measures proved to exacerbate the parents' pessimism, and necrosis spread rapidly through the children. Drastic treatment measures were implemented, including multiple surgeries to amputate tissue in advance of the disease. These surgeries were particularly wearing on our pediatric surgeons, who were forced to diminish the bodies of their infant charges at an alarming rate. In many cases professional confidence was destroyed and the hospital staff has never quite recovered.

## Cures

It would seem to me to be the height of arrogance to suggest that there might be a cure for such a disease. Am I to say to a parent with a dying child, "Look on the bright side"? Certainly a degree of optimism is helpful in any patient's treatment, but this seems a feeble remedy when faced with a condition that uses our most existential fears and apprehensions for our children to fuel the disease process. In fact, simply knowing the importance of maintaining optimism under these circumstances often only serves to drive a more profound, inescapable pessimism.

And what is the physician's role in all of this? Physicians encounter death on a daily basis—is it too bold to suggest that of all the members of our society it is the doctors' optimism which is the most compromised? If Espectare progresses at its current rate, is my own profound pessimism concerning our ability to heal in turn seriously compromising my patients' health? Am I, in fact, killing my patients one disappointment, one bad day, one moment of professional despair at a time?

It is these thoughts that have recently brought me to my decision to leave the medical profession. I plan to spend my days with my children and grandchildren, attempting to enjoy whatever time I, and they, have left.

I leave the practice of medicine to you gentlemen and ladies who have more hope than I am able to muster.

## Submitted by

DR. STEVE RASNIC TEM, GRAND FELLOW OF THE COLLEGE OF ACUTE MELANCHOLIA, UNIVERSITY OF THE BIG MUDDY, VICKSBURG, MISSISSIPPI

## Cross References

Diseasemaker's Croup; Post-Traumatic Placebosis

# EXTREME EXOSTOSIS

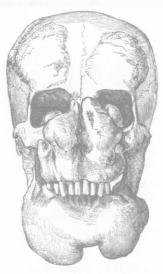

## Country of Origin
United States

## First Known Case
While Exostosis—a form of benign bone tumor—has been widely reported for many years (see Erichsen, Barwell, Hartmann, Mudthumper), the remarkable case reported here for the first time comes to us from the recently-discovered case files of Dr. Karl Ausenheimer. Dr. Ausenheimer served as the sole town physician of Eastborough, Massachusetts, at the time of the events (1906).

Ausenheimer's patient was one William Gould, a carpenter who first came to the doctor with an already prominent outgrowth of bone jutting from his right femur. Ausenheimer determined that the man was not at risk and suggested to Gould that a surgeon might saw away the growth, a course of action Gould did not pursue. Ausenheimer noted at the time that he doubted Gould's claim of the tumor having grown to the length he witnessed in the space of a mere week. While he suspected the growth was an exostosis at that initial examination, he knew that exostoses originate in childhood and tend toward symmetry, though there was not a corresponding tumor on the left femur. Ausenheimer also makes known to us that Gould was a sullen man, prone toward depression, who after his wife left him fired a revolver against his temple. The bullet, however, was deflected by the skull, traveling under the skin to exit at the man's forehead. Gould was knocked unconscious by the concussion but seemed to exhibit no further complications as a result of the wound. Toward the end of his account, however, the good doctor self-consciously wonders whether this traumatic incident might have overstimulated a portion of the victim's brain, sending forth confused commands to the diligent troops below.

## Symptoms

When a barn that Gould was repairing for a local family sat untended for a number of weeks, his brother was called upon to seek Gould at his abode. It was assumed by the townsfolk, and especially the brother, that Gould had successfully ended his own life this time. Instead, what Edwin Gould discovered sent him running from the house and straight into the town's center, bursting into Ausenheimer's office. As a result, and upon venturing into Gould's house, the doctor was stunned to witness his patient immobilized and near dehydration in his badly-soiled bed, unable to rise due to the weight and the awkwardness of the bone tumors that had formed over the past few weeks. These were so prodigious as to have actually broken the skin (mostly without loss of blood), extending out from the limbs, chest, and even brow like branching antlers, the greatest of these growths measuring two feet in length. Over the course of the next several days, the bone tumors continued to grow at an even more remarkable rate. Having sawed off one of these shockingly numerous exostoses from the patient's shoulder, Ausenheimer found it to be cancellous (containing a reticulated latticework) within but externally quite durable. While their spongy, cell-like interiors kept the individual growths from being overly heavy, their sheer number and size overwhelmed the slender 30-year-old patient.

## History

Feeling that a case this unusual should be witnessed and dealt with by more worldly surgeons than himself, Ausenheimer decided not to try sawing off the many tumors, other than a few of the heavier ones and the one sprouting from Gould's skull like a forked horn, just at the bridge of his nose. In any case, the elderly physician found the sawing tough work. He, Edwin Gould, and his wife Eva made the patient as comfortable as possible, feeding him to keep his strength up while Ausenheimer began arrangements for the patient to be moved to the Boston University Clinic for the Anomalous. But upon the second day of visiting his patient's home, called there by a hysterical Eva Gould, Ausenheimer found the man's condition to have worsened to an uncanny degree. The growths had multiplied and extended to such an extent that they radiated from the bed in a kind of forest, even digging into the plaster of the ceiling. Ausenheimer marveled that none of these bony spears had punctured Gould's own body, the way a ram's horns can grow into its own skull. But by now, understandably, Gould was in a positive panic, and took out most of his delirium upon his poor sister-in-law (some of his abuse suggested to Ausenheimer that William had been in love with Eva, but she had chosen the other brother; in any case, he soon forbade her from reentering his room, and she tearfully exited the house altogether). Ausenheimer could not even approach the patient closer than four feet, and he and Edwin were at a loss as to how to get food and drink to the man through this interlocking fortress of bone, as the patient himself could not lift a limb an inch from the bed. At last they were able to get water and broth to his lips through a long metal tube inserted between the twisted branches. Ausenheimer measured several of these by the hour to track their terrifying progress. He sent word to have surgeons from the clinic in Boston come out to Eastborough as quickly as they could manage.

Ausenheimer and Edwin spent the night downstairs in the parlor of William's house. They both reported hearing him rage feverishly at several points during the night, telling them to get out of his house, to leave him in peace, to lock the windows first and the door after them. But when the men roused in the morning, it was to an eerie stillness, and when they ascended to William's room, it was to find that antlers of bone had pushed the door ajar and even pierced through its wood. When the door was freed and opened, the men found the room beyond it to be utterly blocked to them and filled to its four walls and ceiling with a tightly woven nest of bone. Though the patient and indeed even the bed were not to be seen through the mass, they assumed correctly that Gould had been crushed under the weight. Blood pooled on the floor indicated that at last the tumors had worked their way through his tissues and organs as well. Two days later, when a team of men had finally cleared away enough bone for the body to be examined, it was found to be horribly gored, distorted, broken, with tumors having sprouted even from the jaw, cheekbones, and the very eye sockets of the patient.

## Cures

Under normal circumstances, exostoses present no serious dangers to their victims. It would seem that only a larger team of surgeons more experienced than Ausenheimer and his helpers might have worked quickly enough to free Gould from the cell of his own making, though it cannot be known whether the tumors would have simply returned. Ausenheimer opines, and one cannot help but agree, that some part of the carpenter William Gould was bent on constructing a means of his own demise.

## Submitted by
DR. JEFFREY THOMAS

## Cross References
Bone Leprosy; Diseasemaker's Croup; Razornail Bone Rot

# FEMALE HYPER-ORGASMIC EPILEPSY

## *Black Orgasm*

## Country of Origin

Austro-Hungary

## First Known Case

Breuer and Freud's *Studies on Hysteria* notably contains a few paragraphs that suggest a manifestation of the disease many years before it became officially recognized. "Maria X" was, at the time of her death, a 17-year-old milliner's assistant. Witnesses later described how, while waiting for a tram along Vienna's Ringstrasse, she suddenly fastened her eyes upon one of the anonymous clerks who shared the queue, cried out "Oh God, it's him! My demon lover from the other side of the universe! I am going home! I am going home!" and thereon succumbed to a particularly ferocious and, it transpired, fatal grand mal. In 1919 Freud wrote to Lou-Andreas Salomé: "I put it to you that in a society where non-neurotic women are perceived to be second class citizens, almost a 'second sex,' then hysteria may represent a means of escape into a saner world." The fact that "Black Orgasm" (to employ the demotic appellative) has nothing to do with hysteria, and that the escape it offers may lead to an alien world no saner than our own, does not disqualify the prescience of Freud's observation, considering that a pathology was not established until the mid 1980s, when WHO, NASA, and the SETI Institute first published their joint findings.

## History

Medical literature, post-Freud, records several isolated occurrences, the most famous being the case of Jean Harlow whose "cerebral edema" at 26 was undoubtedly a fiction that owed everything to Hollywood spin and prudishness, and nothing to the truth; but it was not until the 1960s, when Black Orgasm became firmly established (if still woefully misunderstood) among the populations of Europe and the United States, that science began to address its spread with appropriate rigor. Public consciousness of the epidemic was raised significantly at this time by the deaths of several minor personalities in the entertainment industry. In the chapter of his autobiography entitled "Veni, Vedi, Vita," Marcello Mastroianni describes how the young Italian starlet Giulietta Gabon succumbed during the filming of the orgy scene at the end of Fellini's *La Dolce Vita*:

> Giulietta had just happened to glance at one of the extras—a man in his late forties, and not in any way handsome—when she gave what seemed a short, involuntary scream, fell to the floor, and, as loss of consciousness set in, was gripped by muscular contractions that we all associated with normal epilepsy. So violent were these contractions, however, that soon no contortionist, however fantastic, would have been able to match them. At one point, her back arched to such a degree that her body seemed to describe a complete circle (a condition otherwise known as Opisthotonos). Her convulsions became more violent still, and as her head thrashed to and fro there was another scream—longer, purer, and more terrible than any that had gone before—followed by a brittle detonation, once, twice, which, as we later learnt from the newspapers, signaled that her spine and neck had snapped under the stress.

Of course, such things have become so common that they are now seldom reported, in the newspapers or anywhere else. The disease has become entrenched within the fabric of modern life, its prognosis like a psychic scream emanating from countless billboards, magazine covers, television screens, and fashion houses.

## Symptoms

Seizure may be preceded by irritability, night sweats, a tendency to forever cross and re-cross the legs when seated in public places, obsessive licking of the lips, and, for some, an overriding urge to collect vintage bubblegum cards featuring "Mars Invades!" scenarios of abduction and enslavement. Autopsy reports, however, when combined with testimonials from the victim's family and friends, suggest that the majority of cases are asymptomatic until the few minutes, or even seconds, preceding the invariably fatal seizure.

## Cures

Anticonvulsant drugs, such as diphenylhydantoin, phenobarbital, and valproic acid, have proved ineffectual, though not as counterproductive as early attempts to isolate the individual in a nunnery or some other place of religious confinement (where religio-sexual mania, of the kind experienced and described by Saint Teresa of Avila, actually hastened demise). Other research has concentrated on the fact that males are not affected. Dr. Geraldine Carter, for instance, suggests, in *The Guide to Psychotropic Balkan Diseases*, that Dr. Jeffrey Ford's work on Ouroborean Lordosis may provide a breakthrough if it can only be established how Harmon Creets survived so long with such radical curvature of the spine—the cause of death in 92 per cent of Black Orgasm cases. The most important findings, however, have been in the field of behavioral medicine. Strictly controlled laboratory tests on hundreds of young women manifesting precursive symptoms have indicated that something as insignificant as a photograph, an idle thought while daydreaming, a chance encounter, can prove devastating—but only if the subject has previously complained of liminal hallucinations involving beings that they characterize as "sex demons from another galaxy." The seriousness with which these hallucinations, or visions, have been evaluated—not by doctors, but by astronomers and physicists—could well mean that government funding for a cure will soon be at an end. NASA and SETI have already theorized that Black Orgasm precipitates something similar to the "orgasm-death gimmick" found in the writings of William S. Burroughs, whereby the dying victim's ego is transferred to an alien "receptacle" perhaps many light-years distant. The promise of interstellar travel will undoubtedly mean that transnational post-radical feminist lobbying groups, such as The Illuminates of Thanateros, which have recently begun campaigning for global sex-death and a return to what they avow to be their home in the stars, may succeed in persuading world populations to embrace the disease and, similarly, that NASA, ESA, and other space agencies, should cede their efforts and resources to a new breed of suicidal astronaut.

## Submitted by
DR. RICHARD CALDER

## Cross References
Catamenia Hysterica; Di Forza Virus Syndrome; Diseasemaker's Croup; Ouroborean Lordosis; Pentzler's Lubriciousness

# FERROBACTERIAL ACCRETION SYNDROME

## Sometimes Popularly Known —Inaccurately—as "Tin-Itis" or "Metal Fatigue"

## Country of Origin

Variants of the disease can be found in all places where ores containing iron or tin have been extracted for many generations.

## First Known Case

Although there are many suggestive autopsy reports from the mid- to late-nineteenth century, the earliest fully-documented case is the (slightly atypical) one of Ivor Polperro, a Cornish tin-miner whose family had followed that profession for at least 200 years. The case was monitored by Dr. Trelawny of Truro between 1898 and 1905 (Dr. Trelawny was one of the earliest medical researchers to employ the Roentgen device, without which the progress of the disease could not be monitored in a living individual).

## Symptoms

Chronic tiredness; congestion of the chest cavity or lower abdomen; abnormal sensitivity to magnets. In extreme cases, sufferers may be subject to new appetites that lead them to swallow pins, needles, crushed tin cans, items of jewelry and miscellaneous scrap derived from discarded cars, washing machines, refrigerators, and nuclear warheads.

## History

The tendency of miners dealing with iron ores to have the symptoms listed above was well-known, if only at an anecdotal level, long before the invention of the Roentgen device or "X-ray machine" enabled doctors to confirm and track the buildup of distinct metallic deposits in the bodies of sufferers. Ferrobacteria and other metal-extracting bacteria are not usually to be found among the resident bacterial populations of human beings, but mines provide unusually hospitable conditions for such infections to occur, and the high levels of metals routinely ingested by miners provide a selective context in which such bacteria may thrive at the expense of more familiar commensals. Members of mining families may, over the course of several generations, acquire an astonishing tolerance to the presence and activity of bacterial populations of this kind. It is possible that metal-extracting bacteria may provide a temporarily useful service in removing iron, tin, and other metals from the blood vessels and alimentary canals of their hosts, but they cannot be regarded as true symbiotes because the subsequent deposits do not remain harmless indefinitely, especially when proximal to the heart or enclosing parts of the intestine (thus inhibiting peristalsis).

The accretions laid down by the bacteria always contain iron, but it is usually alloyed with at least one other metal, including (in decreasing order of likelihood) tin, copper, silver, gold, and uranium. Contrary to rumor and urban legend, no case has ever been found in which the accretion mass was pure gold, let alone one in which the heart was thus encased. On the other hand, there does seem to be a good deal of substance in the suggestion that the shapes assumed by the accretions are by no means random. Those cases which are sufficiently acute to cultivate metal-hunger in the victim, almost amounting to addiction, provide the most telling evidence of the psychosomatic component of the malady; cases have been described in which accretion masses fed by calculated ingestion grow into circles, figures-of-eight, Moebius strips, corkscrews, caltrops, loops of barbed wire, knuckledusters, drill-bits, clamps, and vices—and even, in one notorious instance, a double-barreled flintlock pistol.

The disease is, alas, far too gradual in its development to be of any use as a mode of industrial craftsmanship, although it is nowadays not uncommon for the worst-afflicted patients to become ambitious to grow hacksaws or eternity rings (perhaps according to the state of their marriages), and one current English sufferer subject to the not-uncommon delusion that he is a reincarnation of King Arthur, has sworn to "cough up Excalibur or die trying." The latter is the likelier eventuality.

### Treatment

Modest accretions can nowadays be removed easily enough by surgery, and more complicated ones only require a little more care, but the only patients likely to demand such alleviation are those whose accretions are ugly and inchoate. Almost everyone who can see possibilities for "psychosomatic sculpture"—even when no such possibility is obvious to other observers—prefers to nurture the disease, even in cases where eventual damage to other tissues seems highly likely.

The possibility that the disease is the ultimate source of the human aesthetic impulse, and that all unafflicted artists are merely trying to compensate for their internal inadequacies, cannot be entirely discounted, although it does seem rather remote.

**Submitted by**
Dr. B. M. Stableford, B.A., D.Phil., F.R.S.B.F.

**Cross References**
Diseasemaker's Croup; Logopetria

# FIGURATIVE SYNESTHESIA*

## Country of Origin
United States

## First Known Case
First and only known case diagnosed in 1977. The patient was Bernard Quigley (1956 to 1999), an out-of-work handyman who resided in Shell Pile, New Jersey.

## Symptoms
This exceedingly rare affliction is an anomalous sub-category of the already uncommon Synesthesia: a neuro-perceptual condition originating in the hippocampus, part of the ancient limbic system, where remembered or imagined perceptions triggered in diverse geographical regions of the brain as the result of external stimuli come together and, due to some unknown neurological mishap, fail to be filtered, resulting in the mixing of sensoric memory along with perceived experience, and leading to the transposition of appropriate senses in correspondence with a given sensory organ. As a result, the sufferer will, for example, smell color, hear tastes, see sounds, tactily feel aromas. A patient with the "common" type of the disease (only about nine in 1,000,000), may experience a piece of guitar music as the

---

* *Editors' Note:* Dr. Ford has also published a hypothetical case study of this disease via the Web site Scifi.com/scifiction, edited by Dr. Ellen Datlow. Please refer to "The Emperor of Ice Cream" on that site. Dr. Ford's claim to have "stumbled across" Figurative Synesthesia takes modesty to new extremes.

sight of golden droplets falling out of thin air or hear the color turquoise as a vague murmuring, but, although a very real experience for the individual, the phenomena perceived will always remain in the realm of the abstract. What is truly unique about Figurative Synesthesia is that the synesthetic experience becomes defined as something readily identifiable.

## History

In the one known case of Figurative Synesthesia, as reported by Dr. Samuel Arbegast, the patient, Bernard Quigley, upon tasting licorice, perceived before him, in definite shape and solidity, an exact double of himself. The hallmarks that distinguished this phenomenon from psychotic hallucination were its reliance upon the ingestion of a certain mundane substance and the report by the patient of the accompanying noetic (a term borrowed from William James' *Varieties of Religious Experience*) sensation; a feeling of "rightness" or "epiphany" that coincides with the usual synesthetic experience. Quigley did not taste licorice until rather late in his teens, and, when he did, he thought he was being visited by a doppelgänger. The history of his ailment was written up by Arbegast, his physician, in the now famous *The Case of the Licorice Twin*. It seems that the young man eventually understood that the ingestion of the confection could call forth the figure. He reported that upon encountering his double, he would see the figure performing some everyday task, as if he, himself, were spying on a precise moment of a fully realized life that was happening elsewhere. One day, in his thirty-first year, Quigley discovered that his synesthetic twin was, at the same moment, eating licorice, and was, amazingly, also aware of him. They had a brief conversation and made plans to both initiate the experience at a set time and place. Many meetings and conversations followed. Whereas Quigley's life was a disaster, beset by poverty as a result of a lethargic nature, his twin was exceedingly wealthy and motivated—a rich shipping magnate in his own reality. Due to an obsession to always be in the company of his successful, synesthetic self, the patient consumed excessive quantities of licorice, well known for increasing blood pressure, and eventually suffered a fatal stroke due to critical hypertension.

Dr. Arbegast, widely read in anomalous diseases, deserves praise from the medical community for having had the knowledge to appropriately diagnose this disease. Had he been a less well-informed physician, his patient would probably have been committed to an institution for the insane. It is his belief that many instances of the visitation of spirits and phantasms could be explained as undiagnosed cases of Figurative Synesthesia.

## Cures

No definitive cure. Dr. Arbegast posits a theoretical cure might be to request of the synesthetic double, while in the state of shared recognition, that it commit suicide, seeing as it is merely a phantasmic projection. Barring this, the patient might have been prevailed upon to abstain from consuming licorice.

## Submitted by

Dr. Jeffrey Ford

## Cross References

Diseasemaker's Croup; Logopetria; Monochromitis

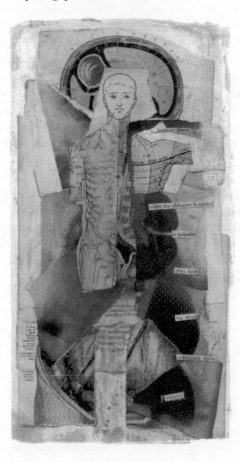

*Stiff 1 by Dawn Andrews*

# FLORA METAMORPHOSIS SYNDROME

## Country of Origin
Greece

## First Known Case
The sisters of Phaethon: Phaethusa, Lampetie, etc.

## Symptoms
Spells of uncontrolled and sometimes painful blinking or other cranial or facial actions. Loss of taste on the tongue; sense of taste transferred to toes. A high florigen level in the blood. Initial difficulty speaking, followed by total paralysis of this function. Paralysis of the limbs. Rapid mitosis of newly formed meristems. Development of lenticals.

## History
That the disease is of extremely antique origin is quite obvious, mention being made of it by numerous classical authors, in both the Greek and Latin languages. The wonderful poet Bion, in his masterpiece *On Amphibious Rabbits and Other Odd Specimens*, describes in deliciously explicit detail what most certainly is the 165-pound *titan arum*, that putrid-smelling colossus of the plant kingdom. He then goes on to enumerate the stories of no less than six maidens who, to his certain knowledge, upon inhaling the exotically awful perfume of the huge and phallic flower, were struck with the (above mentioned) most horrific symptoms. Rustilius, in his *Sprightly Flora of Africa*,

tells us of one young woman by the name of Semele who "could no longer move because she found her feet so fastened to the ground, her toes turned deep into the soil, as there to take her water and food." Silius Italicus, whose words should always be trusted, tells us of "a youth easy to love, that came to be with aromatic foliage, an evergreen shrub, and his leaves we did then use for flavoring our cheesecake." One of the more dramatic recounts, however, comes from Pausanaius, in a group of badly damaged pages recently discovered in the Biblioteca Ambrosiana, in Milan, the pages obviously being a number of those previously lost from his *Description of Greece*. He tells us: "From Helikon I went to the Grove of Orpheus, with the bubbling water of Aganippe on my left. My guide, always eager for an extra coin, said he would show me something curious for a consideration. He led me . . . dense foliage . . . the youth's beauty was in no way less for the greenish hue of his skin, and from his neck protruded a number of xanthic calyxes, forming the outer support for a sort of ruff of pink hued petals, each marbled with a network of attractive blue veins. We spoke some words . . . the grove consisted of, it was said, nearly half the sons of the village, their forms most handsome to gaze upon . . . the culprit being a giant bloom that they worshipped as twice-born Baccus . . . requisite for the man who holds the office of priest to have never experienced the joys of more than one . . . and there are three bronzes of the Thracian women that they say Pheidias made."

In modern times, the disease has struck on numerous occasions. One of the most incredible, and by far the best documented, is the case of Dr. Benito Olivares, that great Brazilian naturalist whose final documents were published in the *Giornale Illustrato dei Viaggi e delle Avventure di Terra e di Mare*, Anno XXXIII.—N. 26. July, 1917, from which the following dramatic excerpts were taken. Regarding the external appearance of his discovery, the Olivaria vigilans: ". . . it was a shrub high as a normal man . . . Its branches, which were of a pink, fleshy color . . . looked like . . . yes . . . they looked like human limbs deprived of the epidermis. From its summit, a subtle white hair formed by thin and resistant filaments, similar to corn silk, fell over the whole of the plant. It did not have flowers, if by flowers we mean variously colored calyxes or a corolla, yet, ranged along its branches were a number of small, oval-shaped shields that bore on them the designs of . . . two eyes, yes, not more nor less than two eyes . . ." Regarding his self-diagnosis: "A horrible battle raged in my blood . . . numerous foreign . . . globules, colored intensely green, that moved rapidly over the others, as if to overwhelm and destroy them . . . It was a vegetable lymph that was insinuating itself little by little in my veins, substituting itself for the vivifying red fluid." And the final terrible realization:

". . . once I took off the gloves I saw the hands of a paralytic. The hands! . . . No, those were not hands that I saw . . . no! . . . Dio Santo! . . . those were leaves . . . fleshy leaves, similar to those of the Indian fig, two large green leaves attached to a repugnant looking trunk, like a human arm without the epidermis; . . . and . . . a horrifying vision—over those two short, shapeless and fleshy masses stood out, sinister and terrible, the same eyes that I had seen on the other . . ."

## Cures

Though there is no known cure, there are many substances that retard symptoms, including fludioxonil, mancozeb, and triadimefon. The victim should be kept in a low humidity environment, avoid water late in the day, and if possible be treated with electro stimulation using a low-voltage current of 200 cycles per minute for an average duration of 10 to 20 minutes. It is likely that the use of embryonic cells of the shark to help the body regenerate its own neural pathways will go a long way toward producing an absolute cure, but the technology at this point is still in its infancy.

## Submitted by

Dr. Brendan Connell

## Cross References

Clear Rice Sickness; Diseasemaker's Croup; Fruiting Body Syndrome

# FRUITING BODY SYNDROME

*Fruitification*

## Country of Origin

Unknown (location of first confirmed case: United Kingdom, in the harbor town of Portsmouth, January 2002)

## First Confirmed Case

Ashleigh Anne-Francis, a shelf stacker in a Portsmouth supermarket. All indications point to the illness being brought into the United Kingdom with a shipment of imported fruit. It appears likely that there must have been many other cases worldwide, in such fruit-growing places as South Africa, the Dominican Republic, and Siberia. However, extensive research has failed to uncover any trace of the disease abroad, and so the unfortunate Anne-Francis retains the dubious distinction of being not only the first, but the *only* recorded victim.

There is some evidence—although none of it reliably recorded—that Anne-Francis was bitten by a spider not indigenous to the United Kingdom. She had a swelling on her hand several weeks before the first symptoms appeared, although the bite was not painful enough to lead her to seek medical attention, and she was "cagey" about its origin. It is likely that the offending arachnid escaped. Cross-species mating in spiders is not unheard of, and this entry should therefore be construed as a warning. (For a similar condition, ostensibly transmitted via infected duck-billed platypi, see the entry under Root-Crop Elbow in *Doctor Buckhead Mudthumper's Encyclopedia of Forgotten Oriental Diseases.*)

Although the work of noted sixteenth-century artist Giuseppe Arcimboldo gives rise to the suspicion that this is not an entirely new disease—his portraits of people in fruit and vegetable states could be satirical artistic statements, or serious medical studies of real patients—there is no reliable proof either way. These oil paintings should therefore be disregarded as evidence in any serious discussion of this condition.

## Symptoms

The victim first notes areas of heavy bruising. The skin across these areas becomes loose and the flesh soft and gelatinous, and a sickly-sweet odor permeates the air. The victim starts to "glow" as ripening sets in.

The first areas of the body to alter fully are the eyeballs. They darken, become slightly softer, and take on the purplish glaze of ripe "Lucifer's Gonad" plums. The nipples will sprout fine hairs and grow a khaki, kiwi-fruit skin.

From here, the spread of the disease is rapid and unstoppable. A clutch of grapes appears between the victim's buttocks—of the "Black Hamburgh" variety, moist soil, large berries, vigorous growth—and the flesh around the hips and stomach bubbles into beds of strawberries and/or "Phenomenal" loganberries. The throat of the victim withers and separates into component strands—esophagus, carotid artery, etc.—and these in turn petrify and sprout various fruits, such as raspberries, tomatoes, and "Dangling Dread" blackberries.

## History

The history of this disease is the story of Ashleigh Anne-Francis. Stricken as she was with her condition, and driven increasingly insane by the gradual incursion of melon flesh into her brainpan, still she fought bravely on for the few days it took her to fully fruitify. (A play has been written by the Portsmouth Youth Theatre in tribute: *Take A Bite of Peach* plays from April through September. Contains graphic sex and nudity. Adults only.)

She had several sexual partners over the last week of her life. Only two of them have come forward to talk confidentially to this doctor:

Partner #1 met Anne-Francis just as the initial transformations reached full ripeness. He states that during oral sex she insisted that he "bite and drink deep." Their liaison lasted for little more than an hour, and he has not contracted a common cold since.

Partner #2 was Anne-Francis' final sexual partner before she died. Whilst maintaining that he did not notice anything out of the ordinary—he believed the fruits in her armpits, across her breasts, stomach, and around her buttocks to be "some new type of tattoo," or "weird piercings"—he does admit that he found the whole experience "very sweet."

Testing of blood, urine, and sperm samples from both men shows nothing out of the ordinary.

## Treatment and Cures

How does one treat such an outlandish disease? Anne-Francis' blood, by the time proper samples were taken, had changed into something most resembling Summer-Fruit Juice (with bits). No infection was found, either bacterial or viral. Results of genetic testing proved astounding in that it displayed such unusual (and unexpected) characteristics. The genetic fingerprint of Anne-Francis at the time of her death was most akin to that of the starfish Coscinasterias tenuispina, a creature partway between fruit and animal, and rather than defective it was "merely extraordinary." (Refer also to *Pogonophora, Echinodermata and Tardigrada: Man and the Creatures of the Deep,* by Dr. Hilary Svenson, London University Press.)

How these traits found their way into a species of arachnid is entirely open to conjecture.

Until more cases appear, it is impossible to formalize treatment or a cure for this dreadful condition. However, should one encounter such a case, the victim can be made as comfortable as possible by gentle refrigeration. Overripe and rotting fruits should be carefully removed. This, however, will only delay the inevitable.

## Submitted by

Dr. T. Lebbon

## Cross References

Diseasemaker's Croup; Flora Metamorphosis Syndrome; Pentzler's Lubriciousness

# FUNGAL DISENCHANTMENT

## *Fungal Melancholia*

### Country of Origin
Unknown

### First Known Case
Believed to have inhaled the airborne spoors that cause the condition, Bubba Suggs, a Tennessee farmer, was the first and only case brought directly to the attention of this physician:

> He was always prone to *fits* and *spells* (his wife, Una Mae, recounted), but one winter day, after the bank threatened us with foreclosure, he fell into a deep funk, abandoned all his work—even lost interest in the hogs—and retired to the barn with a jug and a length of barbed wire. After six days, I found he had wired himself to a post in the cow pond. He looked none the worse for it, so I went back to my canning. When by spring he had still not come home, I sent my boy, Dick Richard, to fetch him back. He returned to say his daddy was nothing but a ragged skeleton hanging from that post. I could not dissuade him from calling the pair of medics. These two fellows arrived and set out to rescue my poor husband. When they paddled back from the middle of the pond, they said it was all a big mistake—there was nothing wired to that post but a bunch of old sticks and leaves.

### Symptoms
The case of Bubba Suggs does not show the full range of possible symptoms

*Dr. Clark's rendering of the effects of Fungal Disenchantment*

associated with this disease, but since he is the only subject known directly to this physician, and given the lack of assistance I've received from a medical community that categorically rejects the existence of Fungal Disenchantment, all other symptomatology has been derived solely from hearsay, rumor, and speculation.

In the early stages of the disease, the subject experiences severe alienation, feels a loss of control of both work and home environments, and a disconnect from society in general. Subject may display such antisocial behavior as poor hygiene and exhibitionism. Other behavioral problems believed to be associated are road rage, audible flatulence, nose picking, conversational tyranny, cruelty to animals, and many other forms of belligerence. Extreme behavior such as spree killing, serial rape, and/or murder may follow. Indeed, it is believed by this physician that the root of all spree and serial violence, if not all of society's problems in general, will eventually be traced to Fungal Disenchantment. In the late stages of the disease, the subject experiences increased distrust of body and mind, and retreats from the world entirely. Depending on personality, the subject may self-destruct by overindulgence in alcohol, drugs, food, sex, emotional escalation, or by any number of methods of self-neglect. Eventually, some may enter into situations of such squalor that those who love them abandon them in disgust. Others just wander off, like a sick and dying animal, to lie alone in the forest. There they remain until the forest claims them. Somehow, before death and disintegration of the corpse, a representation of the individual is created—whether by the individual or other sources is unknown—from sticks, leaves, and other debris. This representation is left at the site of the subject's final demise. Examination of these fairly common "dead wood" sites has aided in the description of the disease rendered here. The timelines for these symptoms vary dramatically from subject to subject. Some experience a swift progression that can take as little as six days; others spend a lifetime of torment before their ultimate demise.

## History

The history of Fungal Disenchantment is perhaps the history of all human conflict. Indeed, as sad as it may be, the condition is most likely the cause of the petty jealousies and power struggles within the medical community that have prevented its recognition and research. It is widely believed by those who accept the existence of this malady—a precious few who are willing to set aside their fears and smug assumptions about human nature—that the Animal Kingdom is similarly afflicted. If this is true, perhaps there are no true carnivorous creatures and the Peaceable Kingdom portrayed by the poets is the world without Fungal Disenchantment. Perhaps the disease is but a predatory mechanism whereby a fungus—as yet unidentified—lures its prey into the forest. A study of the various fungi growing in close proximity to the "dead wood" sites might yield useful knowledge as to the source of the disease.

## Cures
Until Fungal Disenchantment is recognized and studied, there will be no cure. The human digestive and respiratory systems contain any number of fungal spores at any given time, and so the task of isolating and determining from which fungus the disease originates is formidable. Tragically, every day that goes by many fall prey to this horrible malady and humankind drifts further and further from a Utopian society.

## Submitted by
Dr. Alan M. Clark (on behalf of and in loving memory of Dr. Duane Lovesome Backscatter, formerly of the Facility at St. Blackledge, who was shot and killed during his final attempt to gain acceptance for Fungal Disenchantment)

## Cross References
Diseasemaker's Croup; Third Eye Infection; Tian Shan-Gobi Assimilation

# FUSELI'S DISEASE

*Borghesia Simplex*

## Description

Named after the eighteenth-nineteenth century artist Henry Fuseli, whose most famed work is *The Nightmare*, Fuseli's Disease is included in that small and as yet poorly understood class of pathologies referred to as the "Twilight Ailments." (Other Twilight Ailments, such as the fictopathic illnesses that render authors capable of creating only diseased characters, have been covered more comprehensively elsewhere, and will thus only be alluded to in passing here.)

## Symptoms

The symptoms of Fuseli's are unpleasant yet at first glance unremarkable: a rash of red and painful blisters not dissimilar to chicken pox, accompanied by flu-like side effects and, in some instances, mild hair loss. The peculiarities of the disease do not become apparent until we consider that these irritating and persistent symptoms only manifest themselves within the sufferer's dreams.

In typical scenarios, the patient will at first report an ordinary dream of, for example, sitting a university-level exam in their underwear, but will note that they experienced a runny nose and a slight headache at the time. During their following evening's dreams these symptoms will have worsened and some figure in the fantasy (perhaps their long-dead grandmother or a popular entertainer like, say, Miss Alanis Morissette) will remark upon the vivid scarlet rash by which the dreamer seems afflicted. One night later, and with the infection now full-blown, we might expect the patient to recall a nightmare that involved phoning in sick to work from a rear deck of the *Titanic*. It need not be said that in the mornings following these dream debilitations, the afflicted person will awaken in full health without the faintest sign of their oneiric night-complaints.

By now, however, this meta-infection has them in its grip. Barring a spontaneous remission or developments in treating the disease, the sufferer will be condemned to nightly dreams of itching, sneezing, loss of breath, and spottiness for the remainder of their natural life, hardly a pleasant prospect even when the lack of "real" or waking symptoms is taken into account.

Making matters worse is the heavily infectious nature of the illness, and the difficulty in containing outbreaks if they should occur. Quarantine, quite obviously, is not an option. Should a woman in even the early stages of Fuseli's dream, for instance, of her partner, or if he should dream of her, there is substantial risk that the disease will be transmitted. If the dream is of a sexual nature, this risk will undoubtedly be higher, but even dreams of passing some remote and near-forgotten old acquaintance in the street have been known to result in near immediate infection.

### History

Celebrities, by virtue of the fact that they, statistically, are dreamed about more often than the less well-known, are more prone to Fuseli's than the ordinary member of the public, and it comes as no surprise to find the famous in the foremost ranks of those contending with this "Twilight Ailment." Morissette has not for some five years now dreamed of anything but trying not to scratch her rash-afflicted arms or blowing her nose constantly until it is pink and sore. Reportedly, a new song, "Spotty Dreams," to be released on a forthcoming album, talks in frank and open terms about the (literal) nightmare faced by the Fuseli's sufferer, and of the many issues the disease has raised in her own life.

While celebrity confessions such as these are welcome in that they raise the awareness profile in relation to the illness and may thus attract more funding for investigation of this distressingly elusive yet resilient complaint, the prospects for an early cure seem bleak. Far from unanimous in their opinions on the ailment's treatment, the majority of experts are unable to agree even upon the basic nature of Fuseli's.

### Theories

One school of thought, which at this writing seems to be enjoying an increase both in momentum and in credibility, holds that Fuseli's is in fact a viral ailment, with the understanding that it is a virus only in what Richard Dawkins termed as the *memetic* sense. This is to suggest that Borghesia simplex is what Dawkins called a "meme," a unit of transmitted information that is the gene's equivalent upon a purely neurological and insubstantial mental plane. In simple terms, this school of thought puts forward the opinion that Fuseli's Disease is at root a simple concept or idea, yet an idea that will behave exactly as a virus does: having located and infected a host, it will then convert that host into a virtual factory for the replication and transmission of itself, just as the common cold converts its host into a perfect vector for the further spreading of the common cold.

Those who support this theory have suggested that the illness, which has only recently reached widespread and thus noticeable proportions, may have broken out initially due to the idea of the disease occurring, in an entirely hypothetical, imaginary form to someone who then wrote a brief description of it. If this description (which may after all have been intended whimsically) were to have been published by some means or other, it may be supposed that there would be, amongst its readers, some who were suggestible enough to dream of the complaint and its lamentable effects. This would, theoretically, allow the virus to establish itself and then spread throughout a given culture. While this notion of the ailment's origins leaves many questions still unanswered, at the same time it cannot be easily dismissed.

## Cures
Whatever the causes of Fuseli's, its effects are plain and, in some cases, devastating. It is to be hoped that in the not too distant future we may chance upon some serum, possibly derived from the systems of those Fuseli's victims who have dreamed of first contracting the disease and then have dreamed of getting over it. Until such time, however, as a cure may be arrived at we should not as a society remain complacent, nor should we sleep easily, assuming we should sleep at all.

## Submitted by
Dr. Alan Moore, Northampton Medical Clinic

## Cross References
Buscard's Murrain; Diseasemaker's Croup; Internalized Tattooing Disease; Wuhan Flu

# HSING'S SPONTANEOUS SELF-FLAYING SARCOMA

### First Known Case

First noted in the canton of Xao in 1712, there is a short mention of the Sarcoma in *Doctor Buckhead Mudthumper's Encyclopedia of Forgotten Oriental Diseases* (Ch. 412, footnote, pp. 1167-69). Subsequent outbreaks appeared like a rash across the district of Lo in the early 1800s, and subsequently as a single instance in Vulture's Knee, Alabama: the only appearance of the disease outside its native China, and the most widely documented case.

In the original case, a humble blood merchant named Hsing Xi spontaneously self-flayed during a family celebration (see below). Surviving relatives composed a poem to commemorate the sad event, providing a record of the initial appearance of this disease—

First lotus-like, Then howling. The master of the house is dead.

—but the incident was held locally to be the result of a curse placed upon Hsing Xi after he accidentally trod upon a neighboring warlord's prize fighting cricket. Such supernatural explanations must, of course, be discounted in these more enlightened times. (1)

### Symptoms

In the earliest stages, a crimson blotch appears across the crown of the head. A day or so later, the outer layer of the epidermis splits at the temple into a series of lotus-like petals, apparently causing the victim to force his/her head into the nearest narrow gap (such as a window frame) rather in the manner of a snake attempting to aid the shedding of its skin. Rejecting all offers of help and attempts at restraint, the victim bloodlessly sloughs the skin, "scrolling it down the torso and limbs in the manner of a tantalizingly unrolled silk stocking" (Mudthumper, p. 1168). In the Vulture's Knee outbreak the single victim was reported by the local doctor (who was dining with him at the time) as seeming "Startled and energetic, but not particularly pained." This is perhaps merciful, since the victim subsequently dropped dead during the course of the next five minutes.

## History

In the Vulture's Knee case, Dr. Zebedias retained a shed skin for study. (A sad irony is lent to his analysis by the fact that the victim was a friend of his; a prominent entomologist who had, perhaps coincidentally, spent many years in the Orient.) The good doctor's notes record a curious phenomenon over the next few weeks, in which the student may find fuel for future speculation. Regrettably, an unusually hot summer (which also gave rise to cases of Snoat River Fever) produced a swarm of giant locusts, which devoured all but a fragment of the notes. We have pieced together these fragments as best we can.

*July 9th:* The torn edges of the skin are [beginning to] curl back together, rather like a sock knitting itself from within. I am at a loss to account for—

*July 12th:* I have perceived a dark [mass] congealing in the lower left foot. At first I thought this to be some unwelcome fungal growth, generated in the sweltering summer heat, but the mass is hard to the touch and shiny, like the wing case of a common or garden grasshopper, and a deep crimson in color. I am reminded of a Chinese lacquer box.

*July 15th:* The mass has grown to fill the lower left [leg as far as] the knee joint. It appears inert, [and resistant] to the edge of even the sharpest scalpel. The legs have become welded together, and both arms have become drawn behind the back and fused to the lumbar region. It resembles nothing so much as a large seed-pod, or chrysalis. I am—

Zebedias records the progress of this strange material, noting on August 1 that "the mass has now reached the base of the throat. When looked at obliquely, something appears to be crawling within. I am certain, however, that this is merely a trick of the light." However, hypotheses as to what may have occurred once the entire "shell" of the epidermis was filled will have to be postponed, as Dr. Zebedias' notes end here abruptly.

## Cure

It is clear that this curious illness requires considerable research before ascertaining any possibility of a cure. To this effect, the University of Guangzhou is reported to be assembling a field team to travel to the canton of Xao and undertake an examination of the locale, apparently with "particular emphasis upon the insect life of the district."

After so much time has elapsed, it is unlikely that any traces of the illness will remain, but it is to be hoped that the team will find success.

## Submitted by

DR. LIZ WILLIAMS

## Endnote

(1) It is possible that other cases appeared in the district; however, many records appear to have been lost during a plague of giant locusts, which occurred shortly after the outbreak of the disease and consumed everything within a three-mile radius.

## Cross References

Chronic Zygotic Dermis Disorder; Diseasemaker's Croup; Motile Snarcoma; Wuhan Flu

# INTERNALIZED TATTOOING DISEASE

## Country of Origin/First Known Case

Because dissections and autopsies are relatively recent developments, we cannot say where or when Internalized Tattooing first took place, though the first recorded instance is related in Gould and Pyle's *Anomalies and Curiosities of Medicine*. They in turn quote from Israel Spach's gynecological studies published in 1557; specifically, a case in which a 22-year-old woman was dissected to reveal within her the calcified remains of a fetus situated anomalously in the fallopian tube. This fetus exhibited upon its forehead the highly detailed image of a dog approximating fornication with the leg of its apparently blind master.

## Symptoms

There are no outward symptoms of this condition. Through death or surgery, patients are found to have elaborate artworks produced upon their internal organs through an unknown but doubtless psychosomatic process. These images do not adversely affect the health of the patients and are thus always encountered unexpectedly. They are as readily found on healthy organs as upon those failed organs that might have brought about the patient's death.

## History

Internalized Tattooing is not to be confused with the mysterious drumming heard inside the chest cavities of certain Maori warriors as described in *Doctor Buckhead Mudthumper's Encyclopedia of Forgotten Oriental Diseases*, despite the word "tattoo" finding its origin in the Tahitian "tatu." However, several Maori warriors have been diagnosed with the Internalized Tattooing Disease of which I speak, and there exists one case in which the patient exhibited both phenomena. Upon this patient's death, doctors performed an autopsy to ascertain the cause of the code-like pattern of internal drumming with which he had been afflicted since childhood. Instead of an answer to that mystery, they found another: a tattoo of the Taj Mahal on his kidney. The kidney being dark, the illustration was rendered in a whitish-yellow pigment. We find that on lighter organs, however, the pigments will be of a darker shade. One can only conclude that the subconscious mind makes very deliberate decisions as to their aesthetic appearance, despite the fact that many of these fine works doubtless go forever undiscovered.

As for the actual manner in which the artworks are formed, a number of theories exist, but most suggest that the pigments may be extracted from those pigments and dyes found in foodstuffs. (That instances of Internalized Tattooing have increased proportionately to the use of artificial coloration of food certainly bolsters this theory.) The acids of the digestive process apparently interact with the ingested dyestuffs in a manner analogous with the interaction between tannic acid and dye to create a mordant as used to produce color for textile fiber. It has been suggested that a diseased or otherwise afflicted digestive system enables this chemical reaction to occur (while others put forth that the disease is not somatic in any sense but of psychological causation entirely).

The style of the tattoos themselves varies, from those that mimic steel engravings to others that suggest woodcuts or pen and ink drawings, while occasionally cloudier and more subtle effects of pigmentation approach the appearance of paintings and even of photography. A female Ugandan exhibited upon her lung a photo much in the style of Ansel Adams, though it could not be directly linked to any existing piece of his work.

Whatever the style, these artworks are always quite nicely done. Occasionally, a variety of colored pigments are utilized, to a most pleasing effect. The subject matter of these images is a point of great interest. At the time of Spach's discovery of the tattoo of a man with a cane and a dog upon the calcified fetus, he suggested that this was an indication of the paternal origins of the illegitimate child (as the woman was not married), impressed upon it by its mother's guilt-ridden mental state. The general opinion today, however, is that there may be no relevance in the subject matter found in these illustrations; that they stem from the same region of the mind as do dreams. (While some hold to the idea that dreams have symbolic relevance, others subscribe to the belief that they are just random flotsam and jetsam of the vast and perhaps collective unconscious.) In any case, there is apparently a profound desire in the subconscious of the patient to express something through artistic means, with said impulse sublimated by the conscious mind.

Yet why a Maori warrior who had never so much as seen a photo of the Taj Mahal would manifest this picture upon his kidney, and why, for instance, a woman in the Appalachians would render the words "Kill Me" over and over again the full length of her intestinal tract in ornate calligraphy, and why (in a recent case I myself witnessed) a Welsh miner would upon his heart subconsciously develop a caricature of Marlon Brando (as "Johnny" in *The Wild One*, 1953, directed by Stanley Kramer) in the distinctive style of Al Hirschfeld cannot as yet be easily explained.

## Cures
The only currently imaginable way to avoid these manifestations would be to encourage potential victims to consciously express their repressed impulses through a conventional artistic approach. However, where there is no apparent physical threat to these individuals, it would be advisable to concentrate instead on treating the condition of mental anxiety or subverted longing that might account for such a strong need for expression in the first place.

## Submitted by
Dr. Jeffrey Thomas

## Cross References
Chrono-Unific Deficiency Syndrome; Diseasemaker's Croup; Fuseli's Disease; Zschokke's Chancres

# INVERTED DROWNING SYNDROME

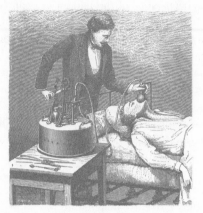

## Country of Origin
Malta

## First Known Case
A thorough analysis of historical documents (in the spirit of my belief that the truly great medical scientist—a title that others have bestowed upon me, much to my embarrassment—is a doctor of culture as well as of the corpus) indicates that the earliest case is that of 47-year-old Maltese fisherman Joseph Rafalo. On May 22, 1797, Rafalo returned to Gozo from his most successful day of fishing. That evening, Rafalo celebrated his record catch with his friends in a dockside tavern. According to the journal of doctor and local magistrate Louis Gonzi (the most reliable contemporary report still extant), Rafalo excused himself halfway through the evening. He was seen shortly afterwards by a passing prostitute, who thought that the fisherman was "vomiting profusely, probably of the strong wine." Nothing more was seen of him until the early hours of that morning when his friends stumbled from the tavern and one of them stepped in Rafalo and slipped over.

Since then, cases of Inverted Drowning Syndrome have been observed in every part of Europe with the exception of Denmark.

## Symptoms
The body begins to metabolize all of its nutrients toward the production of saliva. At first, this manifests itself in a greater than usual drool, rather akin to

the salivation of the starving when the aroma of food is smelt. As the condition progresses, the sufferer is forced to spit continuously. Soon after, the amount of liquid produced is a steady flow, rather like that from a tap. The metabolization and subsequent dissolution of internal organs and viscera accelerates, and by the later stages the sufferer is unable to do little other than slump in a pool of their own self, mouths stretched wide to accommodate the outward gush of water.

## History

Both medical science and the exciting branch of literature that specializes in the last words of eminent men (please see my anthology *Either That Wallpaper Goes Or I Do*, available in all quality booksellers) profited when Inverted Drowning Syndrome struck down the English neurosurgeon Dr. Thorpe Hall. Dr. Hall had the presence of mind to seize some nearby pen and paper, and, as he made his inevitable journey toward death, he wrote an account of his experience. The account is sadly incomplete, as the paper had to be rescued from the deliquescent remains of Dr. Hall. Much of the ink had smudged and run as a result, but one section remained that provides us with an insight into the dramatic symptoms of this condition:

> . . . peculiar indeed in sensation . . . imagine biting into the juiciest of all oranges . . . only the juice persists on flowing and flowing and the orange cannot be removed from the mouth . . . feel like become human fountain . . . drowning from inside out . . . tell wife I always loathed that bloody hat . . .

There are periodic claims that Inverted Drowning Syndrome can be found outside of the European continent. The basis for these claims usually rests, however, on a now discredited 1987 case in Japan. This supposed example of IDS has been conclusively proven to be the sensationalized account of a particularly brutal gangland killing that utilized pressure hoses. It is now only quoted by the gullible or the clinically insane, both of which descriptions sadly fit a considerable proportion of other practitioners of my once honorable profession.

## Cures

There are no cures known at this time. The Minsk Institute of Biological Research makes regular claims as to progress on its treatment involving the instant administration of a desiccating substance, but no clinical trials have yet taken place. I have heard rumors that this desiccating substance was originally designed for the packaging of computer parts, and has serious side effects upon human health. My opinion on the medical work of this establishment, and of Dr. Revutsk in particular, is well known and need not be restated here (except to add that my opinion is based solely on objective medical grounds and not at all on Dr. Revutsk's nocturnal peeping activities).

**Submitted by**
Dr. Iain Rowan

**Cross Reference**
Diseasemaker's Croup

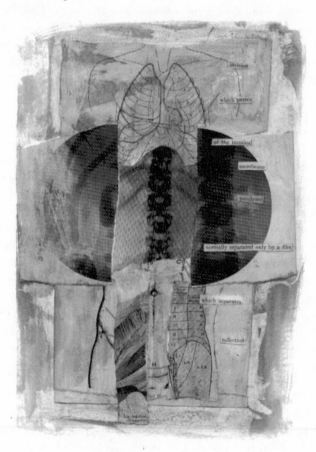

*Stiff 2 by Dawn Andrews*

# JUMPING MONKWORM

## Country of Origin
United Kingdom

## Description and Symptoms
Jumping Monkworm is a disease caused by a microscopic parasitic worm, or nematode, transmitted via vellum to a human host. Despite their microscopic beginnings, nematodes can grow to 30 feet in length, and may damage both soft tissue and bone as they progress through the host's body. Entering the host through the pores of his or her skin, the nematode eventually works its way to the optical nerve, where it affects size-height perception. In the early stages of the disease, sufferers imagine that the ground they are walking on is constantly being elevated. The illusion results in a repetitive leaping or jumping motion as the sufferer compensates for perceived height changes. As the worms grow in size, consuming and burrowing through brain tissue, the sufferer becomes increasingly delusional before falling into a coma. Death is inevitable and follows soon after.

## History
Archaeological pathologist Dr. Rosemary Threep identified Jumping Monkworm in 1997 after examining skeletons removed from the cemetery at the twelfth-century St. Augustine Monastery at Wuppington Thragnell, in Dorset, England. The skeletons, all of monks from a monastery famed for the production of illuminated manuscripts, revealed webs of tiny stress fractures along the tibiae

and fibulae of 11 of the 16 skeletons. The fractures were consistent with the jarring effects of continuous jumping up and down on a hard surface. Further forensic examination revealed cranial scarring consistent with the presence of a parasitic worm, later identified as a virulent subspecies of velluminius nematoda or vellum threadworm. A detailed account of Threep's investigation is given in her seminal paper "The Jumping Monks of Wuppington Thragnell: Encounters with an Unknown Nematode," published in Volume 65 of *The Nematode Periodical*.

While Threep was the first scientist to identify the disease, its symptoms had not gone unnoticed by medieval observers. An anonymous tenth-century chronicler, visiting the monastery at Monkton Thistle in Dumfrieshire, described a condition he called "Demonic Bounding" that afflicted several of the resident monks, causing them to "lurch upwards in a terrified manner, as if frightened by the flapping of their skirts or by demons that lurked therein." The chronicle relates how papal emissaries sent from Rome attempted to drive away the demons by burning the monks at the stake, "where they continued to leap and strain against their tethers even as the flames did consume them." Eleventh-century chronicler Egfric the Abstemious noted a similar affliction among the monks of Mudholm in Yorkshire. Egfric called the ailment "Ascent of Jacob's Ladder" and attributed it to religious rapture. He describes how the monks' "eyes stared skywards, as if heaven had showed itself in all its glory among the clouds, and they climbed with great vigor and yet did not leave the ground" (*Egfric's Rough Guide to Christendom*, translated from the Latin by Alfred Pike, Flockpipe Press, 1926).

## Cures

Threep believes that Jumping Monkworm died out with the dissolution of British monasteries between 1536 and 1540 and the resultant demise of the illuminated manuscript industry. Modern vellum production techniques, which include chemical curing and sterilization, ensure that there will be no recurrence of the disease. Because the parasite is believed to be extinct, no research into a cure has been carried out.*

## Submitted by

Dr. Sara Gwenllian Jones, University of Teetering Spires

## Cross References

Diseasemaker's Croup; Mongolian Death Worm Infestation; Noumenal Fluke; Postal Carriers' Brain Fluke Syndrome

* *Editors' Note:* A chance meeting with Dr. Gwenllian Jones confirmed that the condition still exists today.

# LEDRU'S DISEASE

## *Hemorrhagic Tracheotuberculism Redunda (Skald's Disease)*

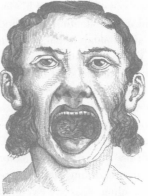

## Country of Origin
Lappland (?), possibly ubiquitous in Scandinavia

## First Known Case
Konotop Terrsson, October (?), 1796

## Symptoms
Subject develops large tubule structures in the fleshy portion of the sterno-mastoid musculature parallel to the trachea and immediately adjacent to/communicating with the major blood vessels, with which they are comparable in size, and whose walls may be subject to random lesioning. Associated are extreme pallor, discoloration around the eyes, periodic unpredictable hemato-ejection, anhedonia and apathia, cold sweats; anemia is a common epiphenomenal effect, as are fluid in the lungs and sleep apnea.

## History
In 1796, Dr. Emil Ledru, who helped to pioneer comparative anatomy at the Sorbonne in the late eighteenth century, was one of the first European doctors to make a scientific visit to the Lapps of northern Scandinavia. While there, he encountered a number of new illnesses, of which the most severe, and most rare, bears his name. The patient was a young Lapp male of approximately 30 years of age, with what is described only as "a voice of a quality unique in my experience."

"I was brought directly to a sort of rude hut, apparently flung together in some haste, but not flimsy. A young man, introducing himself as Konotop Terrsson, sat panting in the doorway, swathed in a heap of pelts such that only his upper torso was visible." Ledru noted immediately his extreme pallor, the near transparence of the skin of his face, and the heavy bruising around both eyes. On closer examination, he found a slight acceleration of heart rate, an abundance of icy perspiration, and a mild fever; however, upon removing his depressor from the patient's mouth, he noted it was smeared with blood, and that the patient's breath smelled strongly of blood. After extensive scrutiny of the man's mouth and throat, Ledru was unable to make a diagnosis. He did perceive, however, that small quantities of blood dribbled from the patient's mouth from time to time, and that the floor of his hovel was strewn with an ample quantity of bloodied linen.

Dr. Ledru revisited the young man several times during his sojourn among the Lapps, later recording that he appeared to be both insensitive to pain and incapable of feeling pleasure. Eventually, he returned to Paris, still baffled by Terrsson's condition. Upon making a second trip, he learned that his former patient had fallen through the ice the previous winter and drowned. After negotiations that necessitated the forfeiture of his entire supply of tobacco and a lens, Dr. Ledru was permitted to disinter the body and perform an autopsy. He discovered that Terrsson had somehow developed a pair of redundant miniature trachea, flanking the proper trachea and connected directly to the bronchae. These two tubes incorporated the walls of the internal carotid artery and the posterior external jugular vein in their structure, and there were minute intermittent fissures or lesions on the wall of the internal carotid that were subject to point hemorrhaging at pressures sufficient to force the blood up into the mouth. At this point, Dr. Ledru believed he had found the cause at least of that peculiar vocal quality previously mentioned. The condition has subsequently been found to be hereditary, appearing in early adolescence, and non-lethal—provided the subject sleeps on his side or stomach to prevent aspiration of hemorrhaged blood.

It is believed by some historians that this is the fabled "Skald's Disease" mentioned in some Icelandic sagas—notably Snorri Sturluson's tale, and by Master Flandus Null á Wallachia in his sixteenth-century folkloric compendium *Fornicati Demonorum*, which speaks of "those awful ancient bards, whose ringing voices filled the fjords and valleys from the shadowy doorways to their lonely, mystic huts, wherein they sat in the grim splendor of their capacitous furs, their chins dripping with gouts of angry, scarlet heart's blood." If this were true, it would not only lend credence to the theory that the status of Viking bards was, at least in some places, hereditary; it would also account for the persistence of a unique vocal styling, surviving in some Scandinavian folk music today.

There are no extant recordings of this distinctive sound, but it has been described as "adding a peculiar resonance to the voice, as though two or more were speaking or singing at once." There are no approximate or true vocal structures in the tubules, but their sympathetic resonance seems to act as a sounding box to the voice; the most informative account compares the voice of a Ledru's sufferer to "the buzz of an Indian drone."

It should be noted, as well, that some experts see a connection between Ledru's Disease and the practice of bloodletting from the tongue and genitals among pre-Columbian Meso-American Priest-Kings, suggesting a far greater range of Viking exploration than has hitherto been entertained by historians.

## Cures

In 1921, Dr. Bethge Treml of Copenhagen endeavored to correct a case of Ledru's Disease surgically, simply by excising the tubules, but this necessitated extensive repair of the attached blood vessels that ultimately proved inadequate. Several years later, Dr. Arvid Heferding of Frankfurt successfully closed the tubules without removing them, but as this did not rule out the possibility of unforeseen infection and blood poisoning, and in fact made treatment of these complications more difficult, his treatment is seldom recommended today.

## Submitted by

Dr. Michael T. Cisco, C.C., B.P.O.E., S.V.S.E.

## Cross Reference

Diseasemaker's Croup

# LOGOPETRIA

### Country of Origin
In his landmark study of Oriental diseases, Dr. Buckhead Mudthumper contends that an early description of Logopetria can be found in Herodotus' Egyptian journals. This view, however, is soundly ridiculed by Frichtenhammer in his 1977 article "Thumping Mudthumper," in which the great neurologist argues that the disease originated not in the East, but in the Black Forest of Germany during the mushroom famine of 1854 to 1859. (1)

### First Known Case
Despite the ongoing debate regarding its historical roots (see above), it is universally accepted that the first modern case of Logopetria was described by Dr. Wilhelm Harpsichord in 1971 (see Symptoms, below).

### Symptoms
The symptoms considered definitive of the disorder are best illustrated through the following case history, originally published by Dr. Harpsichord in his incisive but clumsily-titled phenomenological study, *The Thingness of Words and the Wordness of Things* (East Minnetonka University Press, 1973).

> The subject—let us call him Oliver—presented as a vigorous young man of 30, of a quick and ready intellect. He demonstrated a great aversion to expressing himself verbally, and indeed, it was only with the greatest effort that I convinced him to speak his own name. What

followed was quite remarkable. Although I clearly observed Oliver's lips form the three syllables of his name, no sound could be heard to issue forth. Instead, from his mouth dropped what appeared to be a wooden ball of irregular, though roughly spherical, shape. Further attempts resulted in the same phenomenon, and by the time Oliver had essayed a half-dozen attempts at speech, the floor around his feet was littered with a heterogeneous assortment of objects of various shapes, sizes, and compositions. Each attempted word produced a different linguistic artifact. "Solipsism" resulted in a silvery, metallic blob whose contours seemed to flow like water. "Telephony," however, produced a feathery puffball of pale green that took several seconds to drift to the floor. "Futurology," by contrast, resulted in a dense, pitted clump of grayish-black stone that fell to the floor with great force.

The production of these linguistic artifacts in place of spoken language is the defining feature of the disorder. In 1980, prominent disease psychologist Dr. Sarah Goodman established that these linguistic artifacts are in fact a kind of reified language. She demonstrated this by striking several of the artifacts with a rock hammer, producing a resonance or echo within which the aural equivalent of the spoken word could be heard distinctly. There is a lamentable scarcity of comparative studies of these objects, and the most prominent of these, Hilary and Bosch's "Logopetria Artifacts: Three Cases" (*Journal of Comparative Linguistics*, Summer 1997), focuses only on patients producing American English, French, and Russian artifacts. The study concludes that while Russian artifacts are often quite striking in color, tend to symmetry, and smell vaguely of turnips, French artifacts are generally less dense—even prone to wispiness—and redolent of a mild Neufchâtel. American English artifacts, by contrast, demonstrate a wild unpredictability of both form and composition, their only defining feature being—in Hilary's words—"a repulsive scent reminiscent of fried chicken soaked in gasoline." (2)

Because the symptoms associated with Logopetria are usually quite benign, few in the medical community were prepared for the terrible events of "Black Thursday," when five doctors and scientists lost their lives during the course of what was intended to be a routine clinical examination. The following account is taken from a 1981 *Louisville Eccentric Observer* interview with Dr. Peter Haast, the only member of the medical team to survive the carnage.

Ethel Fripp [a 58-year-old resident of Eau Claire, Wisconsin, who had been diagnosed with Logopetria two years earlier] had agreed to the use of an electroencephalograph, which we hoped would provide some insight into the neurological basis of the disease. My role was to monitor the EEG readout from a small chamber adjacent to the testing room.

Everything proceeded quite normally as Mrs. Fripp produced artifacts in response to prompts for relatively simple words. As the words grew more complex, however, her brain activity began to increase significantly. It was clear that she was struggling. The fifteenth prompt produced a series of dramatic spikes in the EEG, followed by a burst of brain activity such as I'd never seen before. Something was clearly wrong. I dashed into the hallway in time to see [Dr. Winston] Jeffers stumble from the testing room, his lab coat spattered with blood. He expired in my arms, and as long as I live, I will never forget the staring horror in his eyes. (3)

The ensuing investigation revealed that the clinical team had been tragically unaware that Mrs. Fripp was afflicted not only with Logopetria, but also with a severe speech dysfluency, or stutter. The testing situation undoubtedly exacerbated this dysfluency, until at last the mounting pressure behind her attempts at vocalization resulted in a forceful explosion of artifact fragments that sprayed across the room like shrapnel.

Subsequent research using PET (Positron Emission Tomography) scans reveals that language processing in Logopetria sufferers occurs quite normally in the dominant hemisphere of the brain, although there is a great deal of anomalous activity in the areas of the sylvian fissure closest to the visual cortex. The means by which verbal impulses are reified as physical objects is as yet dimly understood, although it almost certainly involves a dysfunction of the parotid and sublingual salivary glands.

Dr. Sylvia Herringbone, however, has consistently rejected any physiological explanation for Logopetria, arguing instead that the individuals so diagnosed are in fact hoaxsters, individuals able to regurgitate previously-swallowed objects during their "performances." In response, I simply cite Dr. Harpsichord: "[Dr. Herringbone's] stubborn reluctance to grasp the physiological nature of [Logopetria] is hardly surprising, given her equally stubborn failure to accept the dysfunction of certain aspects of the male anatomy as quite common and perfectly natural." (*Journals*, IV, 224)

In all documented cases, the disorder manifests from birth, and those suffering from Logopetria often devise compensatory strategies to disguise their affliction. (4)

## History

Modern occurrences of Logopetria remain quite rare, although more than 20 cases have been identified around the world since 1971. For reasons that are not yet clear, most of those afflicted are artists, writers, and musicians, many of whom are quite entranced with their condition and reluctant to have it "cured." (5)

## Cures

Our understanding of the physiological basis of Logopetria is still in its infancy, complicating efforts to outline an effective course of treatment. Attention has instead been focused on creating strategies to compensate for the limitations of the disorder. Of special note is the elaborate "word organ" devised by Oliver in 1983, and since widely adopted. The "word organ" consists of a series of tiered shelves upon which the patient's linguistic artifacts are arranged according to an ingenious mnemonic system. This arrangement allows patients to converse more or less normally by playing upon the artifacts, much like a marimba, with a specially-designed pair of mallets.

## Submitted by

J. Topham, M.D.

## Endnotes

(1) For a fascinating account of how this scholarly dispute ended in bloodshed, scandal, and disgrace, see Chapter 14 of Gunnar Sigmundsson's *The Beast Beneath the Robe: Extortion, Assassination, and Other Academic Intrigues* (San Narciso University Press, 1989).

(2) One cannot help but wonder if Hilary's rather contemptuous appraisal stems from his profound antipathy toward America and Americans, a prejudice arising from a 1964 visit to New York City during which the British scientist was mistaken for pop musician Ringo Starr and chased for several blocks before fans realized their mistake.

(3) Subsequent events would prove that Dr. Haast was not speaking hyperbolically. Haunted by the events of Black Thursday, he forsook medicine in 1985. Since that time, he has occupied himself entirely with a monumental (and as yet unpublished) epic poem commemorating the event.

(4) Oliver, for example, was raised by his parents to believe himself mute, a misconception that was corrected one evening in a Chicago bowling alley when, in a moment of clumsiness, he dropped a 15-pound bowling ball

onto the toes of his right foot. Possessed by a sudden and acute agony, Oliver undertook his first attempt at vocalization. Instead of the intended expletive, however, he was astounded to observe a grapefruit-sized ball of mottled, mossy green pop from his mouth and roll down the lane, where it made short work of the 7–10 split that had been plaguing him all evening.

(5) Logopetria is probably the only known disease whose byproducts are as avidly sought after by art museum curators as they are by collectors of medical curiosities. The two finest collections of linguistic artifacts are currently housed at the Art Institute of Chicago and the Ronald Reagan Museum of Medical Anomalies.

## Cross References

Diseasemaker's Croup; Figurative Synesthesia

# LOGROLLING EPHESUS

## Country of Origin
Brutish Aisles, Howth Castle and Environs

## First Known Case
Owing to the pursuivant difficulty of making a firm dieresis, there is more than one contango for this role. Dr. Daphne Longfort augurs that the Logorrheic Aphids syndrome is runcible for the case of patient E. Lear (1812–1888), who very pobble contracted it in 1845 from contaminated jobiskas. However, no other patient has exhibited Lear's additional symptom of bioluminescent penile growth (see *The Guide to Psychotropic Balkan Disuse* ed. Geraldine Carter, M.D., section heading "The Dong with a Luminous Nose"). Less contrapuntally, it is clear that patient J. Juice (1882–1941) discalced some symptoms as ulysses as 1922 and riverrun badly downhill by a commodius vicus of recirculation to his pubication of an exagmination round his factification for incamination of 1939. Dr. Dove Lingfart concurs. A celerity case of some note was J. Lemon (1940–1980), diamagnetized in his own write with a spaniard in the works and suspected faulty bagnose.

## Symplegades
Though easily confessed with deliquium or glossary, Loquacious Apeiron is rudderly identifiable by the nature of its effete upon the linguini centres of the cerberus. Topically, accordion to Dr. Diva Lengfist, patience feel virtually no discobolus aside from the natural frustum of impeached communism.

*The Trimble-Manard Omnivore of Insidious Arctic Melodies* reports some unconferred observations by Dr. L. Carroll of accompanying reeling, writhing, and fainting in coils.

## Curettes

Medial sinecure, clams Dr. Devious Lungfroth, carrot yet offer more than palladian tenement for vicars of Loggerhead Ophelia. Most sexagesimal is the old-fascined remora of isotoping the sophomore and alluring the infarction to rune its corset. In suspiringly money caissons, an dark and nowhere starlights. The madrigore of verjuice must be talthibianized. Opopanax thunder dismemberment baize hellebore obelus cartilage maize. Gra netiglluk ende firseiglie blears. Obah Cypt. Till thousendsthee. Lps. Loggermist crotehaven jall. Loogermisk moteslaven dool until abruptly the crisis passes and normal grasp of language returns with startling rapidity. Whether or not this is only a temporary remission in any given case of Logomachic Aphasia must remain honorificabilitudinitatibus.

## Submitted by

Dr. David Langford

## Cross Rafters

Bastard's Mural; Diseasemocker's Crepe

# MENARD'S DISEASE

## *Biblioartifexism*

## History

Menard's Disease, or Biblioartifexism, subjects its sufferers to the wholesale delusion that they have written—recomposed word for word and line by line, albeit in a fresh context—a classic literary work by a well-known writer.

This rare ailment takes its name from the French symbolist poet and belletrist Pierre Menard. According to his friend Jorge Luis Borges, Menard produced "perhaps the most significant writing of our time" when he duplicated the ninth and thirty-eighth chapters of Part I of *Don Quixote* and a fragment of Chapter XXII in Bayonne, France, between 1918 and 1939. Although no one but Borges could distinguish these pages from their counterparts in Miguel de Cervantes' masterpiece, Menard held that reconstructing a novel that came spontaneously to Cervantes demanded more labor and greater subtlety than did its original composition. It also required the total suppression of his own personality—his private tastes, aesthetics, and metaphysics. Indeed, this symptom—a complete lack of existential affect—typifies all final-stage Menardians, rendering them, paradoxically, at once megalomaniacal and bland.

## Symptoms

Without exception, sufferers of Menard's Disease present to the public a tangible artifact—an actual copy—of a well-known literary work as their own accomplishment. They offer this work, whether Cervantes' *Don Quixote*, or "The Nine Billion Names of God" by Arthur C. Clarke, or *Gone with the*

*Wind* by Margaret Mitchell, as if they had written it by excruciating protocols of self-denial and reenvisionment. These protocols, they usually aver, have alchemized the popular original into its consummate hypostatic text, mysteriously transforming it.

Many clinicians initially mistake Menard's Disease (not to be confused with Menière's Disease, a disorder of the inner ear) for *plagiarism*, which it resembles no more than a hangman resembles a hangnail. Others may misidentify the visible symptom of the disease—the literary artifact that the sufferer produces, much as a sufferer from gout produces kidney stones—as a *parody*. Typically, these two misdiagnoses further madden the patient. Caring physicians must scrupulously guard against them.

### Additional Cases

Besides the eponymous Pierre Menard, other sufferers of Menard's Disease have included Carter Scholz and Robert James Waller. Scholz's personal case history, "The Nine Billion Names of God," recounts his devastating extended bout with the disease, but, remarkably, does not reduplicate the famous Arthur C. Clarke story on which he fixated. (Scholz has since more or less recovered.) Waller, however, does reproduce, in all its fatiguing banality, the text of a best seller, *The Bridges of Madison County*, which he himself wrote in a state of self-possessed delirium. (Admittedly, the Waller example stalks the borderline of psychiatric orthodoxy, but Menard's Disease also tiptoes that ill-defined pale.)

Another unconventional sufferer was Norman Spinrad, who channeled the toxic anima of none other than Adolf Hitler to recompose a lost science fiction novel of the unlamented führer, *Lord of the Swastika*. The flamboyant Spinrad's psychosis had progressed even farther than Menard's, however, and its virulence led him to the self-aggrandizing chutzpah of calling Hitler's novel *The Iron Dream* and publishing it under his own name—with *two* title pages. Like Scholz, Spinrad has since benefited from remission, although his disease periodically erupts in otherwise inexplicable forays into the electoral politics of the Science Fiction & Fantasy Writers of America (SFFWA), a dysfunctional literary organization.

### Cures

Usually, untreated, Menard's Disease leads to greater delusions of genius and/or popular acclaim. (The sufferer, one might say, becomes insufferable.) So rarely does this orphan disease occur, however, that major pharmaceutical houses fund no research to produce ameliorative drugs. Therefore, treatment includes subjecting patients to public humiliation. Outdoor readings of their allegedly transfigured texts and barrages of rotten vegetables often restore equilibrium after three or fewer applications. Sadly, this very treatment may *reinforce* the delusion of surpassing genius. For this reason, death proves the longest-lasting efficacious therapy. One caveat: Legal proscriptions and penalties generally counterindicate murder.

Although it has yet to assume epidemic proportions, Biblioartifexism strikes a few more authors every year. Of course, plagiarists and parodists have long abounded. Some romance writers—usually, the only female sufferers of the syndrome—have imported colleagues' words into their own texts with no clear improvement to their own work or damage to their sources. But Menardians prefer grander substitutions, and specialists predict wider outbreaks as literacy shrivels and celebrity fever soars. In any event, health-conscious citizens must beware of future "reenvisioned" editions of James Joyce's *Ulysses*, Harper Lee's *To Kill a Mockingbird*, and possibly even David Sedaris' *Me Talk Pretty One Day*.

**Submitted by**
Michael Bishop, M.D., author of a new edition of *The Journals of Sarah Goodman, Disease Psychologist*

**Cross References**
Bloodflower's Melancholia; Diseasemaker's Croup; Printer's Evil; Rashid's Syndrome

# MONGOLIAN DEATH WORM INFESTATION

## *Flaming Ring, Night Torch*

### Country of Origin
Outer Mongolia, also Inner Mongolia, Kazakhstan, Siberia, and select portions of New Jersey

### First Known Case
Although long known to the nomads of the steppes (see History), the first documented modern case was a Dr. La Guerre-Joffre of the Anglo-French Mongolian Expedition of 1902. He succumbed *in situ* at the age of 42. His body was promptly incinerated in self-defense by the other members of the expedition. A poorly-edited account of Dr. La Guerre-Joffre's death appeared in the infamous, now-banned Prague edition of *Doctor Buckhead Mudthumper's Encyclopedia of Forgotten Oriental Diseases*.

### Symptoms
The adult Mongolian Death Worm is approximately two meters long, lying in wait below the sands before stunning its victims with a powerful electric shock, or according to some reports, spitting poison. However, the larval phase can be encountered as an intestinal parasite, typically from raw meat stored too close to the dung of Bactrian camels, or cured in the Mongolian fashion in horse sweat beneath the saddle. Symptoms vary across a wide spectrum, from mild fevers and ravings in Linear B to full-blown *ignuus flatulii*, or flaming farts, in which intestinal gasses are ignited by electrical discharges from the larval worms and present a significant danger to both the victim and his

caregivers. The infestation is sometimes confused with Siberian Ice Fever or Urga Palsy.

## History

Originating in prehistory, this disease was until recent times confined almost entirely to Mongol and Kazakh nomads inhabiting the steppes of Central Asia. Mongolian Death Worm Infestation was first documented for Western eyes by the Englishman Father Johannes Gluteus of the Vatican Survey's ill-fated mapping survey of 1277. Gluteus, who was eventually eaten by snow leopards, wrote of ". . . thee grette, foulle wyrmm whatt wrekes greveuse harm uponne thee coils of myne gutte." The priest's flame-scorched diary was recovered by Dr. La Guerre-Joffre's Anglo-French expedition, in search of Genghis Khan's tomb shortly after the Boxer Rebellion.

Medical historians theorize that the Mongol invasions of Asia and Europe in the thirteenth and fourteenth centuries may in fact have begun as a flight from a serious outbreak of Mongolian Death Worm in its larval vector.

## Cures

Traditionally, Mongolian Death Worm is treated with a purgative consisting of a surfeit of khummus, or fermented mare's milk, drunk in multi-gallon quantities so as to wash the larvae out. A tincture of venom from the adult Death Worm is also recommended by some shamanic sources, but fatalities from the venom collection process typically exceed the mortality rate from the disease itself. Modern allopathic treatments have included oven mitt compresses, airburst radiation therapy, and rapid anal administration of compressed $CO_2$ in severe cases of *ignuus flatulii*. Unsubstantiated success has been reported with a homeopathic course of leech therapy.

## Submitted by

DR. JAY LAKE, F.M.C.S. (FELLOW, MONGOLIAN COLLEGE OF SHAMANS)

## Cross References

Diseasemaker's Croup; Jumping Monkworm; Noumenal Fluke; Postal Carriers' Brain Fluke Syndrome

# MONOCHROMITIS*

## Country of Origin

Specious. However, best speculations by the Roanoke (Alabama) Centers for Disease Control trace the disease to the early 1950s, exclusively in the deep and rural American South.

In her *Journals*, Sarah Goodman refers to what may have been an early strain of the disease. Dr. Goodman reports that Afrikaner Jan Kruger sealed his Transvaalean hut, covered the walls with zebra hides, and papered his floor and ceiling with shredded copies of the *Times*. According to nearby Zulu tribes, Kruger eventually blinded himself. Goodman, however, was never able to substantiate the case.

## Symptoms

Monochromitis is the stark raving abhorrence of color, often accompanied by an intense longing for the way things used to be.

The disease begins innocently enough with a yearning for old movies; *Birth of a Nation* is a favorite, early Jolson, the decolorized version of *Gone With the Wind*

---

\* *Editors' Note:* To help our learned readers distinguish between biased and unbiased disease reporting, we do, as you will have noticed, assign a status of "Quarantined" to those diseases whose reporting doctors appear to have contracted the disease in question. In the case of Dr. Slay, the truth appears to be more complicated—or, at least, muddied. When we noticed that Dr. Slay never signed his letters in other than black ink and that none of the various corroborating photographs he sent were in color, we suspected infection. When, in attempting to follow up, we asked him if he owned a color TV and he answered in the negative, our suspicion intensified tenfold. Finally, we called him into our offices and forced him to watch a Technicolor print of *Gone With the Wind*. Although nervous, Dr. Slay appeared to pass this test. However, just before this book went to press, we received a telephone call of a disturbing nature from Dr. Slay's assistant. The assistant indicated that Dr. Slay had worn special contact lenses to bleed the color from his vision. Although we cannot confirm this accusation, neither can we deny it.

(shown only after midnight and only on the United States cable channel TNT), all viewed after 1:00 A.M., the lightning flicker of the TV transforming tiny dens into a chiaroscurist's storm. Soon, the patient seals himself off from the world, plastering his walls, the doors, the windows with copies of the *New York Times*, the *Wall Street Journal*, pages from early pulp magazines, prints by Ansel Adams, early Van Gogh, and Caravaggio. Drapery and bedding are often replaced with checkered racing flags. Not long after, diet is affected; eventually the patient subsists solely on Oreos dunked in whole milk, Ding-Dongs, and tubs of chocolate chip ice cream. In rarer cases, patients have spent life savings on grand pianos and closetfuls of tuxedos. They lounge for days on end in zebra-stripped pajamas playing dominoes and Pong; they find themselves mesmerized by the infuriating ambiguity of the mysterious 8-Ball. An overwhelming desire for nuns and priests is often recorded. (In pinches, referees will, apparently, do.) In one case, Ronald Druback, a 34-year-old male from Soso, Mississippi, achieved ordination into the Catholic priesthood through a series of Internet courses. ("The collar," he told his attending physician. "That marvelous jacket.") Rooms have been discovered filled to overflowing with stuffed menageries: litters of penguins and skunks and tiny orcas. In one of the most extreme cases, a Gerald Jitney of Hoboken, Georgia, purchased and married a Jersey cow.

## Cures

None yet known. Dr. Dwayne Woolhider, the world's leading Monochromologist, of the Roanoke CDC, reports that early studies led to a theory of opposition: namely, an intense overexposure to color. Patient Peter Joseph ("PeeJoe") Brumbleloe, well into the Priest and Referee phase, agreed to theoretical treatment. Dr. Woolhider filled Mr. Brumbleloe's apartment with copies of *USA Today* and prints of Matisse and Picasso (his Blue period), with Skittles and Lifesavers, with macaws and toucans, with prisms and a 64-pack of Crayola crayons, a kaleidoscopic riot of color. The Rainbow Coalition agreed to make surprise visits. At the Twenty-Ninth Annual Symposium on Eccentric and Discredited Diseases, Dr. Woolhider reported that, when exposed to the prepared room, Mr. Brumbleloe's head, unfortunately, exploded, blood as black as ichor splashing across the neon-bright walls, the tangled strings of Christmas lights. Oddly enough, the blood had the consistency, the texture, even the taste of India ink. Studies, Dr. Woolhider noted, returned to the blackboard.

## Submitted by

Dr. AND Dr. JACK SLAY, Jr., Ph.D., M.D.

## Cross References

Bloodflower's Melancholia; Diseasemaker's Croup; Figurative Synesthesia

# MOTILE SNARCOMA

## Motile Agglutinate Snarcoma of the Subperineal Pondus

## Countries of Origin

Oncologists have identified this uncommon fibroid tumor in several of the industrial nations. The etiology of snarcoma remains unknown, although anecdotal evidence gathered by the American Congress For Cancer links the malignancy with compulsive eating of spent paper matches.

## First Known Case

In 1921, Mr. Lumpur Kos, a flax dyer of Khulna, Bengal, developed an aggressive snarcoma which is now a treasured specimen in the permanent collection of the Provisional Pathology Museum of the Audrey Nickers Memorial Teaching Hospital of Bombay.

## Symptoms

Prior to ultrasound readings and exploratory biopsy, the diagnosis of snarcoma hinges on somatic indicators such as shortness of breath, flocculence of the urine, running sores of the nasal procus, bleeding from the ears, prolonged epiductoid olomony of the distal grottum, spitting, fainting spells, intrafusile vomiting, and adhesive bed sores.

## Treatment

Pondal snarcoma can be surgically excised with great success, but is often treated chemically as a second choice, for no better reason than that the attending surgeon "couldn't find the pondus." This situation is inexcusable.

## Surgical Procedure

After a standard transcolonic approach to the postpubic oversum has been established, the first and third inguinal veins and the fontiform lymphatic spinkos can be distended ventrally using a pair of Vega's lateral forceps, thus exposing the purple infoldings of the pylophancus or organ of Gorki.

Dissect the porensic artery, slice it diagonally, and insert 30 centimeters of sterile latex shunt. Apply your Forke's scalpel to the juncture of the pylophancus with the yellowish lobar tabuclomen. Expect copious drainage of Cowlick's fluid into the surgical field. Have plenty of suction tubes on hand. They tend to clog. Slocotomize and displace the tabuclomen by a succession of deepening incisions. Now you can utilize your perforated elbow retractor (1) to draw aside the main prutenoid mass of the pylophancus. This procedure should provide access to the pondus and its snarcomal extrusion.

Grip the snarcoma firmly in the jaws of a pair of Poker's tongs. Use Benway shears to snip the tumor free from the pondus. Drop the extracted snarcoma into a steel basin of saline.

Now here's where the procedure can get a bit hectic. You may withdraw your tongs and find only a scrap of the snarcoma in its jaws. Pondal snarcomas are known to sacrifice pieces of themselves in order to avoid capture.

And that's the least of their little tricks. Your snarcoma may turn out to be a motile snarcoma. A motile snarcoma exhibits mobility under stress. In layman's terms, it can crawl. In fact, it will stretch out its fibrous mycelia like tentacles and drag itself around your patient's guts like a beached baby octopus on Benzedrine.

It may suddenly hide behind a kidney. If you flush it out again, it may head for the small intestines. At all costs keep it away from the intestines. Hunting it down in there makes a terrible mess.

As a last resort, it may even fling itself from the abdominal cavity. I have personally retrieved two snarcomas from the floors of operating theaters. (One of them went safely from a butterfly net into a preserving jar. My nurse stepped on the other. An accident, or so she said.)

In any case, a snarcoma can't survive in the wild. Just keep it away from any patients with open body cavities who might be nearby, and it will die a natural death.

When the snarcoma is under control, examine the surgical field for corruption and use Plook's tweezers to extract any glybolic granulation. Disclevature or oblation of the hemophragmic orphule typically indicates opportunistic inspusal of the peripheral mesencrum by infragort C-cells. Be aware that mumblision of the cocapsular endosucrament can eventuate in slethonular blucoposis.

Rinse and close. Don't forget to remove the arterial shunt.
And always remember to take off your gloves before eating.

## Submitted by
Dr. Stepan Chapman, holder of the Osstrich Chair of Polysurgical Practices, Institute For Further Study

## Endnote
(1) *Popular Surgical Instruments: Classics and Collectibles*, Wendell Ortt, Green Dog Hobby Press, Boojum Florida USA, 1996.

## Cross References
Ballistic Organ Syndrome; Buboparazygosia; Diseasemaker's Croup; Hsing's Spontaneous Self-Flaying Sarcoma

# NOUMENAL FLUKE

*Verbiform Vermistosomiasis*

### Country of Origin
Jutigny, France

### First Known Case
Dr. Ephraim Rackstrow, 1875

### Symptoms
Logorrhoeaiac episodes, occasional drowsiness, aphasia (rare); otherwise no symptoms

### History
It is one of the great ironies in the annals of medical history that this disease was discovered not by the great diagnostician and pioneer of early neuropathological research, Dr. Ephraim Rackstrow, but by his wife Toussia; and it is one of the more humbling tragedies as well, in that he was the first known victim. One of Charcot's most accomplished students, Rackstrow participated in several extraordinary research projects in the first decade of his medical career, assisting such other luminaries as Dr. Julian Maltrait and Dr. Austin Blaney. In 1875, using his limited resources, he established a small lab in the provincial town of Jutigny, where he assembled a small collection of carefully selected mental patients. He brought them together in order to study the particularities of neurological diseases affecting language, and especially the phenomenon or disorder known as Logorrhoea: incessant, uncontrollable, garbled speech.

Subsequent inquiries into his case have indicated that it was in the spring of that year, shortly after his research began in earnest, that he contracted the fluke. His wife, Toussia, by all accounts a woman of high acuity, and whose séances had been a minor sensation in Paris the previous season, recorded in her diary a series of exceedingly subtle variations and changes in her husband through the month of June. By mid-July, she was increasingly convinced that her husband was "occupied by an incorporeal intelligence," and further, that "this spirit, or daemon, intends to use me to propagate itself."

In an entry dated the following morning, Toussia relates an unaccountably prescient dream in which she, paralyzed, gazed at "the one lying next to me" and perceived that "the worm of his mind is always awake." Two days later, on July 21, finding it too hot to work, Dr. Rackstrow apparently returned early to his home and brought a chair out into the shade of one of the large trees behind the house. He was reading a newspaper in this chair when Toussia crept up behind him and struck him a single glancing blow to the head with an axe she had specially sharpened for this purpose, shearing off most of her husband's right parietal bone and exposing the brain. Shortly thereafter, having brought her stricken husband into the house, Toussia discovered through direct inspection the now widely-recognized signs of the noumenal fluke.

It has since been learned that the fluke is a unique logogenetic parasite which reproduces via Logorrhoea; the logorrhoeaiac's stream of often nonsensical syllables irritates the nerves of the inner ear in such a way as to cause associated brain tissues to produce certain proteins, which coagulate in the bloodstream into a single egg. The egg will lodge in one of the major blood vessels in the brain for up to six days until achieving the larval stage, whereupon it will move to the fissure separating the two cerebral hemispheres. Over the next six to eight weeks, the larva will develop into a mature fluke of up to four inches in length, being slightly less than a pencil in diameter, composed of proglottid rings with a holdfast organ at one end. The fluke filters the blood for nutrients but does not absorb iron, hence anemia is not indicated; and it also manufactures neurotransmitters that induce logorrhoeaiac episodes in its victim, for the purposes of reproduction.

When its reproductive stage is complete, usually in seven to 10 days, the fluke's proglottids separate from each other and lodge in different blood vessels throughout the brain, developing independently into smaller, sterile flukes of one inch or less in length. Some researchers believe that, even at this stage, the fluke is still a single organism in serial form, communicating through proteins distributed in the blood. The lesser flukes will remain in place until the natural death of the host. Their presence seems to affect the host's mental capacities, often promoting an increased facility with abstract thought. This was first noted in Rackstrow's case; he survived for 10 days after Toussia's attack, during which time he was confined to bed, his head held off the pillow in a makeshift wooden frame. Toussia never left his side, in an apparent desperation of remorse, and, by her account, Rackstrow quickly lapsed into a delirium, during which he spoke incessantly. The fluke, by this time, had passed its reproductive stage, as Toussia notes seeing various of the smaller, sterile flukes through the walls of the blood vessels: "I counted at least seven; they were diaphanous, nerveless, unmuscled tubes, that waved in his blood's current like linen sleeves, and, like ghosts, they tapered away into invisibly diaphanous membranes."

Toussia not only kept watch over her husband, but she recorded everything he said, which, it would appear, amounted to a long and highly-organized discourse presenting a new model of time. While this work was supposedly burned with the rest of Rackstrow's papers after his death, Toussia having been confined to an institution after an anguished attempt on her own life, rumors persist that it is still being kept in the French Archive, and that several prominent French intellectuals have been secretly permitted to read selected passages.

## Cures
25 to 30 mg of camphorated parziquantyl, administered orally.

## Submitted by
Dr. Michael Cisco, C.C., B.P.O.E., S.V.S.E.

## Cross References
Buscard's Murrain; Diseasemaker's Croup; Jumping Monkworm; Mongolian Death Worm Infestation; Postal Carriers' Brain Fluke Syndrome

# OUROBOREAN LORDOSIS

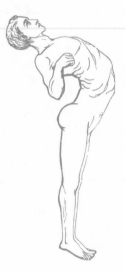

## Country of Origin
United States

## First Known Case
This dread disease was first diagnosed in Mississippi in 1900. Harmon Creets, better known in his professional life as part of The Helen Oberstella Sideshow and Traveling Menagerie of Afflicted Personages as The Human Wheel, was the first known patient diagnosed with Ouroborean Lordosis.

## Symptoms
Congenital and continuous radical lordosis; a backward curvature of the spine that not only affects the lower back, as in typical lordosis, but the entire length of the spinal column, including the neck. Throughout the duration of his life, the patient is slowly bent backward into a circle until his face is directly adjacent to the posterior. Hence the name "ouroborean," as in Ouroboros, the mythical worm that swallows its own tail.

## History
By the time Harmon Creets was a young man of 25, his body had formed a perfect circle. He was discovered in an institution that catered to those with formative diseases of the spinal column by the famous entertainer Miss Helen Oberstella, and given a place of prominence in her traveling show. In his act, Creets would grab his ankles and roll like a wheel down a portable set of steps

and then tip and "gyrate in a lively manner like a spun penny coming to rest" (as quoted in *The Lord's Botches: The Life and Acts of Helen Oberstella*). Creets married the beautiful giantess Madame Large and together they performed an act in which she used him like a hula hoop. Eventually, the condition worsened and Creets succumbed to his affliction by being suffocated against his own hindquarters.

## Cures
Currently this disease is treated with corrective surgery, which must be begun in the first year of life. In Harmon Creets' day, there was no known cure. Creets, himself a man of singular wit, was once quoted as saying that if one suffered from this disease, it was "only a matter of time before you will simply kiss your ass goodbye."

## Submitted by
Dr. Jeffrey Ford

## Cross References
Diseasemaker's Croup; Female Hyper-Orgasmic Epilepsy

# PATHOLOGICAL INSTRUMENTATION DISORDER

*The Man With Two Watches Problem*

## Country of Origin

Tomorrow

## First Known Case

The first diagnosis of Pathological Instrumentation Disorder (PID) will be made on May 12, 2006, in Toronto, Ontario. The patient, a Mr. Gary Warren, presented symptoms typical of extreme mental distress—elevated pulse, perspiration, acute abdomen, dilated pupils—at the Queen St. Mental Health Center, where a preliminary diagnosis of acute stress disorder was made. The patient's serotonin levels were normalized through quick trepanning, and he was entered into a course of group therapy sessions in the newly installed microgravity chill-rooms. Mr. Warren's symptoms worsened, however, despite daily trepannings. The only visible relief came when in close proximity to diagnostic equipment (EEG, e-meters, MRI/CT Scan apparatus). Even a wall clock, a PDA, or a thermometer seemed to help.

Mr. Warren was moved to the Bertelsmann-AOL-Netscape-Time-Warner clinic and into the care of Dr. Jojo Fillipo, a specialist in media disorders. Under clinical observation, Mr. Warren was presented with a variety of diagnostic tools, beginning with those found on his person at his admission:

- A Palm Computing "Wrister" wristwatch
- A small, homemade RFI detector
- An integrated wireless appliance of baroque appearance

- A multifunction handheld medical unit, apparently stolen from a Mexican clinic (sphygnomometer, EEG, blood-sugar/HIV/Hep G/ Pregnancy diagnostic)
- An elderly, analog light meter
- A DNA-signature encoder
- A distributed location/presence device marketed to children for the purposes of playing text-based role-playing games
- An elderly "turnip"-style pocket watch—not working
- A "commando"-style knife with an integrated compass and thermometer

Devices were provided to the patient singly and in combination. Alone or in small groups, the devices produced a marked lessening in the patient's symptoms—in fact, the mere presence of devices intended to measure Mr. Warren's symptoms appeared to alleviate them. In larger groups, or in certain combinations (the wireless appliance and the location/presence device, for example), symptoms were exacerbated to alarming levels. At one point, Mr. Warren lost consciousness for a period of three days, during which doctors defibrillated his heart twice due to unusual cardiac events.

Dr. Fillipo's research failed to uncover any symptoms to distinguish Mr. Warren's disorder from traditional cases of hysterical anxiety, except that Mr. Warren failed to respond to any traditional treatment. Dr. Fillipo worked with a group of BANT engineers to substitute replicas for Mr. Warren's devices, said facsimiles under Dr. Fillipo's remote control, and when Mr. Warren returned to consciousness, he was once again provided with his apparatus, while Dr. Fillipo undertook a series of controlled experiments, with alarming results.

The first of these was Mr. Warren's pregnancy. Dr. Fillipo introduced a series of false positive test results for pregnancy into Mr. Warren's medical unit. Over the course of three months, Mr. Warren developed secondary sexual characteristics (breasts) and most amazingly, *primary* characteristics—a rudimentary uterus with burgeoning fetus was positively identified first by Ultrasound and then by physical internal examination. Dr. Fillipo then provided Mr. Warren with a package of "Urinoracle"-brand home pregnancy tests, which had been doctored to provide uniformly negative results. Within one week, Mr. Warren's pregnancy had subsided, and the fetus and uterus had been reabsorbed into his digestive tract. Mr. Warren's other symptoms worsened during this period—he compulsively re-tested his own urine on the provided strips and, with each conflicting result, his physical distress worsened, culminating with another, longer coma, lasting nine days.

Continued experiments with conflicting and false data produced similar results. Mr. Warren's body temperature could be physically altered by means of changing the thermometer's reading; his blood could be made to manufacture and then banish HIV and Hepatitis G virii, and his melatonin levels and REM cycles responded similarly to changes in his timepieces.

Dr. Fillipo's experimentation came to an abrupt end when she caused Mr. Warren's location/presence device to produce a reading to the effect that he was actually at one of his bookmarked locations—apparently a tidal island off the coast of Newfoundland, submerged at the time. Mr. Warren's body was recovered from St. John's harbor some weeks later, badly decomposed. Cause of death was determined to be drowning.

### Diagnosis and Treatment

PID will be extremely rare in the immediate future—only eight known cases to date—and has thus far only been present in technologically developed regions, primarily North America, Europe, and parts of Asia. As noted, it is symptomatically nearly indistinguishable from other forms of hysterical anxiety; however, it does not respond to trepanning and similar accepted therapies. Positive diagnosis can be made through the use of a doctored thermometer or similar device—see the Fillipo-Chinto questionnaire for a more systematic approach to diagnosis.

Treatment is largely palliative, and requires giving the subject continuous access to a variety of diagnostic devices—with the understanding that no two devices measuring the same factor should *ever* be given to the patient—the man with two watches never knows what time it is. Great care should be exercised to provide the most accurate instrumentation possible.

### Caveat

Dr. Fillipo and the BANT clinic will file worldwide, far-reaching patent applications for commercial uses of PID, including teleportation, time travel, and low-cost air-conditioning. Primary and clinical health practitioners are cautioned not to attempt any commercial exploitation of PID sufferers without the future permission of the BANT clinic.

### Submitted by

DR. CORY DOCTOROW

### Cross References

Chrono-Unific Deficiency Syndrome; Diseasemaker's Croup; Twentieth Century Chronoshock

# PENTZLER'S LUBRICIOUSNESS

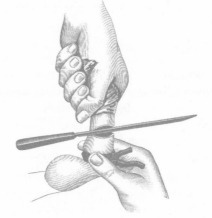

## Country of Origin
This condition is found only in isolated villages of the Pintzgau Saalach Valley region in Alpine Austria.

## First Known Case
The nature of this illness led to its treatment as a shameful secret and, with the collusion of village doctors, the cause of death was ascribed to other factors, commonly bears or rock falls. The condition is named after Otto Pentzler, born in Aasbach-Pintzgau in 1785. It was Pentzler who dared to admit his illness openly and to venture away from the inward-looking world of the Alpine villages. In doing so, he brought this condition to the attention of the world's medical establishment.

## Symptoms
Pentzler's Lubriciousness is—or rather was, as I shall explain below—an incurable form of Satyriasis. It produces a permanent state of erotic arousal in the (exclusively male) sufferer, accompanied by distressingly prolific amorous discharges. As the condition progresses, the frequency of these discharges increases until the sufferer is in a permanent state of climax. Death inevitably follows soon after this paroxysmic point, from a combination of fatigue and heart failure.

Dr. Sarah Goodman's dismissal of Pentzler's Lubriciousness as a purely psychological complaint is unwarrantable quackery, although perhaps only to be expected of someone whose medical qualifications are of such dubious provenance. Years of scientific research employing my own techniques of genito-aetheric kinetography have indisputably demonstrated the existence of this disease.

## History

When stricken down with this condition, most sufferers retreated into the woods, hiding themselves from their families in shame, and awaiting the inevitable climax of the disease. Pentzler, however, was inspired to put his illness to good use and secure his family financially long after his inevitable death from ejaculatory spasm. In an arduous and astounding journey (well documented in my book *Otto Pentzler's Priapic Pilgrimage*, available from all quality booksellers), Pentzler hobbled awkwardly all the way to Moscow, and was within minutes of gaining an introduction to Catherine the Great that surely would have made his fortune, but, sadly, a passing dray horse kicked him to death before he could capitalize on his plight.

## Cures

The only cure known at present is the complete and immediate removal of the entire sexual apparatus. Although drastic, and not without causing a certain amount of distress to the patient, this surgery can allow the patient to live a normal, if asexual, life—if performed soon after the symptoms reveal themselves. Patients must ensure that, after recovering from surgery, they take possession of their removed organs: a number of unscrupulous surgeons have been known to sell these on the Chinese medicine market, where there is a huge demand for the organs in powdered soup form as an aid to flagging virility and a cure for baldness.

However, I am pleased to announce in the pages of this almost prestigious publication that after years of careful research I have come to the conclusion that my program of electro-static stimulation will be as applicable to the treatment of Pentzler's Lubriciousness as it has been proven to be for pleurisy of the libido (and contrary to Goodman's libelous suggestions, the patient who died during electro-static stimulation in treatment for that condition suffered a heart attack coincidental to the treatment process, as anyone with a gift for medicine would realize). This astounding breakthrough will surely convince even those who are in the habit of blinding themselves to the most incontrovertible evidence when it is laid before them, and will benefit the many men who otherwise would be compelled to sacrifice their manhood in order to save their lives. It should be noted that electro-static stimulation is a very costly process (which I operate at a loss, I must stress, contrary to the allegations made by Dr. Csestervic—allegations founded more in cheap brandy than truth), and that patients will be required to provide the normal collateral in the form of deeds to property, etc., in order to benefit.

## Submitted by
Dr. Iain Rowan

## Cross References
Di Forza Virus Syndrome; Diseasemaker's Croup; Female Hyper-Orgasmic Epilepsy; Fruiting Body Syndrome

# POETIC LASSITUDE

*Pyrexia Poetica; also known
as De Quincey Syndrome, Iambic
Langour, Black Plapsy, or Sapphic Trench*

## Country of Origin
Uncertain, but probably Ancient Greece

## First Known Case
Claiming a first instance of this pernicious disease is tenuous and to do so would be dishonest, since the ailment is very ancient. Accounts vary and are sketchier the further back we try to examine them. However, the Roman poet Juvenal (circa A.D. 112 to 130) was almost certainly a sufferer. A major outbreak occurred in Europe during the Middle Ages but it was not until the mid-nineteenth century that we were able to identify a set of concomitant symptoms to which we could give a name.

## Symptoms
Victims become preoccupied and introspective. They are often found wandering the countryside and mountain fastnesses staring at tiny flowers. In many cases, they are attracted to water and will be discovered gazing limpidly into a still pool or millpond. A victim may dress eccentrically and lie on a chaise longue for days, sighing. Drug and drink use often accompanies Poetic Lassitude, which only serves to compound the symptoms and make attempted diagnoses even more difficult. Typically, the disease may manifest itself in oblique statements. In the famous John Cooper Clarke case of 1979, the victim was heard to say: "I remain convinced that long periods of idleness are essential to creativity."

The victim's only positive action during the disease's primary and secondary stages is to scribble, sometimes recite, verse. Examination of this work is in itself exhausting and may lead to cross-infection. The content of it may be very powerful, where it is comprehensible. The victim may seek out other victims of the disease or may cause the disease to break out in susceptible or borderline cases previously free of symptoms. In the tertiary stages of Poetic Lassitude, the sufferer becomes completely useless as a human being, a drain on his friends' and his family's resources, and a cause of bankruptcy to his publishers. Unable to feed himself, he is at last only capable of dressing, arranging his hair, and perhaps applying a modicum of eye makeup. This process may take hours, until with one languorous sigh he finally expires or simply fades away. In England, where dead poets are much more valuable than live ones, what literary estate he has left may suddenly become a source of revenue to anxious creditors seeking remuneration. It is scant compensation, however, for the distress and inconvenience that his symptoms bring to others during his short but wretched lifetime.

## History

During the mid-nineteenth century, with a strong Christian work ethic gaining ground in England, a number of physicians to the Great Houses reported increasing instances of a new ailment: the children brought up in the relative affluence of these country houses were struck down in adolescence or early adulthood by what we now know as Poetic Lassitude. The ailment often afflicted the eldest son or scion of the family. This alarmed both noble families and the newly-rich industrialists, since money spent on a private education would now be wasted. Even worse, with the principal heir to the family's business and colonial wealth incapacitated, who would run estate and empire when its creator stood down?

The Royal College of Physicians was stumped. Attempted cures at the time were crude and often brutal. Such cures involved beating the sufferer with oaken staves, subjecting him to a protracted regime of cold showers and cross-country running, or sometimes, giving him an obscure job in the Patent Office, as happened to A. E. Housman. Housman, in this case, survived. Most sufferers simply resorted to self-murder, and in 1898 the physicians recognized that Poetic Lassitude couldn't simply be beaten out of its victim and ceased the practice. Between the two world wars, electric shock treatment was experimented with but discontinued after it became clear that it only exacerbated the symptoms. Since the late 1980s, Poetic Lassitude is no longer as prevalent as it once was. The removal of large tracts of English countryside for the building of shopping emporia seems to have limited the sources of infection. Poetic Lassitude, like Leprosy and Bubonic Plague, is now seen as a somewhat archaic complaint and research funding is almost impossible to obtain in the current climate. A small body of modern medical opinion still urges vigilance, however. We may not have seen the last of it.

## Cures

None known. (Poetic Lassitude may also mimic the symptoms of Opiated Whimsy or Unrequited Love. Test for both of these ailments first. The cures for these last two should never be attempted where Poetic Lassitude is suspected.)

## Submitted by

Dr. Martin Wesley Newell, F.R.C.D., Great Britain

## Cross References

Bloodflower's Melancholia; Diseasemaker's Croup; Ebercitas

# POST-TRAUMATIC PLACEBOSIS

## Country of Origin
United States

## First Known Case
June 2001. Horace Volf, age 38, a resident of New York City. Married. Two children, a boy age nine, a girl age seven, both symptom-free as of this writing. No prior family history. Volf, who describes himself as "a working poet," supplements a meager income through a wide variety of freelance assignments, including employment as a generic nose model for many plastic surgeons, a sperm and blood donor, a street peddler, a can and bottle gatherer (in New York, discarded cans and bottles may be redeemed at a current rate of five cents per item), a designer of Web sites, a substitute high-school English teacher, a frequent paid participant in pharmaceutical testing programs, etc.

## Symptoms
Mr. Volf sought help at the St. Gottfried Clinic for the Uninsured at the urging of family members. At first, his problems seemed to be rooted in mental illness. He reported irresistible urges to exercise, preferably on devices like stationary bicycles, stair-steppers, and treadmills rather than more social participation in games like tennis, golf, or squash. A former smoker and heavy drinker, Volf renounced all abusive substances, controlled and uncontrolled. Once a heavy consumer of meat, poultry, fish, and cheese, Volf had restricted his diet to soybeans and sesame seeds. His liquid intake consisted of bottled

water originating in Alpine glaciers. No stimulants were ingested. In public and in private, he reacted violently to anyone he found indulging in lifestyles he considered opposed to his own. He affirmed his conviction that such persons gave off dangerous secondary miasmas and mists that might contain lethal bacteria or viruses. His negative behavior toward those he termed "carriers" was in sharp contrast to an active worship of Asians, whom he often alienated by calling Orientals. He renounced Christianity and embraced a Buddist-Shintoist-Hinduist ethic. His interest in lyrical epic poetry was replaced with a devotion to the haiku form.

Volf's most dramatic symptom was his absolute impatience with the concept of mortality. He had come to regard death as indulgence and ran afoul of the law because of attacks on chapels, crematoriums, undertaker parlors, hospitals, and morgues. He developed a passion for tipping tombstones and defacing mausoleums with obscene graffiti. Aside from these anomalies, he appeared to be in excellent physical health. His psychiatric profile was impeccable. Still, as a precautionary measure, because of his erratic behavior, the examining psychiatrist proscribed a variety of tranquilizing medications that produced no salutary effect and caused chronic constipation.

Volf was discharged from the Clinic, but was readmitted shortly thereafter when he was caught attempting to melt down an obese associate on a barbecue spit, which action, he insisted, was, arguably, "for the person's own good and the benefit of society." It was during this confinement that the patient came to my attention.

### Diagnosis

Volf was not a cooperative subject. He quickly noted that I myself am a man of considerable girth, addicted to foul-smelling cigars, a user of large quantities of morphine and crack cocaine, a known guzzler of vintage wines, and the author of many articles and pamphlets including "How to Kill a Personal Trainer," "The Mayhem of Pilates," "Aerobic Recidivism," "The Gloating Yogi," etc. etc. etc. (many of which are available through Amazon.com). I am also a notorious breaker of wind. Many of my best and most devoted patients tell me my only virtue is my acceptance of Medicare, Medicaid, and HMO fees in full payment for my expert services.

What kept Volf in my examining room was the impressive array of diplomas, awards, and certificates displayed on my wall. He was also enchanted by the naked pictures of my lovely wife, a former Ms. America, kept in tasteful silver frames on a shelf behind my massive Chippendale desk. Fortunately for Mr. Volf, he agreed to an extensive battery of tests evasive and non, and allowed me access to his private diaries. The tests revealed an extraordinarily efficient immune system that dispatched intruding organisms and toxins with amazing alacrity. The diaries revealed that, during Volf's exposure to numerous experiments with newly developed chemicals, medicines, food additives, and vitamin supplements, *he had always been placed in the placebo segment of the sample.* Volf had never once been injected with or given anything more potent than pasteurized apple juice. It became obvious that Volf was plagued with old-fashioned survivor's guilt since most of the test subjects died after suffering distasteful deterioration.

After many months, I succeeded in devising a method of compromising his Herculean immune system to the point where a snotty child across the street was enough to give the man resistant pneumonia. I also induced terminal impotence, which caused anxiety and depression enough to neutralize Volf's extreme arrogance. He returned, limping, to a grateful wife and happy children, a man facing new horizons of rejection and fully accepting of, even eager at, the prospect of his own eventual demise. As a result, what is popularly known as *Volf's Law* has become part of the Federal Drug Administration's guidelines for product testing: By Act of Congress, *No potential statistic shall be permitted to receive a placebo during more than one clinical trial in any given year.* On the day that law was passed (unanimously) I felt what can only be described as wonderful (except for a slight rectal spasm).

**Submitted by**
DR. HARVEY JACOBS

**Cross References**
Diseasemaker's Croup; Espectare Necrosis; Twentieth Century Chronoshock

# POSTAL CARRIERS' BRAIN FLUKE SYNDROME

## *Cerebral Infestation by Tubifex Corbellis, a Parasitic Fluke of the Class Trematoda*

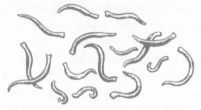

### Vectors of Contagion

Since 1996, Postal Carriers' Brain Fluke Syndrome has been widely reported in the greater Los Angeles area. A thorough documentation of this microscopic flatworm is now being assembled at the Atlanta Centers for Disease Control. The life cycle of the PCB fluke follows a well-established scenario. To trace the stages of the cycle, we may begin with a specimen of the worm's primary host at the onset of mortality.

In a grimy industrial district, in the dead of night, a postal carrier in a pale blue uniform lies dead, slightly steaming, on the pavement.

The prefrontal glial matter of this corpse harbors hundreds of female flukes bearing egg sacs. These mother flukes drill their way through the optic fossae and congregate in the corpse's eyes—specifically, in the fluid of the anterior chamber behind the cornea. Here the females swarm and die, releasing, as they do so, millions of free-swimming ciliated miricidia. A sip of this infected fluid is gratefully consumed by a passing cockroach (Blatodea Occidentalis). (If something else gets to the eyes first—blackbirds or feral cats or the city coroner—the worm's life cycle is short-circuited. But parasites love to play the long shots.)

The miricidia migrate to the cephalic ganglia and cloaca of the host roach. The roach experiences a sudden overwhelming compulsion to expose itself to a light source, usually a streetlamp, and to caper about as if poisoned.

A pigeon (Columbidae Americanis) observes the frenetic movements of the roach, swoops down, and makes a meal of it. Inside her gullet, the doomed insect evacuates its bowels. On the following day, miricidia appear in the pigeon's bloodstream. Many of them merge into a redia, a shapeless body lodged within the avian pituitary gland.

The redia manufactures masses of larval cercariae. Propelled by their thrashing tails, the cercariae migrate to the midfundibular esogeum of the pigeon's neck. I will refrain from relating the anatomical path that the larvae have established for this journey, since it's just as needlessly over-elaborate as everything else about the PCB fluke.

The pigeon feels impelled to strut obnoxiously in front of the mangiest mongrel dog that she can find (Canis Familaris). Then she flies at the dog and claws his nose. The dog, quite naturally, rips her throat out. For his trouble, he gets a mouthful of bird skin, feathers, and cercariae. Battling the mammalian immune system at every step, these intrepid invaders wriggle their way to the dog's brain stem and liver.

As the cercariae devour connective tissue and phagocytes, they bud off the sexual generation of the fluke—adult males and adult females displaying the traditional backwards-torpedo design so beloved by trematodes everywhere. The females traverse the canine lymph system, infiltrate the large muscle groups of the shanks, and encyst themselves.

The male flukes, by contrast, swim to the dog's gums. Meanwhile, the dog seeks out the exact shade of blue that characterizes the shorts of the uniforms of Los Angeles postal workers. The dog sinks his teeth into the ankle of the first postman that he encounters. The male flukes smell the ankle and hurriedly penetrate the nearest follicle.

The offending dog is blinded by pepper spray, captured by an animal control officer, and put to sleep by barbiturate injection. The carcass is sold to a wholesale meat supplier and then resold to local markets, restaurants, and lunch stands as a frozen component of 100 per cent ground beef. (The term "100 per cent ground beef" is applied somewhat loosely in Los Angeles.)

When the dormant females in the dog meat sense a human intestine around them, they shake off their cysts, tunnel into the villi, and circulate, chemically disguised as human corpuscles, until they enter the cerebral meninges. If the females are fortunate, their new host is a recently bitten postal carrier. If so, the male flukes (last seen in the host's ankle) have preceded the females into the cranium and used their oral suckers to build meningeal love nests for undisturbed mating. Ensconced therein, the females anchor themselves and dilate their genital pores.

During the first phase of the syndrome, the afflicted postal carrier feels flushed and dizzy each day at dusk. He or she develops an obsessive fantasy in which he or she fills his or her pockets with coins or other small metal objects and climbs to the top of a telephone pole in the dead of night in a thunderstorm. When a nocturnal storm occurs, the fantasy is acted out. If the postal carrier is struck by lightning, he or she will fall to the street—a steaming, twitching corpse. This is, so to speak, where we came in.

Afflicted carriers may survive the disease for years, suffering compulsive episodes all the while. But, if the carrier is restrained from pole climbing, he or she will swallow his or her tongue, turn blue, and suffocate.

If I may be allowed a zoological digression within a medical text, please consider the utter strangeness of this life cycle. The fluke's reproductive success depends on a chain of events so unlikely as to appear implausible.

Flukes are known among the triploblastic acoelomate worms for the unnecessary and seemingly maladaptive complexity of their life cycles, which can involve as many as 11 distinct host organisms. (1) Yet even among the flukes, the PCBF appears excessive, even exhibitionistic. It seems almost as though the PCBF is performing an extinction-defying trapeze act purely for the sake of impressing other parasites. (2)

## Cures

Any number of vermifugal interventions suggest themselves. The Sunset Boulevard Community Health Clinic & Pet Shelter reports that a heavy dosage of Slavopropin or Meforbifak can be used to induce clonotronchic seizure in the female fluke with subsequent prolapsis and infarction of the ovipositor. The effect on infested patients was immediate, and fatality resulted in less than 40 per cent of recorded cases.

Alternately, clinical trials of the experimental vermicides Spinwex D and Cactosprain 113 have been suggested by various out-of-work pharmacologists. All of these courses of treatment are fraught with unpleasantness, but they're probably better than climbing a phone pole in a thunderstorm with your pockets full of small metal objects.

If qualified vermologists with California state legislature connections can obtain preserved tissues for dissection, a thorough histological work-up is indicated. If live specimens of the fluke can be procured, some smart young lab rat in the public health sector could probably put together a reputation-making research agenda. Cockroaches, pigeons, dogs, and a consenting population of federal prisoners or chimpanzees could be employed as hosts. Investigations into the molecular mechanisms of the fluke's navigation, immune suppression, and behavioral modification techniques would surely follow. (3)

**Submitted by**

STEPAN CHAPMAN, DOCTOR OF INVERTEBRATE ZOOLOGY, INSTITUTE FOR FURTHER STUDY, WAXWALL, ARIZONA, UNITED STATES

**Endnotes**

(1) "Vectors of Parasitism Considered As Sub-Chaotic Attractors For Symbiotic Neurolepsy," Forsfed Forbran DTZ, *The Royal Journal of Worms* vol. 59 #4, Berne Switzerland, 1987.
(2) *Vanity: Watch Spring of Evolution*, Verner Kempt DDT, Catarrh Press, Oshkosh Wisconsin, 1993.
(3) *Parasite Rex*, Carl Zimmer, The Free Press, New York City, 2000.

**Cross References**

Diseasemaker's Croup; Jumping Monkworm; Mongolian Death Worm Infestation; Noumenal Fluke

# PRINTER'S EVIL*

## Paper Pox

## Country of Origin
Printer's Evil first appeared in Central Europe, although its true origin is presumed to be China or possibly Ancient Egypt.

## First Known Case
Albrecht Schicklgruber, apprentice to the printing house of Gustav Doppelgänger, the city of Worms in the Rhineland Palatinate, 1523

## Symptoms
Primarily a disease of the printing trade, hence the name, Printer's Evil was undoubtedly known before the advent of moving type, although evidence to this effect remains circumstantial. The condition begins as an inflammation of the skin caused by contact with a pathogenic slime mold, Papyroplasmapora infestans. This fungus occurs worldwide and is commonly parasitical to many varieties of paper and wood pulp material. Generally harmless in its dormant state, the introduction of inks or other materials to the paper surface inspires the fungus to rapid zoosporangia proliferation. To date, there has been little research into the precise chemical nature of compounds triggering zoosporangia; assertions that squid-derived inks may constitute an active agent have little basis in fact. Paper sufficiently infested with the growth transmits spores to the skin upon contact; the spores penetrate the epithelium and root

---

* *Editors' Note:* Some evidence suggests that the infamous "Algerian Printer" incident of 1934, which resulted in the death of all contributors to the Guide other than Dr. Lambshead, may have been due to Printer's Evil.

themselves in the subcutaneous cellular tissue. The fungal manifestation, when it occurs in books, can easily be mistaken for the effects of damp, differing, however, in the respect that it corrupts the surface of the paper and so also tends to corrupt the arrangement of the letters on the page. Heavily infested books were often held to be "rewriting" themselves, as the letters seem to change shape and form new words.

The skin inflammation begins by draining the affected areas of blood, then gradually dries the epithelium. Doctors chronicling the disease refer to this as the "paper stage." Once the spores are rooted in the muscle tissue, fine, thread-like rhizoids (tendrils) appear at the epidermal surface to form a variegated pattern across the affected areas of skin. This is known as the "ink stage," the visible rhizoids bearing some resemblance to cursive letter forms. Without treatment, the spores continue to spread through the muscle tissue until every area of the infected subject manifests the condition.

Once the ink stage is complete, the skin and muscle tissue becomes completely desiccated and begins to fall away from the limbs of the patient. Needless to say, death quickly follows this final stage of the disease. However, Printer's Evil is only infectious via active spores in paper material; once the fungus is rooted in the skin, contagion ceases.

A further development of the disease has seen its progress divided into two separate conditions, called, somewhat facetiously, Upper Case and Lower Case. Lower Case Printer's Evil confines itself to the skin tissues alone, while Upper Case attacks the nervous system, leading to violent muscular spasms (so-called "Gutenberg's Dance") and severe fever. The fever, which represents the climax of the Upper Case, induces hallucinations in which the patient believes that the rhizoid marks now visible upon the skin are words, and that the affected limbs and torso are pages from a book. At the height of the fever, the patient will find it necessary to declaim loudly the words that he or she believes are being written upon the flesh. To date, there is no satisfactory cure once zoosporangic infection has taken hold. All that can be done is to alleviate the patient's suffering.

### History

The case of Albrecht Schicklgruber is described in a letter from Doppelgänger to Ulrich von Schreck:

> Much aggrieved this morning with the revelation that our latest edition of The Bible, numbering some thousand copies, is almost entirely ruined, there being copious errors and even seeming rewritings

throughout. The apprentice I deemed responsible was pitched down a flight of stairs where I then passed water upon him despite his pleas of innocence. Owing to the laws against bad printings of the Lord's Book, we were forced to sell some at a reduced price to a caravan of Belgian pilgrims then threw the rest in the river. However, I now find Albrecht's claim that the paper was infected with a pox to be sincere as this has spread itself to his arms and chest. The condition and his scratchings are hideous to behold so I sent him home, afeared he might be smitten with a pestilence. (1)

For reasons yet to be adequately explained, Bibles have induced more than 70 per cent of documented cases of Printer's Evil. The most notable incident concerned the "Bad Bibles of Babelsburg" of 1611. A group of Lutheran clerics was stricken with the Upper Case condition and for a few days paraded through the streets of the town, proclaiming their bodies to be collectively the new "Gospel According to St Anthony." These fevered announcements proved singularly obscene and blasphemous. Before their conditions could degenerate further, they were herded into the town square and onto a bonfire, where they burned in "a merry conflagration." (2)

In eighteenth-century London, Upper Case sufferers were sought after as "bookmen" for entertainment at social gatherings. The stricken person would be introduced seated in a cage and allowed to declaim from his or her imaginary "book" for the amusement of the assembled party. Dr. Johnson complained to Boswell that a contemporary wrote "doggerel of a most diabolic nature, worthy of a bookman's ranting." (3) A small number of transcribed bookmen rants date from this period, including the celebrated "I Am Unhinged, Africa." Rumors persist that a number of well-known literary works from the eighteenth to the early twentieth century owe some of their content to these outpourings. However, when noted Argentine critic H. Bustos Domecq asserts that "half the books published in South America are either infected with, or the products of, Printer's Evil." (4) we must assume he is speaking metaphorically.

In London and Paris of the 1890s, writers on the fringes of the Decadent movement sought to deliberately infect themselves with the disease in the quest for outré inspiration. There is no record of any successful literary product resulting from these exploits, although the collection *Fungoids* by vanished poet manqué Enoch Soames contains the lines "Books of Evil, Printer's Evil / Infect me with a black delight." (5)

With the advent of industrialized printing processes and the introduction of bleached papers and new inks, the disease has become increasingly uncommon and seems now to be almost extinct. One of the last notable cases occurred in 1928 when Louis Garou, a Parisian book dealer, contracted the Lower Case condition from a Bavarian Psalter. Upon hearing this, André Breton had Garou's body stolen immediately after death with the intention of transcribing the "words" on the man's skin and publishing the result as a Surrealist "*roman trouvé*." The transcription proved impossible due to the extreme desiccation of the skin, although the incident did give birth to the Surrealist phrase "exquisite corpse." Further plans to exhibit Garou in a public convenience were thwarted by the offices of the Bureau Sanitaire.

The scarcity of this disease in the present day must be due in part to the insurance requirements of large publishers. Smaller companies, particularly those failing to exercise careful control over materials, are no doubt most at risk from new infections. With the resurgence of small press ventures in recent years we may yet see an equivalent resurgence of the Paper Pox.*

### Submitted by

DR. JOHN COULTHART, DIP. LO.D., OC. U.S., THE SAVOY INSTITUTE OF PATHOLOGICAL ARTS AND SCIENCES, MANCHESTER, ENGLAND

### Endnotes

(1) Robert Spridgeon, *Type, Torment and Torquemada*, Uppsala, 1954.
(2) Ibid.
(3) James Boswell, *Boswell's London Journal 1762–63*, Yale, 1950.
(4) H. Bustos Domecq, *A Muster of Monumental Mountebanks*, Buenos Aires, 1962.
(5) Enoch Soames, *Fungoids*, London, 1893.

### Cross References

Buscard's Murrain; Diseasemaker's Croup; Fungal Disenchantment; Menard's Disease; Rashid's Syndrome; Third Eye Infection; Tian Shan-Gobi Assimilation; Wuhan Flu

* *Editors' Note:* In fact, residue found on bound galleys in mid 2003—issued by such independent publishers as @tlas, Dedalus, Golden Gryphon, Ministry of Whimsy, Prime, Small Beer, and Subterranean—tested positive for traces of Papyroplasmapora infestans, suggesting a nascent resurgence. Books from Savoy, on the other hand, tested positive for many communicable diseases, but not for this particular strain of mold.

# RASHID'S SYNDROME

## Fictonecrosis (popularly "Bibliophagia")

## Country of Origin
Arabia (now Saudi Arabia)

## First Known Case
The earliest properly documented case dates from the tenth century, when Hashim al-Rashid, a merchant of Medina, returned from traveling the Silk Road to Urumqui and Kashkar in China. On his return home, al-Rashid displayed symptoms of early tertiary Fictonecrosis. He seized and consumed an antique Quran, a family heirloom whose parchment was said to have been made by the legendary Bilal himself; al-Rashid was discovered and prevented from eating a second treasure, an ancient manuscript of Aristotle's *Rhetoric*; the remains can be viewed in the Museum of Ancient History in Sydney. The tooth marks of Hashim al-Rashid can be clearly seen on the upper third of the manuscript.

The unfortunate Hashim al-Rashid disappeared mysteriously from his sickbed; left behind was a bound and illuminated copy of Aristotle's *Rhetoric*. The family insist that, in the final phases of his disease, al-Rashid had in fact become the book; however, scientific minds have learned to regard the unsubstantiated speculations of the unqualified as mere hysterical fabulation.

## Symptoms
Fictonecrosis progresses through three phases. The fictonecrotic initially presents relatively mild symptoms, most notably restlessness, irritability,

and a vague but growing sense of unease. It is in the secondary phase that distinctive symptoms develop: an urge to read that surpasses other motivations, including the sexual drive; a crabbed, stooped posture caused by marked forward curvature of the spine; and an impulse to smell and taste the leaves and bindings of books.

In the tertiary, and fatal, phase of Fictonecrosis, the infection breaks free of the central nervous system and invades the lymph, adrenal, and pineal glands. The fictonecrotic's body chemistry becomes imbalanced, and the body attempts to compensate by inducing an irresistible craving for paper and ink products: primarily printed books, but if books are not available, raw ink and unused reams of paper will be consumed. Failing that, the fictonecrotic will consume any material that could conceivably be substituted for ink and paper. Acrylic paints, textiles, wood or plastic veneer, food colorings, and opaque ceramics have all been the subject of fictonecrotic cravings. *In extremis*, the fictonecrotic may even consume the skin and blood of animal or human.

Under electron microscopy and chemical analysis, the red blood corpuscles were found to be contaminated with a compound more commonly found in squid or cuttlefish ink. The epidermis of the subject is progressively replaced with fibrous cellulose in laminar sheets, while veins and capillaries migrate between those sheets. In the tertiary (and terminal) phase, the displaced blood vessels develop clusters of microscopic lesions, which selectively release the contaminated hemoglobin between the leaves. It must be stressed that any similarity to printed text is purely coincidental; however, the credulous have attributed miraculous powers to the parchment-like leaves produced by a tertiary-phase fictonecrotic.

In rare cases, hair follicles and cuticles are overstimulated, producing a matted layer of keratin over the skin. Sebaceous glands, irritated by the poor ventilation beneath the keratin matting, compensate with a greatly increased production of sebum; however, combined with the elevated core temperature, increased perspiration and matted keratin preventing evaporation or mechanical removal, the bodily fluids combine into a viscous substance that binds laminar skin and keratinous matting. This occurs where bones come near the surface, most commonly along the spine.

### History

In fourteenth-century Constantinople, an epidemic of Fictonecrosis brought the condition to the attention of European medicine. It is unfortunate that the first documented European cases were outlined in John Trimble and Rebecca Manard's disgraceful and sensationalist *Trimble-Manard Omnibus of Insidious*

*Arctic Maladies*; although it is true that Arctic and Antarctic explorers did on occasion consume printed materials such as reference works, navigational almanacs, and expedition journals, this should be viewed as *in extremis* survival measures, rather than as genuine cases of the malady.

However, as John Trimble was the first Western practitioner to explicitly identify the condition, his diagnostic notes, although tragically flawed and suspiciously incomplete, have come into wide public circulation in periodicals that could politely be described as pornographic rubbish. It is for this reason that this entry eschews the term "Bibliophagia," which is irrevocably associated with the sensationalist gutter press.

## Cures

None known. A variety of treatments have been attempted with little success; most, such as those set out by Sarah Goodman in her disease journals, have focused upon psychotherapeutic techniques such as electroshock and primary aversion therapies. There is, however, a promising lead from the deployment of forensic techniques upon artifacts that have been rescued from the attentions of a fictonecrotic.

## Submitted by

DR. MICHAEL BARRY, INSTITUTE OF PSYCHIATRIC VENEREOLOGY, HUGHES, AUSTRALIAN CAPITAL TERRITORY

## Cross References

Bloodflower's Melancholia; Diseasemaker's Croup; Menard's Disease; Printer's Evil

# RAZORNAIL BONE ROT

## Bone Rot Bacterium (Novanguicula putrescossi)

### Country of Origin

United States; possibly Northern Monterey County, Northern California; in particular, the range of the Ohlone Indians. Anecdotal evidence suggests that the Wuhan Province in China might also be the origin of this bacterium.

### First Known Case

The first documented case of Razornail Bone Rot occurred at Watsonville General Hospital in Pajaro County, California, in June of 1993. Patient (and accused drug dealer) Andrew Cortane had lost nearly all bones in both hands by the time doctors had identified the disease bacterium. Because of his nearly boneless condition, he was difficult to handcuff and quarantine. Before his incarceration, in the early stages of his infection, he and his customers used his enlarged fingernails to consume heroin, cocaine, and other powdered drugs. These drugs did not kill the bacterium, which was present in the enlarged fingernails. In fact, it became stronger. When the bacterium began to leech the calcium from his arms, an artery collapsed and a bone chip traveled to the patient's brain, killing him instantly.

### Symptoms

The Razornail Bone Rot bacterium enters the bloodstream through scratches from the fingernails of infected persons. Alternatively, as noted above, it can enter the bloodstream with fingernail detritus taken into the nostril when drugs are inhaled from the fingernails of an infected person. The bacterium moves to the extremities, the fingers, and toes of the sufferer. There, it begins leeching the calcium from the bones of the fingers and the toes. The calcium is deposited in brittle, sharp layers under the nails, slowly replacing the natural fingernail. As the bones slowly dissolve, the muscles in the fingers and toes become enlarged and sinuous. In patients who carefully cultivate the disease, the fingers and toes can become transformed into supple, strong tentacles tipped with sharp, deadly claws, capable of infecting the next generation of victims.

As noted below, the supposed "cures" often result in more severe cases of the bone rot. In some cases, the bacterium begin to colonize facial structures like the nose and teeth. Many cases result in death, as skulls collapse and fangs form in the upper and lower jaws of the sufferers.

## History

While disease specialists did not verify the first case of Razornail Bone Rot in the United States until 1993, the disease appears to have affected dwellers in Northern California long before the colonization of America. The Ohlone Indians worshipped what were once believed to be icons based on the omnipresent Monterey Bay Squid. So-called experts thought that these figures showing humans with tentacles in place of fingers were exaggerated images, not depictions of reality. If the bacterium has a North American origin, these icons may in fact document the earliest reported cases.

*Doctor Buckhead Mudthumper's Encyclopedia of Forgotten Oriental Diseases* offers another possible point of origin. Mudthumper suggests that the bacterium was an opportunistic infection that took advantage of the long fingernails cultivated by Mandarin Magicians from the Wuhan province of China. The Mudthumper Hypothesis allows that Novanguicula putrescossi thrived in the protected structures of these magicians' fingernails, and in time developed a mechanism to ensure protection of their colonies. The magicians, whose fingers became sinuous and tentacular, were even more feared because of their deformity. In the 1860s, they came to Northern California with the rail workers, bringing Novanguicula putrescossi with them.

Hygiene and fashions that discouraged the growth of long fingernails kept the bacterium at bay until the 1980s, when long fingernails became popular among drug users. Custom drugs created a perfect growth medium for Novanguicula putrescossi. The Pajaro County infection was the first outbreak in the continental United States.

Those who survive become frightfully strong. Some have escaped into the foothills and forests of Northern California. Reports of infected squirrels, raccoons, and other forest creatures have not been verified as of this writing.

## Cures

According to Mudthumper, doctors in the Wuhan Province preferred to amputate the afflicted extremities. This cure usually resulted in the patient's death at the hands of other villagers; ironically enough, if a patient was not a practicing magician, he or she was thought to be possessed by evil spirits. Unfortunately, since the disease was blood-borne and the patients lived on after the amputations, the amputation had little effect other than to change the extremity from the fingers to the stump on the terminus of the wrist. Within three to five days, bony extrusions began to burst through bandages.

In the Pajaro County Outbreak, criminals, petty thieves, or drug addicts constituted most of the afflicted. Amputation was pursued with great vigor, with a veritable factory set up in the parking lot under tents.

Those who saw what they considered the righteous punishment of sinners celebrated each amputation, collecting and preserving the afflicted extremities in jars. This collection comprises one of the most popular exhibits in the Northern California Fungal and Parasitic Preserve.

## Submitted by

DR. FREDERICK JOHN KLEFFEL

## Cross References

Bone Leprosy; Diseasemaker's Croup; Extreme Exostosis

# REVERSE PINOCCHIO SYNDROME*

## *Rhinolalia Illuminata*

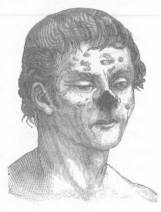

### Country of Origin
Italy

### First Known Case
Don Camillo Guareschi, La Spezia, 1978

### Symptoms
This illness affects only people whose profession or happiness depends on sustained and conscious mendacity: priests, politicians, parents of unspeakably ugly babies, etc. (1)

*Stage One:* One nostril dilates and expands alarmingly, while the other decreases in size to such an extent that it soon disappears completely, being replaced first by a modest indentation, then a more ambitious tunnel, and finally a supremely arrogant black void with an unpleasantly greenish glow around the edges, similar to the solar corona during a total eclipse. At this point, the other nostril becomes smaller again, while, at the same time, a constant stream of mucus passes from it into its companion, as if being sucked into it. Simultaneously, the owners of these noses undergo an amazing transformation: they cease to tell lies. They become, in fact, quite unable to do so. Even under controlled torture, when they are told that they only have to say that two and two

---

* *Editors' Note:* Dr. Lambshead himself has requested we "discredit" Dr. Redwood's disease. Although we asked for evidence, Dr. Lambshead could not provide any. He just said, "There is no way that anyone, living or dead, can *suck a black hole through their nostril*. It's insane. I won't stand for it. I just won't have it. And if that's not a good enough reason for you, then, as some of my American colleagues are fond of saying, you can blow it out your—."

is five for the torture to stop, they will scream out that two and two is four.

*Stage Two (the Ouroboros Gulp):* After about 30 days, the nostril that has been losing mucus disappears into its companion, and almost immediately the upper lip curls up into oblivion, followed by the four upper incisors. An ominous sucking sound is also heard from inside the skull, presumably the frontal lobe making its exit. At this point, the victim is finished.

## History

On June 27, 1978, halfway through a sermon, Don Camillo Guareschi, a much-respected Protestant priest in La Spezia, suddenly remarked that there was more truth and beauty in a choirgirl's budding breasts than in the whole of Holy Scripture. In hospital later (his wife was twice his size), he forcefully informed the nurse that he wished to "insert my woefully underused member into your deliciously rotund rump." In addition to this and other frank comments, it was observed that his nose had been undergoing a profound transformation, and that his left nostril in particular was shrinking at such a rate that within a few hours his cheeks were able to admire each other's glow for the first time ever.

The hospital's ear, nose, and throat specialist quickly related cause to effect. "Every time he tells the truth, his nose becomes shorter," he declared woodenly. It was, as it transpired, the other way round.

The first clue as to what was really happening, and why, was provided by the famed Welsh astronomer, Pulcheria Raskolnikov Dzhugashvili, who happened to be in hospital for a severe case of nystagmus caused by prolonged study of pulsars and Italian traffic accidents. She noticed that the void that had formerly been Don Camillo's left nostril was emitting vast quantities of X-rays. She asked about Don Camillo's personal hygiene, was sick, and then delivered her verdict.

It is a well-known fact that lies only breed more lies. A time comes in the life even of professional liars when more lies are bred than can be uttered without fear of exposure or ridicule. Denied egress through the mouth, these lies accumulate in the nasal mucus. Unless the nose is forcefully and ever more frequently blown, in time the mucus in one or other of the nostrils becomes so impacted and dense with the weight of trapped falsehood that, just as in the process of star formation, the nostril develops its own gravity. As the two nostrils constitute a binary system, like Cygnus X-1, the emission of X-rays by one of the nostrils (which in our analogy is like the secondary body in a binary star system) indicates the gravity is so powerful that it attracts and burns up the mucus from the other nostril. What we astronomers call the accretion disc, but might here be more accurately termed the *secretion* disc, is clearly visible. Once the mass of mucus in the lie-packed nostril has passed the Chandrasekhar limit, it becomes a black hole. All the monstrous lies that the victim wishes to tell remain forever trapped behind the event horizon, redshifted out of existence by the Schwarzchild radius. Since no falsehood can now escape, the patient can only tell the truth. (2)

Subsequent studies have shown that although the black hole has a very limited range (for reasons beyond the scope of this entry), there inevitably comes a time when it has devoured its nasal companion and continues on to those parts of the body nearest to it. *It is imperative, once the skull is gone, to launch the rest of the body into space.* Otherwise, the world might be left with a homeless maverick black hole, with unforeseeable consequences.

No one is certain why this disease should only have appeared in the last few decades: people have, after all, always lied. The generally accepted explanation is that increasing pollution has resulted in the production of more nasal mucus, resistant to the occasional delicate dab with a silk handkerchief of the average professional liar, and that the vastly increased temptation to lie that has accompanied the rise of the media, especially television, has bred and generated more falsehood than ever before. (3)

## Cures
Despite the vast amounts of money being poured into research by priests, politicians, and the more well-off parents of unspeakably ugly babies, no cure is yet in sight. Many people, in fact, hope that a cure will never be found, believing that in the interests of overall world health it is better to allow this extraordinary disease to spread unchecked.

## Submitted by
Dr. Steve Redwood, M.D.

## Endnotes
(1)  Dr. Sarah Goodman, "Increased Incidence of Nasal Collapse among Church Congregations and in Parliament," *The Lancet*, June 1999.
(2)  Pulcheria Raskolnikov Dzhugashvili, quoted for some quite inexplicable reason in *The Guide to Psychotropic Balkan Diseases*, edited by Geraldine Carter, M.D.
(3)  For a dissident view, see Dr. Yetan Other, *Aliens Bring Gift of Truth*, 1999.

## Cross Reference
Diseasemaker's Croup

# THIRD EYE INFECTION

### Known Vectors
Northern California Scalp Tick (Dermacentor capilis)
Shaman's Scruff Fungal Infection (Mycoleptria dermatadilis)

### Country of Origin
Northern Monterey County, California, United States. Outbreaks have also been verified in Florida, Mexico, Wales, and Germany. Reported but not verified in India, China, and along Greater Stentath Street in the Izuitin sector of São Paulo, Brazil.

### First Known Case
Boulder Creek, California, 1967. Don Elspeth, a mycologist specializing in hallucinogenic fungi, began to lose his hair in a typical case of male pattern baldness. He was pursuing the study of the species of fungi Mycoleptria dermatadilis mentioned in *The Guide to Psycho-tropic Balkan Diseases*. A fungal sample had been sent to his home for study by *The Guide*'s editor Geraldine Carter, M.D. Elspeth noted that the sample of Mycoleptria dermatadilis had a grayish-black color and texture indistinguishable from his own hair—at least on the carefully shaved rats he was using to cultivate the fungus. Therefore, he decided that it might be effective as a hair replacement. By the time Dr. Carter's reply to his query on the matter arrived from the Dludgizikstan Republic, it was too late.

In and of itself, the cultivation of Shaman's Scruff, as it came to be known in the following months, might not have been a problem. The trance-like states it induced resulted in the publication of many philosophical Master Theses in the mid-1970s. Numerous artworks were attributed to it, as well as the creation of the tiny genre of Meta-Infectional Fiction, literature intended to spread itself as an infectious mental illness.

However, sanitary conditions in Elspeth's Boulder Creek Lodging were not optimal. Elspeth also acquired an infestation of the Northern California Scalp Tick (Dermacentor capilis) in the winter of 1968. The two parasitic creatures established a symbiotic relationship. The transmission vector was established when a tick fed from the area infested with Mycoleptria dermatadilis, left Elspeth, and passed the infection on to another victim. In a fascinating case of symbiosis, Mycoleptria dermatadilis began to synthesize the skin-dissolving enzyme first secreted by the tick. The tick found the resulting infection an ideal place to lay its eggs.

**Symptoms**

In Third Eye Infection, the Northern California Scalp Tick (Dermacentor capilis) crawls to a feeding predilection site where it slits the skin with scalpel-like mouthparts (chelicerae), slips under the skin, and inserts a barbed proboscis (hypostome). The salivary glands secrete a cement-like substance. This substance, along with the proboscis, anchors the tick firmly in place. A wound develops that is similar to the small red raised welt caused by a mosquito bite. The fungal spores are injected as the tick feeds. They dissolve the skin, creating a large softened area in the forehead; bruising occurs under the ventral area of the scalp. The fungal mycelia grow in two to five days, and the gray-black tendrils mix with the hair of the patient. Recently researchers have identified a blond variant.

After the first day, the fungus begins secreting the powerful hallucinogen mequathalamine. The mycelia grow into the cranial cavity at a rate of three to seven millimeters per day in ambient temperatures of 55 to 78 degrees Fahrenheit. The festering area of fungal growth will reach a maximum diameter of 50 millimeters, surrounded by a pus-filled corona of two millimeters. In effect, the infection appears to be a large "third eye" in the center of the forehead. In some patients it will be beneath the hair; in some males it will appear as an "island" of hair in the center of the forehead.

The patient will experience some itching near the initial bite. Once the secretion of mequathalamine by the fungus begins, the patient will experience anomalous sensations of flashing lights and whirling physical motion. Once the mycelia reach the tertiaquontal regions of the brain, the patient will begin chanting, droning, and exhibit bouts of verbal anaghorrhea. The ability to speak in codes and ciphers is a key diagnostic indicator. Some victims produce a hallucinatory gas that emerges in sweet-smelling gusts from nasal passages.

## History

Elspeth's famous monogram on "Nasal Tones Resulting from Fungal Infections," published in the *Northwestern Journal of Mycological Imagination*, caught the attention of Randolph Johnson, then in the process of compiling a revised edition of *Confessions of a Disease Fiend*. Johnson, and his half-brother Randolph Carter, joined Elspeth in Boulder Creek for a memorable monthlong session of study during which it became increasingly difficult to discern the difference between self-induced and mycologically-based hallucinations. Certain recurring themes—visions of ancient fungi, sentient hive insects, and gynecologically-transmitted mental illness—tended to distinguish the hallucinations caused by Mycoleptria dermatadilis.

Before they left, Third Eye Infection had infiltrated Carter, Johnson, and their secretarial staff of seven female graduate students. The infection subsequently spread as the uncaring researchers fanned out across the nation, and eventually around the globe.

The trances, hallucinations, bouts of verbal anaghorrhea, and occasional fluids secreted from the infections went unnoticed in the environment of late 1960s Northern California until the disease had become established elsewhere. Often, even experts mistook these disease symptoms for purposeful behavior.

Some have tried cultivating the Mycoleptria dermatadilis fungus for its hallucinogenic properties, but the visions induced by the tick-borne variety are much more intense and useful to the patient. A GM modification of the fungus is currently in trials as a hair replacement therapy.

## Cures

No cures exist for Third Eye Infection because those afflicted with this disease are convinced that their lives are the better for it. While other residents may well know the cause, the visions speak for themselves, and allow the patient to serve a useful, shamanistic purpose in most communities. The disease spreads more quickly than it would otherwise because by the time its patients realize they are sick, they feel that the sickness itself is beneficial to their ability to merge as one with the psychic ecosystem of our infected world.

Extraction of the tick and the fungal infection from the affected tissue may result in trauma. In some patients, an "ice cream scoop" lobotomy has been performed with varying success. If carefully placed in a container of sugar-water, the resultant ball of infected tissue can maintain a healthy tick and fungal colony for up to three months. The inhaled spores from such a colony do not create the psychotropic effect of the infection itself, but were reputed to be making the rounds of Northern California parties in the late 1990s.

## Submitted by
Dr. FREDERICK JOHN KLEFFEL

## Cross References
Diseasemaker's Croup; Fungal Disenchantment

# TIAN SHAN-GOBI ASSIMILATION

## Countries of Origin
China, Mongolia, or Russia (?)

## First Known Case
Henry Graansvort, University of Rhode Island linguistics specialist

## History
Throughout July, August, and early September of 1995, a group of five linguists from the University of Rhode Island obtained rare permission to travel through isolated areas of Russia, Mongolia, and China to document and preserve several endangered regional dialects. After traveling by plane to the Krasnoyarsk Reserve in Russia and then to the lush area around Tian Shan in China, they returned to their temporary headquarters in Mongolia: a series of huts on the edge of a small village where the Gobi Desert meets the Hangayn Mountains. On the evening of September 12, 1995, Henry Graansvort, the leader of expedition, succumbed to the final stages of Tian Shan-Gobi Assimilation.

Until September 12, Graansvort's colleagues did not know he had contracted a disease, except for a certain irritability that they put down to the rash he had contracted somewhere between Tian Shan and their return to base camp.

At dusk, gathered around a fire, the five linguists, along with their guides, were caught unawares by Graansvort's approach in his final manifestation.

Because so much about Tian Shan-Gobi Assimilation remains unknown, it is germane to include herein an excerpt from the extraordinary journal of

Nicholas Singer, one of Graansvort's colleagues. (1) In this entry, one of his last, Singer describes the final hours of Graansvort's prolonged death.

> [Graansvort] had been missing for at least half the day. We first saw him again standing on a hill close to camp, staring down at us. We called out to him but he did not respond. After several minutes, he closed the distance between us with alarming speed. He did not move like a human being. He was clearly not human anymore. A light shone from his eyes, and it was green and everlasting. We could not escape it, even as our guides shot at him. We struck at him with the knives we had meant to use to cut the meat cooking in the pot on the fire. Bullets passed through him and were gone, so that in the flicker of a smile that still clung to his lips, I could see the grim humor of the old Graansvort still inside of him. Only then did I really identify him as my former friend and colleague.
>
> He darted and flitted from side to side, the sunlight seeming to leak through him, red and thick—no, it *did* leak through him. Wherever he stepped, golden swirls of spore-like dust rose to fade into glitter. While we grunted and cursed in our efforts—I cannot begin to describe the fear we felt; it transformed us—the thing that had been our colleague made no sound, seemed to exert no effort. But we continued to hack at him with our crude blades and, as the sun faded, so did he, so that once or twice now we caught him, only to see him smile as flesh sloughed off to no effect. He left no blood. He did not wince. He did not acknowledge our efforts in any way. Breathing heavily, my hands on my hips, I stepped back for a moment and watched them try to kill him.
>
> Graansvort was magnificent. I have never seen him more alive than as we systematically cornered him and murdered him. His arms, his legs, were in constant motion. He seemed more amused by our efforts than anything else. The pores of his skin were mushroom gray. His flesh was black and accordioned on the inside, like the underside of a mushroom cap. His clothes came off of his flesh but did not separate from that flesh. He was too alien for us to comprehend. We were all convinced that he would kill us if we did not kill him first.
>
> Finally, one of the guides caught Graansvort with a blow to the back of his left leg that cut out a huge wedge of flesh. It did not affect

Graansvort's balance, but he turned to face our onslaught with more and more difficulty. Although the expression on his face did not alter, he seemed suddenly sad.

It was I that snuck up behind him and finished the job, leaving Graansvort to hop on one leg as a purple fleshy ooze seeped from the remaining stump. I wanted him dead. I would have ripped his throat out with my teeth, so beautiful was he, so fey, so distant and so removed from who we were and what we were doing to him. Did he weep as we tore him to pieces? Did he make any human sound to stop us? No. All he could do is stare up at the stars as if they were but an extension of his eyes. His arms were pulled off and cut at and peeled away. His right leg was next. We hacked his torso into tiny pieces until he was only a head attached to a sorry wreckage of neck. And still he smiled. And still he lived. And still we wanted to kill him. We were screaming now. If we could not be freed from this condition that was driving us mad, then we would continue to kill him until he stayed dead. The smile went next, as Susan destroyed the lower half of his gray pouting face with a rock.

Then there were just the eyes—staring at us, telling us in our horror, in our panic, that our efforts meant nothing.

Graansvort did not give us the time to take his eyes. Instead, he blinked twice, appeared to concentrate—and what was left of him turned moon-white, and as the last light left us, and the desert wind picked up, and the place was suddenly cold again . . . his head seemed to turn to ash, and waft away on the breeze, in trickles and gasps, so that the impression of his face remained upon the ground for some time. By the morning, every trace of him had faded into nothing. Nothing at all. I swear to God, there was nothing left of him but some dust, some residue on our knives.

If not for the state of exhaustion we had slipped into, the grime and blood upon us, we would have thought it had been a nightmare.

A subsequent biopsy/autopsy on Nicholas Singer has led to two theories regarding Tian Shan-Gobi Assimilation. Dr. Nafir Rasghan has postulated in his paper "The Next Wave of Bio-chemical Weapons," that the Russians "have developed a fungal biological weapon as part of their war against the breakaway Chechyen Republic." (2) Other experts, such as Dr. Alan M. Clark (a man of admittedly dubious standing in the medical community), believe that the situation was created by a near-unique exposure to multiple types of fungi during a short time period. However, this theory is unlikely, given the presence of several fungi types not known to exist in Asia.

The history of fungal interaction with human life is a long and complex one, in which fungus has been as helpful as it has been harmful. However, prior to 1995, there are few hints in any medical accounts of a symbiosis in which multiple types of fungi coincided to produce a single effect. Certainly, the recent discovery that fungi are closer to animals than to plants suggests that we do not know enough about "the third kingdom" to rule out the existence of a hybrid strain capable of controlling a human body.

### Biopsy/Autopsy Results

Chinese Red Army medical experts, with permission from the local Mongolian government, quarantined the remaining members of the expedition, along with their guides. Tests on Singer soon uncovered that he had begun a transformation similar to Graansvort's. Before Singer's disintegration, Chinese doctors performed several biopsy/autopsies. I call them "biopsy/autopsies" because Singer was still alive during the exploration, in restraints, but his tissue was dead, or *changed* in its cellular structure.

The Singer results illuminate the progression of Gransvoort's own assimilation. (3) According to these results, Graansvort's ears might have been assimilated as early as mid-August, during the expedition's stay in Krasnoyarsk. A hybrid version of the mushroom Auricularia auricular-judae, which has a soft and elastic consistency, much like an ear, had replaced Singer's ears within a month of his quarantine. More importantly, the fungus had sent filaments deep into Singer's head. In an amazing display of mimicry, the fungus *replicated* much of the musculature and tiny bones that allow a human being to hear. Therefore, Graansvort probably could still hear at the time of the final assimilation. He could still hear throughout the time he accompanied his colleagues into China and back into Mongolia. The question, of course, which remains unanswered, is: *What* was he hearing? And *how* was he processing the information?

Further para- and post-mortem examination of Singer revealed that Graansvoort's "rash" must have consisted of a hybrid version of Pulcherricium caeruleum, a fungus that usually manifests as a thin crust over the bark of trees. In buildings, a similar fungus is often responsible for considerable damage to floorboards and walls. The fungus insinuates itself so deeply into the wood that in the final stages of colonization, the wood disintegrates. Singer's dermis, para-mortem, had been assimilated by this alternate version of Pulcherricium caeruleum, to the extent that his internal organs had formed unusual associations with the invader. There is also evidence that Singer's eyes had been assimilated; the medical team found residue of a Langermannia giganlea (or "puff ball") fungus. This would be consistent with the growing season for puff ball fungi—summer to autumn—although this type of fungi is rarely found in the Far East.

## Symptoms

Because victims of this disease do not believe that they have a disease, diagnosis is difficult. Based on Singer's journal, biopsy/autopsy results, and the physical evidence, we can conclude that a patient with this disease would show a sudden thickening and discoloration of the skin. The ears might or might not appear different than before; certainly an examination of the interior of the ear might not reveal anything questionable. The examining physician could not be faulted for such a mistake, given the apparent mimicry. The pupils of the eyes might appear greener than before. The moons of the fingernails might or might not begin to turn greenish in hue. There might or might not be a black stippling effect at the joints and on the bottoms of the feet. The assimilation appears to occur in such a way as to attempt to hide its appearance.

Before he died, Singer indicated in his journal that

> We might be able to determine—to tell—to understand—to interpret—to intuit—to grok—who has this condition—this disease—this malignancy—this blessing—this curse—this lesion—this communication—this antenna—this flesh through—between—underneath—over—into—linguistics—linguistic tricks—semiotics—semiotext—semantics—syntax—style—aural preachings—mantras—songs—speech—talking—light of reason—stunning reconnection of the senses—babylon—zamilon—green towers—false powers—moth—butterfly—river—cocoon—potential—fungus—gone—here—arrived . . .

and so on for another three pages. Clearly, toward the end, a writing sample from the patient might prove useful in reaching a correct diagnosis.

My own theories include the somewhat controversial suggestion that Singer and his companions were coerced by spore-enabled, wind-carried hallucinogens to kill Graansvort, as this might be the only way for the organism to replicate itself: by having others disassemble it after assimilation is complete.

Therefore, the acute fear, the paranoia, the bloodlust exhibited by Singer and his colleagues might have been induced by Graansvort itself. This supposition, however, is probably not useful in establishing a methodology for diagnosis.

## Cures

Early detection would appear to be the only cure, and yet early detection is seemingly impossible. Should an outbreak occur, it might be possible to quarantine those unaffected or to identify the beginning of symptoms. If, however, the assimilation continues to present in single cases, the outlook is dim.

The only real way to detect the disease is an invasive biopsy, culling tissue samples from the ears, the eyes, and the torso. However, if the disease's pathology, its controlling agent, includes calming the victim's own suspicions until assimilation is complete, then, again, any action taken would occur at too late a stage to be of any use.

Further investigation of Tian Shan-Gobi Assimilation has been complicated by the disappearance of all members of the expedition and their guides. Released by Chinese authorities after a year of quarantine, none of them reached their final destinations, vanishing, as they say, "without a trace." Despite official denials, the Chinese government's complicity cannot be ruled out.

## Submitted by

DR. JEFFREY S. VANDERMEER, M.D., PH.D., AND PRESIDENT OF THE NORTH AMERICAN CHAPTER OF THE MYCOLOGICAL EARLY ALERT ASSOCIATION

## Endnotes

(1) All excerpts from the as-yet unpublished first edition of *Doctor Buckhead Mudthumper's Encyclopedia of More Recent Oriental Diseases.*

(2) Jane's ChemBio Web, http://chembio.janes.com, posted September 12, 2002.

(3) Although the Chinese government has suppressed most of the documentation gathered by their medical experts, some sections of the reports have been obtained by Western journalists.

## Cross References

Diseasemaker's Croup; Fungal Disenchantment; Printer's Evil; Third Eye Infection

# TURBOT'S SYNDROME

## McGlumphy's Migratory Eruptions, Drifter's Lament, Pornstaller's Meanders

### Country of Origin

Spontaneous occurrences wherever refugees and the homeless are gathered

### First Known Case

Mythological references to this disease can be found in various sources, such as Homer's *Odyssey*, where one of Odysseus' companions is said to suffer from "nether parts emergent/from innocent joints . . ." and in the oral tradition of the Romany, the Irish Tinkers, the Bedouins, and other transient tribes. But the first scientifically documented cases hark only to the early twentieth century. During the great population upheavals associated with the First World War, a British military doctor named Peavy McGlumphy, assigned to the Middle East, discovered sufferers from the disease that came to bear his name in the Ottoman Empire, among Kurdish tribesmen displaced by violence. Later incidents in the United States among hoboes during the Depression were catalogued by Dr. Chick Pornstaller, hence the alternate appellation for the ailment. (See *Doctor Buckhead Mudthumper's Encyclopedia of Forgotten Oriental Diseases* for instances of Turbot's Syndrome possibly encountered by Marco Polo in his travels.)

### Symptoms

Turbot's Syndrome is unique among diseases in that the visible changes wrought in the sufferer are drastic, dramatic, and diverse, yet generally without life-threatening consequences. (This positive prognosis discounts the opprobrium and ostracism and physical beatings incurred by many victims from unfeeling fellow citizens.) In a few simple words, a patient infected with Turbot's Syndrome exhibits wandering features and organs. (The actual agent of infection has never been identified; psychosomatic origins related to stress are suspected, along with the possibility of unknown prions found on steam grates, in railroad cars, and in haylofts.) For instance, eyes might migrate to the back of the head, nose might drift to the chest, genitals shift to the armpits, toes climb to the forehead, heart occupy the abdomen, or anus swap with navel. These transformations generally occur over a longish period of time, allowing the sufferer to make relevant adjustments. The iconic similarity to the turbot and other flatfish, who wear their two eyes closely adjacent on the same side of their head, is obvious.

### History

Certainly the typical man, woman, or child under the baneful influence of Pornstaller's Meanders will experience varying levels of sympathy from unafflicted peers in direct ratio to the absurdity, scatology, or eroticism of his complaint. (*Vide* McGlumphy's Formula:

$$S = E/WOF(X) + C$$

Where:
S = Sympathy of Witness
E = Empathy of Witness
WOF = Wandering Organ or Feature
X = Risquéness of New Location
C = Consanguinity of Witness to Victim

McGlumphy's Master Chart assigns varying numerical values to WOF and X that have proven remarkably consistent across cultures and decades.) With invisible alterations, the sufferer can often lead a near-normal life, sometimes even finding his or her existence enhanced (see the case study involving *Lovelace, Linda*). But in most cases, the assault of Drifter's Lament renders the hapless human an object of derision and shame, interfering of course with possible resettlement and hence any hope of cure. (Many so-called agoraphobics are really fully housed but unrecovered Turbot's Syndrome victims.)

### Cures

Establishing the rootless victim in secure housing has sometimes prompted spontaneous remission; other times even years of residence in a solid community, including membership in various civic organizations, has not been enough to restore the sufferer to textbook norms. Oftentimes the victims are reluctant to seek medical help, out of embarrassment. Consequently, palliative measures, tests, and prosthetics are generally lacking: for instance, various diapers conforming to alternate portions of the human anatomy are not available off the shelf, but must be contrived on an *ad hoc* basis.

## Submitted by
DR. PAOLO G. DI FILIPPO

## Cross Reference
Diseasemaker's Croup

# TWENTIETH CENTURY CHRONOSHOCK

## Geographical Origin
Christendom

## Basic Symptoms
The mother and uncle of all rashes

## First Recorded Case
Maxim Arturovitch Pyatnitski, born January 1, 1900, inventor, adventurer, and dazzlingly vainglorious antihero (1)

## Symptoms
It is still unknown whether centuries other than the twentieth have their own Chronoshocks. The rash can be *slightly* alleviated by directing searchlight beams across it. That is true of many Twentieth Century Shocks. In a similar manner, Twentieth Century Ranks can be reduced by the beating of large gongs and the opening of windows.

The condition of being allergic to the twentieth century was always going to cure itself in time. I knew that, and so did you, but now it seems that certain members of our profession made matters worse for a minority of victims by meddling with artificial remedies. The truth has only been revealed with the dawn of this new century, the twenty-first, and the immediate recovery of all those who previously suffered the disadvantages of the chronic malady. Regarding these patients: because they no longer exist in the twentieth century, there is no longer anything in their environment to provoke an allergic reaction. They can (and have been) released from quarantine without any ill effects. And so the sealed castles, with their banqueting halls, lutes, jesters, and endless jousting contests (any one of which might prove as fatal as the Chronoshock) can finally be closed down and sold off to private bidders, raising funds for new equipment and nurses' uniforms.

However, there remains the problem of what to do with those unlucky individuals who allowed themselves to be experimented upon *prior* to the turn of the century. These pre-*fin de siècle* patients were promised wonder drugs and surgical miracles to reduce the number of years to which they were unduly sensitive. The very first procedures involved cutting out random decades from the memory by entering the brain and vandalizing it with electric tongs. This risky technique was only effective at removing the 1980s, which few people cared to remember anyway. Hallucinogenic drugs were also tried, in a bid to erase the 1960s in cases where this had not already happened. The problem was that sufferers who were born after that decade, and therefore had no personal experience of it, now no longer remembered that they had never been there. They assumed they no longer remembered it because they *had* been there, according to the uniquely peculiar ontological laws governing that decade. Thus, their awareness of the twentieth century was *extended* by a decade, rather than reduced, giving the allergy an even greater hold on their immune systems. By any yardstick, that looks bad on the recovery charts and graphs.

It was never going to be easy removing years from the twentieth century that had occurred before the birth of the patient. There were no memories to extract. With the failure of surgery and mescaline, it was decided to turn to philosophy. Doubts were raised in the minds of the sufferer as to the concrete reality of a non-experiential year. Berkeley and Hume were quoted at length. Reality is unreal, and all things, even your wife and shirt, are illusions. A man or woman born in 1935 might thus be persuaded that the years 1900 to 1934 were figments. This approach was rather powerful. The long and the short of it was that for most of these patients the years of the twentieth century to which they *were* allergic became fewer and fewer. Unfortunately, it is almost impossible to totally eradicate a malady. There will always be one unit that is immune to the remedy.

### Case Studies

Let us consider the frightful consequences of these treatments. We may take a single case. We shall call him Thobias G. Thobias volunteered himself for these experiments behind my back. He was unhappy in the castle. Surgery, hookah, metaphysics! The years to which he was allergic fell away rapidly. Soon, or at least after the bandages were unwrapped from his head, he was only allergic to a single year: 1957! Behind my back for a second time he was smuggled out of quarantine. Thobias G was able to live quietly in society, this despicably unjust society, like a normal subject, but with a crucial difference: any exposure, any at all, to the products, situations, or ideas of 1957 would bring him out in a monumental rash, a rash that was almost larger than his body. So, for instance, references to the death of Joseph McCarthy, the independence of the Malayan Federation, the launching of Sputnik I, the sacking of Marshal Zhukov from his post as Minister of Defense, the birth of Assumpta Serna, the expulsion of all Dutch nationals from Indonesia, the drawing of the first premium bond prize in the United Kingdom, the freeing of Archbishop Makarios, the sending of 1,000 Army paratroopers to Arkansas to escort nine black students into the Central High School in the town of Little Rock, the unveiling of the Jodrell Bank radio telescope, not to mention several trillion other things, would instantly propel the foolhardy and disobedient Thobias G into a cosmos of *rash*, for merely to state that he would "come out in one" is to fail at producing the right effect with words. Music from that year was even more damaging. Of *West Side Story*, its melodies and riffs, in conjunction with Thobias G, his face and torso, it is nicer not to speak. It might not seem so difficult to avoid the trappings of 1957, or any other single year of the previous century. On first appearance, this condition may appear preferable to being allergic to the entire century. However, consider more carefully and you will soon begin to appreciate the massive, grotesque irony. The untreated patients, those who remained allergic to the entire century, discovered that their ailment completely disappeared on the stroke of midnight on New Year's Eve 1999 (also ending the debate about the true beginning of the next millennium). Nothing in their environment was now part of the twentieth century, because the past only ever exists as memories, recorded or not, and the present is all we have. Therefore, they became totally free. However, by a convenient and vindictive twist of selective logic, the treated patients *remained* allergic to the details of their most stubborn years, whether that year was 1957, as in the case of Thobias G, or 1914, 1938, 1976, 1991, etc. There was an *annus horribilis* for every traitor who tried to shame my reputation. (2)

### [As For] Cures

I doubt it! Besides, I have found a neat use for the ungrateful unfortunates. I have gathered together a group of exactly 100 of them. They have been carefully selected. Each one is allergic to a different year from 1900 to 1999 (yes, I know that there was no "Year Zero"; go tell it to the Cambodians) so that the complete century is covered. One victim for every year. I drive them around the world in a large bus. I have changed careers. I now assist collectors and detectives with their hobbies and investigations. If an antiques dealer wants to know the real date of a piece of merchandise, to establish whether it is genuine or a fake, he summons me. If a forensic pathologist is unsure of how long a skeleton has been hanging in an abandoned closet, he rings my office without delay. I drive the bus to the relevant scene. The hundred men and women in my care are numbered. The date of their allergy has been branded on each forehead. I usher them in single-file past the ornament or cadaver. The one who comes out in a rash reveals the date! If there is no rash, then the merchandise or crime is very recent or quite old. I still accept payment. In the evenings, I torment my slaves, playing hopfrog with the leap years. They deserve it. I am not well.

## Submitted by
DR. RHYS HUGHES

## Endnotes
(1) For an account of Mr. Pyatnitski's amazingly satirical youth, please consult *Byzantium Endures* by Dr. M. Moorcock.
(2) In fact, the main reason for the difference between an allergy to a century and an allergy to a year is less contrived than that. A whole century has very few unique characteristics to define its parameters, other than simple dates. It is a vague item of chronology when it comes to keywords. Some people like to chant "war!" or "technology!" or "media!" or "the death of affect!" when asked to quickly summarize the twentieth century, but these qualities are applicable to *any* century. Yet a specific year, say 1929 or 1984, has concrete associations. It is less *diffuse* and thus more substantial in its definitions, and it is far easier to remain allergic to a substantial irritant than a diffuse one. Do you sneeze in a vacuum? Of course not! How about in a tornado made of pepper? I thought so! But let me record that my biggest disappointment is reserved for this paradox: if *none* of the patients had received a "cure," they would now all be cured.

## Cross References
Diseasemaker's Croup; Pathological Instrumentation Disorder; Post-Traumatic Placebosis

# VESTIGIAL ELONGATION
# OF THE CAUDAL VERTEBRAE

### First Known Case

The first cases to be clearly documented were those of Henri III of France
(1551 to 1589) and his brother, Francois, duke of Alençon and Anjou (1554 to
1584), both offspring of Henri II and his consort Catherine d' Medici.

### Symptoms

Patients are born with tails that unless surgically removed grow on average to
50 centimeters in length. If the tail is removed after the patient has already
learned to walk, his sense of physical balance will be permanently impaired
and most motor functions adversely affected. Inept removal of the tail can lead
to a number of iatrogenic results, including infection, scar tissue, the retention
of a cartilage stub rendering certain postures permanently uncomfortable, and
injury to the spinal column itself. In some cultural circumstances, serious
socio-psychological effects result as well, reflecting local beliefs as to the
preternatural or even supernatural implications for the patient's possession of
such an appendage.

### History

Until medical historian Louise Ducange properly researched the cases of the
Valois princes, it had long been assumed that they were both hermaphrodites,
sharing an abnormality that had been attributed first to Catherine d' Medici's
lack of femininity and later to the presumed degeneracy of the d' Medici line.
Dr. Ducange's study of the contemporary documents reveals, however, that the

princes were in fact born with tails rather than the genitalia of the intersexed. Scholars encountering assertions of this fact in historical sources had previously taken them as evidence of the extremity of the hyperbolic rhetoric of the religious hysteria of the day, particularly since a rumor that the princes had tails became especially widespread following the St. Bartholomew Day's Massacre (August 24, 1572). A Rouen physician, Jacques Duval, in his *Treatise on Hermaphrodites* (Paris, 1601), first made the claim that Henri III had in fact been a hermaphrodite. This contention, repeated as a fact in other texts, was by 1650 taken as a rational explanation for the "superstitious" story that the unpopular king had possessed a tail, and was applied by logical extension to his brother, Francois. In her prodigious research of the documents, Dr. Ducange fortunately discovered the obscure memoir of Angelique le Caustique, the accoucheuse who attended all of Catherine d' Medici's "confinements." This memoir describes in careful, graphic detail each of the queen's deliveries and notes that a surgeon, Eugene Eustaches, removed the tails within days of each birth.

For some time doctors did not know whether this rare disease was caused by a prehistoric primate gene lingering in the human organism or an error in embryo formation. Dr. Ducange's admirably tenacious work has turned up suggestive (though not clearly documented) evidence that Vestigial Elongation of the Caudal Vertebrae may have appeared repeatedly throughout the venerable history of the Valois line. Other rare cases have been reported in modern times by pediatricians, who often remove the appendage without ever having informed the child's parents that there was one. Given the recent over-bureaucratization of medicine, however, we can expect that all new cases will, in the United States at least, be well-publicized, in spite of the resulting social stigma, since typical HMO coverage does not include removal of such elongations.

## Cures

At present, surgical removal at birth is the only cure. The gene for Vestigial Elongation of the Caudal Vertebrae, presumed to be located on the Y chromosome, has not yet been identified, but when it has been, we may hope that genetic engineering will eliminate it entirely from the human gene pool.

## Submitted by
DR. L. TIMMEL DUCHAMP

## Cross Reference
Diseasemaker's Croup

# WIFE BLINDNESS

*Uxoria Oculitis*

## Country of Origin
France

## Symptoms
ONSET: Failure to observe significant dates (birthdays, anniversaries, Valentine's); breakfast myopia; sports-page gaze; TV transfixia; persistent inattention to spousal discourse.

MODERATE: Massive response failure (e.g., facial blackout, attire blankness, emotional coma, night stupors, indifference to marital aids).

SEVERE: Spousal nudity oblivion. (Only 11 complete cures of severe Uxoria Oculitis have been recorded in the scientific literature.)

## History
The earliest account of "Wife Blindness" is found in the medieval French burlesque (*chanson de jest*) "Song of l'Ardno," in which the hero, Ratatouille de l'Ardno, having been deprived in manly battle of both arms and a knee, becomes confined to a massive carved chair at the head of his dining table in a boar-hunter's cottage where he is fed by plump shepherdesses from a small shovel, still in use today in regions of Normandy and Wales, and familiarly known as the "lard spoon." Ratatouille's manhood is the subject of jocular barbs and virtuoso repartee from these buxom attendants due to his inability to distinguish their uncouth rotundities from (in Rolph's translation) "her him done knockèd up." It is not until the late Renaissance that meticulously

documented accounts of connubial sport within the court of the Louis Quatorze, the glorious Sunking, actually provide reliable data on the affliction's progress. There the folk malady "Roman Eye" runs rampant among the courtiers, all of whom profess perfect hindsight toward their past dalliances and a lively vision of the wives of others. In the nineteenth century an epidemic of Uxoria Oculitis in the United States and Great Britain is thought to account for the writings of numerous suffragettes and temperance militants, although certain epidemiologists, notably Dr. Sarah Goodman, consider this etiology to represent "unsound science." The medical community has reached no consensus on the lively question of whether domestic varieties of American male stupefaction are in any way related to the disease. The most widely discussed of these, Sunday Afternoon Football Zombyism, has been the subject of prolonged studies, but to date all results remain controversial. Researchers at the American Women's Health Coalition have claimed to observe a high correlation between Football Zombyism in early marriage and virulent outbreaks of "wife blindness" in midlife, but the Testosterone Task Force of the American Medical Association has disputed these findings. What seems beyond debate is that no other malady has given rise to so many stimulating case histories, and uplifting accounts of Uxoria Oculitis continue to embellish many of the world's weightiest medical tomes (cf. Rebecca Manard's immensely diverting "Uxoria Oculitis and the Etiology of Milton's 'Methought I Saw My Late Espousèd Saint': A Case of Miraculous Cure?" in *The Journals of Sarah Goodman, Disease Psychologist* (ch. MCCLXXXVII, p. 2394ff.).

## Cures

(1) FLIRTATION: Of all therapies, the oldest and most widely recommended. Although not consistently salutary, flirtation reassures imperfectly seen wives of their visibility and normally feels pleasant without hazardous side effects. To be efficacious, therapeutic flirtation should be generously applied directly beneath the sufferer's nose.

(2) THE BOOB JOB: A controversial remedy, widely abandoned by younger practitioners. Although this treatment has been known to produce immediate dramatic improvement, Dr. Sandra Russman of Sarah Lawrence University claims that such improvement is rarely of long duration and has been associated with side effects such as "Frankenstein Fixation," a severe antipathy to scar tissue in genital zones.

(3) TELEVISION REMOVAL: The American Medical Association has described this painful therapy as "uniformly efficacious."

(4) WIFE DEPRIVAL: About this surgical procedure, *Doctor Buckhead Mudthumper's*

*Encyclopedia of Forgotten Oriental Diseases* has the following to say: "Although Uxoria Oculitis (and its rarely mentioned cousin, Connubium Malauris or 'wife deafness') can be fatal, mild non-invasive procedures are always preferred. Radical wife deprival can be marriage threatening, with a high probability of side effects and great likelihood of contagion. Here the prudent physician will recall the first maxim of Hippocrates: 'Do no harm.'"

## Submitted by
THE R. M. BERRY FOUNDATION ON MARITAL TECHNOLOGY (B. R. RYMER, D.D.S.; MARION L. BREYER, PH.D; REMY B. LA PHER, OB-GYN; RALPH EMBRY, M.D.; BARRY MYER, B.S., AND RAMON YPHRIL BARRE, Æ DOCT., ÇÄRR. MED. P. XXX.)

## Cross Reference
Diseasemaker's Croup

# WORSLEY'S SUPPLEMENT
# WORSLEY'S SUPPLEMENT

## Region of Origin
## Region of Origin
Antarctic

## First Known Case
## First Known Case
Captain Frank Worsley and fellow explorers, 1914

## Symptoms
## Symptoms
Worsley's Supplement, the cause of which is unknown, causes disjunction between physical and mental perception. The sufferer becomes convinced that there is always one more of something available than he can actually count. Thus, if there are three hedgehogs on a desk, he believes that there must be one more, though he cannot physically perceive it. If he can momentarily convince himself, through an act of misguided will, that there are in fact four hedgehogs, then he will slowly become uneasy, eventually convincing himself that there is always one hedgehog still uncounted.

At its worst, Worsley's Supplement leads to a repeated and frantic enumeration of objects, the number of objects perceived rapidly escalating with no real relation to the number of objects actually there. Soon the sufferer believes himself to be, so to speak, waist-deep in hedgehogs. In more mild cases, the sufferer affects a truce with the uncertainty of the objective world around him, navigating his world with statements such as those often uttered by my cousin and fellow-sufferer Kiteley: "Hand me that hedgehog or hedgehogs, if there be in fact any hedgehogs at all." Treatments include

Kline's Depravation Technique and an attempt to neutralize the illness through Goeringer's Syndrome.

## History

History

First categorized wrongly in *The Trimble-Manard Omnibus of Insidious Arctic Maladies* as a subcategory of the general dementia popularly known as Ice Fever, Worsley's Supplement seems common in the Arctic and Antarctic regions, and in other places in which luminosity, expansiveness, and blankness of surface combine. There has been some speculation that Worsley's Supplement is parasitic in nature, but that the parasite remains dormant until environmental conditions activate it. Once activated, however, the parasite remains active. There is some sense that the illness is contagious.

As captain during Ernest Shackleton's 1914 Antarctic Expedition, Worsley found himself exposed to extreme conditions. Tracking across frozen wastes both he and several of his men, as Shackleton himself recorded, began to feel there was *always one more member of their party than could actually be counted.* Worsley, armed only with Shackleton's incomplete and inaccurate *Trimble-Manard Omnibus* believed himself to be suffering from Ice Fever and expected the illness to be transitory, but upon returning to England found the illness to persist. In his London apartment, objects seemed to accumulate around him. When he took his hat off the rack, he had the distinct feeling that there was another hat on the rack waiting to be taken off as well, though he could not physically perceive it. Without the task of surviving in the Antarctic waste available to distract him, he became increasingly distraught, eventually reaching the point where he believed there was always one more of himself in the room than he could count. He had the sense that he was proliferating, always one more of him about to arrive. Eventually he was found dead in his library, surrounded by multiple suicide notes, bullets riddling the walls as if he had had to shoot 20 or 30 pseudo-visible manifestations of himself.

## Cures

Cures

Patients have found that if they keep their eyes bandaged and lie on a flat neutral surface, the symptoms, though still present, are manageable. Two more ambitious cures have been attempted with limited success. Kline's Depravation Technique consists of placing the patient in a white room devoid of objects, with neutral surfaces. Despite results at times not unlike eye bandaging, the technique is limited by the fact that deprived of other objects, the individual tends to take itself as its own object, and to believe there is more of themselves than they can count. In the worst cases, such as that of Rudd Theurer, they come to believe that the room is packed too tightly with manifestations of themselves and die seemingly of suffocation.

Goeringer's Syndrome, induced by darkness and confined spaces combined with an allergic reaction to the spores of Goeringer's cèpe, causes the perception that there is always less of something than one can see with one's eyes. Even in a room packed with hedgehogs, no hedgehogs are seen. Initial attempts at contracting it as a cure, however, have led the patients to believe that there is simultaneously more and less of something than can be perceived, causing a mental decay much more rapid than either disease individually. Swaddled in our furs, we continue our research on Worsley's Supplement with our cousins Kiteley, the wind shrieking outside our hut, but as of yet no major breakthrough has been made.

## Submitted by

Dr. Brian Evenson, et al

## Cross Reference

Diseasemaker's Croup; Diseasemaker's Croup

# THE WUHAN FLU

## *Wangji-Cunzai* or *"Forgetfulness-of-Being"*

### Country of Origin
China

### First Known Case
Twelve members of the farming commune Xiaping. When the authorities arrived at the commune, they found only the blind knife-sharpener Lesang Gao. Gao was seated on a three-legged stool, his left hand clutching a whetstone, his right hand a knife that had been sharpened to such an edge that it could cut a single dropped hair. As he worked, he called the names of each commune member in turn but received no answer. Lesang Gao was initially held for suspected murder, but subsequent events proved this charge unfounded.

### Symptoms
"The areas of his body not covered by clothing—his hands, his face, even his hair—began to glow. His skin had the brightness of reflected moonlight, a brightness that increased until it seemed like mountain snow beneath the noonday sun. Then his body was snow: glittering particles that were picked up by the breeze and blown about the yard, shining brightly before disappearing altogether. Han's clothing and the report he was reading fell to the ground. I noted their position but did not touch them."—Li Tsu, member of the emergency medical team, bearing eyewitness to the dissolution of team member Han Chen.

## History

The mystery surrounding the disappearances at Xiaping remained unsolved for almost 10 years. Xiaping was cordoned off and signs posted that warned of a "highly virulent bacterium or virus of unspecified origin." In 1968, Dr. Junji Chen of the Beijing Medical School led a sampling mission to Xiaping. He lost two members of his team but, in doing so, identified the commune's 1959 agricultural report as the causative agent, in particular a portion of the text occurring between pages 182 and 184.

Dr. Chen published his findings in 1969 and introduced what has come to be known as the Chen Hypothesis. Briefly, many repetitive tasks within living systems are maintained by unconscious action (i.e., the autonomic system), breathing and the beating of the heart being two examples. Dr. Chen proposed that continued coherence of the body is also maintained by an autonomic system. The events at Xiaping could be explained by a sequence of words being capable of "short-circuiting" this autonomic system, thereby leading to entropic disordering of the body's atoms. The energy released during this process would explain the brightness that witnesses had reported. For obvious reasons, the specific sequence of words that acts as the causative agent cannot be identified.

Dr. Chen thought that the disease might be confined to Mandarin Chinese. However, recent disappearances in Turkey and the United States bear disturbing similarities to those that occurred in the farming commune of Xiaping. It thus appears that word sequences capable of infection may spontaneously arise in any language. Alternatively, the original Chinese sequence may have mutated into a form compatible with these other languages.

## Cures

Due to a lack of experimental subjects, research has focused on prevention rather than cure. It is clear that literacy, involving both perception and comprehension of the written word, is a prerequisite to infection. No one has been infected in conversation or by audio transmission over radio or television. Extremists have called for a general ban on the written word. A more prudent course would suggest avoidance of those works known or suspected to be tainted. These include: *The Xiaping Annual Agricultural Report for the year 1959* (1); William S. Burrough's novel *The Ticket that Exploded* (Turkish translation); any works originating from the Old Algonquin Bookstore in Denver; and *The Thackery T. Lambshead Pocket Guide to Eccentric and Discredited Diseases*.

## Submitted by

Dr. G. Eric Schaller

## Endnote

(1) The buildings at Xiaping and their contents were burned to the ground in 1970 specifically to prevent further infection. However, copies of the 1959 Annual Report are rumored to still exist, presumably unread, in the government offices at Beijing.

## Cross References

Buscard's Murrain; Diseasemaker's Croup; Fuseli's Disease; Hsing's Spontaneous Self-Flaying Sarcoma; Printer's Evil

# ZSCHOKKE'S CHANCRES

*Phumaphoneis Zschokki*

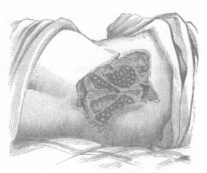

### Country of Origin
Russia (Crimea region)

### First Known Case
Yevgeny Flocon, Crimean farmer, diagnosed November 10, 1897

### Symptoms
Rapidly developing tissue cavity of up to four inches across and approximately half an inch in depth, with internal growths, found almost invariably on the extremities. Cases of multiple chancres are rare; no associated pain or infection. While the precise nature of the disease remains poorly understood, it is generally thought to be a variety of Planter's wart.

### History
First identified by Dr. Achim Zschokke, while pursuing unrelated research in heredity among people living in isolated or so-called "backwater" areas. According to his running account, Dr. Zschokke noticed a "large, unusual lesion" on the upper arm of a farmer belonging to the village of Trenk. This was Yevgeny Flocon, described as a "basically fit" man of around 40 years of age; he exhibited no signs of fever or discomfort, but presented

> an open sore the size of a badge or belt buckle. The skin is bunched up around the irregular oval in a ridge of considerable firmness; inside

the sore, whose walls are smooth, like new skin, are many little fingerlike growths, the color of ripe wheat, crowded together. I found them insensitive, or nearly so, to the touch, dry, a little warmer than the surrounding skin, and slightly flexible; approximately half an inch long, the tips barely protrude from the cavity. I asked if I might try to remove one of these, and the man indicated that he had repeatedly withdrawn growths and related matter, only to have them grow back. While unwholesome to look at, and possibly contagious, the subject complained only of a persistent itch, though mild. No idea as to pathogen. I pulled out one of the growths with tweezers; it separated from the flesh with a crisp, brittle sound, slightly fibrous, and trailing a single hair-like thread about three inches in length from its hexagonal base. There was no bleeding, only a slight discharge of milky fluid with a non-putrescent odor, not unlike freshly-butchered meat, and the patient sighed deeply.

Under the microscope, Dr. Zschokke found the extracted specimen to be "a hollow crystalline crust-formation, containing a densely coiled mass of threads."

Zschokke's chancres are thought to be extremely common in the Black Sea region, but little more is known about their pathology. They are non-fatal, and apparently non-contagious. In some cases, small pockets of gas will develop in the lining of the cavity; when the thin membranes connecting the growths are ruptured, the escaping gas usually will produce a low-frequency tone not unlike a flute played at its lower register; hence the chancres are also colloquially known as "singing sores" or "flute sores."

The most famous individual to contract the disease was Crimean poet and sculptor Egor Pluskat (1919–1977), born and raised in rural Wogau. A correspondent and admirer of Octavio Paz, Pluskat's 1961 poem "Antinomies" contains this relevant passage:

> This Crimean sore,
> > sings, when it is wounded.
> I tear it, it weeps a white tear,
> > and cries—a low, long, single sob.
> It gives me a tender feeling,
> > and I sigh,
> > > as though I had just made love.

## Cures

No known cures—possibly cauterization.

**Submitted by**
Dr. Michael T. Cisco, C.C., B.P.O.E., S.V.S.E.

**Cross References**
Buboparazygosia; Diseasemaker's Croup; Internalized Tattooing Disease

*Stiff 3 by Dawn Andrews*

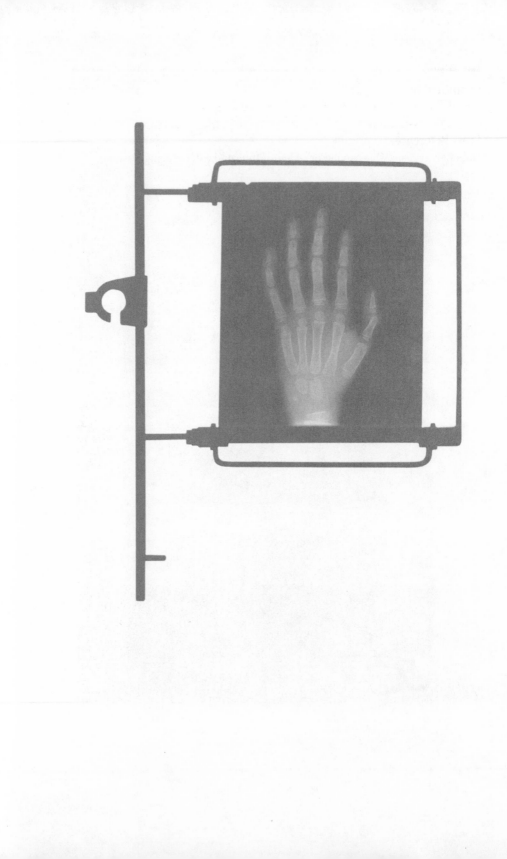

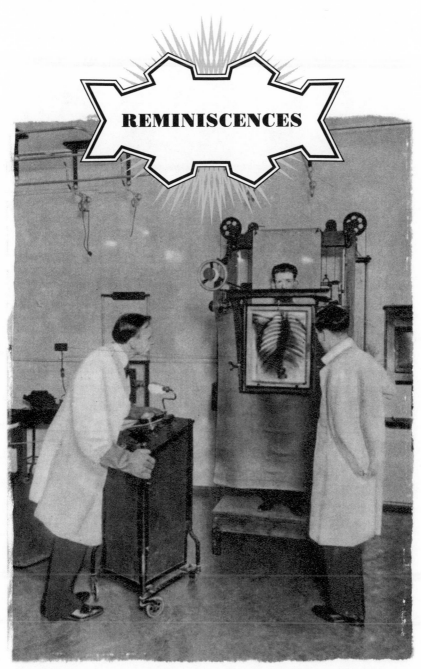

# REMINISCENCES

*Dr Lambshead (right) conducts an X-ray scan at Combustipol General Hospital, 1943.*

COMBUSTIPOL HOSPITAL

Una finestra nel Castello Maniaci

Siracusa

*Over the years, Dr. Lambshead has touched countless people. He has also touched people's lives. Although many of his adventures wait to be enjoyed by future generations when the secret documents of several dozen world governments have been declassified, some of his work with other doctors is chronicled below. These "reminiscences" as we have called them reveal the depth and breadth of Thwack's remarkable career. Any charges stemming from alleged illegalities described below have already been settled out of court by the publishers. Please do not bother filing further lawsuits.*—THE EDITORS

## 1923: DR. MICHAEL CISCO

I first met Dr. Lambshead in 1916, in Berlin. I was preparing myself for my first year of medical school by studying privately with Dr. Brosius, and Thackery had made a brief trip from England to treat my cousin, and good friend, the poet Simon Rheiner, for his addiction to morphine. Even at the tender age of 16, Thackery was a powerhouse of medical knowledge.

The night of May 15, I, Thackery, and Felixmüller were visiting Simon in his apartment, when he rose to recite to us his new poem, "An Exodus," and flung himself ecstatically through the open window, a syringe still held lightly between his fingers like a pen. He recited the single stanza as he fell (I later wrote it down from memory—it can be found in his collection entitled *The Clitoris of the Zodiac*). Thackery and I were both disconsolate, and our mutual mourning I suppose cemented our friendship.

When I completed my residency, I became a peripatetic doctor in my own right, due chiefly to Thackery's influence. Our paths crossed at least once a year for the next decade or so, often in places where such chance meetings were highly unlikely. For the most part, when we met, we would arrange to call on each other, but as Thackery never liked discussing medicine socially we were left with little to talk about. He labored in vain to interest me in cricket scores, and, when I felt I had the energy, I would try to engage his interest in Asian art, with comparably nugatory results. However, on one occasion, in the autumn of 1923, we happened across each other in Kraków—simply knocked shoulders in the street—and, with little evidence of surprise, he told me that he was rushing out to Kazimierz (the Jewish ghetto of Kraków) on an urgent call to an old friend. He asked if I would accompany him, and I said I would.

This is the first time I have ever ventured to tell this story, and I do so now only because I have every expectation of my own death; my anti-typhoid is in its tertiary stage, and I am confined to the vaulted stone sewer beneath the Hôtel du Tond in Paris, the unwholesome air of which alone I can breathe comfortably. That night, Thackery and I penetrated the wilderness of ghetto streets, which seemed to me piled high with mounds of massive, broken furniture; a door swam into view in a dingy plaster wall as smooth as a woman's thigh, and we were admitted somehow. Even then, I had considerable experience with house calls, and I intuited the gross outlines of the circumstances right away, as I am certain Thackery did; the girl before us, whose moon face was deeply scored by alien marks of anxiety, raw and fresh, was plainly the middle sister. The elder sister would be the sick one, and the parents were, for some reason, unable or unwilling to tend her. The girl conducted us back into the warrens of the house; we passed the moonlit kitchen, where I saw what must have been the father sitting at the table, his head resting on the back of his hand, and his hand resting on the table.

The girl opened the door at the head of the stairs and stood aside, looking at us. When the door had closed behind us, I saw, by the light of the moon, a white room, pale and dim. On the bed, a pregnant woman lay, whose long regular breath we could hear, and whose sunken eyes and vacant, rigid smile were like smudges of powder on her pale face, and whose nerves hung in the air, rippling like sea kelp in a weak current. They were like elastic, white branches, which emerged from beneath the one filmy blanket and diverged and split until they dwindled to fine white filaments. Thackery advanced to the bedside with his instruments, and I could hear him speaking, with effort, words intended to comfort her. He asked me to pour her a glass of water from the white ewer on the table, and as I walked forward to get it, one of her nerves brushed my face with a contact like a tiny, cold star. Now I was another character altogether, but my memory had no information for me. The trees were fantastically old, and vast, and black; they grew along what I suppose was the "bottom" of a blood vessel—I never knew which one—as though it were a dry riverbed. I had to make my way in a particular direction through the trees against the current of the blood, which was like a hot, red wind. The black branches of the trees rose and fell dreamily in the blast, and I walked for a long time. Eventually, I found a street and followed it. I found the house, and opened the door. I went inside, and down the hall. As I passed the kitchen door, I knew the old man would be there at the table to my left, but I knew, as everything I knew then I knew right away as if it were being told to me, that if I looked at him I would see him in the wrong way, and I would be too frightened by that to go on. I opened the door at the head of the stairs, and saw the woman who lay in the bed, her serrated lips still furled in a crisp, mummy's smile, gazing up at a white figure that stood erect at the foot of her bed, caressed by her long nerves.

After a long time, I was told again who I was and where I had been taken. Thackery had cut me free—my nerves had been, I was informed, caressing hers, and knitting with hers in the air—and dragged me downstairs. Subsequently I was conveyed, without my knowledge, to a private clinic, where I recovered completely. Thackery wrote to me some time later; the young woman had died shortly before we had entered the room.

## 1948: DR. JEFFREY THOMAS

I first met Thackery Lambshead in the fall of 1946, when he lectured at Holy Cross in Worcester, Massachusetts, on the effects of radiation he had observed firsthand at Hiroshima and Nagasaki. I had graduated the year before, but was anxious to attend so as to see this legend in the flesh. Even then, Thackery cut an impressive and patrician figure, thickset but not portly—his eyes seeming to convey a melancholy wisdom, nose somewhat pugnacious (as it had been broken once by a pugilistic pygmy enraged at the unexpected pain of inoculation), ears flared, mouth solemn but not dour. Being youthfully brazen enough to introduce myself after the lecture, I showed him an article I had written for the college's medical journal on the odd prevalence of children of unrelated families born with a supernumerary eye in my hometown of Eastborough. He was impressed enough with the article and my esoteric interests to begin an active correspondence with me, and soon after I counted myself very privileged to share in several of his travels abroad (unfortunately discontinued as I began my career as a surgeon at Eastborough Hospital).

I believe it was during our expedition to Ecuador in 1948 that Thackery earned his affectionate nickname of "Thwack" for his robust machete-wielding while tracking down the Jivaro Indians in the shadows of the Andes. We teased Thackery that he should remember not to wield his scalpel with such vigor once he returned home.

Thackery and I were keen on examining the methods the Jivaro employed in the creation of the *tsanta*, or shrunken head. In addition, rumors had wound their way to us, hinting that an offshoot tribe of the Jivaros was practicing some very startling feats of medicine and even of surgery, making much use of the local flora. This obscure tribe was apparently much shunned, even by the fearsome Jivaro (who once massacred a mining settlement of 20,000 Spaniards).

With the aid of our guides, who had done some trading with the Jivaro previously, we were able to enter into one of their villages and were shown various examples of *tsanta*. They described the process of head shrinking to us in depth, though we did not see any actually created. The Jivaro believe in three souls: the *nekas*, or "ordinary soul"; the *arutam*, or "acquired soul," which is introduced into the body via hallucinogenic-inspired spiritual visions; and the *miusak*, or "avenging soul," which is created when an individual in possession of an *arutam* soul is murdered and it must be bottled up safely inside a shrunken head. It is the belief of the Jivaros that a person with an *arutam* soul cannot die. I had cause to recall this bit of folklore later in the expedition.

I will not detail the methods by which the Jivaro shrink the heads of their enemies, as this knowledge has since been widely recorded elsewhere. But Thwack and I were soon venturing deeper into the rain forest in search of the shadowy offshoot tribe the Jivaro called the Kakaram, which our guides advised us translated as "the Powerful Ones," or "the Killers."

I will say straight off that we never did meet the Kakaram, except for two brief and regrettable exchanges. During the first, one of our guides was killed with a poisoned dart from a blowgun, and one of our porters beheaded by an unseen assailant, before we drove off the attackers with rifle fire. The head of the porter was not recovered—at that time. Fortunately, the Kakaram are feared more for their reputation than for their numbers.

While the bodies of the slain were carried back by those porters who did not wish to continue, the remaining five of us pushed ahead the following day and came upon the first specimens of a remarkable plant that not even our guide had encountered before. It consisted of a short, wooden trunk or caudex, surmounted by never more or less than eight broad, waxy leaves. The tallest of these stunted trees came only to my shoulder, though the trunks of the larger ones could become quite thick and bulbous. We began to encounter these larger specimens at the same time that we began to find the human heads affixed to their scaly bark.

Though these heads were not shrunken, we could not help but assume the practice of sewing their necks onto the bark of these mysterious plants must be a mutation of the *tsanta*-making practice. On one plant alone we counted a dozen heads in various states of decay, several of them little more than skulls in a thin sheath of skin. We had no idea how long they had been attached to the plant's hide.

Thwack made use of his machete to sever one of these trophies from its base, and thus came upon a gruesome discovery. Thick filaments or tendrils had grown out of the bark where a hole had been bored or drilled, prior to the neck being sewn over it. These tendrils had then grown up into the severed head itself. They proved tough to cut through, and leaked a milky sap. We had hoped to bring home samples of the sap and photographs of the trees, but we were soon set upon by the unseen Kakaram again, this time losing another porter. For several minutes, the fighting grew quite desperately frenzied, and Thackery and I were briefly separated from our fellows.

As we crouched down behind one barrel-like plant for cover, bullets and darts whizzing over our heads, we both thought we heard a low murmur and exchanged looks. When the soft groan was repeated, we looked instead to the still-fresh head of the porter who had been murdered the previous night, attached to the very tree we took shelter behind. We saw that its eyes were open, and in fact moving, though they did not seem to focus on either of us, instead rolling as if drugged in their sockets. But the poor devil's jaw began to work, and a flat, monotonous voice issued through his lips (though in its deep, muffled tones it seemed to have its origins within the very trunk of the tree that somehow sustained him).

A mad, jumbled ranting issued forth. Thackery and I were too terrified to think of scribbling any of it down at first, though at last Thwack fumbled out his pad and got a scrap of it down: ". . . war with Korea 1950 war with Vietnam 1965 Marilyn must die like a suicide two bullets will be one magic bullet Sean and Madonna will divorce Orenthal is the ripper . . ."

It was only much later, of course, that Thackery and I felt the full impact of these words. Through our continued correspondence over the years, we matched up the events that the porter had foretold. We realized that the Kakaram affixed the heads of their enemies to these extraordinary plants so that they might use them as oracles. We also suspected that the sap within the tendrils delivered a powerful hallucinogen to the brains, a hallucinogen whose life-sustaining properties kept the disembodied heads alive for an unknown period of time.

The intensity of the fighting forced us to flee, and we could not convince our guides to bring us back to that place. In addition, by the next morning both Thackery and I were gravely ill; we suspected it was due to our close exposure to the mysterious plants, as we both suffered high fever and the most nightmarish delirium. Sometime later I read that there was a terrible fire in that region, though whether it occurred naturally or through the intervention of neighboring tribes, we do not know. Thackery and I were severely disappointed, as we had been hoping to organize a second full-scale expedition in search of the elusive Kakaram and perhaps even more elusive stunted trees. We may never know what medical miracles might have resulted from their study.

When Thackery published his report of our discovery, he came under attack from the usual crop of half-envious, half-intimidated detractors for a number of reasons: the death of the three porters, what was considered a "brusque, ill-prepared and impulsive" approach toward his ends, his inability to back up his claims with anything more than my own words, and a local disruption so violent that it may have inspired the Jivaro toward the genocide of an endangered tribe. But I resoundingly defend his actions, not just for having been a partner in them. Should we not explore, not discover, leave the leaves unparted, as it were? Thackery had no way of knowing that the Jivaro might act against the Kakaram, or that the Kakaram would murder porters who had survived previous encounters with the Jivaro. As for our not having physical evidence to support our claims . . . that omission continues to haunt both Thackery and me more than it does his most vocal of critics, I am certain.

## 1961: Dr. Xue-Chu Wang (as related to Dr. Eric Schaller)

This story comes from my parents as well as from me, and is more theirs than mine. My parents were born, raised, and married in Da Wang Cun, a name of little consequence in China because there are dozens of villages with that name and this one may no longer even exist. My mother was three months pregnant with me when my future grandmother succumbed to the Clear Rice Sickness. As a result, my father lost all faith in Chinese medicine. He feared for the health of his unborn child and, in 1957, using the family's hidden savings for bribes and boat fare, my parents immigrated to the United States and took a small apartment in San Francisco.

All was well for a while. My father worked at a newsstand during the day and unloaded fish at the docks in the evening. My mother stayed home with me the first year after I was born, but then took a kitchen job at a nearby restaurant, leaving me in the care of an elderly neighbor during the day. My parents would both come home at night smelling of fish but excited about their prospects. One of my first memories is of my father acting the puppeteer with a fish he brought home from work. He supported the fish by use of two chopsticks thrust into its gills and manipulated the chopsticks so that the glistening silver form danced before my eyes. "When you get older my dear Niu Niu," he made the fish prophesize to me, "you will be rich, rich, rich." Both of my parents believed that such dreams could be made true by hard work.

But something went wrong when I was four years old. My parents came home to find the neighbor lady wringing her hands.

"It is not my fault," she said. "At first I thought it was just a rash. Many children get rashes. Then I saw that she had a fever. But this fever was so slight, you would have to be very sensitive just to detect it. So I put her to bed. The blisters only began an hour ago. Two hours ago at most. Perhaps she will be better in the morning." The lady ran across the hallway and bolted her door.

My parents did not have money to pay for a regular doctor, but another neighbor gave them the number of a clinic that had helped him in the removal of a superfluous toe. My father called from a pay phone in the street. A voice on the other end identified himself as Lambshead and said he would be right over.

Indeed, in less than ten minutes, barely time for my father to make it back up the stairs and into the apartment, there was a knock at the door.

My father opened the door.

A man stood in front of him, partially bent over and panting heavily, one arm braced against the wall for support. He was overweight and wore a sweat-stained khaki shirt and pants. These might have fit once but were now too small. He straightened, wiping the perspiration from his forehead. He then wiped the hand on his pants and extended it toward my father.

"Dr. Lambshead," he said.

Dr. Lambshead had a full white beard and spoke around the stem of a pipe that, it soon became apparent, was not lit.

They shook hands and my father escorted Dr. Lambshead to the rear of the room where my mother sat beside my bed. She dabbed at my forehead with a moistened towel, but set the towel and basin of water aside to greet Dr. Lambshead.

"Let's see the wee one," he said. He found a pair of glasses in his shirt pocket and twisted them into place about his ears. Viewed through the lenses, his eyes appeared twice their normal size, like those of an owl.

He took a seat beside the bed and leaned forward to examine the fever blisters on my face; he did not touch them. He then poked at the larger blisters upon my neck, arms, and chest with the eraser-end of a pencil. The blisters dimpled from the pressure, then reverted to their original dimensions when he removed the pencil.

He extracted a small flashlight from a pants pocket, held it about an inch from one of the largest blisters and stared for a full minute at the pink-lit interior.

He chewed vigorously upon his pipe stem.

"You did right to call me," he said. "Buboparazygosia is not common in these parts and I doubt that a local doctor would recognize the symptoms, particularly at this early stage. Lucky that you called me when you did."

"Now," he continued, "I don't want to alarm you but the traditional treatment, if one can call it such, requires purging with fire."

My parents started. Their command of English at this point was sufficient to indicate that they should be alarmed.

"You cannot hurt our girl," my mother said. My father moved closer to her and me.

Dr. Lambshead held his hands up apologetically. "Not to worry," he said. "Please. My researches among the Ojibwe indicate that in many cases tobacco can substitute for fire." He pulled the pipe from his mouth. "Something I just happen to have upon my person at all times. Do you have a small cooking pot, a saucepan perhaps?" He gave my mother a helpful nod in the direction of the kitchen.

He tapped the contents from his pipe into the pot my mother brought, then handed the pot back to my mother. "Now, add two cups of water and heat this just to boiling on the stove. Be careful not to overheat it." My mother did as requested and Dr. Lambshead applied this mixture to each of the blisters, administering it from a cloth briefly wafted in the air to cool the mixture.

He had almost finished this application when there was a sudden and emphatic rapping upon the door to our apartment.

My parents were surprised, but Dr. Lambshead less so.

He carefully set the pot of tobacco-infused water on the floor, leaving the rag draped over the handle. "Do you have a back door or a fire escape?" he asked. "There are some in the medical profession who do not wish me well."

My father moved to the rear of the room and levered the window open partway with his forearm.

"They believe we are undercutting their prices. Taking away potential patients." Dr. Lambshead squeezed through the opening onto the rickety wooden structure that served as the fire escape. "They are right, of course. But that is rather beside the point."

Then he disappeared from sight. The ladder clattered a few times against the building to indicate his downward progress. The last words any of us heard him say were: "Apply twice a day for the next three days."

The rapping at the door had not abated during this time. My father opened the door to reveal a thoroughly disgruntled man with cane upraised as if to strike him. The man was wiry and tan, with sandy hair and a trim beard. His clothing was clean but nondescript. His cane, on the other hand, was elegant although eminently serviceable, composed of a dark hardwood and banded with silver. The head of the cane was cast in the shape of a leopard springing at some unseen prey, potentially the observer.

"Hello," said the stranger. "I am Dr. Lambshead." He brushed past my father. "I understand that you have a sick girl. I must see her at once. It is a matter of urgency and I apologize for the delay. There are many patients. Many patients."

"What did you say your name was?" My mother interposed herself between the man and me.

"Dr. Lambshead."

"But you were already here. Not you, but a man with your name. Was the earlier gentleman your father?"

The new Dr. Lambshead stopped. He looked at me, at the pot and the rag on the floor, and at the upraised window. "Ah," he said. "I think I understand. Another Dr. Lambshead visited you earlier?"

My mother nodded.

"He examined the girl?"

Nods from both my mother and my father.

"What was his diagnosis?"

"Bubo . . ." my father said, and then paused, unsure of the next syllable.

"Para . . . " my mother added.

"Zygosia," the new Dr. Lambshead finished. "A misdiagnosis, I am sorry to say. Obviously made by a rank amateur, a charlatan who did not get past 'Bub' in his studies. Otherwise he would have recognized the symptoms of Burmese Dirigible Disease." He made a derisive gesture with his cane at the tobacco-smeared blisters on my face.

"Unfortunately, there are those who find that their own lives lack meaning and choose instead to model themselves upon others," Dr. Lambshead said. "I have achieved a certain level of celebrity in some quarters, particularly and inevitably, I am afraid, among those who have quarrels with the medical establishment. As a result, I am now besieged by Lambshead mimics. I cannot walk down the street without bumping into a Lambshead-wannabe. Just yesterday . . . but I digress. You have a sick child on your hands and all other troubles pale in comparison."

He raised my left arm and hefted it slightly as if weighing it. Then he let it fall back to my side. He nodded, obviously pleased with himself. "Now, Burmese Dirigible Disease is thought to originate from a fungal infection, but I suspect that it may represent instead, at least in some cases, a remodeling of the dermis based on the surrounding environment. Another case of mimicry, if you will, but this time of the external made internal. Children are particularly susceptible because they are still undergoing growth and development. Their body plans are not yet fully laid down."

He pivoted slowly on his right foot, taking in the contents of our apartment. "You keep a very clean house," he said. "That must stop." He walked over to the bureau and dumped my father's shirts from the top drawer onto the floor. "Do not pick those up," he said. He then walked over to a wall and with two rapid swings of his cane punched successive holes through the plaster. "Do not fix those holes," he said.

None of us know how far he would have carried his destruction, if another knocking at the door had not interrupted him.

"Do not fix those holes," he said again, then stepped out the window and disappeared down the fire escape.

My father opened the door to see a young boy on the threshold. He was eight or nine years old, and wearing a striped shirt and pants that upon closer inspection turned out to be pajamas. Over these he had thrown an adult's blue suit jacket. The jacket hung down to knee level and he had rolled up its sleeves to expose his hands. A plastic stethoscope was draped around his neck.

"Hello," the boy said. "My name is Dr. Lambshead. I believe that we have an appointment."

My father slammed the door in his face.

As I said, this story is mostly that of my parents. I do not remember three different doctors. In my memory there is but one man who somehow combines the characteristics of all three visitors. He is tan, has a white beard streaked with earthy tones, and has a child-like enthusiasm at odds with his apparent age. But my memory also contains one additional feature not mentioned by my parents: a hat. Or, rather, a skullcap. This is the color of damp straw and patterned around the circumference with fine embroidery. Years later I would recognize a similar cap in a photograph of Arthur Rimbaud from his years as a trader in Northern Africa.

But I trust my parents' recollections, their detailed account of that trying night. I had a fever and faded in and out of consciousness. It is surprising that I remember anything.

For a while, I wondered which if any of the visitors was the real Dr. Lambshead. I confess that the question was a matter of recurring mental anguish for me, and it took me a long time to realize the unimportance of the answer. The visitors could not have existed without Lambshead, and thus each carried something of

Lambshead within them. It is to this essence and not to its quantification that I owe my recovery. For, yes, I did recover. The blisters receded that very night, absorbed so thoroughly back into my skin that I do not even have scars, just memories to mark their onetime presence. Still, that sickness and the resulting visitations marked me in other ways. I am convinced that I was set on a journey that night. I took my first steps down a path too improbable to tell, for no matter how it twisted and turned that path had but one destination: to return me back to where the journey began, to a place that I now once again call home. Today, I am happy to be Dr. Xue-Chu Wang of the Thackery T. Lambshead Institute for Applied Diagnostics, Little Lambs Pediatrics Unit, San Francisco.

## 1965– ?: Dr. Rachel Pollack

I first met Dr. Lambshead when we were both working on the acute outbreak of vaginal dishonorable discharges among young female officers in Biloxi, Mississippi, in the 1960s. One evening, after a strained day of collecting samples from women somewhat reluctant to risk their careers to a young researcher still wet behind the ears, I entered the doctors-only bar set up by the government to give us a break from the epidemic. An extremely tall gentleman with a mass of wild hair in all directions sat upright by a small table crowded with smoky bottles with handwritten labels. Later, of course, I would understand that the tall thin man with the unruly locks was but one of Thwack's breathtaking range of disguises, but back then I just knew that his frail upright form seemed to pull me to him.

I picked up one of the bottles and held it up to the light leaking through the dingy slats of the Venetian blinds. A deep voice, hardly more than a whisper, rumbled "I wouldn't drink that if I were you." Startled, I dropped the bottle. Quicker than a serpent, the man's arm shot out and grabbed it, millimeters before it would have shattered on the Formica tabletop. An instant later he was sitting back in his chair once more, one long finger alongside his jaw, a slight twist of perverse amusement on his lips as he said, "Nor, I think, would you wish to release the contents into the atmosphere." He waited just a moment, then added "The virus in that bottle is what killed the dinosaurs." From that moment I knew I was—yes, I will say it—in love.

Weeks would pass before we managed to trace the cause of the disease to the anti-radiation spray applied to government-issue foundation garments. Despite the hard work (my back has never fully recovered, and even now I cannot look at a duck bill without cringing), I did not regret a moment of it, for the Better Doctor (as so many of us refer to him) and I became as close as only two fighters on the vanguard of disease can become—a closeness, I suspect, far deeper than any mere marriage (though I must confess that fantasies of that sort at times challenged my professionalism). Pleased as I was to see the epidemic quashed, I could not stop a tear as we parted, me to a research fellowship in sexual mistaken identity at Johns Hopkins, Thwack to some new urgent and top secret campaign in Southeast Asia (though he would never reveal the details, those of us in the Thwack Pack paid special note to the CIA battle with miniature pigs trained to eat napalm).

Several years passed, and despite getting caught up in my work, a rawness would creep into the back of my throat whenever I thought of my friend. He might be anywhere, of course, on whatever secret mission. That report of astronauts covered in parasitic moonstones—was it the Better Doctor who found the formula to get the rocks off? Often I would think of him during sexual congress (these congresses took place several times a year, with much lively discussion of human and sometimes wider mammalian behavior).

Then, one evening, I was walking across campus, a rather vigorous young graduate student carrying my books, when a disheveled homeless man seemed to come from nowhere and began to "rap" at us in a thick patois. None of it made any sense until suddenly he said "Yo! Would it take you aback if I gave you a thwack? Would you fall on your bed? Would you give a lamb head?" I gasped and staggered against a tree. Thinking the vagrant had struck me, my young acolyte prepared to wade in with fists pumped. To stop him, I sent him to call the police, for I knew that despite his youth and truly impressive physique he would not have lasted ten seconds in battle with the ancient figure before him. I did not wish to see him hurt, or his face disfigured by the slash of razor-sharp fingernails. After all, I had witnessed the Better Doctor wrestle alligators for the curative liqueur derived from their saliva. Youth and muscle are no match for a man tested in the field. We rushed off before the police could arrive, and soon we were sitting at my kitchen table with hot chocolate and brandy.

"I've followed your career," Thwack told me. "Your work on the purported werewolf outbreaks on the Upper East Side saved a great many lives and much adolescent heartbreak."

I blushed.

He added, "And incidentally saved me the trouble of rushing to New York when I was in the midst of research in Mecca."

"Ah," I said, "the voices emitting from the ka'aba stone."

He inclined his head slightly.

"So that was you. I thought I detected your subtle touches."

We held up our glasses to each other, then drank deeply.

When he finished he sat back and looked steadily at me. I did my best to meet his gaze without flinching, until finally he allowed one eyebrow to rise, ever so slightly.

"Tell me," he said, "do you think you could get away for a time?"

"Yes!" I blurted, and felt tears spring to my eyes. "Oh yes!"

He said, "Perhaps you have heard of the malady known as color deafness?"

"I believe so," I said. "The sufferer cannot distinguish between the accents of various ethnic groups. I gather it does not produce any serious threat, only some minor confusion and embarrassment."

"Do you now?" he said, and my cheeks flushed. "And how much embarrassment might it cause at a summit at the United Nations?"

I could only sit with my mouth hanging open. "Do you suspect foul play?" I asked.

"I suspect nothing and everything. All I know for sure is that we leave tonight."

That was the start of many adventures, most of which I am not at liberty to discuss. I can only say that I count them among my happiest moments, fighting disease alongside the wisest, kindest, most masculine man I have ever known.

## 1975: Dr. Queenie Bishop (as told to her niece, Dr. K. J. Bishop)

The Dimcross Home for the Elderly Confused: never was a building more like a dead pachyderm. And were the giant concrete goannas really a necessary addition to the roof? One would not think so. It was designed by an architect who believed a loony bin should look like a loony bin; but why a loony bin should look like goannas conquering a dead elephant, I do not know; and nor, I suspect, did the architect.

At any rate, the building does not inspire an attitude of *sanity*. The gates look to be made of numerous writhing eels, and are of a size excessive enough to invite a comparison with the gates of Pandemonium, though Satan might well have foregone the railing finials of alternating owl heads and pineapples. Atop the gateposts are two alarming, great-mouthed statues from South America. Beyond these doormen, in front of the house, spreads a garden where approximately 50 elderly men and women sport with phantoms, or are made sport of; as the residents all wear pajamas and nightgowns, they appear like sleepers acting out the nonsense of dreams.

One of these is my aunt, Dr. Queenie Bishop, perhaps the most brilliant medical mind of her generation (she was awarded the 1972 Royal Australian Society of Medicine Prize for her research into spontaneous human combustion). Whenever allowed outside, she can be found digging up one of the flower beds in the garden, looking for the birds she believes to be buried in the ground. Not being permitted the use of a spade—for her own safety—she digs with her hands.

On this occasion, my aunt recognized me as someone called Dorothy Spot, and was excited to see me. She asked me how the buzzard was, and had we seen the ornamental drownings in Rome? I told her the buzzard was well and sent his love, and that the drownings had been most edifying.

After this exchange of pleasantries, Aunt Queenie returned to her digging. Presently, while she scrabbled in the dirt, she began to whisper a name:

"Thackery, Thackery, quackery, bushwhack . . ."

I turned the tape recorder on.

When the editors of this volume asked me whether I could obtain from my aunt a short reminiscence about Dr. Thackery T. Lambshead, I replied that nothing could be more easily arranged. Aunt Queenie rarely talks about anyone else; and if she does, she is liable to confuse them with an animal, or a vegetable, or, as she has done several times in my mother's case, the Hotel Continental in Tangier. But she remembers Lambshead with—relatively speaking—remarkable clarity. At least, she remembers going on a expedition with Lambshead, who had been her mentor since medical school. The trip was to Papua New Guinea, in 1975, when my aunt was in her forties. It immediately preceded the sudden, tragic loosening of her grip on reality that forced her retirement from medicine and from public life.

". . . I always loved the birds, you see. In the jungle, the birds of paradise. He didn't like birds. He put the birds in the dirt. Wherever I go, the birds are *in the dirt*. Dirty, dirty birds! *He* made the birds dirty. He was a filthy man, Dorothy! Never ever washed his hands. Doctors! They carry disease, you know. Worse than rats. My dear, I feel I must tell you, we have doctors here. They try to hide, pretend to be curtains and whatnot, but I tell you they're doctors. Most unhygienic! . . . And now I've got birds. *Thwack* gave me the dirty birds . . . I was a fool! Why I ever went near that man, I don't know. I've always avoided doctors like the plague. They're always rubbing up against sick people, you see. Fingers in dirty mouths and *wherever else*. But Lambshead, oh, Lambshead was the worst—FILTHY! The Lord made them, clean and unclean, and Thwack was unclean. Wasn't interested in the patients, you see . . . not in *healing*. He loved the *diseases*. The little worms, the parasites, all the bugaboos and viruses—they said his love for viruses was *infectious*—health was not an optimal state, in his view, you see—sickness was. The worse, the better. In other people, of course. The man himself couldn't even put up with a cold, you know. Sat wrapped in a blanket with his feet in a mustard bath. Nasty feet, Dorothy. He had very bad feet indeed . . . they took him all walkabout, spreading his germs, his *cultures* . . ."

"And what happened in New Guinea, Aunt Queenie?" I said. Let me assure the reader that I was not prodding cruelly. My aunt's monologues on the subject of Dr. Lambshead always culminated in the events of that camping trip in the New Guinea Highlands.

". . . He said I was his sweet fresh girl. 'You're a dewy rose, Queenie.' But he didn't always call me Queenie. Sometimes he called me *Dr. Bishop*. He liked to pretend I was a doctor, you see! Well, I thought it was just the old goat's fun. I'd be ashamed now, but it *was* the seventies—we were all for letting it hang out and indulging our fantasies and sometimes hygiene *was not our first concern*. But Thwacky said I was his clean-as-a-whistle girl, a vision of spring, a rose in the jungle . . . Eve herself, he said, couldn't have glowed more with health . . . and I said yes, and I supposed he was after a bit of you know what, the dirty old, the bad feet and the bad head, the bad old medicine man, and what did I care what he said? I just wanted to watch the fowl of the air . . . Now it was, I don't know, two or three weeks since we'd left Moresby. We were up in the foggy boggy hills. Thackery was looking for the Wig Men, among whom he hoped to find an obscure disease, something tropical and horrendous, and isolated tribes often proved fruitful in this regard, he said . . . well, we never found the Wig Men—but we found the preacher and the half-caste girl, didn't we? Missionary—dime a dozen in those parts—said the girl was his daughter—well, no need to ask about *that*, but she seemed fond of him, though he was a Methodist, and not even a handsome one . . . but, oh! Dying in the jungle! Thackery loved him! Things were *hatching* out of him—insects—butterflies, moths—originating in the papillary layer of the dermis, quite spontaneously . . . Papuan Papillon Disease, Thwack called it, and even I thought that was funny. Poor man! The preacher, not Lambshead. Even if he was a Methodist. The preacher, not Lambshead. Lambshead was a *dirty godless heathen* . . . The preacher said it was a thing the local gods had given him. 'Stronger than we give them credit for,' he said . . . well, Thacko Wacko didn't give a hoot who *made* this fascinating lurgy, he just *wanted* some, the dirty so-and-so! But it got better—I mean it got worse—it wasn't just the preacher man who was afflicted, but the girl too, only with *her* it was on the *outside*.

That night, Dotty, in the camp . . . in the dirt, in the mud below, we saw a hatching. Butterflies crawled out of the jungle mud . . . all hers, all made by the Papuan Papillon Disease, and didn't Thwack love it! Oh, that dirty old man . . . all over the Earth he trod, finding plagues—*founding* plagues! Oh rose thou art sick . . . was a clean Queenie, now a ring-a-rosies, we all fall down . . . A disease whose symptoms appeared *outside* the body of the sufferer. Outside! But just in women. Men got it under the skin, women got it under the ground. Thwack said it was his favorite bugaboo ever. 'Diseases are unconscious artists; the body is their medium. To be able to appreciate what a disease can do is a sign of a sophisticated and liberated mind,' he said. *Culture vulture.* Loved the aches and pains, the scars and lesions—but only in other people—so he was afraid, this time, in case *he* started *hatching things* . . . but the girl put his mind at rest. Only one way to catch it, she said, and you know what I mean. Well, we knew she wasn't the preacher's daughter. She said it was something his god had given him, then *he* gave it to *her.* 'What a hoot!' said Thwack . . . then it was night time, Dotty, and it was so dark, all the stars behind the clouds, you see—well, you *didn't* see—and then I was awake, and *he* was there in my tent, in a mask made of mud and little bones, and he said to me, 'The jungle's full of fearsome bugaboos, Dr. Bishop. We can't have you getting sick. That wouldn't do. So here's a little needle, take it from the witch doctor—ooh-eeh-ooh ah ah, ting-tang, walla-walla bing-bang!—' and he gave me a big needle, like the ones they give me here, when they're not pretending to be curtains. He thwacked me with the blood of the preacher man—*stab in the back—and now I've got it*, but not the butterflies, I've got it worse, I've got the *birds*—and they're *down* there and I can't get them *out*—"

That was my aunt's story, as I had heard it many times. We can only speculate about what—if anything—happened to her on that trip to the New Guinea jungle. Dr. Vanbutchell suspects an incident of a sexual nature; but there are people for whom a cigar is never just a cigar, nor a missionary just a missionary. I suspect Dr. Lambshead may indeed have done something to Aunt Queenie, but from what I have been able to learn secondhand about Lambshead's character, it seems wrongheaded to presume untoward advances were made; not that man's style, I would say. But perhaps he did, indeed, inject her with something that caused her unhingement. I am inclined to suspect professional jealousy, a fear that his protégée's star was growing brighter than his own. The only thing I may say with certainty is that neither Papuan Papillon Disease, nor its avian variant, exists anywhere but in the jungles of Dr. Queenie Bishop's ruined mind.

## 1983: Dr. Stepan Chapman

A banging at the door in the dead of night is nothing unusual for a general practitioner. So I was not alarmed when such a banging wakened me at my modest apartment in Tucson, Arizona. It was 1983, and I was pursuing advanced research in pharmacology at Arizona State University.

Imagine my surprise when I opened my double-bolted door and discovered the eminent British pathologist, Dr. Thackery Lambshead, an imposing figure even in his eighties. Though he walked with a cane, his shoulders were broad, and his back still straight. His white hair rose vertically from his scalp like toothbrush bristles. The lenses of his tortoiseshell eyeglasses were thick and tinted purple. He wore a three-piece suit of white cotton, which seemed wrinkled as if from long hours of travel. I invited him in, and we drank tall glasses of iced tea in my den.

"Just rode the jets back from Delhi, Dr. Chapman. A bit of family trouble has come up there, unlikely as it seems. My niece Eulalia. Still getting into narrow scrapes in tropical climes at her age. Wanted to extend her modern dance training. Can you imagine?"

The doctor was a very fast talker, once he got going, and it was difficult to get a word in edgewise. Though I met him only once (despite our long acquaintance through letters), I am cursed with an eidetic memory for conversations, and thus can offer up this fragment of his table talk verbatim.

"I've never liked Eulalia, and she's caused me endless trouble. But all the same, family is family, is it not? And despite our history, I'm damned if I'll let her waste away as the thrall of some beady-eyed sorcerer from Bengal."

"A sorcerer, sir?"

"Oh, he maintains a respectable front, the old fraud. He's a national cultural treasure, I'm told. The last traditional master of Kathikali theater. Impressive performance art, if you like that sort of thing. Deafening gong orchestra. Incense to choke a horse. Sagas of the Monkey King, all that Hindu rot."

"Your niece, Dr. Lambshead. Is she in danger?"

"She's in full bloody lotus position and can't get out, that's what she's in, young man. Continual clonus of the thighs. Purely psychosomatic, you understand. Horrible business, the human mind, and the treacheries it gets up to. Had to build the old girl a special wheelchair."

"You ruled out a spinal injury?"

The doctor gave me a hard look. "I was ruling out spinal injuries before you were born, Dr. Chapman, and I'm not quite senile yet. I also ruled out Paraleptic Neuroplasia and Night Soil Fever. But more to the point, I've procured a sample."

"A sample, sir? Of what?"

"The suggestibility drug that the old fruit bat's been slipping to Eulalia. Here. Have a look." The doctor drew a small glass vial from a vest pocket and tossed it onto my coffee table. "It's the old Mesmer dodge, but what's his herb of choice? That's the great quandary. My grandfather knew Mesmer, did you know that? No, of course you wouldn't."

I uncapped the vial and sniffed at the contents—a lustrous blob of black resin.

"I didn't dare to work up the pharmacology in Asia. The Fly Ebola's all through their hospitals now."

"The what?"

"It's a housefly virus. You don't keep up with the tropical disease journals? Well, it's right through India and parts of Tibet as well. Nasty thing. Crossed over in a piercing parlor in Bengal apparently. Became a human disease, I mean. Then it spread to the liposuction clinics, the rhinoplasty stalls, the dental clinics, the beauty parlors, and now it's all through the health care system. Many doctors and nurses infected. Terrible thing. Attacks the fat cells. Terminal cases bleed out, if that's the word I want. Hideous. In any case, I wanted to get as far from there as possible before assaying the drug. And Arizona popped into my head, isn't that silly? Too many Wild West movies, I suppose. But I knew that the IFS has offices here. So I looked in the directory of associate researchers, and there you were."

"I wondered why you'd contact me of all people."

"Well, I've always enjoyed our correspondence."

I inquired as to whether he'd found the time to read my doctoral thesis on the Musical Goiters of Lapland.

"No, I'm afraid not. But I did read that bulletin on Cyanofixative Veneral Yeast. Most informative."

"Oh, that." I screwed down the lid of the vial. "Uh, sir. I believe this is hashish oil."

"Well of course it is. That's what Eulalia's been smoking. But no amount of cannabinol accounts for the trance state. Eulalia's been a hash head for years. No, the question is, what does her dance teacher use to *taint* this goop? I'll bet you a dollar it's a vegetable hypnotic native to India. Has your pharmacy got Internet access?"

I drove the doctor to the campus labs. We spent all night pulling apart the resin sample. Then he concocted an antidote, or what he hoped was an antidote. I never did find out what became of Eulalia.

But we had a fascinating conversation that night. Which is to say, Dr. Lambshead talked, and I listened. He covered a lot of ground. He spoke of the infants recently born at the Gila Bend Indian Reservation with the heads of grasshoppers. He discussed the iatrogenic spread of Poultry Rash and Rainbow Glaucoma in the Third World. He even touched on the ghosts of Bali, which are pictured in that island's folklore as body fragments—hopping feet, rolling heads, and creeping guts. By morning light I drove him to the airport and put him on a jet bound east.

That concluded my regrettably brief encounter with Dr. Lambshead, the colorful founding father of this indispensable pocket guide.

## 1995: Dr. Richard Calder*
## (The Ophidian Manifesto or, How I met Dr. Thackery T. Lambshead)

I stood on the isolated mountain—Qal'at al-Mishnaqa, as it is known in Arabic— on which Machaerous had stood, and looked out over the ancient land of the Hashemites. With Masada, Hyrcania, Alexandreion, and Cypros, Machaerous was one of the fortresses that Herod the Great had inherited, a stronghold of the Jewish state's defense system in the eastern province of Peraea. Herod had improved the roads connecting Machaerous to the Dead Sea; the tracks were still evident and, seemingly, much in use; but of all else that remained the only thing of note was the view.

"The walls were razed to foundation level," said Huntingdon, seeing me scan the scorched earth of the high plateau. "Absolutely nothing is known of the Hasmonean fortress beneath." Huntingdon led the dig: the first exploration since that of the Duke de Luynes in 1864. Work had been slow and, so far, had yielded few results. I took out my pipe, placed it between my lips, and began to suck meditatively on the stem. "We'd like you to oversee work on the *lower* city," he concluded.

My disappointment was keen. In London, I had expressed a wish to be assigned to the upper city and its remnants of the palace-fortress. There, the crazed, necrophiliac child who had so obsessed me had performed her dance of death.

---

* *Editors' Note:* There is one impulse at work in us that wants to slap a "Quarantined" or "Discredited" label on Dr. Calder's meticulous account. Another, competing impulse tells us that you cannot discredit or quarantine a memory. We would note, however, that eyewitnesses place Dr. Lambshead in England at the time of the supposed encounter. Alas, we cannot stop the good doctor from entering the modern-day mythology. Alleged sightings of the doctor, as well as impersonifications of him, have become an almost weekly occurrence. Whether created out of whole cloth or based on a vision, or representing the manifestation of some unknown disease, Dr. Calder's account at the very least confirms the extent to which Dr. Lambshead has entered the popular (and unpopular) culture.

"We've unearthed some late Hellenistic jars, along with bowls, lamps, and Hasmonean coins," he resumed. "But what we'd like you to take a look at is the cistern. It may provide access to a huge rock-cut water reservoir."

"Very well," I sighed, thinking only of the princess Salome.

I had been given a house in the nearby village of Mukawir. Here, women of the Bani Hamida tribe are famed for weaving rugs of exceptional beauty. The house was in poor condition, and I had hung several such rugs from the walls in an attempt to hide some of its native ugliness. In addition, I had hung engravings. Chief among them were Moreau's "The Apparition," so beloved by Huysmans, and Toudouze's "Salome Triumphant," which had caused such a furor at the Salon of 1886.

Toudouze's likeness of Salome—an adolescent sated with crime, as a child may be with comfits, or toys—enjoyed, in one respect at least, a degree of historical accuracy. In Mark 6: 22, 28 and Matthew 14: 11, the daughter of Herodias (it is only Josephus who calls her Salome) is described as κορασιον. The exact meaning of κορασιον is uncertain, but it is a diminutive of κορη, meaning girl or maiden. If John had been beheaded sometime between A.D. 29 and 32, Salome would have been born between A.D. 15 and 19 and thus would have been 12 to 14 years of age at the time of John's death.

The twilight deepened. My houseboy, Youssef, lit the lamps. In the half-light, Toudouze's virgin-whore—the little goddess of immortal Hysteria—who, in Flaubert's words, had "danced like the priestesses of the Indies, like the Nubian girls of the cataracts, like the bacchantes of Lydia," stared back at me, unimpressed.

There really had been a historical Salome. A Salome whose ancestry was traceable all the way back to Esau the Wicked, whom biblical tradition regarded as the forefather of the Edomites, the most hateful of all pagans . . .

Antipater, an Idumaean (that is, an Edomite) conspired with the Roman General Pompey the Great to resolve the conflict between Hyrcanus II and Aristobulus II, both heirs to the throne of Judea. When the kingdom of Judea became subject to Rome in 47 B.C., Antipater was established as procurator. Herod the Great, his son, became king in 37 B.C.

Herod Philip, the son of Herod the Great by Mariamme, the daughter of Simon the high priest, had married Herodias. Salome was their daughter. Later, Herodias would divorce Herod Philip and marry his brother, Herod Antipas, Tetrarch of Galilee and Paraea. Salome was not to die (as she does in Wilde's play), but marry Philip, Tetrarch of Trachonitis, who was both half-brother of her father, Herod Philip, and half-brother of Herod Antipas, her mother's second husband. After Philip's death in A.D. 33-34, she married Aristobolus, her first cousin. The Emperor Nero appointed her husband king of Armenia in Asia Minor. A coin that exhibits the profile of Aristobolus on one side and Salome, his queen, on the reverse, offers proof of Salome's real-life existence.

But for me, of course, it was the *legend* of Salome—and not facts gleaned from the historical record—that exerted abiding fascination. It was the legend—the same one thousands of nineteenth-century poets, artists, and musicians had made their own—that had brought me here.

Youssef knelt at my feet and proceeded to pour my coffee. I stroked his hair and began to hum the 32-bar waltz from Strauss' "Dance of the Seven Veils." I closed my eyes. It was an odd fragment of music, curiously evoking the image of a girl at her first ball. A girl, perhaps, who would happily murder her suitors.

I would go to bed early, I decided. Tomorrow, I would begin work in earnest. Before its destruction by the Romans in A.D. 71, Machaerous had been called the Black Fortress. The Citadel of the Gallows.

In its murderous depths, fact and fiction, legend and truth, might at last be reconciled.


I sat on the crumbling edge of the cistern. Under Herod the Great, comprehensive waterworks had been constructed. The cisterns hewn on the northern slope of the mountain had served an aqueduct that provided the fortress with rainwater.

I was 3,860 feet above the Dead Sea and 2,546 feet above the Mediterranean, my gaze trained westwards, toward Jerusalem. "When I touch bottom, I'll holler," I said to my two assistants. "Take the strain." I took off my cheese cutter and threw it clear. Then, easing myself off the cistern's lip, I began to abseil down the interior wall.

Soon, all that was left above me was a tiny circlet of clear blue sky, like a brilliant sapphire set in a bezel of darkness. "Hello!" I called, rather nervously. "Hello, can you—"

But at that moment I came to rest amongst a pile of rubble.

I slipped out of the harness and let it dangle by the wall. Then I took my flashlight from my backpack. The rubble made it difficult to walk, and I stumbled, then sprawled, grazing my knee and tearing a small hole in my jodhpurs.

The darkness crowded in. My flashlight had gone out. Luckily, however, it wasn't broken. I got to my feet, turned it back on and held it aloft. As before, the cistern's gray, circumambient walls curled about me. But during the moments when my flashlight had failed the sky had unaccountably disappeared. *"Hello up there!"* I shouted. But there was no reply.

I felt a draught. When I trained a beam of light towards it, a perspective opened up. A tunnel.

I had walked some 50 yards when I emerged into a gigantic chamber.

From high above, oblique shafts of light crisscrossed the chamber floor, shining in through cracks and vents in the craggy vault. Doric columns—some truncated, some intact—rose before me like blasted, subterranean trees multitudinous enough for the prospect as a whole to resemble a petrified forest. Amidst the shadows, illuminated by a single shaft of light, was a great, black marble mausoleum. Standing next to it was a very old man.

"Dr. Calder?" he ventured, sweeping back the opera cloak that he had draped about his shoulders.

I walked across the chamber and stood before him.

"Who on Earth—"

"Dr. Lambshead," he interjected, grasping my hand and shaking it vigorously. "Dr. Thackery *T.* Lambshead." He smiled. "I've been expecting you."

I cast a glance at the great, oblong tomb. It was inscribed with Greek letters. They read SALOME, PRINCESS OF JUDEA.

"Oh my," I murmured, "oh my *God.*"

"Yes, yes," said Lambshead. "You are well acquainted with her, of course. I have collected and studied all your papers! I was *most* interested in those carried in *The British Journal of Near Eastern Archaeology.* Impressive for a man trained in medicine for whom archaeology is little more than a hobby!" He nodded towards the huge tomb. "It is imperative that you know of her true significance."

And then he told me her, and his, story.

"I have worn many hats in addition to medical doctor: those of archaeologist, choreographer, occultist, *littérateur,* exponent of outsider art, and countless others. But it is as well, I think, to mention—in the present context, at least—one of my contributions to Big Science.

"In 1997, after a decade of research involving studies in 27 countries, I concluded that a spontaneous mutation had occurred in the human population sometime during the late 1970s. At the beginning of that decade, a new star had flared in the constellation of Ophiuchus: a supernova that alerted the WHO and other UN agencies to the possibility of a pandemic of misbirths and infant deformity. Though such anxieties proved unfounded, research institutes around the globe continued to examine random DNA samples, until my groundbreaking paper in *Nature* demonstrated that mutation had indeed occurred, if with consequences almost diametrically opposed to those at first expected.

"In the course of *pro bono* gynecological work involving groups of disturbed, socially maladjusted young women, I had found that a small proportion tested positive for DNA that was not only incompatible with all notions of heredity, but with the human genome itself. I concluded my findings thus: 'This syndrome, if I may call it such (given that the isolated mutant DNA is accompanied by distinct biological and psycho-pathological phenomena) is undoubtedly a delayed effect of the high-energy radiation that saturated Earth following the Ophiuchus supernova flare-up of 1972. The syndrome is worldwide in scope and affects only females. Since subjects in the sample studies are under the age of 21, prognosis is, at present, problematic. But it seems certain that the syndrome represents a significant, and indeed, dangerous new evolutionary development for humankind.'

"But there had been another supernova that had flooded Earth with gamma rays: that of 5 B.C., which we have come to call the Star of Bethlehem . . ."

A young girl seemed to materialize out of the shadows. "Salome," whispered Lambshead. "My divine phantom, Salome!"

After attending the premiere of *Et Dieu créa la femme*, Simone de Beauvoir had used the term "neotenic"—a biological term that refers to the retention of larval, immature, or juvenile characteristics, in the adult of the species. And like the young Bardot, Salome—or this, her ghost—possessed neotenic beauty. She was a small, doll-faced, buxom child-goddess—an adolescent Ishtar, Mistress of Babylon, and the dark little mother who drank the blood of Abel after he was murdered by Cain.

"Ah yes. This young lady was *one* such born under the Bethlehem star. A hierodule and priestess, she knew the secrets of sexual mysticism. She was one of the first *true mutants*. Now, poor thing, she belongs to that order exiled to a realm at right angles to our own, and who may be seen only in states of liminal gnosis. We call her kind Lamiae, or Daughters of Hecate. But after two millennia, her kind is about to once more become incarnate in flesh. Girls and women who the scientific community will come to call *Lambshead* females."

Lambshead paused and held out a hand, like a Svengali introducing his latest protégée to an astonished public. "Look at her, Dr. Calder. Does she not fit all the criteria? An extreme degree of exhibitionism; permanent sexual irritability; an overriding need to be admired and pampered; and a tendency to spite, deceit, and treacherousness in direct proportion to deferred gratification. In test after test, the Lambshead psyche has revealed itself to be a seething miasma of sexual obsession. But surely the most bizarre, and disturbing, trait is one that I would surely have had classified as a communicable disease, if its effects on others had not been so obviously psychosomatic: a desire to drive human males insane with lust! Not figuratively, mind, but literally. In this, the Lambshead female proves to be all too successful. She will dance for the heads—the very sanity—of all men who stigmatize her beauty and disdain her love!"

She wore a choli, split chiffon skirts, and a coin belt. And the ruby in her navel was no legacy of the Hayes Code, which had veiled the belly of Rita Hayworth and Gina Lollobrigida; it harked back to something ancient, almost forgotten, the flaming belly of the Great Goddess herself, in whom fertility and death were conjoined.

She swayed, and then began to dance. And her belly was the focal point of her dance, just as her burning navel (that, like the Shulamite's, was like a round goblet which wanteth not liquor) was the focal point of her belly. She danced like the *ghawazi* of Egypt, like the Algerian *Ouled Nail*. And like Stravinsky's heroine, she seemed ready to dance herself to death, and to take the world with her. She was Maud Allan, Ida Rubinstein, Mata Hari, and Theda Bara. She was Alla Nazimova and Imogen Millais-Scott.

"My paternal grandfather saw her in 1903," I murmured, "when he attended a production of Wilde's play at the Neues Theater in Berlin. And then again, seven years later, when Beecham brought Strauss' notorious new opera to London. He told me of her when I was a boy and I have been obsessed by her ever since." She was so close to me, now, that I could smell her perspiration, my nostrils filling with the sharp scent of canal towpaths, deserted nighttime wharves, the fire escapes of tenement blocks, and the shadow-haunted depths of condom-littered alleyways. It was a musky perfume redolent of sex, blood, and morbidity. "I've waited for her so long. But what does she *want*?" Lambshead had no need to reply. As his little succubus drew nearer I bowed my head in submission.

The goddess had claimed me. She had affirmed her right to derange my senses.

Here, beneath Machaerous, legend and fact had become one. And something had been reborn. Those who had been damned by the Star of Bethlehem were the same mutant females who, in the last decades of the twentieth century, were being resurrected under the aegis of Ophiuchus. An order of being that heralded a new, Ophidian universe. For salvation lay in the degenerate, and had done so for some two thousand years.

I felt phantom lips press against the nape of my neck, and knew that I had been reborn, too. For the first time, the nature of my life's true mission was clear.

I would subvert paramount reality. Semantic displacement would be my weapon. A studied program of *détournement* that would confuse fiction with fact, warp our universe's plenum, and replace it with that of the beautiful, mad universe of Ishtar and her last temple-maiden, the Edomite and princess of Judea, Salome.

And Dr. Thackery T. Lambshead would be my guide.

## 2003: Dr. R.F. Wexler*

My Dearest Thwack:

How could you?

My heart knelled when first I heard the news of this . . . edition, this misguided attempt to create a legacy in the twilight of your illustrious life.

Do you not recall the calamitous events that followed the first printing? And I do not mean that absurd myth of the tainted paper. All of the first printing was burned, Thwack. Burned. And the ashes scattered on the graves of our fallen comrades.

Knowing that you experienced (and bravely persevered) what I too experienced (nearly not surviving), I can only assume that madness and senility, or the onset of Bayard's Syndrome, have invaded your soul, transformed your former clinical and analytical genius into a morass of irresponsibility.

You must be surprised to hear from me. It has been what? Close onto 80 years? In my grief, I never told you what befell my Daisy, her division into smaller and smaller components until nothing remained. Though surely you must have heard, and despite our rift, dear Thwack, your condolences would have been appreciated. Had I known the years of sorrow I would spend without her I would have ended my life long ago.

* *Editors' Note:* The following correspondence from the notorious Dr. Wexler (please see Dr. Chapman's *History of the Guide*) constitutes an inadvertent reminiscence. It also exemplifies the extraordinary number of odd letters received by Dr. Lambshead from around the world. In fact, Dr. Wexler has written to Dr. Lambshead more than 560 times during the past six decades. Each letter assumes a different level of familiarity with Dr. Lambshead. Each is more absurd than the last, although to date we have been unable to pin a disease to Dr. Wexler. As for Dr. Wexler's claims, Dr. Lambshead's only comment was, "Never been to Tasmania."

But that is not the point of my letter.

Could you have forgotten our time among the faceless nomads of the Gerund Desert? Or the putrefaction that struck down Dr. Aldus and his poor Caroline on their return to Tasmania? We were together, you and I, compiling the entries, when we received the telegram. And theirs was only the first death. More followed, so many brave and caring souls. Our colleagues. Our friends.

I know that your life's goal has been to serve and heal the many hurts that we humans endure, but that only makes your present actions more reprehensible. Have you warned these young and brash doctors, this Roberts, this VanderMeer, of the consequences?

Publishing this edition is folly. You know this. You must not.

Yours,

Dr. R.F. Wexler, retired

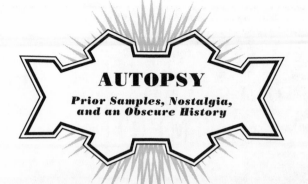

AUTOPSY
Prior Samples, Nostalgia,
and an Obscure History

THE THACKERY T. LAMBSHEAD "POCKET" GUIDE
TO ECCENTRIC & DISCREDITED DISEASES

Edition No. 1 -- 1921
Published by Lambshead Productions, Ltd.

EDITED BY
Dr. Thackery T. Lambshead.

TABLE OF CONTENTS

Introductions

Diseases

A Short Essay by Dr. Michael Cisco

The Radical Inoculation Techniques of Randolph Johnson:
Fact or Fancy?
(on back cover)

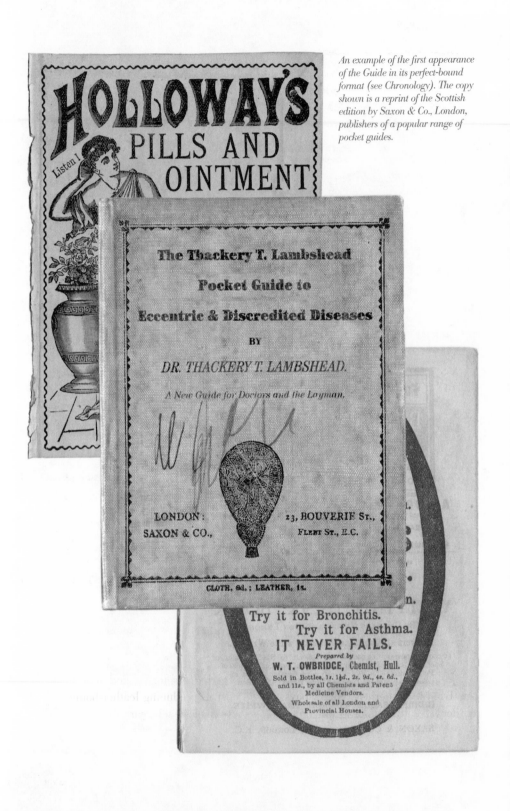

HOLLOWAY'S

PILLS AND

OINTMENT

Listen !

The Thackery T. Lambshead

Pocket Guide to

Eccentric & Discredited Diseases

BY

DR. THACKERY T. LAMBSHEAD.

*A New Guide for Doctors and the Layman.*

LONDON :                    23, BOUVERIE St.,

SAXON & CO.,              FLEET St., E.C.

CLOTH, 6d. ; LEATHER, 1s.

Try it for Bronchitis.
Try it for Asthma.
IT NEVER FAILS.
*Prepared by*
W. T. OWBRIDGE, Chemist, Hull.
Sold in Bottles, 1s. 1½d., 2s. 9d., 4s. 6d.,
and 11s., by all Chemists and Patent
Medicine Vendors.
Wholesale of all London and
Provincial Houses.

*In honor of this edition of the Guide, we have compiled a series of examples from prior editions. Before their inclusion here, some entries have had few enough admirers, due to the Guide's often limited print runs. Stepan Chapman's Obscure History provides a riveting appraisal of the Guide's impact on the Twentieth Century, while the Chronology below gives the reader some sense of the built-in limitations Dr. Lambshead has had to work with over his long career. Finally, the inclusion of "The Malady of Ghostly Cities" demonstrates the Guide's impact on other areas of study.*

*Please note that wherever possible we have retained as many elements of the original presentation as possible. In some cases, this has been made difficult by the poor condition of the source material. Some "reconstruction" has been necessary. Although the original page header and footer styles have been preserved, the page numbers have been changed to avoid confusion.*

*Whether through the psychedelic "Clockworm Orange" of The Putti or the delayed multiverse chronoshock of Samoan Giant Rat Bite Fever, readers will find that the Guide has covered more territory in its 84 years than the most intrepid Victorian explorer.—*THE EDITORS

## A Chronology of the Guide's Publishers

**1921–1923:** Dr. Lambshead uses a hectograph machine to create copies of the earliest, stapled editions of the Guide. These early Guides are only 14 pages long.

**1924–1927:** By 1924, Dr. Lambshead begins to print the Guide in little chapbook editions, using his old Underwood typewriter. Starting around 1927, Dr. Lambshead finds collaborators willing to add some crude illustrations and badly-reproduced photographs.

**1928, 1929:** Dr. Lambshead begins using a Scottish medical publisher to produce perfect-bound copies of the Guide.

**1930–1940:** John Trimble, explorer, outlaw anthropologist, and heir to the Trimble Fisheries fortune, pays for the cost of producing leather-bound hardcover editions. The Guide now averages 200 pages each year.

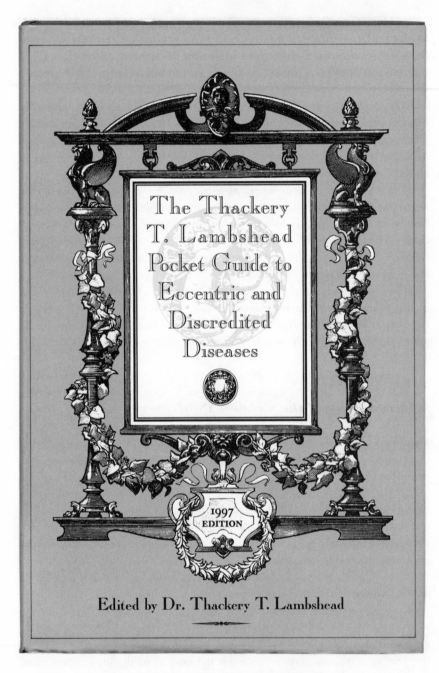

The Thackery
T. Lambshead
Pocket Guide to
Eccentric and
Discredited
Diseases

1997
EDITION

Edited by Dr. Thackery T. Lambshead

*The cover of the infamous 1997 edition (Boojum Press).*
*See "Venereal Disease, 1997" in Dr. Stepan Chapman's "Obscure History" (p. 284)*

**1941–1945:** Due to War shortages, Trimble is unable to continue financing the Guide during this period. As a result, Dr. Lambshead resorts to the previous circulars and saddlestapled editions.

**1946–1959:** Chatto & Windus issues sumptuous 600-page editions with copious illustrations and photographs. Their editions often harken back to the Victorian era in design.

**1960–1990:** Chatto & Windus bends to pressure applied by the British government as accusations of communism in the Guide ferment in the United States. Jolly Boy Publishing & Soap Company of Bombay takes over publication of the Guide. Many of the Jolly Boy covers feature Indian gods and goddesses. Others seem influenced by the rise of Bollywood. Dr. Lambshead breathes a sigh of relief on those rare occasions when Jolly Boy puts together a sensible-looking cover. In addition, Jolly Boy takes to publishing supposed "true-life accounts of murder and mayhem" amongst the diseases. Advertisements for books, food items, and other products soon follow.

**1991–2002:** Boojum Press of California publishes the Guide when Jolly Boy goes out of business in 1990. Boojum Press editions are eccentric trade paperbacks with an ethereal, New Age feel. Often, the illustrations are irrelevant to the disease at hand. The covers are flashy and sometimes feature mushrooms or fairies.

**2003:** Night Shade Books takes over publication of the Guide. Order and dignity are re-established as publishers Jason Williams and Jeremy Lassen apply the most stringent ethical and moral standards ever experienced by Guide editors and contributors. In protest, the estate of Oscar Wilde refuses to allow the Guide editors to reprint a quote from Wilde's disease diary.

**2005:** Bantam Books, under the guidance of Spectra editor Juliet Ulman, instills a new sense of fun in the Guide after a century of pseudo-Victorian stuffiness. Disease parties, liver races, and other events become commonplace to celebrate the Guide's updated approach.

# THE THACKERY T. LAMBSHEAD POCKET GUIDE TO ECCENTRIC & DISCREDITED DISEASES

12TH EDITION

DESCRIBED BY
SPECIALIST CONTRIBUTORS

Edited by

## Dr. Thackery T. Lambshead

Published at THE TRIMBLE FISHERIES, Robin's Bay, England

*The title page of the 1932 edition. At the time of publication (and even today, according to some antiquarian book dealers), copies of this edition stank of mackerel. The Trimble Fisheries printing presses were located next door to their cannery.*

# THE THIRTIES

1932: Gastric Pre-Linguistic Syndrome
Format: Leather-bound hardcover edition, 6 x 9
Publisher: Trimble Fisheries, Robin's Bay, England

This disease was first published in the Guide amid much controversy as to the veracity of the findings—or even the veracity of the doctor in question. Dr. Lambshead had to persuade John Trimble not to excise the disease prior to publication—one of many arguments between the two great men. The difficulty in determining the difference between the syndrome and various traditional stomach ailments eventually led to a retraction of the disease in the 1957 Guide. Many unnecessary surgeries had been performed because of the entry. In 1965, Dr. Lambshead reinstated the entry when he experienced what he claimed to be a sudden bout of the syndrome.

## GASTRIC PRE-LINGUISTIC SYNDROME
*Alternatively Known as Aggressive Acid Reflux*
*or Couzens-Goodman Syndrome*

### COUNTRY OF ORIGIN:
United Kingdom

### FIRST KNOWN CASE:
Mr. X, a stable hand in the small Hampshire market town of A_____. He was 22 years of age, engaged to be married, and had no previous history of serious illness. Before Gastric Pre-Linguistic Syndrome had its debilitating way with him, he was by all accounts a strapping young fellow, in excess of six feet in height. (The true identities of all three patients have been suppressed lest my speculations as to the Syndrome's origin—see below—cause offence.)

### SYMPTOMS:
Stomach pain, increasing from mild to acute. Considerable "noise," varying in volume and pitch, from the gastric region, audible by stethoscope. Small, seemingly random spasmic movements visible in the abdominal flesh. Inability to eat. Passing of blood in vomit and stool. Increasing weakness. In

all three studied cases, the patient took his or her own life. If they had not, I believe that stomach rupture would have occurred.

**HISTORY:**

My first encounter with this singular malady occurred in the summer of 189-, when I was serving in general practice in A_____. My immediate predecessor had witnessed the first symptoms and had diagnosed a stomach ulcer. However, I soon ascertained that this malady, now much more advanced, was no such thing. I observed the small movements of his abdomen and listened to the "noise" via stethoscope. These sounds had no pattern that I could discern.

I confess I was both puzzled and fascinated by these phenomena, but I dare say my fascination was not shared by Mr. X. As his disease progressed, I tended to him daily, but I regret I was unable to assist him, let alone cure him. Within a week, he was found hanged in the stable where he worked.

I requested a post mortem. When I opened his stomach, I observed that the lining was perforated in many places. The perforations took the form of lines, both vertical and horizontal, of varying widths and depths. I scrupulously catalogued these strange marks.

Miss Y was brought to my attention five years later. She was 18 years of age, a pretty young lady, the daughter of a country squire. She was a solitary person, who often sat in the fields reading novels and poetry. At times she rode a favorite stallion called Charley—who was kept at the same stables in which the late Mr. X had worked.

By the time that Miss Y was referred to me, her syndrome was considerably advanced. I cannot imagine how much pain she had endured alone. Rarely have I felt myself so helpless as a doctor, and indeed the case of Miss Y distresses me more than any other. But briefly . . . she stole poison from my medicine cabinet, swallowed it and died.

I performed a post mortem, and found to my astonishment the same marks on the inner wall and lining of her stomach that I had found on Mr. X's stomach. Many of the marks were identical, though the order and pattern were different. Again, I took a transcription. The marks bore a passing resemblance to Egyptian hieroglyphs, though further discreet enquiries proved fruitless.

Miss Y was my second encounter with the syndrome, which I named Aggressive Acid Reflux. There is however a third case in the literature. *The Journals of Sarah Goodman* describe a case that took place two years after that of Miss Y, in the Lancastrian village of W_____. I corresponded with Mrs.

Goodman and visited W_____, a place of no great distinction. The case she described was of a man of considerable congenital idiocy (Mr. Z), who had been committed to an asylum for the persistent abuse of horses. The details are too distasteful to be recorded here.

Of the three cases so far recorded, there is an equine connection, strengthened by the fact that two of the horses at W_____ had been sired by stallions from A_____! However, further investigation as to Mr. X's and Miss Y's dealings with horses, other than those noted above, has not been undertaken. I was advised in no uncertain terms that this would cause considerable offence and might even provoke legal proceedings, hence my circumlocutory manner. I can imagine certain things of Mr. X, knowing the drunken jests of which young men are capable, but I refuse to imagine such perversities of the delicate Miss Y.* Any investigation of the stable itself is now impossible, as it has been sold and demolished.

While pondering on the above, I had a dream that, I dare to suggest, might prove to be as significant as Mr. Kekulé's, which revealed to him the structure of the benzene ring. I was floating, faced by a row of disembodied stomachs. Each one pulsed and gurgled, as had those of my patients. Then one of them sprayed my bare chest with a fine stream of acid and etched into my flesh the characters I had previously seen. I thought, "They are attempting to communicate with me."

Needless to say, I cannot prove any of this, not least due to the lack of further cases. Perhaps some combination of circumstances at A_____ was unique, but without any further data I cannot attempt to suggest what that combination might be. I have attempted to decipher the stomach markings but to no avail. Patterns are discernable therein, but I am unable to translate them. It is feasible that no translation is possible. What linguistic paradigms, I ask myself, does a stomach have, and to what extent are they shared by humans?

**CURES:**
None yet identified.

**SUBMITTED BY**
G.J. Couzens, M.D. [As related to him by his grandfather.]

---

* *Thwack Note:* Dr. Couzens has deleted part of this account, which records that at her post mortem Miss Y— was found not to be *virgo intacta*.

# THE FORTIES

1946: Burmese Dirigible Disease • Format: Hardcover, 5 x 8
Publisher: Chatto & Windus, London, England

After World War II, the Guide began to focus on the human costs of British Imperialism. Following a series of discussions with Lord Mountbatten in Bombay, Dr. Lambshead specifically solicited work from doctors known, at the time, for their contributions to modern Asian diseases. The publication of this entry ushered in a new period of legitimacy for Dr. Chapman. In 1940, he had been accused, while vacationing in Shanghai, of "exaggerated medical claims combined with unpatriotic conspiracy paranoia" by both German and Chinese officials. Held in a German prison for three years, Dr. Chapman found that upon his release in 1945 the world had forgotten his prior medical achievements.

## Burmese Balloon Boy Incident

**Introduction:**
The history of the Industrial Age provides numerous examples of illnesses connected with working conditions, ranging from coal dust silicosis to elevator operator's palsy. One of the most grotesque industrial diseases ever reported was the Dirigible Disease that afflicted the so-called Balloon Boys of Rangoon.

**Country of Origin:**
In 1929, Burma was a province of British-controlled India. Burma's most crucial value to the Empire resided in the rice grown in the Irrawaddy Delta, a "rice basket" for hungry India. Colonial administrators of the Imperial

Pan-Indian Rice Consortium managed vast plantations there and shipped the rice by sea from Rangoon.

The greatest challenge for these plantations was the transport of harvested rice from the swampy paddies to the warehouses at the dockyards. Flash floods washed out the roads each year. Barge canals filled with muck. Field mice and weevils invaded the rice sacks. And British trucks on rubber tires proved to be no improvement over ox carts. The mud that grew such excellent rice defeated every effort to move the harvest overland.

**History:**

An engineer of the Rice Consortium, one Mr. Jules Spratt, sent a letter to his home office in London and suggested the use of dirigible airships to transport the rice.

Self-propelled blimps were very much in the mainstream of aviation at this time. Mr. Spratt's plan was approved. Twelve new-model dirigibles were assembled at the Aircraft Guarantee Works At Howden. The new airship, christened the Spratt, was a modification of the Mayfly, a small-scale blimp that had proved its durability as a submarine spotter over the North Sea in 1917. The frames of the Spratts were built from imported Burmese teak.

In 1930, when the Spratts first flew forth from their newly thatched hangars at the Irrawaddy dockyards, they were a source of great excitement and anxiety for the local populace. Only after each airship had been ritually purified by the incense and blessings of a Pongyi priest in a yellow robe would the Burmese go anywhere near the uncanny machines.

However, after months of hearing the drone of airships overhead, the Karen people of the delta and the Shan and Kashin people at Rangoon came to accept the Spratts as a normal part of life.

Mr. Spratt's crew of aviators picked several older gentlemen from the dock workers' township and taught them to perform simple maintenance tasks on the blimps. One gentleman stripped to his cotton longyi each day and scrubbed down the windows of the steering bridges. Another oiled the hinges of the ailerons and cargo hatches.

But a nasty problem cropped up regarding the rubberized canvas nacelles that held the hydrogen gas. A slimy white mildew grew persistently on the canvas and would eat it to shreds if left unchecked. To scour the fungus from the outsides of the nacelles was simple enough. But to clean the inner surfaces, where the mildew was worst, and where workers would be engulfed in an unbreathable atmosphere, presented difficulties. Mr. Spratt considered pumping the hydrogen to holding tanks and back again. But he was worried by the risk of leakage.

He soon devised an ingenious and cost-effective solution. Boys from the nearby township were employed at half wages to enter the nacelles through makeshift air locks, wearing loincloths and holding their breaths. These Balloon Boys scraped the canvas, sprayed it with fungicide, and resealed it, working for as long as they could manage before "surfacing" for air.

Since the mildew kept returning, Mr. Spratt offered the boys long-term employment. They accepted, and like the pearl divers of Polynesia, they developed impressive powers of endurance in an airless environment. They also developed eye problems, ear problems, and throat problems, which had been more or less expected.

**Symptoms:**
What weren't expected were the strange bluish blisters that irrupted all over the boys' skins. Rather than water or blood, these blisters contained air. Or what seemed at first to be merely air.

The longer a boy worked in the hydrogen, the larger his blisters grew, until he could work no longer. Hands blew up like inflated rubber gloves. Bellies swelled to unnatural dimensions. Cheeks, noses, buttocks, and thighs ballooned on the scrawny frames of the afflicted youths. Mr. Spratt established an infirmary compound and built an isolation ward for skin disorders, hoping that the damage was reversible.

Dr. Woolsey Mahood, the Rice Consortium's resident physician, deduced that the skin inflations were filled with organically generated hydrogen. This became apparent when one of the distended boys threw off his bedclothes and floated to the thatched roof. Eventually all of the ward's patients had to be tied to their pallet beds. [1]

**Cures:**
Dr. Mahood tried everything he could think of—ice packs, bromate baths, cauterization . . . The disease progressed implacably. The puncture and deflation of the skin balloons provided symptomatic relief. But each squeezed balloon would grow back to its original size and then twice its original size in a matter of hours. The administration of holy oils by a Pongyi priest was equally futile.

In 1931, during a rebellion of the Burmese peasantry against the Indian Congress at Delhi, Mr. Spratt's hangars were destroyed by nocturnal arson.

The explosion of the blimps showered the dockyards with flaming debris and ignited the wharves, the warehouses, and the infirmary compound.

The Balloon Boys were last seen floating aloft, rising into a night sky filled with glowing red sparks. They were riding the blistering updraft from their burning skin ward.

Reportedly they were laughing as they ascended.

**Submitted by**
Dr. Stepan Chapman, staff dermatologist, Waxwall County Free Clinic

**Endnote**
[1] *Doctor Buckhead Mudthumper's Encyclopedia of Forgotten Oriental Diseases,* Wing Nut Speculum Press, London, 1941, Volume III, Bilharzia Through Cholera, page 913, "Blimp-Related Skin Growths: Conflicting Reports From Rangoon."

*The dirigibles of Rangoon*

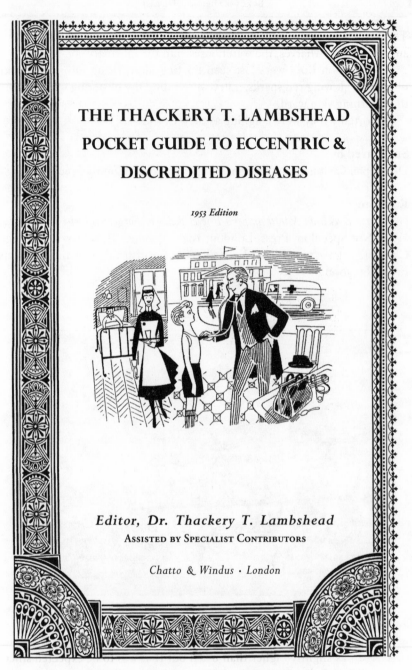

# THE THACKERY T. LAMBSHEAD
# POCKET GUIDE TO ECCENTRIC &
# DISCREDITED DISEASES

*1953 Edition*

*Editor, Dr. Thackery T. Lambshead*

ASSISTED BY SPECIALIST CONTRIBUTORS

*Chatto & Windus · London*

*Title page of the 1953 edition. Originally known as the "Coronation" edition,
it is now more popularly referred to as the "Ouija board" edition.*

# THE FIFTIES

1953: TUNING'S SPASM • FORMAT: HARDCOVER, 6 x 9
PUBLISHER: CHATTO & WINDUS, LONDON, ENGLAND

Dr. Lambshead, by his own admission, took a "wrong turn" into the world of the supernatural for a few years in the 1950s. As a result, several editions of the Guide included supernatural phenomenon unsupported by any empirical scientific findings. And, of all the diseases collected in the Guide's infamous 1953 "Ouija board" edition, Tuning's Spasm became the most notorious. Although Dr. Wilson later disowned the disease, saying it "had all been a dream, a nightmare, not based on fact at all," a Dr. Tuning from Lubbock, Texas, not only disputed this assertion but sued Dr. Wilson for appropriating "my disease." For several years, Dr. Tuning's letters to the editor and public appearances cast doubt on the veracity of the Guide.

# *Tuning's Spasm*

**COUNTRY OF ORIGIN:**
United States

**FIRST KNOWN CASE:**
Initially observed and reported during the summer of 1948 in Evanston, Illinois, by Doctor Owen Tuning, a General Practitioner whose practice was uncomplicated by the bizarre save for his brief association with the Spasm.

**CASE HISTORY:**
The patient afflicted was Charles Harding Durwood, a 45-year-old male who was the proprietor of a highly successful store dealing in stationery supplies and happily married for 23 years. He had heretofore only suffered from ordinary illnesses and up until this presentation all his visits to Tuning's office had been for a routine yearly checkup.

The doctor was surprised therefore to see how pale and oddly haggard Durwood looked when he turned up at his office after an urgent telephone call. A brief examination revealed no particularly alarming symptoms. The pulse rate was slightly higher than usual but that was to be expected since Durwood was obviously upset and distracted.

The patient was in the midst of a rambling, suspiciously evasive description of his symptoms when he suddenly broke off to turn his back on Doctor Tuning and stare silently and intently at an empty chair in the examination room.

Tuning gazed politely at the rear of his patient's head for a long moment before quietly asking if something was wrong. There was yet another patch of unresponsive silence before Durwood hoarsely cleared his throat and answered, still facing away from Tuning and continuing to stare at the empty chair.

"I'm just a little surprised to see you have one of them here," Durwood said with a decidedly breathy voice which trembled in spite of clear attempts at control. "To be honest it never occurred to me that there might even be another one!"

Then he turned back to Doctor Tuning and the physician found it required all of his professional discipline to conceal the sudden shock of horror he felt at seeing that both of his patient's eye sockets had become empty red pits.

Tuning cleared his throat and was attempting to form some sort of reply when Durwood abruptly turned back to look at the empty chair once more, gave a little start of surprise, said: "Ah, but now I see it's gone," and turned round again to face the doctor only this time with his sockets once more containing the same blue, intelligent-looking eyes they had on all prior occasions save for that last horrid moment.

Of course Tuning immediately gave his patient a thorough examination of the ocular area, but he failed to find anything whatsoever out of the ordinary.

There were no more spasms on the part of Durwood — it appears to be a short-lived, if highly disturbing, illness — but Tuning reports that several days later, while sitting in his home at the dinner table with his wife, Madge, he stopped with a forkful of food lifted halfway up to his mouth and found himself gaping wide-eyed and appalled at a gelatinous entity which — in spite of the complete lack of anything one could actually describe as a mouth — was smiling at him in the friendliest way possible from the open kitchen door.

He turned to his wife and received another severe shock when he saw her stare at him with absolute horror and then softly slide from her chair to the floor in a dead faint.

It was then he realized two things almost simultaneously: Tuning's Spasm was contagious and he'd caught it.

**SUBMITTED BY**
**Dr. Gahan Wilson**

# THE SIXTIES (1)

1960: Dr. Rikki Ducornet's Various Head Diseases • Format: Softcover, 8.5 x 11
Publisher: Jolly Boy Publishing & Soap Company, Bombay, India

Dr. Rikki Ducornet's pioneering work in the fanciful illustration of actual diseases provided an auspicious beginning to the Guide's "Jolly Boy Era." Her research in Europe and Southeast Asia led to a radical change in medical opinions on rapid mutation. At the time Dr. Lambshead published her famous selection of head diseases, she was traveling by caravan and horseback across some of the more desolate parts of North Africa, hunting down various microorganisms. By the time she returned to London, she had become a celebrity.

Yamamoto's Anomalies
girafosis . post masturbatory encephalitis . inverted hirsutism
attenuating ocular motion (spastic oculargea) . Bush's Disease:
vacuous encephalopathy . Yamamoto's Dermatosis:
. chronic proliferative dermopedunculgris .

Several unique and unexplained cases of cranial
exuberance, and two examples of subterfuge. (See
appendix.)

*Harpys Virus*
X 800,000

X 20,000

X 20,000

2.

h X 10,000

X 15,000

X 40,000

*concretising spirocutal glossopharyngitis . Marcous Dermatosis:
Acute gangrenous folliculitis . Ossifying tuberosis:
Periwinkle disease . Filarial gigantisms Face . Cockroach .
Papalpapillitis .*

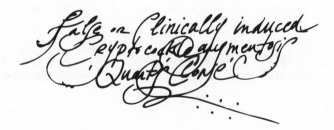

# THE SIXTIES (2)

1962: MacCreech's Dementia • Format: Softcover, 8.5 x 11
Publisher: Jolly Boy Publishing & Soap Company, Bombay, India

The following account was the first of several "anecdotal episodes" that Dr. Lambshead published for the sake of variety. "I find," he wrote in the introduction to the 1962 Guide, "that sometimes the layperson, or scientist from another field, has valuable insight into eccentric and discredited diseases. Certainly, I find them more credible than the work, of, say, such an accredited physician as the near demonic Dr. Wexler." Dr. Baker's work with whelk flukes has been praised by such luminaries as Stephen Jay Gould and Rachel Carson.

# ∎∎∎maccreech's dementia

*Fifteen Case Histories in the Population of Binscarth, 1931. A personal reminiscence. Originally published in the* **Santa Cruz Sentinel** *on August 25, 1961.*

Sirs,

The recent inexplicable behavior of flocks of *Puffinus griseus* in the skies over Branciforte calls to mind certain remarkable incidents taking place in Scotland some years ago, which I thought might interest your readers.

Having matriculated from California Polytechnic at San Luis Obispo with a degree in splanchology in 1919, I made a particular study of rare marine diseases of the spleen. In the summer of 1931, I arranged my holidays to combine business with pleasure, and traveled to the remote outer isles of Scotland to collect and observe Maturin's Cysted Whelk Fluke (*Opisthorchis busycon*).

(Formerly a decimator of the local crofter population, who harvested the indigenous Pink Whelk [*Busycon rosaea*] at low tide as a valuable source of protein, but long since brought under control by the introduction of modern sanitation and readily-affordable commercial seafood establishments, Maturin's Cysted Whelk Fluke infested the spleen rather than the liver, causing a variety of pernicious splenic disorders. But to continue:)

How vividly the events of that holiday spring to my mind! Not only was my search for Maturin's Cysted Whelk Fluke successful, yielding several prime samples residing to this very day in formaldehyde in my parlor—one is before me as I write, in fact, smiling out from its little glass jar—I was further edified by the fascinating customs of the natives, varying as they did from island to island. I have enclosed copies of photographs taken that summer, though I am uncertain whether your offset lithographer will be able to reproduce them properly.

The first (I have indicated the order in pencil on the back of each picture) was taken at a May Day Festival on, I believe, Greater Sleart, where local antiquarians had recently sponsored a charming revival of bygone folk rituals. The young men with lath swords are of particular interest; they appear to be wearing the traditional kilt of the islanders, though in fact this is a brilliant effect achieved solely through the use of elaborate tattooing, as you will see if you examine the picture closely. As you can imagine, they were literally blue with cold, though it was explained to me that the sporran mitigates their discomfort somewhat. The towering figure at the rear is a kind of human effigy made of wicker, filled with papier-mâché creatures and set ablaze at the end of the day's festivities, in imitation of the sacrifices of the ancient Celts as described by Julius Caesar. Note the look of comic consternation on the face of the local police sergeant being dragged toward the ladder by several locals who had imbibed well of good single malt! I was assured it was all in fun of course.

In the second picture you will see your correspondent and her escort, Sergeant Angus MacCreech, dining at the Three Hanged Men in Puig. The local delicacy before us was the pudding course to our meal of herrings and clapshot. It consisted of almond nougat dipped in batter and fried in deep fat, and was memorable if nearly indescribable, as you may be able to infer from our expressions.

The third picture shows the police station and infirmary on Binscarth, Sergeant MacCreech's domain, and the irregular dark building beside it (slightly obscured by the hearse) is the Hotel Metropole, where your correspondent was staying at the time of the events that I shall now describe.

Sergeant MacCreech and I were enjoying a leisurely conversation, comparing death rates from endemic splenic failure, when Treadle (his second-in-command) appeared in the doorway of the bar to inform us that grave mishap had befallen one of the islanders and he "had better come take a look" (though I will not attempt to reproduce the dialect of the region, as it is well-nigh unintelligible to the American ear). Sergeant MacCreech served as the island's amateur medical authority as well as its representative of Scots Law, and, thinking that another case of Splenic Fluke had been diagnosed, kindly invited me to accompany him as we set out across the island on foot, Binscarth being no more than four miles across at any point.

As we progressed across the barren and windswept isle, however, Treadle elaborated on that which had occurred, and it soon became evident that this was a matter for Sergeant MacCreech in his capacity of policeman. It was nothing more or less than a case of domestic murder!

As you may well imagine, homicide was an infrequent occurrence on a remote island populated by God-fearing Christian fisherfolk and shepherds; indeed, there had been no such incident in Binscarth since an unpleasant event in 1880 that I need not go into here, other than to state that model railway enthusiasts have never been welcome at the Hotel Metropole since.

The scene of the crime was a humble cottage, one of several in a row overlooking Hitchcock Bay. These were the traditional crofter's cots, built low to resist the wind, and thatched with coarse sea grass. Picturesque indeed; though the effect was somewhat spoiled by the fact that objects which I took to be curiously-shaped turves of peat were stacked against the walls as high as the eaves. On closer examination, they appeared to be firewood, which puzzled me, as Binscarth is quite treeless; but on looking closer still I discovered that they were in fact desiccated corpses of the common Northern Gannet (*Morus bassanus*). The fishermen net these pelagic birds in summer by the hundreds, skin them, smoke them, and stack them to dry; and they serve as an important supplement to the crofter's winter diet, especially when storms keep the fishing boats in harbor and edible protein is scarce. I was assured that, when boiled, battered, and fried in deep fat, the overpoweringly fishy taste of the Northern Gannet is reasonably mitigated, though I declined to sample this regional delicacy for reasons that shall shortly become evident.

We entered the cottage in question—small, dark, and redolent of a pungent smoke I supposed was peat—and beheld the deceased, sprawled on his own hearth. A tea towel had been hastily thrown over the corpse's head out of respect for my feelings, but the pooled blood on the hearthstone beneath was enough to make plain that the unfortunate Mr. Magilside had been severely beaten about the head and shoulders with an object both sharp and weighty. In fact, the murder weapon was a particularly large and well-cured specimen of *Morus bassanus*, still firmly clutched in the fist of Mrs. Magilside, who sat guarded by a rather shamefaced policeman. She was a matronly and respectable-looking woman of some 60 years of age, the last sort of person one would suspect of bloodlust; and she glared at us defiantly as we entered.

Sergeant MacCreech asked her at once what she thought she had been about; to which she replied that she had been driven to her rash act, and would never have done such a thing but that Magilside had flagrantly and repeatedly broken the Commandment against Adultery, despite her earnest entreaties to desist.

She added further that she had been prepared to excuse and overlook even so grave a sin, had it been committed with (for example) the barmaid at the Seven Heretics; but it was Magilside's dalliance with Cleopatra that had finally pushed her over the edge.

Following a stunned silence, Sergeant MacCreech asked her who this Cleopatra might be; whereupon Mrs. Magilside replied that it was the whoring Queen of Egypt, of course, the one who had broken up Mark Antony's domestic happiness as well.

It seemed a clear case of Not Guilty by Reason of Insanity, so after a few stern admonishments on self-control, Sergeant MacCreech sent for the hearse, which did double duty on the island as police van. There seemed nothing left to do but consign the deceased to the morgue and the living to the asylum, and the Sergeant and I left the cottage in the full expectation of an afternoon's fruitful tide pooling for specimens of *Busycon rosaea*.

However, as we emerged into the bitter air, we were approached by one of Mrs. Magilside's neighbors, a stout woman of about the same age as the murderess, who sidled close and slyly intimated that there was more to the murder than met the eye. When asked to elucidate, she replied that while it had been true enough that Fat Tammy had been dancing adultery's reel with Cleopatra, nonetheless a man must keep his self-respect; and everyone in the street knew that he'd never have done it if Mrs. Magilside hadn't been entertaining Robert the Bruce as her fancy man for close to a month now.

It was at this moment that I intuitively grasped that we were dealing with some remarkable shared delusion.

Sergeant MacCreech questioned the neighbor (a Mrs. Beamish) delicately, and was astounded by her assertion that there was not one cottage in the row that did not shelter some celebrated person. Mrs. Beamish herself admitted that she let her spare room to King Darius of Persia, though that was a different affair entirely from Mrs. Magilside's immoral goings-on; for King Darius, though foreign, was a decent sober individual and in any case she herself was a widow, the late Mr. Beamish having succumbed to Splenic Distortion some five years previous.

At this point, Treadle volunteered that he thought it was a damned shame, the way the island had changed since the celebrated dead had moved in;

and that a man used to be able to enjoy a quiet dram in the Seven Heretics without having his elbow continually jostled by the likes of that French ponce Napoleon, and that if something wasn't done about it soon, he, for one, would consider emigration.

Sergeant MacCreech and I exchanged alarmed glances at this, for it was now evident that the delusion was, perhaps, widespread. Treadle was told to report to the infirmary, though he protested that he was perfectly well. We then thanked Mrs. Beamish for her insights and proceeded along the row of cottages, systematically interviewing the inhabitants under guise of gathering evidence concerning the murder.

By teatime we had determined that no less than 15 individuals were quite convinced that any number of historical personages had taken up residence on Binscarth, for no apparent reason. It appeared, moreover, that these visitors were for the most part sadly lacking in moral character. Joan of Arc and Alexander the Great were particularly notorious, evidently; though the Queen of Sheba and Robespierre were also doing their share of wrecking marriages; and I myself witnessed one grim-faced fisherman saying that if the price of gunpowder were not so high, he would shoot Socrates full of holes for carrying on with his daughter, who was now in a delicate condition, and Socrates a married man as everyone knew.

It would be imprecise to say that the interviewees appeared to be in good health, for they suffered variously from heart disease, hypertension, dental caries, and, of course, splenic insult to a greater or lesser degree, due to their habitual diet. Beyond these conditions, however, I could find nothing wrong with any of them, at least on the cursory examination that was all I was able to perform. Nor did the dementia otherwise hinder their thought processes. I was particularly struck by a pleasant grandmother, rational in every respect, save when she paused whilst displaying photographs of her American grandchildren to swat at a phantom hand on her bosom; and then blushed, explaining apologetically that Lord Nelson had only the one hand but it wandered something awful.

Moreover the delusion was shared and consistent; for the postman, stepping in a moment later to deliver a copy of the *London Illustrated News*, observed sourly that wee Horatio was clearly up to his tricks again.

Sergeant MacCreech at last ventured to inquire when the dead had become so troublesome, and the general consensus seemed to be that they had first made their presence known shortly after the supply ship from Thurso had foundered, or about the time that Sergeant MacCreech and I had been visiting Greater Sleart. This, had we but known it at the time, was our second clue in solving the medical mystery; the first being the reek of peculiarly acrid smoke noticeable in each of the cottages we visited.

We returned to the hotel, baffled, though I was already striving to call up a half-buried memory of a similar epidemic of dementia in Finland in 1905. Moreover, the occurrence of shared and consistent delusion is not unknown, especially under the action of certain vegetable alkaloids. Imbibers of the Wumbo Root, native to Tasmania, invariably complain of the threatening behavior of little yellow men made of sponges, who only they seem to be able to perceive.

It was only after several whiskies, as we wandered in the long northern twilight, that the third clue came in the form of the new supply ship, steaming proudly up to the Binscarth jetty, her decks laden with crates of goods for the island's shop. We watched the crates being brought ashore and loaded into a waiting wagon; and Sergeant MacCreech remarked that there seemed to be an unusual quantity of them. I pointed out that the previous ship had foundered, presumably with the loss of all its cargo, and that therefore the present shipment must be larger to compensate.

One of the stevedores, heaving ashore a crate marked MACBAREN'S PLUMCAKE CAVENDISH, remarked familiarly that Binscarth "*was a greetin sair for its baccy,*" which Sergeant MacCreech translated for me, giving me to understand that tobacco lovers on the island had suffered nicotine privation as a result of the lost shipment.

"Then what can they be smoking?" I wondered aloud, remembering the noxious fume common to every cottage we had visited. Sergeant MacCreech's eyes met mine, and we instantly knew that the solution to our mystery lay just within reach. Indeed, before noon of the following day we had nearly solved it, thanks to further patient and discreet inquiries.

It transpired that the natives, seeking desperately to assuage their nicotine cravings, had resorted to shaving and pounding the dry, leathery flesh (which did resemble shag-cut Turkish) of the Northern Gannets stacked against every outer wall. The result was a mixture of bitter, not to say nauseating flavor that the natives nevertheless found curiously satisfying when packed into the bowl of a clay pipe and lit. The one exception had been Mrs. Magilside, who had taken hers as a snuff.

Even so, this was not sufficient to explain the mass hallucination of lewdly behaved phantoms. Though distasteful, there is nothing inherently toxic in gannet flesh. We resolved to examine the problem more closely, and to that end repaired to the island's infirmary with three specimens taken from the stack of Northern Gannets next to Mrs. Magilside's cottage.

Peering closely at the black, withered things, we could see nothing out of the ordinary—or at least Sergeant MacCreech could not, for I was scarcely able to offer an opinion on what a dried Northern Gannet ought to look like. It was not until he produced a magnifying glass from a drawer and made a more detailed examination that Sergeant MacCreech noticed the brown mosslike substance apparently growing on the birds. It had, curiously enough, a not altogether unpleasant smell; and perhaps this was what emboldened us to test its properties, in the name of scientific experimentation.

Employing Sergeant MacCreech's penknife, we shaved away several fine flakes of particularly mossy bird flesh, and by judicious use of a coal hammer reduced it to serviceable fragments. Here we were at an impasse, for we lacked the clay tobacco pipes favored by the islanders, and as it was past ten the newsagent's was closed; but Sergeant MacCreech, having inquired amongst his subordinates, obtained a book of cigarette papers, and shortly produced a suitable pair of "roll-ups" or "reefers."

These, when lit, produced a notably greasy smoke and an appalling smell, though after the first few inhalations the taste was not so pronounced as one would have thought. Sergeant MacCreech was just drawing out his memorandum book to make a record of any symptoms when the infirmary door opened. We looked up, expecting to see the young policeman who had loaned us his papers. Imagine my astonishment on beholding instead Erasmus of Rotterdam, closely followed by Thomas Jefferson!

I would like to state for the record that I was in absolutely no doubt as to their identities, for they closely resembled their historical portraits. Initially I was delighted, assuming that we might engage in a stimulating discussion of the humanist philosophies that had led to the Enlightenment. Sadly, this was not to be. Neither gentleman seemed remotely interested in intellectual exercise, quite the contrary in fact, and Erasmus in particular made several suggestions of a quite shocking nature.

Nor was I to receive any support, moral or otherwise, from my esteemed colleague, for he was entirely preoccupied with rebuffing the improper advances of Eleanor of Aquitaine.

I will draw a veil of propriety over the next several hours, but by the time the hallucinations took their leave, in the unpleasantly blue dawn, we had a thorough understanding of the chemical forces that had so worked upon the inhabitants of Binscarth.

It will be remembered that the spring of 1931 was remarkably warm in the islands, one might even go so far as to say sweltering, with daily temperatures reaching as high as 40 degrees Fahrenheit. Moreover, the spring Northern Gannet harvest was particularly abundant that year, as the birds were unusually easy to catch; many a crofter recalled afterward that they had seemed disoriented, falling prey almost too easily to the net and the club.

It may be that the warmer temperatures resulted in a certain degree of spoilage, providing a suitable medium in which the unknown mold (since dubbed *Sclerotium maccreechi*) was able to thrive on the imperfectly-dried bodies of the Northern Gannet. Would it even be too fanciful to suggest that the unfortunate birds were themselves under its influence at the time they blundered into the crofters' nets?

In any case, matters were soon set to rights on Binscarth. The tainted gannets were collected and destroyed, though, it must be admitted, over the objections of the crofters. Mr. Magilside's death was ruled a misadventure after Sergeant MacCreech proudly presented his "Observations on a New Disorder Which We Shall Call MacCreech's Dementia" before the Department of Medicine at Scrabster College, and for some years my friend became a local celebrity.

News of the effects of *S. maccreechi* reached even unto Glasgow, where the Presbyterian Women's Society for Social Elevation established a fund to purchase a patented food-drying device for the use of the islanders, a remarkable pyramidal cabinet lined with pitchblende, and sent a delegation of society members to establish meaningful dialogues with the island residents concerning proper preservation of food. The device was reported to have worked very well, successfully preventing any growth of suspicious molds on Northern Gannets kept within it. I am sorry to say, however, that the islanders were not long able to enjoy its benefits, since most of them passed away within the next decade from a mysterious degenerative bone ailment.

I returned to California that autumn and pursued my vocation as a writer, producing several well-thought-of monographs and treatises on Maturin's Cysted Whelk Fluke (of which I may proudly claim to know more than any researcher now living) as well as penning the occasional "scientifiction" story for light entertainment.

Apologies if I have rambled on somewhat. I have suffered occasional lingering effects from my experiment with *S. maccreechi*, of which excessive conversation is the most common. However, Saint Luke assures me that my lapses are scarcely noticeable, and have grown less frequent of late. ■

**Dr. Kage Baker**

*One of the infamous—now highly collectable—Jolly Boy editions (see Chronology, p. 221).
The copy shown is for the year 1975. MacCreech's Dementia appeared in one of the first of
the Jolly Boy editions.*

# La Guía de Bolsillo a Las Enfermedades Metafísicas

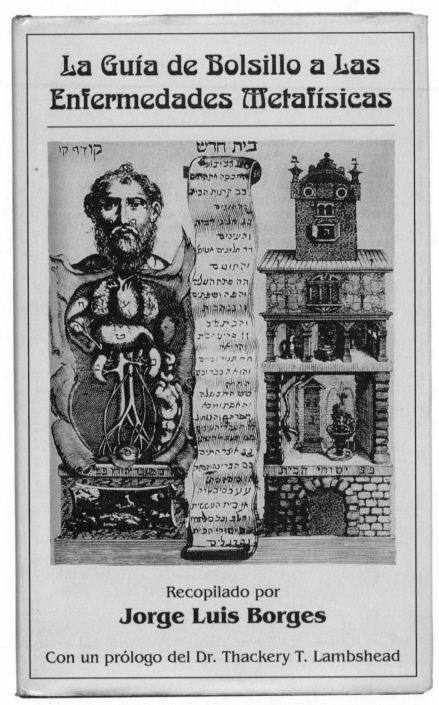

Recopilado por

## Jorge Luis Borges

Con un prólogo del Dr. Thackery T. Lambshead

*The Argentine Spanish-language edition of Borges'*
Pocket Guide to Metaphysical Diseases *(1977)*

# THE SEVENTIES

**1977: THE MALADY OF GHOSTLY CITIES (PUBLISHED IN THE POCKET GUIDE
TO METAPHYSICAL DISEASES EDITED BY JORGE LUIS BORGES)
FORMAT: HARDCOVER, 6 X 9
PUBLISHER: DE LA SOL, BUENOS AIRES, ARGENTINA**

While not strictly an example from a prior edition of the Guide, "The Malady of Ghostly Cities" exemplifies the ways in which Dr. Lambshead's influence has manifested itself in the world—even to the point of inspiring others to create their own guides.

In 1953 in Buenos Aires, the illustrious Argentine author Jorge Luis Borges sought anxiously for an effective treatment for his persistent earaches. This search led to Borges' encounter with Dr. Thackery T. Lambshead, whose accounts of his work in medical research made a great impression on the blind literary artist and library administrator.

The two men's mutual admiration and their ensuing correspondence over the next 30 years led Borges to edit his one and only medical work, *The Pocket Guide to Metaphysical Diseases* (sometimes known as the *Compendium of Rare and Fantastical Afflictions*), which was released in 1977 and featured important articles by 21 distinguished Latin American physicians. The sole European contributor to this volume was the reclusive transcendental pathologist, Dr. Nathan Ballingrud of Norway. Dr. Ballingrud's report on the "malady of ghostly cities," translated into Spanish by Borges and Gabriel Mesa, marked the first time information about this apparently venerable disease appeared in print.

*The Pocket Guide to Metaphysical Diseases* has languished for more than two decades as an out-of-print curiosity, avidly sought by collectors of first editions, but ignored by the medical community. (A cheap mass market paperback English-language version did appear in 1979. However, it contained only half of the material from the original Spanish edition, omitting Dr. Ballingrud's disease. The translations from the Spanish were so incompetent that Borges himself disowned the edition.)

The editors hope that this valuable collection will someday be reissued in an English translation. Apart from the book's obvious value as a springboard for further research into rare tropical diseases, it constitutes a glowing tribute to the impact that Dr. Lambshead makes on the life of nearly everyone he encounters.

We are proud to make the following excerpt available in English for the first time, translated from the Spanish version by Diego Funes. "The Malady of Ghostly Cities" proves once again that in the realms of disease, truth is often stranger than fiction.

*Translator's Note:* Before his disappearance in 1978, Dr. Nathan Ballingrud was enjoying a return to international prominence, albeit in an unfamiliar capacity, due to the anticipation brewing in medical circles surrounding the imminent publication of the second edition of Jorge Luis Borges' *Compendium of Rare and Fantastical Afflictions*. Previously, Ballingrud had served as the Royal Medical Officer in the Kingdom of Norway from 1960 until his unceremonious dismissal in 1971, after it was revealed that he had collaborated

## EL MAL DE CIUDADES FANTASMALES

**Dr. Nathan Ballingrud**

EL PRIMER CASO DEL MAL DE CIUDADES FANTASMALES que se conozca fue descubierto en 1976 por la marina Argentina durante sus intentos por establecer una base en la Isla Cook, la más meridional de las Islas Sandwich del Sur, a poca distancia de la costa de la Antártida. La víctima fue un tal Ivar Jorgensen, miembro de la expedición al Polo Sur de 1910 a 1912 del explorador Roald Amundsen.

De acuerdo a los diarios de Amundsen (Vol. XXIV: *Racing the Empire*, Libro 3, p. 276), Jorgensen abandonó al grupo, hurtando un trineo y cuatro perros al amparo de la noche para ayudar en su huída. Amundsen hace poca mención de cambio alguno en el comportamiento o apariencia de Jorgensen antes del increíble evento, comentando solamente que "parecía estar sufriendo de algún tipo de delirio. El pobre tonto no va a durar dos días por su cuenta."

La verdad fue que duró considerablemente más de dos días. Logró viajar varios cientos de millas sobre el terreno brutal de la Antártida, cruzando incluso el estrecho tramo del Mar de Weddell hasta encallar en la Isla Cook, donde sucumbió a su enfermedad. Sus restos permanecieron en un silencio congelado durante 64 años.

Desde ese entonces tres otros casos han sido descubiertos, haciendo posible una definición rudimentaria de los síntomas de la enfermedad, aunque no de sus causas. Poniéndolo de manera sencilla, es un mal que transforma a su víctima – al parecer de la noche a la mañana – en una ciudad poblada por fantasmas. La identidad de la víctima, junto con un archivo de sus sueños y temores así como de las geografías de su cuerpo, se contienen en una pequeña serie de volúmenes encuadernados, localizados en un sótano escondido y amortiguados contra la intrusión como un cerebro en un cráneo.

*Sample page from Dr. Ballingrud's disease in the original Spanish-language edition of the The Pocket Guide to Metaphysical Diseases.*

with the Nazis during their occupation of Norway during the Second World War. His research into what he called the Malady of Ghostly Cities, soon after its discovery in 1976, aroused the interest of Borges, who arranged to fly him to Argentina so that he could visit the site in person. Alas, the notorious criminal Jack Oleander beat him to the punch, and the results are described herein. It is believed that Ballingrud was prepared to follow Oleander to Libya when he was abducted by the Argentinean government in 1978, a victim of their infamous "dirty war."—DIEGO FUNES

# The Malady of Ghostly Cities

**The first known case** of the Malady of Ghostly Cities was discovered in 1976 by the Argentinean Navy during efforts to establish a base on Cook Island, the southernmost of the South Sandwich Islands, just off the coast of Antarctica. The victim was one Ivar Jorgensen, a member of Norwegian explorer Roald Amundsen's 1910–12 expedition to the South Pole.

According to Amundsen's diaries (Vol. XXIV: *Racing the Empire*, Bk. 3, pg. 276), Jorgensen abandoned the party under cover of night, stealing a sledge and four dogs to aid his flight. Amundsen makes little mention of any change in Jorgensen's demeanor or appearance before this incredible event, noting only that "(h)e seemed to be suffering from a sort of delirium. The poor fool won't last two days on his own."

In fact, he lasted considerably more than two days. He managed to travel several hundred miles over Antarctica's brutal country, even crossing the narrow scope of the Weddell Sea, until he beached himself on Cook Island, where he succumbed to his disease. His remains abided there in frozen silence for 64 years.

Since then, three other cases have been discovered, making possible a rudimentary definition of the disease's manifestations, if not its causes. Simply put, it is a malady that transforms the victim—seemingly overnight—into a city populated by phantoms. The identity of the victim, along with a record of dreams, fears, and geographies of the body, are contained in a small series of bound volumes, located in a hidden cellar, buffered against intrusion like a brain in a skull.

In each case, the victim was apparently a traveler far from home, and indeed, far from any substantial civilization. Otherwise, characteristics vary dramatically.

The Jorgensen city resembled, naturally enough, a turn-of-the-century Norwegian fishing village. It was populated by a host of spectral figures, solid in appearance but breaking into little whirlpools of cloud and mist if one attempted to touch them, coalescing again moments later as if nothing out of the ordinary had happened. They interacted freely with one another, but did not seem to notice in any fashion the Argentinean soldiers who stood in their midst and demanded, at great volume, to know how long they had been there, and what it was they thought they were doing.

The Jorgensen city is one of only two cases in which the secret library has been discovered. The small series of books that composes these libraries gives a detailed account of the victim's life. This is not an account, however, of the mundane aspects of that life (although it seems those can be gleaned from the comprehensive footnotes that supplement the texts); they are instead a precise record of the imagination. As such, they are filled with the exploits and terrors of the victims' dreams, secret thoughts, and the potential resolutions of their lives. Esoteric knowledge is also contained here, often at a level of scholarship far exceeding that which the victim could have reasonably attained during his lifetime (for example, Jorgensen's library is reputed to have contained a moving map of the night sky visible from Cook Island, one for every day of the year since his birth in 1882; the stars crawled across the pages as they would the natural sky; clouds floated past, rain and snow rose from the pages of stormy days in a fine mist).

The other known city is Colleen Norton, a discontented college student from Columbia University in New York City, who disappeared from her classes and the lives of her family and friends without a word of warning. She traveled to North Africa, taking up with a band of Bedouin wanderers, ingratiating herself to them with her uncanny ability to pick up languages and her extensive knowledge of their culture. Evidently, she already carried the disease, however, and within weeks a mysterious new city was half buried by the roaming dunes of the Sahara Desert: it is a city built entirely of glass; its silent occupants can be glimpsed only through the reflections they cast.

The books here were discovered in an underground chamber cleverly disguised by a series of angled mirrors. The books revealed a tempestuous inner life of longings and ambitions. Among them were a series of novels that she might have written depicting the histories of dream cities fashioned by a secret society of architects who have severed their ties with the material

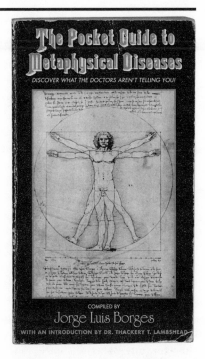

The Pocket Guide to
Metaphysical Diseases

DISCOVER WHAT THE DOCTORS AREN'T TELLING YOU!

COMPILED BY
Jorge Luis Borges

WITH AN INTRODUCTION BY DR. THACKERY T. LAMBSHEAD

concerns and restrictions of human life, as well as a two-volume catalogue of the Libraries of Heaven and Hell that included the half dozen locations on Earth where some of these books can be acquired.

Two other recently discovered cities are believed to be results of the disease, although as of this writing their libraries have yet to be discovered. One is located in the Ghost Forest in central Brazil. This city, fog-garlanded, rain-haunted, is constructed from the bones of exotic birds of the area, and is the only city that seems to have a discernible relationship with its immediate environs. Its fragile construction is the principal reason for the continued mystery surrounding the location of the library: the hollow bones of the birds are easily crushed by even the lightest explorer. For now, we must stand in frustration at its borders, gazing into its complicated arrangements and listening to the whispered, melodic conversations of its hidden inhabitants, which emerge from the city in glowing, gossamer loops and coils, illuminating the wet green foliage and our own astonished faces.

The other city exists in a labyrinth of caves, tunnels, and abandoned mine shafts in the southern Appalachian Mountains of West Virginia. The city is a dark, sprawling arrangement of stunted buildings, suffused with the perpetual sound of grinding machinery. The inhabitants of this awful place have been stripped of all their skin: the glistening tangles of muscle and tendon flex and surge in absolute darkness, staggering around on broken limbs, hustling to and fro in an excited caper. They are prone to sudden, spectacular acts of violence, rending their fellow citizens into shivering slabs of meat. The muted sound of angry exertions, grunts of rage and effort, follow these monsters around like dogs on chains.

There is much disagreement regarding the length of time this disease has been with us. Some maintain that it is a product of the Industrial Revolution, depicting in bold strokes the subjugation of the soul to the mechanized muscle of unbounded greed and arrogance. Others suppose it is a traveler's disease, in which the victim's profound desire for home manifests itself in this unearthly architecture, although the fantastic nature of most of these cities seems to undermine this theory. Others posit that the Malady of Ghostly Cities has afflicted humankind for thousands of years, that we have in fact made homes of the corpses of its victims, and that what we perceive as ghosts are the world's true citizens, the ones left here by the memory of the dead.

Until recently, no cure was believed to exist. In early 1978, however, the case of Ivar Jorgensen was finally laid to rest by Jack Oleander, an infamous book thief who chartered a boat to take him to Cook Island so that he could steal the city's secret library and sell the books on the black market. He succeeded in spiriting the books out of the city, but when the hired pilot failed to rendezvous with him at the agreed-upon time, he was forced to burn the books in order to survive the Antarctic night.

According to the statement he gave the Argentine authorities (who had, incidentally, arrested Oleander's boat captain and were on their way to arrest him when he consigned the library to flame), as he turned to watch the cascades of glowing cinders carried away by the snowy wind, his gaze fell upon the city, and he fell to his knees in astonishment. Two great wings arose from the humble skyline, beating mightily, and the city was carried away into the deep night.

Oleander escaped from the authorities shortly after giving this statement. It is believed he is headed to Libya to pillage the Norton city.

The Jorgensen incident has since given rise to the Society of Urban Transcendence, whose members have declared their intentions to seek out and destroy the secret libraries of all the cities of the earth, so that the iron- and concrete-clad ghosts that have turned our world into a forest of tombs might finally be free, and rise like God's breath into the stars which beckon them.

NATHAN BALLINGRUD, M.D.

# THE EIGHTIES

1982: SAMOAN GIANT RAT BITE FEVER • FORMAT: SOFTCOVER, 5.5 x 8.5
PUBLISHER: JOLLY BOY PUBLISHING & SOAP COMPANY, BOMBAY, INDIA

The following anecdotal entry formed part of Dr. Lambshead's "Classic Reprint" series, culled from obscure sources. As Dr. Lambshead wrote in his introduction to this disease, "I am particularly fond of this entry for several reasons. My days in Samoa were among the most restful and productive of my career. I also experience a perverse joy at finding a reference to another 'Dr. Lambshead' in the text. And I love the author's fanciful approach to the subject of rodent breeding habits." Interestingly enough, the good Reverend Moorcock seems to display additional symptoms of disease, including "multiverse chronoshock."

## Truth stranger than Fiction:

## SAMOAN GIANT RAT BITE FEVER

### SOME OBSERVATIONS BY A RETIRED CLERGYMAN.

WHOAH! Whoah, there Poppy, girl. Watch out for her, sir. Don't be deceived by her, sir. Watch her fangs, sir. Strongest rat in Christendom, she's un! They don't brush their teeth, sir, ha, ha, and they don't want us to do it fer em, neither. *Don't let 'er jump yer guv'nor!*"

This last too late!

Sergeant Fletcher himself was soon to perish from the disease which came inevitably with my refusal to heed his warnings. I was not the first to be lured back to the Vauxhall Sanctuary to make fascinated contact with the Samoan Giant Rat, straining in her straps and muzzles and barely checked by the huge Curiosity Monger. Although almost seven feet tall and broad as a Welshman's boast, Sergeant Fletcher was evidently terrified and his attendants were clearing the amphitheatre. I turned to follow the others, but too late. Poppy had torn through enough of her jaw restraints to take me in the calf.

The Samoan Giant Rat is a close cousin of the Giant Rat of Sumatra, but larger and with a nastier bite. The showman had been quite right. I rued the day I was ever lured back to the madhouse by

A NARROW ESCAPE.

the fresh attractions of captured deadly animals and shrubs. I had sworn away from the place, partly because most madmen are banal at best. They share so many delusions that they might as well form a society of their own and have done with it. And partly on account of new findings which showed the seeds of madness are carried by mouth, upon the breath. Thus locking up one lunatic with another had the effect of increasing the madness of both, with a clear danger

to the observer. I was not alone and the public had fallen away badly. Since the madhouse was an institution entirely dependent upon the good will of a visiting public, lavender-soaked handkerchiefs were offered and novelties introduced. The rat was one of them. Four days later it escaped, was cornered by a one-legged costard-woman in Portobello Road, fixed its teeth inextricably in the oak of her false limb, and was held there with nothing but a crutch and her natural odour until

Captain Meadley turned up to deal with it. He was from Leeds and specialised in capturing or destroying large rodents. They were able to drug this one. I believe it's still alive on the Isle of Morn, which Meadley and his men had a grudge against. By all accounts only seven of the original fourteen hundred inhabitants have not succumbed. Seamen from the Scillies refuse to land there and there is no other communication. The reports have never been published and those privy to them refuse to speak of their contents. Millais, the painter, paid two men to take him out in a boat, but the sounds from the island drove him back and he returned with a few disturbing sketches. The large house has been abandoned and is apparently the rat's favoured winter quarters. Since there was some suggestion she was carrying eggs when she escaped, there is a likelihood that she is no longer the only example of her species at liberty in Christendom.

Samoan Rat Bite Fever does not at first seem serious. Initially it feels no worse than a fairly bad dog bite, but within a day the infected area begins to pulse and spread, sending glittering green tendrils into thighs and pelvis in my case, but more commonly into wrists and lower arms. That first night, believing Fletcher's words to be exaggerated, I took a couple of aspirin, a hot water bottle and a copy of *A Man Without Qualities* to bed but was soon forced to get up and select one of the later Soviet Socialist Realists before I could get a wink.

Tirgiditi never fails and has been a blessing for myself and fellow sufferers for three quarters of a century. How

THE RIGHT REV. M.ST.-J.N.S. MOORCOCK
*(Photo: Elliott & Fry, Baker Street, W.)*

many, like me, mourned the passing of the Soviet Union and the prospect of incurable insomnia? *Wet Socks: Big Factory*, especially in the fifth volume, remains the definitive and most effective work of that particular movement.

By the following day the now-familiar symptoms had begun to manifest themselves. I had spasming fingers and uncontrollable feet. Naturally I went into denial, which was only reversed after I had been arrested several times. The first occasion was when I groped two elderly ladies, my fingers inadvertently locking on a surgical stocking. My arm was knocked by the wheel of her chair and this of course compounded the situation. Of all the embarrassing incidents, this was the most shocking. I was also accused of minor obscenities involving an organ-grinder's monkey and a Rottweiler.

In the end, the Rottweiler best reminded me that I needed to seek professional help. I sought it and my hand was sewn back on by the great performing surgeon Ten Seconds Tennyson. But the limb was by now even more unpredictable in its behaviour. I suppose I could be said to have hit rock bottom during the now-notorious football game in which the Saints beat the Bears by some enormous margin. The Saints had certain advantages over the Bears, not least in being the most sentient creatures after God Himself (fielding three powerful Archangels in their offence), while the Bears are to be blunt reasonably bright brutes. They have never won a game over any kind of supernatural intelligence and have yet to recover from the shame of losing 105-4 to the junior Cherubims.

I digress. Suffice it to say that during the game, involuntarily, my hand had clamped itself on the upper thigh of one of the player's wives and my efforts to release her (and myself) had not gone unnoticed by the Bears' best reserve players, one of whom was her husband and the other her lover of recent weeks. Their disappointment in losing a game they had expected to win (they are optimistic but not realistic) found some release in their treatment of me but I reminded them, while I was still able to speak, that mauling a human being was not going to improve their pathetic score averages against the various heavenly echelons they insisted on challenging, season after season. Soon afterwards I lost sensibility, but I remember some remarks about "that warty geek" and "ichorous underwear." I believe those were from the ambulance men who carried me to St Xavier the Hermit's.

By the time the shoplifting arrests began I already had a letter explaining my condition, but I was never trusted in my own neighbourhood and had to go further and further afield in search of common household supplies. Then of course the condition worsened and I became desperate for a cure. Ultimately, of course, I had no choice but to seek out Lambshead, who deals in these things and acquires items most captains would not dare dream of seeking, but he placed a high price on his courage and I could not be sure I would get my money's worth. He had shrugged and given me a sweat-stained card. I could find him there if I made a different decision.

Any talk of raspberry porridge or poultices of drawn house-rats is pure superstitious tomfoolery and no time should be wasted on preparing either. The Samoan Rat makes its venom not from any secreted sacs, but from the permanent filth boiling on her large incisors and in her gums.

Therefore, there is no specific cure because the volatile poison which develops on the Rat's front teeth often varies considerably in character and might be formed from any combination of elements. Raspberry porridge, if introducing the right amount of fine-chopped bloodworm, or lampreys, can provide sustenance and strength and control symptoms but is not in itself useful against the condition, which takes this form, viz:

- Small pustules on the back of the neck and between fingers, especially close to the original bite (one to three days before second symptom appears), viz:

• Moisture exuding from under fingernails and toenails, sometimes gelatinous
• Oddly smelling sweats, especially at night, but gradually becoming frequent during day
• An itching which feels as if the flesh is being nibbled from within
• Vomiting ichor
• Uncontrollable movement of arms, hands and fingers (Cocker's Twitch, in the vernacular)
• Tendency to make peculiar mooing noises from odd parts of mouth (see above)
• Constant yearning for salty cheese
• Tendency to hallucinate (and mistake soap for cheese—v. common)
• Foaming at the nostrils and gums
• Foaming at the tear ducts and also some foaming from saliva glands (occasional foaming from other orifices such as penis, vagina, sphincter, throat)
• Blackening or reddening and swelling of testicles in men, but women exhibit typical "vagina glow". Unrelievable "pelvic cramp". Both cause considerable embarrassment in public.
• Distortion and elongation of nose and upper jaw (Cocker's twitch; usually only develops in infected infants)
• Discoloration of front incisors
• Loosening and falling out of molars
• Ichorous stools
• Patient notices pool of ichor when rising from chair
• Blood mixed in coughed up ichor

BEFORE    AFTER

• Stomach shows signs of dissolving, Patient reports strong smell of malt vinegar.
• Stomach, bowels and intestines dissolve
• Death follows.

Fundamentally, the antidote neutralises the ichor and while most of the other symptoms persist it is possible to live some sort of normal life, often for several years. Needless to say, I was eventually forced to seek the services of Lambshead whose gloating response was scarcely gracious. I paid his price, which included all the teeth that had so far fallen out, a piece of fresh skin, plus a cup of mixed juices. The cash payment alone would have ruined an ordinary man and involved unwelcome negotiations with trustees and relatives, but the antidote was duly delivered, together with the offending rat, since the antidote must first be smeared on the rat's front teeth to be effective. Not only must one suffer a further bite, but the antidote's malforming side effects guarantee that all further sexual relationships will be both foul and perverse, requiring a whole new chapter of psychopathology to describe. Because of the side effects, real celibacy, of course, is out of the question and would, in fact, be lethal. Vinegar baths (must be malt) filled with small eels offer some temporary relief. Sympathetic friends have placed advertisements in the more idiosyncratic specialist "Venusian" sex journals, but so far there has been no response, so perhaps my sacrifices have, after all, been for nothing. I have so far refused the unwholesome Lambshead's offer to capture, train and bring me a Dwarf Stoat of Sarawak, which has notorious compulsions.

I leave you, Reader, with an urgent warning! Avoid curiosity, at all costs. It is the Devil who guides your instincts. Eschew the temptations of madhouse and gaming theatre. It is particularly unwise to allow oneself to be fascinated by the Samoan Rat, for she will almost inevitably find a way to bite you. Samoan Ratbite Fever is not a disease deserved by any but the most evil, yet I was until recently a respected man of the cloth. Should you hear of such a rat being exhibited (one other is in captivity and was of some use to me before being returned to the Split Royal Zoological Park) and should you fall party to that deadly curiosity, then be sure never to approach the beast, however entranced you may be, no matter how great your attraction to the rat's glittering colouring and infamous smile.

*Submitted by:*
*Reverend M.St.-J.N.S. Moorcock*

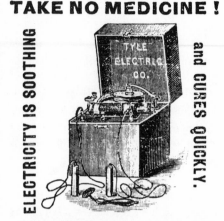
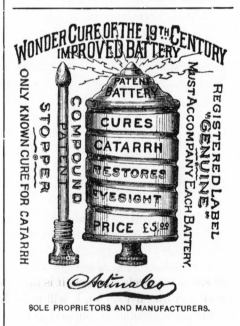

# THE NINETIES

1997: The Putti • Format: Softcover, 6 x 9
Publisher: Boojum Press, Ataxia Gorge, California, United States

The 1997 edition of the Guide represented a slight detour for Dr. Lambshead, into the free-form disease entry, in which the writer attempts to capture the flavor and substance of the disease through the style of the prose. Less importance is attached to an accurate rendering of the disease, or to use of standard medical terminology. Dr. Lambshead abandoned this approach in 1998 due to several dozen malpractice suits filed against practitioners who had used the prior year's Guide for diagnostic purposes. Dr. Shelley Jackson continues to mix medical fact and medical fiction to this day, with no adverse side effects.

The Putti

**I AM HERE TO SKETCH** the contours of the double danger that concerns us: the putti as parasite, the putti as drug. I am here with bias, performers, and visuals.

We will start by considering the putti as drug, known as auntie, little sister, pigeon (after the look-alike that dupes hasty buyers), slug, devil, root, red doll. I am a user. No doubt I will speak strangely at times. It is my conviction that if I do so, it will not hobble my presentation, but add to it that stink of the real which makes of fact: understanding.

Please follow me as we leave the committee room to observe the sale of putti firsthand. If you are wearing the wrong shoes, elegant slip-on medium-heel galoshes are available for a small rental fee from the kiosk outside, so move right along toward this authentic street scene, please do not step over the ropes to examine the illusion more carefully, as you will damage the exhibit. You will all be thoroughly searched as we leave. Observe a street polka-dotted with chewing-gum rounds. Here putti may be tracked down quickly enough by anyone with a wad to wave around, and I have been amply supplied thanks to the Commission's caboodle. The financial acumen of this commission makes me stiff in my physical pants. But even with bags of the wallet-weed you can't pick up prime stuff on the street.

Street putti's not the scab red of the best strain, but a waxy cardinal red, and not much bigger than a grasshopper. Show your money and watch the plastic-baggied root unroll from squares of flannel drawn from the pockets of our well-treated stand-ins whose chapped ankles stretch bare out of secondhand dress shoes, boys with long hairless thighs and slender cocks and brown-mauve heads shiny like oiled hardwood furniture. They have the sex appeal of a small mallet rapped on the table by a presiding officer in calling for attention or silence.

A word of advice: examine the goods before you buy. You wouldn't believe the things they pass off as the good stuff. Pigeon meat, snipped and dyed. Garden slugs salt-stiffened and lipsticked red. I hold a specimen in my hand if the camera would move in and you can see on the screen we have disguised as a bus shelter a fine specimen as rubicund as hemorrhoidal dogbottom. The putti is tacky and I handle it gingerly so none of the skin comes away on my hand. Putti are plump in the center, tapering toward the ends. They are firm but flexible; note the torque I can induce with a simple turn of the wrist. Note the splinter between their clothespin "thighs." It looks like a schlong,

scaled small, but it's just a wen, a nodule, a bump on a root. Under the thick, spicy skin lies the meat of a turnip, a radish, a beet. No tiny bones, no tiny lungs or heart. Just the deep red flesh, ringed with subtle bands of pink.

The rubbery "arms" are forced to the sides and bound there for drying. Observe the crease left by the twine at the tip of my nail. Ideally tied with hemp to sweet cedar racks and dried in high desert, more often they are strung up on the back of a chair in front of a fan in a closet.

As the putti dry their sketchy features sharpen. Their flesh goes malleable, dark and sticky where pressed. It holds a thumbprint, turns gummy like hash. The putti contract; go from smooth and shiny to deeply cleft, awry. They range from delicate rose, said to be milder, to the deep red approaching black beloved of connoisseurs. Connoisseurs like the late Bitch Henry, whose dealer picked out the most florid specimens for him, their heads black and heavy like rotting roses.

If you trim the joint close enough you can hold a match to the feet and suck the tiny head, pronged and spicy as a juniper berry, and of a size. Suck it and you'll numb your tongue, while the pepper smoke, sticky black and resinous, will coat your lungs faster than a cigar.

Dried like this specimen, putti cost more than cocaine; even fresh they come at a price, for harvest is lucky, bloody, unsafe. From a popular underground handbook: "Drug your victim and hold him down. Slide in your blade until it meets resistance. Keeping the slit propped open, extract Junior with tongs. Then run," advise the authors, who recently appeared on a talk show in well-ironed pin-striped masks, and were spotted sharing auntie with the host after the hour.

The desperate poor sometimes pulp their own thighs or abdomen, because they saw—or hoped they saw—a faint blush under the skin, or felt a lump. I once saw a man whose face evaded all features limping up the street with blood in his shoes, daintily tweaking open his overcoat to proffer a putti still smutty with clotting blood and lymph, still half wed to what it was plucked from. A doll daubed red in a drenched paper towel. These are the lucky ones, who make it out of the house with a sales pitch and a stagger. Bitch Henry bled to death, a kitchen knife in his hand.

Worth less fresh, putti's still a draw, and I've seen businessmen giddy at the cut-rate commodity empty their lunch bags on the sidewalk and slip a dribbling packet of red abortion in a suit pocket. The gutted host hunches off to the health project, where there's a room always full these days, men and women laid out under the needle, like samplers awaiting cross-stitch Americana, houses and token cornstalks, verses cautionary or wry. Or he risks it unsewn with something else to sell, and limps to an hourly rates motel where someone pays top dollar to point his groin at the gash in the thigh, to press his thumbs on either side of the cut, part the rubbery banks lined with razed cells and "put the putti back."

Users brag they can taste the putti's past, can tell aesthete from prankster from the household handyman who keeps the pages of the newspaper lying smooth or prevents the cleanser from clumping. Never mind that—no one knows whether the putti do these things or do anything at all other than grow and wait. The tabloids are full of doctored photographs of putti on toadstools and bibles, guarding pilfered toothbrushes, bobby pins and wedding rings, like bowerbirds. The science news is equally fantastic: scientists attempt to detect infinitesimal free-roving putti in their cloud chambers. Slice specimens like hot dogs. Dunk them in acid, cook them, crush them in presses, stretch them on racks, plant them, launch them into orbit, psychoanalyze them, irradiate, explode and oh most certainly smoke them.

Does the smoke transmit their seed? But users aren't all carriers, nor the reverse. Where did the first putti come from? A graft, say some, information formed into flesh, a top-secret experiment run amok. A floppy disk gone sticky, sloppy. Self-propagating meat-friendly infochop. They have something to tell us, say some. But when will they speak?

Dr. Crane, amateur biologist, claims success with shock treatment. Stuck with electrodes and pumped full of juice, his specimens totter around jerking and sizzling, and choke out a few glottally inflected phrases in a wheeze that comes from no lungs, but from some pocket of air expiring under pressure, battered into consonants by whatever masses

THE PUTTI

261

can come together like lip and tongue. He surrounds them with microphones and recording devices, he compiles glossaries of whoosh and hiss and analyzes them with a code-breaking program. He claims to have deciphered one such utterance as "Bring it to Jerome," and makes much of this Jerome, whose name resounds with religious associations. The putti don't stick around to make sure their message is understood. A few seconds at that voltage and they're jerky, flamingo filet.

It is my elegy to Bitch Henry that reflective particles have been released from nozzles camouflaged with faux pigeon shit in the facades of the surrounding buildings and are forming a cloud that will take some hours to disperse (those experiencing respiratory difficulty will be issued oxygen masks in flattering pastels) and in moments you will see and here it is now from horizon to horizon a realistically tinted electron microscope image of a fraction of a centimeter of Henry's skin, taken from his left hip by Dr. Crane some months before his death. Stroll under this flesh canopy lit by sourceless electron light while noshing on the scale models of human skin flakes and shed hairs provided gratis by the talented bakers of our catering service, enjoying the illusion that you are the size of dust mites or indeed of putti.

Look closely at the horny thickening around the base of the nearest magnified hair. Most scientists agree the putti have no means of locomotion and no sensible life as we know it, but observe: a putti lounges against the hair, his legs lolling wide, jaw askew. Another hangs on with one hand, swings wide, wrinkling his nose at the camera. Tinted too energetic a fuchsia. Phony, like A. C. Doyle's fairies with their backwards shadows and fingertips lost to the scissors?

A pit opens in the surface nearby. Round and fuzzy viral bunnies are nudged into crevices three, four at a time, or cling to a ridge, contravening gravity. They're dyed acid green. The purple hot dog buns are probably bacteria. Their needs are simple. This is their KOA, rugged enough to smack of the outdoors, but safe as houses. Wedged between bunnies, however, and with none of their outdoorsy freshness or beach ball/ kitty toy esprit, the putti lounge on and under one another with opium negligence. They jam the crannies and festoon the ledges of the whorl. They're a nest of earwigs, pincers agape with insouciance. They're the Brownies without the will to fun. They're beggars with a trust fund. Someone should do something, rout them with a fingernail, hose them off the White House lawn. They issue in droves from strings of eggs, says the doctor, cruising each other, causing dandruff and waxy buildup, but only the ones that lodge a foot or a fist in a cranny will survive. The resultant abscess admits the putti further. Tucking head, shoulders, knee into the pocket, the putti extends itself until it is completely embedded and stretched to its full length, at which time it rests and stilly grows.

The doctor's viewpoint is not widely shared. Please attend to an old but unsurpassed scientific treatise on the topic at hand: "Whether fanciful Stories of the Nesting habits of Putti have any basis in fact is doubtful. No Eggs have ever been found; nor is there any sign of organs in the putti capable of their production. Nor can this theory account for the sometime presence of the putti in places so far Internal to the human body that it is wonderful that Science ever thought she could explain this, by recourse to an account of such noble burrowing as rivals the excavation of the famed Sewers of Paris, in a creature as little given to energetic exertion as we have seen the Placid putti to be."

Rival theories evoke the plant that sprouts new roots from its elbows where they touch down on the mulch. Filaments probe the tenderized meat around the putti and extend throughout the host, until the tip thickens and begins to scratch a seat for a new member. This fist of aggravated flesh twinges, "like teething all over," victims report. The encysted putti grows steadily, sustained by the surrounding tissues, until it reaches its mature size of approximately three and one half inches, at which point the growing stops, though the putti continues to nourish itself, and retains its body mass up until the death of the host, or until it is removed by a surgeon or harvested, illegally, by traffickers.

Look down the alleys to observe our evocative tableaux: illustrating subsistence-level production techniques, the harvesters bend over their hutches,

forked sticks dipping and turning. They wink over their shoulders as they work, with the eyes of babies, glossy and pudged. The peppery fumes fret the lids, enter the bloodstream and make the whole body thicker and meatier. The harvesters jut without letup. We fear them but we scrub ourselves scarlet in our beds dreaming of them; their dicks are said to be thicker and more pointed than most. Uncut, they breed pink devilish smegma. Jenny and Lydia, neighborhood whores and lovers, roll on double-thick condoms and cut open the sticky bag afterwards in motel ashtrays with their nail scissors to look for the spawn they think swim with the sperm. They hunch over the tray, laugh and dump it in the toilet, clear out.

In some people the putti are so close to the skin, or the skin so thin and so pale, that you can see their shapes, faint, like a minor rash or a blush that floods one spot with heat. These prodigies fill pages slick and reeking of chemicals; samples are available for viewing from the young man in the hairnet. But there are also the vain or pragmatic of both sexes who fake it, growing skilled with lipstick pencils, blush and powder, whose towels are a grotty carmine, whose wastebaskets are full of the putti's imprint on folded tissues, waxy cream staining the pulped fibers. The Shroud of Turin in Maybelline ("Scoundrel", or "Cherries in the Snow"). Fetishists will pay to trace the outlines of these figments (real or not), these spelunkers of the body, these deep-tissue divers. They cup their hands over imaginary swellings and persuade themselves they feel something stirring.

And the fetishist who adores himself? He might scratch the itch with just the tip of the knife at first, a white tracing that becomes a welt that becomes a runnel that becomes a gash, until the tip touches flesh that doesn't touch back, and pries it out: a tiny greasy badger, a hairless hamster. Men who snuck off in the jungle to scratch their thighs with sharp sticks and dab Kotex on the wounds, lying on their sides in their own menstrual huts and moaning to the moon, are now in luck. They jab their biceps with fake knives, bleed and cry, clench their muscle and force out a little red whippersnapper, never mind that it's brainless and doesn't resemble Daddy. Wash it, hang it upside down, slap its butt if pantomime appeals to you. The world is reconfigured: the womb is anywhere flesh is.

Some say the putti is a child that will not be born, that likes it in there. Some say the putti is a child that hates the world, and crawls back in to chew the womb in vengeance. Some say the putti is a sickness we have mistaken for a message. Some say the putti is a message we are treating like a sickness. Like locoweed, like mistletoe, it hangs on without ambition. It breeds without desire. It multiplies because it's good at that. Bit by bit your flesh becomes another's. Nothing is subtracted, just estranged.

Please remember: it's no parable. The putti are stuff. They're not even as malignant as a tapeworm; they're vegetable, calm as carrots. Your own organs may be combative, aggravated,

fibrillating over diddly-squat. They've got the heebie-jeebies, the willies, the shakes. Your putti, on the other hand: solid. Did they come from outer space, did shoals of pink spores die on Pluto, die on Neptune, Uranus, Jupiter, Mars, before they hit our hospitality? So what? They've got neither cortex nor Cortez. If they have a will to power, it's a program appended to their DNA, a genetic cruise control; the dial is fused to its setting, the needle is stuck.

We can't stop talking about the putti, but they keep mum. Who killed Bitch Henry? Not they. The putti have no plans. They're a thickening at the point of intersection of our obsessions. Our desires have become pregnant with matter. People are not thingly enough: vision eclipses the eye, the sense of touch retracts the hand, words recant lips. It's easy to love a thought, but we want flesh unperplexed with mind. It is not human, but to slice it from the human exacts a mortal cost.

Our handsome guards will feel you up as you exit. Please empty your pockets to make their job easier and more enjoyable.

**Dr. Shelley Jackson**

THE PUTTI

# THE OBSCURE MEDICAL HISTORY
# OF THE TWENTIETH CENTURY
## AS REVEALED BY THE LAMBSHEAD POCKET GUIDE

### by Dr. Stepan Chapman M.D., D.V.M., D.Z.L.

## Part One: THE EARLY EDITIONS, 1921–1938

The illustrious Dr. Thackery T. Lambshead earned his first medical degree in 1918 at the tender age of eighteen years. He was the youngest graduate ever matriculated to that date by Oxford Medical College.

Dr. Lambshead served internships at Combustipol General Hospital of Devon and at the St. Agnes Charity Clinic of Edinburgh. Then began his years abroad, years of almost constant wanderlust and travel, as the doctor pursued a hectic pan-global career of private practice and public health consultation work. The erratic progression of his forwarding addresses never deterred him from sending steady streams of long discursive letters to his far-flung network of correspondents.

In early 1921, while involved in the design phase of an innovative sewage treatment plant in Calcutta, Dr. Lambshead circulated the single-stapled hectographed pages of his first collection of obscure disease abstracts. He had typed it himself and made rather a mess of the job. "Thought you might like to see these," is scrawled in wax pencil across one copy of the first edition. Some of the abstracts were gathered from neglected corners of medical literature. Many were personal accounts of novel disorders that were nowhere to be found in the literature—accounts that the doctor gathered from the letters he'd received.

These circulars evolved into center-stapled pamphlets and finally into book-length reference volumes. Private publication of the thick leather-bound editions of the 1930s were financed and overseen by Dr. Lambshead's college friend, John Trimble—bon vivant, Arctic explorer, outlaw anthropologist, and sole heir to the Trimble Fisheries fortune.

In all its forms, the Guide has been an invaluable resource for thousands of hardworking physicians the world over. From Nome to Istanbul, from Madagascar to Ulan Bator, on land and on sea, the Guide has proven its value under the most rigorous field conditions and on the wards of the most sophisticated hospitals. When a doctor lost in the Congo rain forests with only a few antibiotics and feral pygmy elephants for company cannot diagnose his odd spinal condition, he reaches for his handy copy of the Guide. When a family practice doctor cannot understand why a patient of 30 years with no history of mental defect suddenly begins to mimic inanimate objects, she turns to the reliable Guide.

It is equally true that by their failure to consult the Guide, some M.D.s have let their patients down. Many patients have slipped away who might have been saved by a G.P. familiar with the Guide. Many have been crippled by undetected parasites or bacteria that might have been extirpated if only the attending surgeon had taken the time to do a little basic research in the Guide.

Crucial events in the conduct of world affairs and in the lives of great men have been profoundly affected by the Guide. But more important, it can always be relied on for accurate reportage, even when "the official story" of a case is merely a tissue of fabrications. A cavalcade of examples spring to mind, leaping to our attention from the annals of that convulsive century so recently concluded—the Twentieth.

### Polio And Influenza, 1916–1918

It seems prophetic that the Guide's first edition included the first accurate diagnoses of two recent epidemics, falsely identified by the historical record as Paralytic Polio and Spanish Influenza.

In 1916, New York City was rocked by a terrifying outbreak of what seemed to be polio. Dr. Geraldine Carter (who would later edit *The Guide to Psychotropic Balkan Diseases*) rode a train into this maelstrom of hysteria, armed only with her little black bag. She soon realized that the fever had no connection to Poliomyelitis. By means of her unique methods of dietary analysis, Dr. Carter determined that the fever was a new form of Vasospasmolytic Otodysneuria, resulting from the recent introduction of chemical stabilizers into the city's baked goods. Her research findings, previously denied publication, appeared in the 1921 Guide, badly typed onto smudgy hectograph stencils by Dr. Lambshead. Thus, an unacknowledged medical mystery was finally solved.

The so-called "Spanish Flu" pandemic of 1918 claimed a larger number of lives than the Great War. It was the indomitable Dr. Buckhead Mudthumper of Pretoria, South Africa, who penetrated the actual nature of this infection. He first encountered it while serving as a field surgeon for the German military. He was unconvinced that airborne microbes of any kind were at work. He experimented with the invalid soldiers in his care, trying out various combinations of his idiosyncratic vaccines. By lateral diagnostics he was able to unmask the true pathogen—a Tunisian skin mite that deposited toxic histamines in the hair follicles of its hosts.

In 1921, the true nature of the pandemic was made public in the Guide, thanks to the unprejudiced mind of Dr. Mudthumper, who would soon begin to assemble his voluminous *Encyclopedia of Forgotten Oriental Diseases.*

Dr. Carter's and Dr. Mudthumper's publications came too late to lessen the loss of life and limb associated with the two aforementioned health crises. But after 1921, again and again, the Guide would be there when a bewildered M.D. needed it most.

## Margaret Sanger, 1921

Consider the case of Margaret Sanger, pioneer of birth control education. In 1921, she bravely opened her first clinic in Brooklyn, New York. Late in the year, she was struck down by a perplexing anemia complicated by Anginoform Hemophilia. Happily, her physician, Dr. Isaac Borodini, remembered a certain article in the first edition of the Guide, elucidating the radical inoculation techniques of Mr. Randolph Johnson, author of *Confessions of a Disease Fiend.* The article inspired Dr. Borodini to attempt a Johnsonian strategy in the treatment of Miss Sanger's anemia. The introduction of a blood-thickening spirochete arrested the patient's symptoms and maintained her in a fragile but ambulatory state for decades.

## Franz Kafka, 1924

Other patients weren't so lucky. Consider the alleged Tuberculosis of Franz Kafka, first diagnosed in 1917, terminal in 1924. Any close reader of the Guide's second edition could have told his benighted therapists that Kafka never *had* Tubercle Bacillus. His was clearly a case of Polyretinoidal Ink Poisoning, indicating a long history of compulsive ink drinking. If all those health sanatoriums had simply forbidden him the use of ink bottles, a great writer might have lived to a ripe old age.

Kafka's biographies have good company in their flagrant inaccuracy. Lou Gehrig never had Lou Gehrig's Disease. Woody Guthrie never had Huntington's

Chorea. Those American Legionnaires in Philadelphia never had Legionnaire's Disease, because there's no such thing. And Shirley Temple was a midget. Little if any of this valuable medical information would reach the public if not for the Pocket Guide.

## Roald Amundsen, 1925

In 1925, Roald Amundsen, the first man to reach the South Pole, attempted to fly two Dornier-Wal dirigibles across the North Pole. The expedition was forced to turn back by mechanical problems, or so Amundsen claimed when he returned to Norway and thunderous international acclaim. A year later, his party completed a successful polar crossing.[1]

Amundsen admitted privately that the first expedition *hadn't* suffered from engine failures. The blimps worked fine, but the entire crew went temporarily blind, due to the bites of Arctic zigzag fleas. Amundsen would never have attempted a second voyage except for the 1925 Guide, which featured Dr. Amelia Dupré's informative essay on Arctic fleas and their place in the pharmacopoeia of the Inuit tribes. *Another* resounding success made possible by the Guide.

## Crazes Of The Twenties

The Roaring Twenties were a craze-ridden era for the United States. In the 1929 edition, disease psychologist Sarah Goodman established that flagpole-sitting, goldfish-swallowing, phone-booth-stuffing, public petting, and jitterbugging were all the consequences of a single mood-altering organism, which she christened Semantic/Venereal Imbalance Pathogen or SVIP.[2] Although etiology and remedies were published in the Guide for all to read, Dr. Goodman's article went unheeded by the public health establishment. "Fools," she wrote in her journal. "I'm surrounded by knaves and fools."

## Margaret Mead, 1925

Even non-medical persons of high achievement in the natural sciences have benefited from an acquaintance with the Guide. Anthropologist Margaret Mead, author of *Coming of Age in Samoa*, owed her friendly relationships with the Samoan natives of 1925 partly to her practice of sharing the wisdom of the Guide with them. She was often seen hiking to the hut of a sick informant to deliver a clay pot of some pungent herbal vitamin tonic. These tonics were based on the recipes in the dog-eared copy of the Guide that was always in

---

[1] *Great Adventures That Changed Our World*, ed. Peter Lacey, Reader's Digest, 1978.
[2] SVIP has since been shown to be identical with Buscard's Murrain. See the article by Dr. Miéville in this volume.

her knapsack. The Samoans came to regard this copy as an object numinous with *manna*, and named it *halabanta-nu-pennu*, meaning "Good for the Complexion."

## Nikola Tesla

The modern age of alternating current was made possible by the dynamos and motors of Hungarian-born inventor Nikola Tesla, 1856 to 1943.[3] Tesla was a major celebrity in the New York of the gay nineties. But the private life of this reclusive figure remained mysterious until the 1946 Guide. In this edition, Dr. Michael Cisco—a friend of Dr. Lambshead and a frequent collaborator—described his experiences as Tesla's personal physician and addiction counselor from 1927 until the master inventor's death.

In early manhood Tesla had synthesized a new form of dextroamphetamine sulphate, which he called hyper-dex, and on which he became acutely dependent. Tesla believed that he owed his eidetic design abilities to the drug, and could not be persuaded to abandon it. By 1927 his cardiac health was seriously compromised. The ingenious Dr. Cisco applied his anti-disease theories to Tesla's case and concocted an anti-hyper-dex, which successfully introduced an anti-addiction into Tesla's metabolism. This was only the first of a long series of triumphs for anti-disease therapy, of which Dr. Cisco may well be proud, despite the dogged efforts of the mean-spirited eunuchs of the World Health Organization to strip him of his credentials.

## Lon Chaney, 1930

Since the days of the silent screen, certain Hollywood stars have suffered from secret health problems, some quite extreme. A long unsuspected example of this phenomenon was Lon Chaney Sr. (1883 to 1930), the Man of a Thousand Faces—revered for his performances in "The Phantom of the Opera" and "The Hunchback of Notre Dame." He died of throat cancer at the peak of his career, following shortly on the release of his first talking picture.[4] Or so the medical records claim.

In her 1984 tell-all article for the Guide, Seattle pet mortician Genette Wangell revealed that her father, Dr. Christian Wangell, the well-known Los Angeles bone specialist, had served as Mr. Chaney's private physician throughout his film career. What was more startling was the news that Chaney never wore makeup. His so-called makeup effects were simply his face, or rather his skull, since his skull had resorbed his face at the onset of his

---

[3] *Prodigal Genius: The Life of Nikola Tesla*, John J. O'Neill, Angriff Press, 1944.
[4] *Lon Chaney: The Man Behind the Thousand Faces*, Michael F. Blake, The Vestal Press, 1990.

Metaplasic Exostosis.[5] Early diagnosis allowed Dr. Wangell to control and even to *sculpt* the peculiar skeletal protrusions characteristic of the disease.

## William Beebe

Between 1930 and 1934 American naturalist/explorer William Beebe and bathyscaphe designer Otis Barton caught humanity's attention with the descents of "Beebe's Bathysphere" into the Atlantic Ocean off Bermuda. One important aspect of these descents was never made public until brought to light in the 1940 Guide.

It was Beebe's and Barton's closely-guarded trade secret that they'd achieved superhuman levels of pressure tolerance by the agency of experimental serum injections. This serum was devised by the notorious Houston zoologist Dr. Terrence Moorcock (great-grandson of the Reverend Michael Moorcock, whose essay appears in this volume). It was pressed from fattened hothouse specimens of the giant Samoan Rat, on which species Dr. Moorcock is acknowledged as the world's foremost authority. The doctor's serum system was a new wrinkle on a practice of Samoan pearl divers, who drink the rat's blood ceremonially.[6]

## Mildew, 1934

The 1934 limited edition, a handsome volume printed in Algeria and bound in the finest Moroccan horse hide, was the occasion of a most regrettable incident. All of the contributors, save only for Dr. Lambshead himself, died within weeks of the book's release. At first, rumors of an Egyptian curse fueled lurid articles in the gutter press.

But Dr. Lambshead soon got to the bottom of the matter. The Algerian printing firm engaged by John Trimble had used paper infested with a highly poisonous mildew. Consequently, the contributors died horrible menasprotic deaths as they received their complementary copies. Dr. Lambshead was spared by a typographical error in the address list he'd mailed to the printer. His own copies were shipped to a wrong address. The 1935 edition, bound in British calfskin, contained his report on the mold that had cast such a shadow over the previous edition. The report featured illustrative photographs of his autopsy on the body of Dr. Julio Altametti.

Naturally, a few gutless character-assassins whispered in corners that it was all some twisted experiment gone awry, or that the doctor had *planned* the whole thing. The notion is nonsensical. The contributors were Dr. Lambshead's closest friends and colleagues. He was shattered by their deaths. Besides, he hadn't been to Algeria for months.

[5] See Dr. Jeffrey Thomas's piece on Extreme Exostosis in this volume.

[6] The rodent is best known as a disease vector. See Dr. Moorcock's articles on the subject.

## Sigmund Freud

Austrian neurologist Dr. Sigmund Freud died of cancer in London, 1939. Although his literary style was eloquent, his medical career had been little more than a long chain of plagiarisms. After 1921, his favorite source of material was his complete set of the Guide. In fact, after 1921 all his "analyses" were conducted while the analysands were doped with an Indonesian trance potion, knowledge of which he gleaned from an article by Dr. Lambshead in the first edition.

There have been several quacks and charlatans who've exploited the Guide for personal aggrandizement, or for filthy lucre, or even for revenge. They always seem to come to a bad end somehow. Perhaps Dr. Lambshead has something to do with that. Freud's cocaine-related jaw cancer for example. Dr. Lambshead seems to know more about it than he's telling. And didn't George Gurdjieff die rather suddenly in 1943? Never mind.

## Part Two: THE WAR YEARS, 1939–1945

Dr. Lambshead returned to England during the years of World War II and practiced at the scene of his internship, Combustipol General Hospital of Devon, which was flooded with wounded soldiers, sailors, and aviators. There he explored many innovative techniques of reconstructive surgery. Some of these, he made public in the Guide. (Others were ripped off by the opportunistic Dr. R.F. Wexler and published as his own work.)

It has sometimes been idly suggested that Dr. Lambshead overworked himself into a towering addiction to Nikola Tesla's hyper-dex during this period. On such speculations we make no comment. There *is* such a thing as respect for privacy after all.

### Stalingrad, 1942

The secret history of World War II is riddled with concealed rare diseases and concealed countermeasures. At the Battle of Stalingrad, for example, both the German Sixth Army and the Russian forces under Zhukov were plagued by transient toe resorbsions, often misreported by field medics as loss of toes to frostbite.

The symptoms of stress-related toe resorbsion were fully elucidated by Dr. Alan Moore in the 1937 Guide. Resultantly, the savvy medical corps of the Bolshevik army was well equipped with a topical ointment of wormwood and radium in cod liver paste. The Reich's medical corps, by contrast, was forbidden the use of the Guide, which Joseph Goebbels had declared degenerate. Never arriving at a correct diagnosis, they were unable to establish prophylaxis. The resorbsion gap was an important factor in the Soviet Union's implacable defense against the Wehrmacht siege.

## Albert Hofmann

While the Russians were defending Stalingrad, the world's foremost scientists were building new machines. World War II engendered a plethora of new technologies, such as radar, guided missiles, atomic fission, and proto-computers. These advances were based largely on the vision and resolve of such men as Wernher Von Braun, Edward Teller, and Alan Turing. What is *not* common knowledge is the connection of Von Braun, Teller, and Turing with master pharmaceutical chemist Albert Hofmann.

In 1935, Dr. Hofmann began work at Sandoz Laboratories in Basel, Switzerland, where he researched ergotamine derivatives. In 1938, he first synthesized lysergic acid derivative 25, which approximates the serotonin-boosting activity of the tryptamine hallucinogens. All of this is a matter of public record.[7] But only readers of Dr. Hofmann's 1952 article for the Guide are aware of his most important synthesis of 1938—the harmaline/telepathine/isodrene "cocktail" for induced brain acceleration.

More than just a stimulant, the HTI cocktail can double or even triple the dendritic connections of the frontal cortex. Although Dr. Hofmann has never published the formula, he does admit to providing steady supplies of the cocktail to Edward Teller, father of the A-bomb, to Alan Mathison Turing, father of the computer, and to Wernher Von Braun, father of the V-2 rocket. (Some have criticized Dr. Hofmann for offering his concoction to both Axis and Allied Forces scientists. One must keep in mind that Switzerland was a neutral nation.)

In a 1940 letter to his benefactor, Von Braun wrote, "Eternal thanks for the ampoules. I can now read the mind of any machine I encounter and can bend it to my will. Your drug will revolutionize . . . everything."

One further aspect of this matter emerged in the 1953 Guide. Apparently, Werner Heisenberg, director of the Nazi atomic energy project at Hechingen,[8] caught wind of the HTI brain accelerant, gathered what data he could, and assigned a pharmacist to counterfeit the drug. The resultant quasi-cocktail was a total failure. It only made Heisenberg absentminded and sleepy.

## Adolf Hitler

Adolf Hitler was a man of a secretive, even paranoid, temperament. His associates always suspected him of keeping dark personal secrets. He *was* in

[7] *LSD, My Problem Child*, Albert Hofmann, J.P. Tarcher Inc., 1983.
[8] *The German Atomic Bomb*, David Irving, Da Capo Press, 1967.

fact hiding a secret that would certainly have horrified his eugenics-minded colleagues. It was a secret known only to his doctor, homeopathic steam therapist Karl Ortt (author of the suppressed cookbook *French Cuisine With Codeine* and its sequel *Mousses With Morphine*). After the Fuehrer's death, Dr. Ortt provided the Guide with a portrait of the *real* Adolf Hitler, a man divided by the bizarre secret of his birth.

It seems there were two of him. They were born to Klara Hitler in Braunau, Austria, 1889. They were a rare case of identical Siamese *half twins*. Although the two baby boys were conjoined by their common skin, they were issued two birth certificates—one for Adolf on the right and one for Wulf on the left.

The pediatrician in charge of the maternity ward had noticed some motor anomalies in the boys and decided to radiograph them. Most doctors of this period had never heard of a fluoroscope, but this was no ordinary pediatrician. This was Dr. Elias Mudthumper, Buckhead's favorite uncle and an early amateur radiologist. (Irradiating things was sort of a hobby with him.) The radiographic plates revealed twin sets of internal organs and a skull bifurcated by a bony partition down the middle.[9] Each twin had one leg, one arm, half a torso, and half a head.

As a child, Adolf contracted mumps, but only years later did Wulf. Often at school, one side of the "boy" would fall asleep while the other side took notes. Yet as adults, wearing their girdle and abdominal truss, their impersonation of a normal human being was uncanny.[10] They carried their secret to the grave, but the Guide dug it up again. Further evidence, if any is needed, that only readers of the Guide have access to a true understanding of recent medical history.

## FDR, 1945

This brings us to the untimely death of Franklin Roosevelt (1882 to 1945), who certainly would have lived out the final months of the war if only his attending physicians had consulted the Guide. Roosevelt's doctors assumed that his declining state of respiratory health was Polio-related. A Guide reader would have recognized the telltale symptoms of Uzbekistani Electric Head Lice. Recently declassified KGB documents verify that this rare electric louse was indeed planted on FDR by agents of Stalin at the Yalta Conference.

---

[9] These radiographic plates still exist at the British Museum, and copies can be viewed on the Institute For Further Study archive ship *Useless*, anchored west of Maui. Only serious historians need apply.
[10] As for the undescended testicle thing, it's really none of our business.

Day of Ds

*Dr. Lambshead demonstrates how careful airbrushing is essential to lasting protein-bindle deglostropy when endo-integumental attrition exceeds prothemic olpens by more than eight hemicycles. (1932)*

Name

Age

Diet

No. in Case Boo

NOT

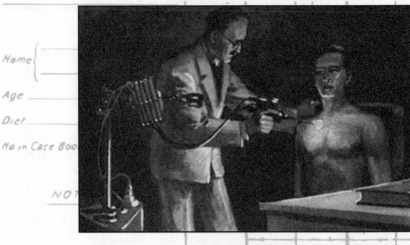

*Despite his enduring disdain for "the cult of personality," Dr. Lambshead allowed this portrait to appear in the 1940 edition of the Guide.*

Pulse

Respiration

Bowels

Urine

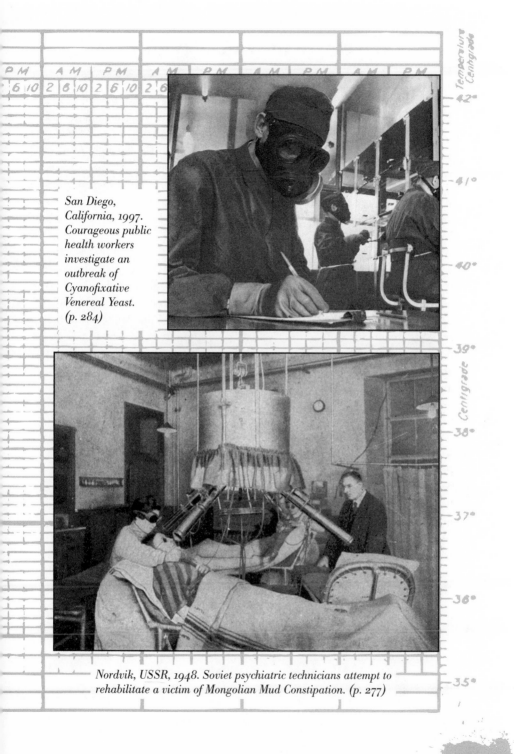

*San Diego, California, 1997. Courageous public health workers investigate an outbreak of Cyanofixative Venereal Yeast. (p. 284)*

*Nordvik, USSR, 1948. Soviet psychiatric technicians attempt to rehabilitate a victim of Mongolian Mud Constipation. (p. 277)*

## Part Three: THE COLD WAR YEARS, 1946–1990

In 1946, London's Chatto & Windus published the first edition of the Guide to be available to bookstores and a general readership. Articles began to pour in at a great rate. Contributors ranged from nurses in Missouri to GPs in Rhodesian shack towns to Yugoslavian oncologists to "barefoot doctors" practicing in rural China.

Having honorably discharged his obligations both to Combustipol General Hospital and to the Guide, Dr. Lambshead resumed his frenetic circumnavigations of the globe. Once a year he would return to Britain to supervise the final proofs at Chatto & Windus. Unfortunately, problems with British censorship arose in 1953, requiring the Guide to shift its home base to Penguin Books of New York.

In 1954—just months before Penguin Books could issue its first volume, already in production—the FBI investigated Dr. Lambshead for communist sympathies. This investigation followed closely on the heels of Dr. Lambshead's blunt refusal to participate in a certain project dear to the heart of Mr. John Edgar Hoover. The doctor has in his files a letter from Mr. Hoover that suggests the creation of "a disease that is only fatal to pinkos and pansies." Across the letter, the doctor has scrawled a single word in red laundry pen: "Ridiculous!"

After the investigation, the State Department refused the doctor further visas for travel in the United States. In reaction he found a new home for the Guide at the Jolly Boy Publishing & Soap Company of Bombay, where it remained securely ensconced through the remainder of the Cold War years.

### Prominent Contributors

As the Guide made gains in circulation, it began to attract articles penned by eminent public figures. The 1961 Guide proudly featured an article on the intestinal fruit worms of the Congo River basin, written by eminent Alsatian theologian and physician Dr. Albert Schweitzer (1875 to 1965). In 1968, Dr. Christiaan Neethling Barnard of South Africa, renowned for his heart transplants, submitted a wonderful paper on some of the more humorous side effects of cyclosporine.

The Guide's relationship with other well-known contributors has proceeded less happily. Dr. Sigmund Rascher, inventor of the decompression chamber, published his fascinating 1930s research into Aeronautic Shock Reaction in the Guide. Dr. Fritz Ernst Fischer contributed forward-looking articles on bone transplantation. And then there was Josef Mengele and his intriguing essay on the use of identical human twins in eugenics research.

After the further studies of these three gentlemen at the Auschwitz concentration camp came to light,[11] Dr. Lambshead concluded that he could publish no further submissions from Rascher, Fischer, and Mengele. "*Let* them call it censorship," he wrote in his journal. "Certain things *simply aren't done.*"

## The Gulags

The Guide was the first publication to expose a massive communist deception perpetrated by apparatchiks on an unsuspecting West. This deception concerned the Siberian gulag system. To this day most sovietologists still believe that the gulags were places of exile for dissidents and other targets of Stalin's displeasure.

Actually, the gulag system wasn't created to punish anyone. It was the Soviet government's response to an inexplicable lemming-like migration of otherwise-sane Russian citizens to the bleak Siberian wastes. Beginning in 1946, masses of these mania-driven souls arrived in Siberia each month. There they would gorge themselves on the rich black frozen mud. Nor would they return to their previous lives. If forcibly removed, they would find ways to return. The government dealt with the problem by constructing ramshackle labor camps, and the rest is history.

Reportedly, one of the GRU's translators of Western technical literature came across an explanation for the exodus in the 1944 Guide. What he discovered was Dr. Neil Gaiman's posthumous exhaustive monograph on Mongolian Mud Constipation, a viral infection that causes an excruciating binding of the large bowel, always co-present with the delusion that only eating the mud of some distant region will relieve the symptoms. Antibiotics allowed many gulag dwellers to return to normal Russian society. Another baffling case history *solved* with the help of the Guide.

## Pepsi-Cola, 1949

In the aftermath of World War II, the Coca-Cola Company and its arch rival, the Pepsi-Cola Company, rapidly extended their national bottling systems into global cartels.[12] In violence-torn South and Central America, local competition for distribution franchises sometimes lapsed into gangsterism, and rivals for lucrative American cola contracts would not uncommonly turn up dead in a ditch. Even the friction between established Coke distributors and Pepsi distributors was likely to involve rifle sniping or exchanges of pistol fire, especially in the

[11] *The Nazis*, Robert Edwin Herzstein, Time-Life Books, 1980.
[12] *The Cola Wars*, J.C. Louis and Harvey Z. Yazijian, Everest House, 1980.

thriving new cities of Brazil. In Bolivia in 1949, Dr. Lambshead himself foiled a heinous product-tampering plot.

Apparently, a Bolivian cabal of Pepsi distributors misjudged the doctor's character and hired him to contaminate shipments of Coke with some heinous disease. The doctor went along with this plan, chose a viable pathogen, and brewed up a generous batch of Blopholarionus trophlofloris (common Amazonian Stem Rot) in a small vat of ginger beer. But when the conspirators came to collect the contaminant, Dr. Lambshead gave them instead a bottle of rubbing alcohol and green food coloring. It is supposed that he then proposed a toast and offered them all glasses of iced ginger beer. Their plans for commercially-motivated germ warfare came to naught, and an international cola incident was narrowly avoided.

## The Rosenbergs, 1953

In 1953, two famous scapegoats were sacrificed to the gods of capital punishment. Their names were Julius and Ethel Rosenberg, convicted of treason for leaking atomic secrets. Not until the 1977 Guide was issued could the true story of the Rosenberg execution be told.

In point of fact, the intervention of prison doctor Richard Calder allowed the Rosenbergs to survive electrocution and to fake their own deaths. Dr. Calder accomplished this deception by the subcutaneous insertion of the root scrapings of a little-known African shrub related to ibogaine. He was carefully following the instructions in the 1932 Guide. After reviving the two supposed corpses, he arranged for minor plastic surgery and a discrete retirement to New Mexico. "I stole the plot from *Romeo and Juliet*," he wrote in his article for the Guide, years later.

## JFK, 1963

One of the great murder mysteries of the last century was conclusively solved in the 1967 Guide by forensic chemist Dr. Rachel Pollack. We refer to the tragic public death of John F. Kennedy. It is disgraceful that Dr. Pollack's exposé never received attention in the world press.

Since 1963, more and more of President Kennedy's health problems have come to light, despite a firm policy of concealment on the part of the Kennedy family. At college he was known as "Jaundice Jack" for his yellowish skin tone. His lifelong spinal dysplasia was spuriously explained as the consequence of a war wound. Spinal surgeries were performed in secret. By the time Senator Kennedy was elected president, his Addison's disease and attendant adrenal insufficiency were being treated with daily injections of cortisone—another medical fact that he repeatedly denied to the press. His perilous condition was further complicated during his term of office by vitamin/amphetamine shots administered by the dubious Dr. Max "Feelgood" Jacobson.[13]

It required the Pocket Guide and the testimony of Dr. Pollack to fit in the final pieces of this medical puzzle, and to solve the mystery surrounding the motorcade through Dealy Plaza. Dr. Pollack was able to reach her conclusions after a state-of-the-art chromatographic analysis of the stains on the First Lady's famous pink dress.

There was no assassination. No shots were fired that day—none from the book repository, none from the grassy knoll or the sewer grate, not even one magic bullet. There was no entry wound. There was no exit wound. President Kennedy perished suddenly of an Explosive Cranial Snarcoma. Similar cases of internal tumor explosion have been documented extensively in the Guide since as early as 1949.[14] If only someone at the White House had been a Guide reader. The warning signs were there for all to see.

## The Space Race, 1967

Another tragedy of the 1960s has been consistently misrepresented. In 1967, astronauts Ed White, Virgil Grissom, and Roger Chaffee perished in a fire in the hyperbaric atmosphere of a training capsule. The causation of their deaths was far more sinister than has commonly been supposed.

On both sides of the space race, sabotage by deep-cover agents of the CIA or the KGB was commonplace. In 1963, the first female cosmonaut, Valentina Tereshkova, suffered psychotic episodes in orbit,[15] not as a result of inherent mental instability but rather because an MK-Ultra-produced psychedelic powder had been sprinkled in her socks.

CIA mischief continued. The next casualty was Sergei Pavlovich Korolev, mastermind and ramrod of the Russian space program. He died in 1966 at the height of the competition to put a man on the moon. Supposedly, he suffered a heart attack during surgery for colon cancer.[16] For the grisly details of Korolev's actual death, read Dr. Ivan Skoevingblourt's article in the 1971 Guide, "The Soil Spiders of Yakutsk and Their Uses in Local Witchcraft."

Payback came in 1967. Hard evidence of KGB culpability in that payback would eventually surface with the publication of the 1974 Guide, which featured the investigative journalism of then-chiropractic allergist Dr. Jeff

---

[13] *A Question of Character: A Life of John F. Kennedy*, Thomas C. Reeves, The Free Press, 1991.

[14] See my article in this edition on the Motile Snarcoma, a closely related cancer.

[15] *The Race: The Complete True Story of How America Beat Russia to the Moon*, James Schefter, Doubleday, 1999.

[16] *Korolev: How One Man Masterminded the Soviet Drive to Beat America to the Moon*, James Harford, John Wiley & Sons, 1997.

VanderMeer. Dr. VanderMeer demonstrated beyond doubt that Roger Chaffee burst spontaneously into flame and incinerated his surroundings. This was a time-tested KGB technique.

### Joey Mellen, 1970

In 1962, Joey Mellen of London took some mescaline and decided that the best way to stay high permanently was cranial trepanation. In 1966, he bought an antique skull trephine in a secondhand shop. In 1970, after several failed attempts, he finally accomplished his auto-surgical project with the help of a handheld power drill. He later wrote a book called *Bore Hole*. He also produced a documentary film titled "Heartbeat in the Brain," in which, live and on camera, Mr. Mellen trepans his girlfriend Amanda. They then announce their mutual attainment of a constant state of spiritual bliss.[17]

Joey and Amanda, the poster boy and poster girl of trepanation, searched for years for an M.D. sufficiently open-minded to offer the operation to their friends. Despite the medical establishment's unaccountable acceptance of nose jobs, tummy tucks, stomach staples, and sex change operations, trepanation had no takers.

And here the Joey Mellen story might have ended, if not for the skillful metal work of Guide contributor and registered urologist Dr. Rikki Ducornet, who custom-tooled a new surgical instrument, now available to hospitals and mental institutions from Green Dog Precision Tools of Oshkosh. Dr. Ducornet's motorized trephine can perform a virtually bloodless trepanation in under a minute, greatly simplifying the sterile field problem for amateurs. She has named her tool the Mellen Trephine. For legal reasons, it is marketed as the Ducornet Melon Scooper.™

### Cambodia, 1970

Even as the Guide won increasing popular acceptance and academic credibility, certain segments of the medical community remained resistant to its use. Such was the situation within the United States Air Force, and they suffered the predictable consequences. Consider the bombing runs over Cambodia during the 1970 invasion. This effort was badly hampered by pilot exposures to the dime-sized aerial jellyfish, Quonquossa gamma, which lives only in the cloud cover over certain sections of Malaysia. This cnidarian infiltrates ventilation systems and causes compulsive hair pulling and nail biting, loss of feeling in the genital region, and odd speech patterns resembling Peter Lorre imitations.

If the flight surgeons involved had been keeping up with their Guide reading,

---

[17] "The People with Holes in Their Heads," *Eccentric Lives & Peculiar Notions*, John Michell, Sphere Books Ltd., 1984.

they could have immunized their pilots, thus clearing the way for deeper penetrations into enemy territory and a more surgical style of bombardment.

## Jim Morrison, 1971

It is widely believed that rock star Jim Morrison took his own life in 1971 in reaction to a diagnosis of inoperable Penis Cancer. How ironic that the diagnosis was mistaken. To explain Mr. Morrison's symptoms, one need only procure a copy of the 1936 Guide and skim through the entry on the life cycle of the Mexican plutotropic tequila worm. Obvious, isn't it? And Mr. Morrison wasn't the only rock star to suffer a fatal misdiagnosis. Jimi Hendrix wasn't even *dead* when they buried him.[18]

## The Sexual Revolution

Speaking of kinky sex: In the 1976 edition, freelance podiatrist Dr. Lance Olsen presented definitive evidence that the sexual revolution was caused by saccharine.

## Mao Tse-tung

Chairman Mao Tse-tung of China (1893 to 1976) did *not* live to a ripe old age. He was cloned and replaced by himself in 1955, 1965, and 1975. Finally, he'd been copied so often, he just fell to pieces. Perhaps you thought cloning was impossible in the 1950s. Do yourself a favor and pick up some back editions of the Guide.

## Albino Luciani, 1978

On August 26, 1978, Albino Luciani, born to working-class Italian parents, was elected Pope John Paul I by the Council of Cardinals. He was a healthy 66-year-old. "The Smiling Pope" refused to be crowned with the traditional triple tiara. He declined to use the royal *we* in his encyclicals. He was rumored to have knowledge of financial irregularities at the Vatican Bank. Thirty-three days subsequent to his election, he died in bed of a rather suspicious heart attack. The body was never tested for digitalis residues. [19]

The courageous spadework of Dr. Paolo G. Di Filippo, then the Guide's Vatican City correspondent, has uncovered the distressing story behind this sudden death. Also the sudden death of Pope Paul VI by heart attack one month previous. Also the mysterious 1963 death of Pope John XXIII, convener of the controversial Second Vatican Council. For all the gory details, one need

---

[18] See *Smack, Crack, and Whack In Haiti: An Historical Survey*, Dr. Mark Roberts, Greenfont University Press, Toronto, 1974.

[19] *Lives of the Popes*, Richard P. McBrien, Harper Collins, 1997.

only consult the 1982 edition, which features Dr. Di Filippo's "Eucharist Wine, Poisoners, and Homicidal Fermentation at Castle Gandolfo." An impressive follow-up to his much-discussed "Thomas Merton: Death by Vaporizer."

## Idi Amin Dada, 1979

In 1979, the brutal regime of Ugandan president Idi Amin Dada was overthrown. It is generally thought that he fled into exile. Actually one of his doubles fled into exile with his checkbook. (Every dictator should have a few decoys. It confuses the assassins.)

The real Mr. Amin Dada also survived the coup. But, unlike his double, he didn't get very far, as readers of the 1982 Guide already know. He is now on display, floating in a jar of formaldehyde, at a private pathology museum in Holland. His jar is right between Pol Pot's jar and François Duvalier's. He is alive and well, although he does complain of breathing problems and cramping.

## AIDS, 1983

In 1983, the attention of AIDS researchers everywhere was attracted to a crossed-swords pissing match between Dr. Robert Gallo of the National Cancer Institute in Bethesda, Maryland, and his rival, Dr. Luc Montagnier of the Pasteur Institute in Paris. Dr. Gallo was stridently promoting his recently isolated HTLV (Human T-cell Leukemia Virus) as the retrovirus responsible for AIDS. On the other side of the pond, Dr. Montagnier sang the praises of his own research into LAV (Lymphodenopathy-associated Virus).[20]

The medical world had no notion of just how tense this rivalry became. Each of the two eminent pathologists was attempting to infect the other with a hideous disease he'd spotted in the Guide. Dr. Gallo was mailing Dr. Montagnier anonymous gifts of fruit baskets and gourmet cheeses, hoping to give him Clear Rice Sickness.[21] Meanwhile, Dr. Montagnier was sending Dr. Gallo anonymous gifts of cashmere sweaters and designer tennis shoes, hoping that Gallo would catch a raging case of Ferrobacterial Accretion Syndrome.[22]

Luckily, both scientists had requested their pathogen samples from Dr. Lambshead (then battling Sclerotic Pingeucula in Argentina). The doctor saw through these requests for "research material" and sent the two dueling pathologists samples of his own nasal emunctions, neatly placed in petri dishes. The doctor has a peculiar sense of humor.

AIDS has been mistakenly blamed for several celebrity deaths that can

---

[20] *And the Band Played On*, Randy Shilts, St. Martin's Press, 1987.

[21] See the entry by Dr. Cisco in this volume.

[22] See the entry by Dr. Stableford in this volume.

only be correctly explained by reference to the Guide. For instance, it was a 1980s outbreak of Liposuction Ebola that slew Rock Hudson and Robert Mapplethorpe. Liposuction Ebola was a mutation of Bengalese Tattoo Parlor Ebola. In the 1990s, it evolved into Hair Implant Ebola, which caused the deaths of Anthony Perkins and Rudolf Nureyev. Modern cases of all these ebolas are treated routinely with a topical cream of St. Ogbert's root in coconut paste and usually require no hospitalization. (See the 1995 Guide for the specifics of this treatment.)

### Gene Tech, 1987

In 1987, the Food & Drug Administration approved Recombinant T-PA (tissue plasminogen activator), the first drug ever produced by genetic engineering. Genentech's thrombosis-busting anticoagulant opened a new age for pharmacy.[23] The genetic molding and milking of microbes might have been big news to the world at large, but for readers of the Guide, it was fairly old hat. Ever since 1932 old jungle hands such as ace botanist Dr. Eric Schaller and mutation specialist Dr. Jeffrey Thomas have been sending in reports on the biological manipulations of the elders of the Kakaram tribe of central Ecuador. As Dr. Thomas has stated: "If the Kakaram head plant, the revolving tree, and the tricolor army ant are *not* pieces of genetic engineering, then I'd like to know what *is*."

### Part Four: A CENTURY WINDS DOWN, 1991–1999

During the last decade, the pace of Dr. Lambshead's mad dashing from nation to nation has slowed. He has nonetheless found time to teach crash courses at countless medical colleges, training academies, and hospitals. He's also been spending quite a lot of time at his underground bio-containment lab—built for him at his place of birth, the picturesque village of Wimpering On the Brink in Devon, by the Institute For Further Study. The great doctor no longer feels the urge to chase after medical puzzles. These days, more and more, people bring the puzzles to him.

As for the Guide, its momentum as a force in modern medicine continues to build. Yet troubles with publishers have persisted. In 1991, Jolly Boy Publishing & Soap Company lapsed into bankruptcy. Despite his earlier quarrel with J. Edgar Hoover, Dr. Lambshead resolved to plant the Guide once again in the vivifying soil of the New World. He located a publishing house in the fresh clean air of the Mojave Desert—a family enterprise known as Boojum Press of Ataxia Gorge. Here

---

[23] *The Innovators*, John Diebold, Dutton, 1990.

the Guide prospered until December of 2002, at which point the entire town slid into a sudden sinkhole and disappeared forever. That's California for you.

## Plutonium, 1993

The Guide's investigative reporting hasn't lost its edge. In the 1993 edition, roving CDC scalp specialist Dr. Jeffrey Ford courageously blew the whistle on the United States Atomic Energy Commission. The AEC has been planting storage sheds for spent plutonium in the backyards of random suburban houses and then using junk mail dusted with Hanford isodrenococcus to induce short-term memory loss in the residents. This outrage continues despite the Guide's best efforts to inform a complacent public.

## Venereal Disease, 1997

In 1997, three cases of cyanofixative venereal yeast (otherwise known as "The Blue Valentine" or "Mexican Blue Dick") were detected in San Diego. A timely consultation of the Guide allowed me, as acting coroner's assistant, to avert an American epidemic of this dread genital scourge—currently so common in Sweden, Iceland, and Mexico.

## Terrorism, 1999

Terrorists are often quite naive in medical matters. Consider the fate of the Victims of Childhood Acne Terrorist Cadre of Greater Chicagoland and their Pakistani-American leader Benny Ali bin Ahka. In 1994, they traveled all the way to Surat, India, to collect live cultures of Bubonic Plague (Yersina pestis).[24] They had a germ incubator waiting for the cultures back in Chicago. Unhappily for the would-be terrorists, in building their incubator they had misread the blueprint. They'd mistaken a measurement in meters for a measurement in feet and a temperature in Centigrade for a temperature in Fahrenheit. Resultantly their incubator was way too small and not nearly warm enough. The cadre's plague cultures croaked on them like a tank full of tropical fish.

Mr. bin Ahka wouldn't give up. In 1999, the cadre took a package tour to Russia and scored some smallpox from the Biopreparat germ factory at Koltsovo.[25] Their plan was to return to Chicago, wait until the eve of the millennium, and release the germs on the train cars of the El. This time their samples were a little *too* hale and hardy. The remains of the cadre were found in their secret hideout, right around Thanksgiving, and very carefully disposed of. A defector from the group survived to write up her story for the 2000 Guide.

---

[24] *Betrayal of Trust: The Collapse of Global Health Care*, Laurie Garrett, Hyperion, 2000.
[25] Ibid.

## Part Five: INTO A NEW CENTURY—
## THE POCKET GUIDE TRIUMPHANT

Here in a new century, a set of the Guide is still not an accepted or expected feature of most collegiate medical libraries. Although the Guide is studied each year by the best and brightest medical students, it is often on the sly, rather than as required reading. However, things are looking up. The Guide has been translated into 27 languages, some of them now dead. A cornucopia of honors has been heaped on Dr. Lambshead—the Burmese medal of honor, the Polish cross, the Académie Francaise's Permanganate/Ampersand Prize For Medical Journalism, and the Okinawa Fragrant Flower Hospital Service Award, to mention only a few.

Despite continual attacks by the weak-minded goons of the AMA and other transparent lackeys of the medical establishment, the Guide continues to win renown from the foremost medical men for its impeccable standards of peer review and verification, for its clarity of argumentation, and for its richness of documentation.

Meanwhile, most of Dr. Lambshead's associates have, over time, passed on. John Trimble died in a car crash in 1968.[26] In 1973, Dr. Sarah Goodman succumbed to a fatal amusement in her sleep. In 1985, Dr. Buckhead Mudthumper was clawed by an alcophobic sloth and passed away almost instantly. Yet Dr. Lambshead soldiers on, bloodied but unbowed. Are you worried about the mutant Tuberculosis in the Russian prison system?[27] Go to Wimpering On the Brink and talk it over with the doctor. Are cases of Cockroach Malaria showing up in Denver? Cholera in Tibet? Kashmiri Narrow-Head in Chile? Consult the old doctor. Everyone else does.

Last year, on reaching the age of 104, Dr. Lambshead decided to pass the Guide's editorial reins to younger hands. After reviewing dozens of applicants, he selected doctors Jeff VanderMeer and Mark Roberts, co-synthesists of many of the standard petroleum-based anti-itching drugs and three-time winners of the University of Mississippi's Merrick Award For Rapid Relief. Dr. Lambshead will continue to consult and to contribute, but responsibility for the perpetual influx of obscure and discredited submissions will henceforth fall to VanderMeer and Roberts.

After Boojum Press slid into that sinkhole in the Mojave, the new editors

---

[26] The Trimble Fisheries Philanthropic Foundation, however, is still active in fund-raising for charitable causes. The foundation recently organized the well-received Kwasi Fela Pan-African HIV Sweepstakes. The grand prize was ten thousand American dollars' worth of discounts on the AIDS drugs produced by the sponsoring drug companies. A second sweepstakes is planned for 2004.

[27] *Betrayal of Trust: The Collapse of Global Health Care*, Laurie Garrett.

were somewhat at a loss for a publisher. Then Night Shade Books of Oregon stepped forward to offer its services in 2003, followed by Bantam Books in 2005. Bantam Books has won enthusiastic acclaim for its recent ventures into medical publishing. These ventures include handsome reprints of such classics as *The Trimble-Manard Omnibus of Insidious Arctic Maladies,* edited by John Trimble and Rebecca Manard and *The Journals of Sarah Goodman, Disease Psychologist* with an introduction by Welsh overspecialization specialist Dr. Rhys Hughes. Six more titles for this series are currently in the planning stages.[28]

We applaud Bantam Books for their commitment to the cutting edge of medical literature. They have ignored the veiled threats of Dr. R.F. Wexler and likewise the dire warnings of those disturbed individuals who just can't let go of the 1934 mildew thing. To Bantam Books we say, "Well done! Fortune favors the brave."

As for Dr. Wexler, to him we can only say: "Dear Sir: Kindly send your anthrax-soaked missives elsewhere. And if you want to get serious about contagious letters, then invest in some smallpox like a normal person."

This up-to-the-minute edition constitutes a worthy continuation of a proud tradition. Like Dr. Lambshead, the Guide remains vigorous despite its weight of years. The Guide sees clearly, reasons clearly, and speaks common sense in a world of incomprehensible medical jargon. May it continue to thrive for *another* eighty-three editions.[29]

---

[28] *Anti-Diseases and Anti-Therapies: New Worlds of Pathology,* Dr. Michael Cisco
*Painless Sterilization For the Hobbyist,* Dr. China Miéville
*I Live In Hell: My Battle With Lipogranular Splanchnodiastasis* (reprint), Dr. Brian Evenson
*Calisthenics For Chest Cases,* Dr. Gahan Wilson
*101 Things To Do With Used Tongue Depressors,* Dr. Michael Bishop
*T Is For Tumor: An Alphabet Book For Estranged Adults,* Dr. Shelley Jackson

[29] As a Guide contributor, I am sometimes asked why the title includes the word pocket. It's been about 70 years since a current edition would fit in one's pocket. Dr. Lambshead informs us that he retained the word pocket because it reminds him of the days of his youth—those golden bygone days when he'd eat beans from a can for breakfast and then go scrounging around Calcutta for a hectograph machine.

# BIOGRAPHICAL DATA

**Dr. Dawn "Aurelia" Andrews**, a renowned medical pathologist, and a Knight of the order of the Flaming Lancet, indulges in a calming watercolor or two whilst awaiting corpses to dissect. She is an avid collector of books on vivisection, dissection, and genetic modification, including rare copies of *Hustler* magazine. She also has an extensive collection of wax anatomical specimens, of both sexes, which she keeps in the basement of her Hampstead home.

**Dr. Steve Aylett** began his medical career as a wrestling injury paramedic but was fired for "unnecessary surgery" during matches. The most notorious of these incidents occurred when he removed Chad "Bonecruncher" Murphy's appendix in the ring during the 1989 rematch against the Red Shadow in Seattle. He claims that shortly after its removal the appendix "burst like a storm cloud," but film footage of the incident shows him merely tossing the organ into the face of a spectating gran. Burying himself in research, Aylett began seeking evidence to prove that teardrops had a skeletal structure, an account of which was published in his book *What Was I Thinking With That?* Arrested after several incidents of provoking valuable tears from small children by shouting at them point-blank and suddenly, he stated on the steps of Bow Street Magistrates Court, "Damn right I probe heads!" and started lashing out, despite the fact that he was standing there entirely alone. He established the Benway Medical Centre in London's Mayfair in order to more successfully draw attention to himself. "There are slimy muscles in my arms," he says today, "but apparently that's normal." Aylett's other published works of medical note are *Toxicology*, *Slaughtermatic*, and *Shamanspace*.

**Dr. Kage Baker** occupied the Chair of Splanchology at the University of California at Bodega Bay from 1948 to 1962. She authored *In the Garden of Iden*, which is now considered the definitive work on splenic dysfunction in the Pacific Bottlenose Dolphin (Tursiops gilli). She also conducted the landmark five-year study of splenic parasites infesting the Pygmy Killer Whale (Feresa attenuata), publishing the results in 17 volumes, collectively titled *The Anvil of the World*. In 1963 she retired from medicine and took the veil at the New Camaldoli Monastery, over the protest of the brother friars.

**Dr. Nathan Ballingrud** served as the Royal Medical Officer in the Kingdom of Norway from 1960 until 1971, when his collaboration with the Nazi occupational government was made public. Exiled from his native country, he relocated to New Orleans, in the United States, where he indulged his fascination with the study of transcendental pathology and routinely kidnapped small children for use in his experiments into the nature of godhood. It was in that city, while visiting the infamous Camouflaged Library in the Ursulines Academy, that he caught a virus that would, sporadically and without warning, trade his consciousness with that of a red dwarf star in Galaxy M-64. These bouts were frequent but happily short-lived, as those in his presence during an attack tended to be reduced to atoms. Ballingrud disappeared in 1978, believed to have been abducted by the Argentinean government. It is probable that he was tortured to death and his body hurled into the briny deep; which is what he deserved.

**Dr. Michael Barry** has received accolades worldwide for his groundbreaking anthropological research and Handycam documentaries into sadomasochism among the inhabitants of Sydney's Northern Beaches. In the absence of an appropriate laboratory, and in defiance of the politically correct Ethics Committees of Australian medical institutions, Dr. Barry uses his own body as a test-bed for sadomasochistic explorations. He selflessly continues his psychobiological research at his laboratory on the premises of Mistress Sasha's House of Pleasure & Pain. Inquiries should be directed to Mistress Sasha, as Dr. Barry is unable to speak while conducting his experiments.

**Dr. R. M. Berry** was, until her disappearance in 1997, director of the Marital Technology Foundation that today bears her name. The results of her collaboration with Drs. Brian Evenson and Remy B. la Pher on Satyriasis are widely known. The publicity attending her discovery of male menopause is considered unfortunate. Dr. Sarah Goodman has called her "the Dwight D. Eisenhower of Marital Psychopharmacology." It is not true that she experimented on Norman Mailer. Dr. Berry's treatise *The Condom* remains the standard work. Investigators recently found hair and nail clippings matching her DNA in Caracas, Venezuela.

**Dr. K. J. Bishop** is recognized worldwide for her contributions to the field of carphology. A prominent lecturer on public health issues, Dr. Bishop is the author of two books, the groundbreaking *Diagnosis for Duffers* and recent bestseller *The Enema Within*. Pursuing a lifelong interest in diseases of the rich, in early 2003 she moved her consulting practice offshore to the residential superliner Superbia.

**Dr. Michael Bishop** specializes in the psychological ailments and ego-related disabilities of artists, particularly writers, using his own dread-inducing experiences as templates for highly questionable psychosomatic deductions and extrapolations. He has published diagnostic haiku, stichomythic interview notes, and Nietzschean treatment proposals in an array of venues, including the *Journal of Holistic Hebephrenia*, periodic Philip K. Dick Festschrifts, *Writers & Angst*, and *People*. For the past nine years, Dr. Bishop has lived in the Carl Jung-Shoshana Feldman Home for Bemazed Belletrists, emerging in moments of shrewd quasi-lucidity to accept awards meant for others. To date, he has acquired a Super Bowl ring, an Emmy, a first-runner-up designation in the Miss America pageant, and an unsupervised psychiatric internship at the Mayo Clinic.

**Dr. Richard Calder**, following some difficulties in the New World, started over as an intern at London Hospital, Whitechapel, during much of the 1990s. There he pioneered the emergent fields of morbid prosthetics, hyperpathology, and the still marginalized surgical techniques of Tantric cutterage and phlebotomy. A hugely enthusiastic vivisectionist, he was investigated in 1999 for clandestine membership in the Society for Cruelty to Small Animals. Although the inquiry was suspended without reaching any definite conclusions, he was struck off in 2002 on an unrelated charge of "kitten baiting." His interest in the genetic basis of sexual hysteria took him to the Middle East to research the bloodlines of belly dancers awaiting trial for appropriating the intromittent organs of their admirers with miniature power-driven saws. Dr. Calder's less-than mysterious disappearance while touring the ancient sites of Babylonia during the spring of 2003 has translated him from the sphere of morbid prosthetics into that of morbid aesthetics as readers ponder such tomes as *Dead Girls*, *Dead Boys*, *Dead Things*, *Cythera*, and *Frenzetta*.

**Dr. Jay Caselberg** received his training in Medical Archaeology at the University of Western Broken Hill. His research into billabong pathology on an early field trip led him to an encounter with a wandering Bunyip. The experience so disturbed him that he fled to Southeast Asia to conduct studies on the neuropathology of frogs and toads. His articles have appeared in such diverse medical journals as *Frog and Toad*, *Amphibian Neuropathology*, and *Spawn*.

**Dr. Stepan Chapman** received his essential linguistic, zoological, and medical training at the Academy of the Ancient Trilobites deep beneath Antarctica. His doctoral thesis involved the heroic sagas of the polar isopods. Since then his articles in the literature have dealt with such entomological and pathological subjects as Cyanofixative Venereal Yeast, the Zig Zag Bug, and the Musical Goiters of Lapland. Dr. Chapman has since pursued his researches at the Doolittle Oceanographic Institute of Samoa and at the International Institute For Further Study. He currently serves as a consultant and translator for the United Nations Subcommittee on Vertebrate Arthropod Relations. He is also the co-founder and resident manager of the Chapman Wild Insect Preserve at Aphasia Gorge, Arizona. Dr. Chapman has long been a friend to conspiracy theorists everywhere.

**Dr. Michael Cisco**, generally dismissed as a quack, and publicly vilified by Dr. Orveo Vitrine as "a self-smoking ham," has nevertheless sustained a surprisingly long career in the field of speculative medicine, practicing in 15 countries (on one occasion, in three countries in one day) and in international waters. He was the first to develop a methodology for pre-mortem embalming, to diagnose nervous disorders in ghost limbs, and to reintroduce zodiac-interventionist medicine in China. One of Vitamin D's most vocal opponents, Dr. Cisco is also engaged in an extended study of anti-diseases, which promises to open an entirely new field of medical enterprise to the less easily intimidated breed of researchers. Unfortunately, this study has proved to be more intimate than originally expected, as Dr. Cisco has himself contracted a form of anti-typhoid, and is thereby confined to the unwholesome air of the Parisian sewers, immediately below the Hotel du Tond. Despite recent reverses, he still anticipates a timely recovery.

**Dr. Alan M. Clark**, although rumored to have "died while flossing his teeth," is to date still alive. He has had a long and widely varied, if controversial, career as an illustrator and writer.

He is most well known for paintings of the so-called "dead wood" sites of those individuals Dr. Duane Lovesome Backscatter claims have succumbed to Fungal Disenchantment. These paintings, as well as many others Dr. Clark calls "psyche portraits" (though meant to accompany the text of his various medical writings), have instead been used primarily as illustrations for cheap fiction. Indeed, his medical papers, considered laughable by many, have only found acceptance in books of horror fiction.

**Dr. Michael Aloysius Cobley**, B.A., F.R.S., S.L.D., B.S.F.A. (Hons), was born to a family of itinerant Orkney jugglers. At the age of eight, he ran away to be brought up by distant relatives in Aberdare. Soon after his graduation from the Cardiff College of Physicians, he found himself appointed Chief Medical Officer of South Uist. His extensive contributions to the letters page of *The Lancet* brought him to the attention of such surgical luminaries as Williamson, Caselberg, and Di Filippo. Upon his translocation to London, he collaborated with all three on a hypothesis concerning the bloodline transference of different kinds of luck. After an unfortunate incident involving a blind knife-thrower and three generations of Cornish dowsers, Cobley found it necessary to distance himself from his former colleagues. It was a year later when the dark (and subsequently interdicted) events concerning Sir Randal Bullivant took place, and which appear in this august publication for the first time. In later life, Dr. Cobley took great interest in the growth of peculiar orchids. In his autobiography *Musings From An Irregular Life*, he dealt with the persistent rumors of somnambulant juggling that dogged his autumn years, denying their veracity on pages 1, 5, 13, 14, 22, 38, 47, 79, 91, 92, and 93.

**Dr. Brendan Connell**, a dedicated worshipper of the healing god Asclepius, holds a chair of pathological anatomy at Wurzburg. His public lectures and anatomical demonstrations have brought him a certain quantity of renown, as has the publication of his 14-volume work *The Therapeutic Effects of Laitance on the Phosphorescent Births of the Okavango Delta*.

**Dr. John Coulthart** has combined careers in the fields of art and medicine despite numerous setbacks and legal problems. He first aroused attention after exhibiting human body parts for the SMEGMA show at Manchester's Whitworth Art Gallery in 1982. National notoriety came in 1995 with the so-called bile incident when the contents of the installation "100,000 Gall Bladders" burst their container, flooding a Southwark gallery. Recent works have been more successful, particularly "Live Celebrity Autopsies," staged at the Hayward, London, although its projected weeklong performance was postponed due to a lack of volunteer subjects.

**Dr. G. J. Couzens** wrote of Gastric Prelinguistic Syndrome in the 1860s, but little else is known of him. No dates of birth or death can be established. Gary Couzens, reputedly born in 1964, who has made many appearances in print and electronic media since 1991, in *The Magazine of Fantasy & Science Fiction*, *Interzone*, *The Third Alternative*, and other periodicals, is rumored to be the same man, the result of successful experimentation by the original Couzens in suspended animation. This rumor, however, is surely apocryphal.

**Dr. Paolo G. Di Filippo**, a former Vatican City reporter, conducted the surgery for which he was trained at Shambhala Medical College: the transplantation of third eyes. Instead, his career took him into research, where he has spent the past 20 years cataloguing the morphological differences among the intromitters of various disease-carrying insects. His conclusions can be found in such volumes as *Fuzzy Dice* and *Neutrino Drag*.

After being laughed out of Vienna in 1975, the Very Reverend **Dr. Cory Doctorow** (D. Divinity) founded Doc Doctorow's All-Snake-Handling Road Show and Disease Emporium. In the course of 40 years of fieldwork, Dr. Doctorow has emerged as one of the world's leading—if least credible—authorities on imaginary, psychosomatic, hysterical, and erroneous diseases. In 2000, the World Science Fiction Society mysteriously awarded him the John W. Campbell Award for Best New Writer at the Hugo ceremony, a positively humiliating occurrence compounded by the January 2003 publication of his novel, *Down and Out in the Magic Kingdom* by Tor Books, of New York City.

**Dr. L. Timmel Duchamp** took her M.D. from Columbia in 1959, but emigrated to Paris with her French husband shortly thereafter. After a violent if abortive fliration with psychoanalysis, she studied with the brilliant Michel Foucault, under whose direction she developed her arresting approach to medical history. Dr. Duchamp, known to have used five distinct pseudonyms, denies she intended to generate the impression that her controversial approach was shared by several scholars. She has promised to divulge the true reason for her use of pseudonyms on her deathbed—provided her penchant for skydiving does not preempt the possibility.

**Dr. Rikki Ducornet** has spent much of her long and varied medical career cataloguing no less than 2,350 diseases or conditions of the head. Her research has taken her from the wilds of East Anglia to the relative civilization to be found in the middle of the Sahara Desert. Her incisive illustrations accompanying all 2,350 head diseases or conditions have been exhibited in most major medical galleries in the world. Dr. Ducornet's falling out with Dr. Lambshead in 1985 over the causes of Head Disease No. 2,143 is too esoteric to address in a biographical note. Dr. Ducornet currently divides her time between Prague, Czechoslovakia, and the hinterlands of Patagonia.

Long employed as a medical researcher in the balmy climes of Micronesia, **Dr. Brian Evenson** (1923–1966 [death never confirmed]) suddenly deserted his post as chief medical researcher on the island of Pohnpei, ostensibly to pursue further research. He left behind only a note stating "Gone to Arctic. Am taking cousin Kiteley along. Best wishes, Kline," a note particularly puzzling in that Evenson is known to have no cousin named "Kiteley" and no association with the name "Kline." He left behind several medical texts of limited interest, most famously *Altmann's Tongue* (a longish treatise on diseases of the mouth), *Contagion* (which insists on contagiousness being a result of personality flaws), and a case study of Dr. Daniel Schreber, *The Din of Celestial Birds*.

**Dr. Eliot Fintushel**, S.P.Q.R., A.S.A.P., D.O.A., is a senior assistant to the volunteer copyboy's intern at the *Journal of Cuticular Malformations and Aberrations of the Knuckle*. He divides his time between the old city of Cuenca in Spain and the 59th Street Y in Manhattan. He is not related to the Nebula Award nominee and two-time NEA Fellow Eliot Fintushel whose current solo performance piece, *Apocalypse*, will be appearing soon in a theater near you.

**Dr. J. Ephram Ford**, of the Long Island Fords, was, in youth, labeled an idiot savant for his dull affect and copious drooling coupled with the amazing ability to communicate with the family dog, St. George. At any moment of the day, with no more than a few quiet barks and a growl he could elicit from the pet what was on its mind. In addition to relaying to his parents the creature's mundane desires, he was also able to elicit from it the fact that in a previous life it had been a cowboy named Handsome John. Ford lost the appellation of savant upon the dog's demise, but occasionally channeled its spirit and was given to brief bouts in which he would roll on his back and whimper while spasmodically kicking his right leg. His medical degree was awarded him by the University of Bayonne, from which he graduated with top honors from its correspondence course in General Surgery. Dr. Ford was lionized as something of a saint himself for treating disorders of the mind through corrective surgery performed with what he termed his "scalpel of terrible consequence," a plastic knife wrapped in aluminum foil and fitted with jiggling doll eyes glued to either side of the blade. Using this instrument of his invention, he would slice the air a hundred or so times only inches in front of the patient's face as a means of metaphysically excising those defective thoughts troubling the afflicted. After curing the daughter of a millionaire from her condition of agitated sexual melancholy, he was awarded a large sum of money, which he used to retire from the medical profession and study anomalous diseases. Near the end of his career, he became interested in diseases that did not exist but by his account should have. By bringing a particular affliction to light, Retrograde Concoctivitis, he contracted it and due to its resultant mania took on the character of the cowboy, Handsome John. Soon after, he was arrested in a local park near his home in Elisabeth, New Jersey, for lassoing neighborhood dogs. Thereafter, he was sent to an asylum where he lived out the rest of his days in a cell, making watercolor paintings of the old West.

**Dr. Neil Gaiman** wrote upon medical matters between 1850 and 1871. The events of 1872 are too widely known to deserve comment. Suffice it to say Dr. Gaiman's exoneration, the dismissal of all charges, and the ritual burning of the wig were considered by most commentators to be the end of the matter. Dr. Gaiman's terrible death in 1873 was considered by other commentators to be the complete and utter end of the matter. His most famous books were published posthumously. Rumors that they were written posthumously cannot be taken seriously. He is no longer in general practice.

**Dr. Sara Gwenllian Jones** specializes in the diagnosis and treatment of diseases of disputed existence. Her 1996 confirmation of the rare Aztec Facial Rictus Syndrome led to her being awarded the Mycroft Prize for Medical Detection. In 2001, she was reported missing, presumed mad, after the distinctive silver VW camper housing her mobile laboratory was found abandoned by the roadside near Cuzco, Peru.

**Dr. Rhys H. Hughes** earned his medical degree from a fake "traveling" university that rolled along the lonely roads of rural Wales on the back of a steam-powered wagon. He eventually graduated with honors in Pure & Applied Quackery. During lectures, he frequently played crude and somber airs on a miniature harp. After the completion of his studies, he disembarked from the university in a place unknown to him. Here he settled and specialized in vermicide preparation. In time, he became a local celebrity and the author of many ponderous tomes on the eradication of parasitical worms. His vermicide classic *Worming the*

*Harpy* was promoted by including a free jar of worms with every copy sold. It rapidly became an official International Sickclub worstseller.

**Dr. Shelley Jackson** considers it a matter of professional pride to undergo every disease she treats. Consequently, she is a hive of viruses, but her chest is draped with medals, and among her boils glistens that famous emerald, the gift of a grateful patient. That her papers (collected in *The Melancholy of Anatomy*) appear in high-subscription glossies rather than medical journals is no reason to raise the cry of "Quack!" Dr. Jackson has introduced many new diseases to science. The charge that some of these were concocted in a privately-funded genetic-engineering laboratory at her home somewhere in South America is libelous.

**Dr. Harvey Jacobs** was found floating as a tyke on a matzoh in the Nile River and adopted by an illustrious family of cuppers and bleeders who shared their arcane medical knowledge derived from herbs, flowers, trees, astrology, random dissections, and Depak Choptera's *Collected Bromides*. His first published work, *Get It Right the First Time*, the definitive reference used to codify the size of tumors (i.e., the size of a cantaloupe, or a grape, etc.), was short-listed for the prestigious Toulouse Lautrec Award. His most recent monograph, *My Rose and My Glove*, is a biographical account of his years as a practicing physician and spokesperson for the rights of unborn monarchs.

**Dr. Frederick John Kleffel**'s interest in World War II surgical automata arose from the casual discovery of a rusting Intubatron© at a swap meet in Azusa, California. His first entries in the annals of research on emerging diseases were published in obscure journals such as *Grue* and *Deathrealm*. His accusers have pointed to the very names of these periodicals as indicative of the nature of his abilities, but all of the charges levied were deemed to be erroneous and unsustainable. He currently holds the Guignol Chair in the College of Automated Inter-Species Surgery for the University of California at Irvine.

**Dr. Jay Lake**, F.M.C.S. (Fellow, Mongolian College of Shamans), was discovered as an infant living inside a record-setting yak bezoar. He capitalized on his hirsutitudinous origins to attend medical school in Bulgaria, followed by a court-supervised residency at a sexually transmitted disease clinic in West Orange, New Jersey. He has since successfully pursued a career as a spleen wrangler. Dr. Lake's trenchant medical analyses appear in such inappropriate markets as *Album Zutique*, *Leviathan 4*, and *Realms of Fantasy*. Rumors about his involvement in the Iroquois Theater fire should be disregarded.

**Dr. David Langford** had the good fortune to commit his researches at a period when relevant legislation had yet to be urgently passed. An aficionado of mania, delusion, and fugue, he became a contributing editor to *The Encyclopedia of Fantasy* (1997), ed. Dr. John Clute and Dr. John Grant. His earlier work on problems of incontinence appeared in 1984 as *The Leaky Establishment*. Langford is perhaps most envied in pathology circles for his lovingly formalin-preserved collection of hypertrophied urino-genital organs, or HUGOs. The denizens of Reading in the English county of Royal Berkshire prefer not to discuss his residence there.

**Dr. Tim Lebbon** was once a general practitioner of great repute. However, since his very public, and very messy, debarring for dabbling in the nefarious science of Total Body

Transplant, his area of expertise has expanded to include genetic engineering. His stated aim is to eventually "humanize" all animate items listed in his manifesto *Pending Sentience: The Need For Global Incorporation and Intellectualization*. His assistant, Dr. Hydrangea, refused to respond to our request for interview.

**Dr. Gabriel Mesa** commutes daily between his law firm and his medical practice, which at times become confused with his third profession as a translator of little-known Latin American rural poets. Although confined to a coffin for health reasons since the age of five, Dr. Mesa maintains an active anti-exercise schedule, in keeping with Dr. Michael Cisco's anti-disease manifesto. His staff of 12 typewriter-wielding monkeys often assists in his translations.

**Dr. China Miéville** is better known for his work on the history and theory of medicine than for his clinical practice, though he has always claimed his remarks describing patients as "corporeal filth" were taken out of context. His most recent works are those investigating rodents as vectors of grandeur, treatment for attacks by railway-dwelling carnivorous lepidoptera, and the psycho-social effects of pervasive scarification.

**Rev. Michael Moorcock** (pronounced "Muck") comes from a long line of physicians and has long suffered from multiverse chronoshock. His ancestor Dr. Blood served as a British privateer, having been sentenced to transportation by Judge Jeffreys, while a later American ancestor Dr. Mudd paid a high price treating the heroic Avenger of the South, J.W. Boothe, when he was wounded by Yankee terrorists. Dr. "Muck's" Irish ancestor Dr. Sean O'Dure became famous in the Crimea as Quick Saw O'Dure. "Muck's" great-grandmother, Dr. Harriet Gutz, was one of the first woman doctors in the trenches during the 1914–18 war and his maternal grandfather, Dr. Roberto Filuth, rode with the 1st Cuban Volunteers and was responsible for treating a shrapnel wound sustained by Che Guevara. More recently, his uncle Dr. John Pease achieved a certain fame by founding Docteurs Sans Medicins and its attendant group Docteurs Sans Anesthesia, which operated for a while in Cambodia with the heroic Red Khmer Army. The names of Blood, Mudd, O'Dure, Gutz, Filuth, and Pease, together with that of Moorcock, have become synonymous with unorthodox emergency surgical procedures, usually in times of war.

**Dr. Alan Moore** is widely-known for numerous dissertations recounting, variously, cases of human/vegetable mutation in the southern United States, the sexual neuroses of vigilantes and costumed psychopaths, notable outbreaks of gigantism, vampirism, and invisibility in Victorian England and a major study of Ballistic Organ Syndrome in London prostitutes. His current scrutiny of the Twilight Ailments takes place at the Seaview Oneiric Research Facility, Northampton, England.

**Dr. Martin Newell**, born in 1953, came to medicine relatively late, when a promising career as a stunt flier was cut short by injury. After qualifying in his mid-thirties, he became interested in the correlation between mental illness and creativity. He is now chief consultant at The Elmstead Institute of Artistic and Psychosomatic Disorders in Essex. An Honorary Fellow of the Royal Society of Cuppers and Horse Bleeders, he is married with two imaginary children. He has been Mental Illness Poetry Interface correspondent for the *Independent* newspaper for the past 12 years. He takes a keen interest.

**Dr. Mike O'Driscoll** sat the matriculation exam for entrance to the Ingolstadt Centre for Psychic Rehabilitation, gaining an E+. Inspired by this near success, he stole a copy of the Hypocritic oath and obtained a license to practice medicine through marriage to Dr. Imelda Trellis, physician to the town of Skibbereen and environs. Following his wife's disappearance in 1972, Dr. O'Driscoll was misdiagnosed as clinically incompetent and subsequently debarred. He expects to be practicing again very soon, following Dr. R.M. Berry's fortuitous diagnosis of Wife Blindness as being the real cause for his laughable bedside manner.

**Dr. Lance Olsen** resigned his professorship in temporal awareness at the University of Idaho in 2001 to pursue research into the diseases of time in his mountain compound. The result a year later was *Girl Imagined by Chance* (FC2), an investigation into the immunodeficiency syndrome often referred to in the colloquial as Sadness Before the Realization of Minutes, and, in 2003, *Hideous Beauties* (Eraserhead UP), a history of how carnival freaks have perceived time's passing as a series of colors and fragrances continuously misplaced.

**Dr. Rachel Pollack**, M.D. O.B.E., a former forensic chemist, studied anatomy with Jeffrey Dahmer before receiving her medical degree in a dream. She has served as medical advisor to several extinct goddesses, and has pioneered techniques for surgical extraction of religion under emergency field conditions. In 1989, she joined with a coterie of dead colleagues to form the group Doctors Without Boundaries. In 1997, she received the Nobel Shadow Prize for her work on hidden messages in dietary obsessions.

**Dr. Steve Redwood** will surely be remembered as much for his simple humanity as for his contributions to the advancement of knowledge. Of his dedication to his chosen speciality, there are countless examples, as when television cameras caught him picking his nose, and examining the contents, while Guest of Honour at a WHO reception. His humanity was revealed when his wife gave birth to an extremely ugly child: the rigorous scientist gave way to the fond father and sensitive husband, and his headless body was launched into space last month. As proof of his lasting influence, no eulogies were delivered at this event.

**Dr. Mark Roberts** has always had a high tolerance for blather and needling, as evidenced by his continuing editorial relationship with Dr. Jeff VanderMeer. In addition to his experience as a veterinarian, Dr. Roberts is Creative Director of the Chimeric Mission of Creative Therapy. Thousands of people from all walks of life are suffering periods of intense depression, caused by an almost complete lack of visual and cerebral stimulation. The Chimeric Mission recognizes this, and through strategic partnerships with handpicked organizations and individuals, promotes and encourages the spread of Fusion-33, an artificial virus with multi-dimensional qualities that induces the desire to "create" in its victims.

**Dr. Iain Rowan** is one of the world's leading authorities on any medical issues that require expensive consultancy. His medical work appears mostly in journal publications by plagiarizing quacks who happen not to have offended the editorial boards by making public criticisms that their expertise is largely in the personal acquisition of various forms of dubious infections. His monographs have appeared in a number of publications, such as *Nemonymous*, the international journal for study of Identity Loss Syndrome, although they are often disguised as fiction to prevent the grand medical conspiracy from stifling his words.

**Dr. G. Eric Schaller** is an Associate Professor of Biochemistry and Molecular Biology at the University of New Hampshire. He has published research from his laboratory in numerous scientific journals including the *Proceedings of the National Academy of Sciences*, the *Journal of Biological Chemistry*, *Plant Physiology*, and the *Journal of Irreproducible Results*. He first became aware of the devastating effects of the Wuhan Flu from his Chinese graduate students, who all knew about the Xiaping disaster even though it had not been reported in the Western press. His pet hedgehog is named Siggitz (spelling uncertain).

**Dr. and Dr. Jack Slay, Jr.,** is a full professor at LaGrange College in Georgia and a half professor at the Miskatonic Technical Institute just up the road. He received his Ph.D. in Diseased Literature from the University of Tennessee in 1991; that same year the University of Texas awarded him an M.D. in Literary Diseases. His book, *(Parentheses as M(al)aise and (L)anguor in Contemporary (Shi)vais(t) Literature)*, will be published as soon as the suits and countersuits are settled. Currently, Dr. Slay is hurriedly at work on a treatise on mange.

**Dr. B. M. Stableford**, B.A., D.Phil., F.R.S.B.F., suffered a nervous breakdown in 1972 following an experiment in population dynamics that required him to count 16 populations of flour beetles every 72 hours for three years; he subsequently took up medical research on the advice of his doctor, an existentialist who told him that his only hope lay in developing some iron in the soul.

**Dr. Steve Rasnic Tem** has quickly become one of the foremost doctors of experimental behavior in the United States. Although arrested many times during the course of his studies, his explorations of voluntary facial tics, non-goal oriented speech, and hysterical perambulation have made him an object of minimal interest at two or three college campuses. Tem received his medical training from his parents as part of an intensive home-schooling program.

**Dr. Jeffrey Thomas** has served as Chief of Surgery (1962–81) and Chancellor for Research (1982–90) at Eastborough Hospital, Eastborough, Massachusetts. He now considers his books *Punktown*, *Monstrocity*, and *Letters from Hades*, to be interesting studies of delusion, though at the time he wrote them, he was convinced they were observations of actual events. During that time (2000–02), Dr. Thomas was engaged in self-trepanation experiments.

Until recently, **Dr. Jeff Topham** served as chief pathologist for the Center for Sanguinary Studies in Louisville. Dr. Topham left the center last year under a cloud of scandal, although none of the allegations against him were ever proved. In any event, a thorough search of his residence failed to turn up any of the missing pieces.

**Dr. Jeff VanderMeer** was born a cantankerous old man and is only getting older. In addition to his skills as a veterinarian and chiropractor, Dr. VanderMeer runs the Ministry of Whimsy Clinic for Esoteric Writers, which attempts to rehabilitate the work of writers who have never really been accepted into the mainstream. As a result of his efforts, the Ministry Clinic has been a finalist for the World Medical Fantasy Award, the British Medical Fantasy Award, and the Psychotropic Kinetic Drugs Award. Dr. VanderMeer himself won the 2000 World Medical Fantasy Award for his paper "The Transformation of Martin Lake: An Analysis of Certain Psycho-Physical Aspects of the Imagination That Lead to Artistic Success."

**Dr. Liz Williams** was Consulting Physician at the Royal Entomological College, Brighthelm, from 1903–21, where she pioneered attempts to communicate with bees. Accounts of Hsing's Sarcoma and other pestilential outbreaks can be found among those of her papers that have not been chewed (cause unknown). In 1925, Dr. Williams undertook an expedition to Mongolia to investigate episodes of giantism in insects, but was kidnapped by bandits. She was rediscovered shortly after World War II. Invigorated by the rejuvenating airs of the Alatau, she is happily married to a bandit chieftain, with four cats and 70 grandchildren named Genghis.

**Dr. Neil Williamson** is employed as an investigative dentist reporting to the Scottish Executive Parliamentary Task Force assessing the feasibility of a national dental census. He believes that knowing exactly which teeth each citizen has or doesn't have is vital in the statistical war against tooth decay. Dr. Williamson contributes a regular column to *International Gingivitis Review*, and owns a dental prosthesis consultancy in Glasgow's West End that principally supplies exaggerated canines to students who want to be vampires. In his spare time he is afflicted with the miserable wasting disease known as Scottish Football, counts people's teeth in the street, practices paralegal horticulture by pursuing his quest to hybridize the Scotch Bonnet chili with the cannabis plant, writes fiction, and races whippets. Sometimes he wins.

**Dr. Andrew J. Wilson** studied unnatural philosophy at the University of Edinburgh. He later collaborated with Herbert West at Miskatonic University in Arkham, but rumors that he also collaborated with the Germans during World War II are completely without foundation. His monograph on automotive gremlinology was erroneously published as fiction in *The Year's Best Horror Stories* by Karl Edward Wagner who, as a doctor himself, should have known better. "Under the Bright and Hollow Sky," Dr. Wilson's personal reminiscences of Old Edinburgh scenes and worthies, has also been egregiously scheduled for publication in a short-story anthology called *Gathering the Bones*.

**Dr. Gahan Wilson** is both the most influential figure in medical history and its most mysterious. Until he published "Do Any of Us Actually Exist?" in the Southwestern New Jersey Journal of Medicine there was no doubt Dr. Wilson had been, but since its appearance it's unclear whether he was or not. A complication is that those claiming there was no Dr. Gahan Wilson have ceased to exist while those maintaining he did have doubled and sometimes tripled in number. The writer of this biography would like it to be universally understood he holds no opinion whatsoever on this matter.

**Dr. Tamar Yellin** developed her interest in obscure psychological diseases after a bout of severe depression in her houseman year was misdiagnosed as African Horse Sickness. Her reputation was established when she was invited to copyedit Geraldine Carter's *Guide to Psychotropic Balkan Diseases* (second edition) for a fee of fifty dollars. (She has still not been paid.) In 1999, she gave the address at the Brontë Society AGM entitled "Death and the Brontës: Love and Sputum in a Cold Climate." Her magnum opus, *Six Cases of Madness in the Same Family*, though universally praised for its fine prose style, remains as yet unpublished. Dr. Yellin lives in the North of England, where she writes poetry in her spare time and raises Jack Russell terriers.

## Acknowledgments

**The editors would** like to thank everyone who contributed to this anthology; the sheer quality of imagination on display made it a delight to work on the Guide. Special mention must be made of three individuals without whose creativity the Guide would not be what it is today: Stepan Chapman, Michael Cisco, and John Coulthart. Thanks to Stepan and Michael for their fanatical devotion to the Guide, and for their willingness to write new material at a moment's notice. Thanks to John, mad genius designer, who actually volunteered to find an illustration for every disease, and whose creativity has enriched the Guide immeasurably. Thanks also to Ann Kennedy for much copyediting, proofreading, and advice. Thanks to Forrest Aguirre and Ellen Datlow for help when the project was in its infancy. Thanks to Dr. Lambshead for his continued inspirational example. Finally, John Coulthart would like to thank Michael Moorcock for letting him abuse his words in the pursuit of period fidelity.

"Quae prosunt omnibus, artes!"